The phone rang.

"Look, I told you—I have to take these keys back. We can start looking for Ramsey in the morning and..."

She stopped talking. She knew.

"No need to look further, dear woman." The words pushed through with a mushy quality. "She will die. Can your limited mentality comprehend this? If the boy spots anyone around, if he so much as suspects the police are after him, he will take her life." The voice slurred and choked. "You cannot imagine what he is." Groaning wind all but drowned out his words. "And for my part, I cannot let you endanger her with your meddling. Do you understand? I cannot allow it."

She leaned over the phone, as though sucked in by his words, and she gripped the receiver so tightly her fingers ached. "If you have any information regarding this..."

Branches rattled in a sudden gust; then the dial tone rose loudly.

"Hello?" Panic settled on her. *Get him back on the line. Try star sixty-nine.* Her numbed fingers stabbed at the buttons. *Get him talking, get him to say something useful. Act like a cop for once.*

In the distance, she could hear a phone ringing. Not over the instrument, but faintly through the windows behind her. She replaced the receiver, and the ringing ceased.

The phone booth outside.

Other *Leisure* Books by Robert Dunbar:

THE PINES

THE
SHORE

ROBERT
DUNBAR

ISURE BOOKS NEW YORK CITY

For Carl, who loved a good scary story…
late at night on the roof…
with the wind off the Hudson and the sky full of stars.

A LEISURE BOOK®

July 2009

Dorchester Publishing Co., Inc.
200 Madison Avenue
New York, NY 10016

ISBN 10: 0-8439-6166-X
ISBN 13: 978-0-8439-6166-9
E-ISBN: 978-1-4285-0699-2

The name "Leisure Books" and the stylized "L" with design a
trademarks of Dorchester Publishing Co., Inc.

Printed in the United States of America.

10 9 8 7 6 5 4 3 2 1

Visit us on the web at www.dorchesterpub.com.

Author's Note

This book is entirely a work of fiction, the characters imaginary, the town of Edgeharbor based on no actual place. Only the Jersey Devil is real.

THE
SHORE

...the sea,
Delaying not, hurrying not,
Whispered me through the night, and very plainly
before daybreak,
...the low and delicious word...
DEATH...
Hissing melodiously,
But edging near...rustling at my feet,
And creeping thence steadily to my ears...
DEATH...

~Walt Whitman

PROLOGUE

Pines glow, branches clawing at moonlight as the car hurdles past.

She turns up the radio, but music dissolves in static as she fiddles with the dial. Only a religious talk program emerges clearly. Switching it off, she rifles the glove compartment for a disk.

At last, jazz trombone smokes through the interior of the convertible. Though tension still sings in her neck, she sighs. Hellish shift tonight—the faces of the players, desperate and sweating, swim in her mind. One more year of this, she thinks, and she'll go back to school; then she laughs aloud, wondering how long she's been telling herself this. She increases the pressure on the gas pedal, and bristling shades stream around the car, melting in the periphery of the headlights as the road throbs beneath her.

A sign flashes past. Instantly the channel narrows, and she eases up on the gas. A tall tree seems to writhe in her headlights. Fringed and tufted with needles, its limbs seem to reach for the fleeting brightness.

Darkness coils like a river, and a chill seeps through the canvas roof. The music swells with anxious melancholy.

Her high beams scythe the night. No one uses this road much. It has been almost an hour since she glimpsed house lights or even another car, and isolation makes the night seem chillier. Yet she cracks the window to let freezing air whistle in. Her lungs still burn, and the acrid stench of tobacco clings to her clothing. Above the windshield, skeletal trees vault, endlessly frigid and unsullied, as her mind drifts on the music.

The road twines through the pressing tangle, widening again, sloping up toward a house on a rise, the convertible now a shadow among shadows. As the woods fall away, a few more dwellings gather at the top of the hill. Some little town, she guesses, but still raw, still clean.

The road humps downward, and suddenly the sea spreads before her.

Her shoulders relax, and the charred rasp in her chest eases. As the car bounces past, shocks squeaking like mice, a big old house with gabled windows peers blindly. Cranking the window shut, she slows the car to a crawl. Black conifers claw over ledges and rocks, edging onto the shoulder of the road.

There—a gap in the scrub growth.

Tires skitter off the graveled edge of the dirt trail and wallow in softness, things crunching beneath the wheels. A moment later, she eases the convertible out onto a small beach.

Private probably, but not posted, at least not that she can see. Not that she cares much anyway. Not tonight. What's the worst that could happen? Silencing the wail of music, she sets the hand brake. It's been months since she found a spot this perfect. Hardly any beach at all really, just the trees, then the rocks and then surf—right there. She clicks off the headlights.

Waves flicker.

She listens to the muted hiss, relishing it. The dash lighter pops. Briefly rummaging in her bag, she lights a joint and inhales deeply, then zips up her coat, brushing an ember off the sleeve. It's a new coat, too expensive for her. A gift. Like the car. Her teeth clench grimly, and she shoves the door open. Cold floods in. Hunching her shoulders and lowering her chin, she clambers out. Normally, on a night like this, she might only sit in the car and watch the ocean, maybe play a CD. But tonight she needs to walk, if only for a moment, if only as far as the rocks. Pines seethe in the wind, and the door slams softly.

Shale and beach grass crackle underfoot as she heads for a blunt wedge of stone. The raw materials of creation seem to have been abandoned here. Lumpish boulders squat. Scrub growth struggles onto a thin strip of gravel, not so much a beach as a shoal of crushed shells, primeval, unfinished. In the wind, sparse sand grits loudly, and waves slide against the rocks with a tumbling whisper.

Planting her suede boots firmly, she imbibes the scent of the sea. It smells impossibly ancient, like vapors from the dawn of time. Hypnotized by faint luminescence, she stares at the waves. She tokes on the joint, then squeezes out the tip, as the wind prowls through rocks to pounce, whirling the mass of black hair around her face like a satin veil. The cold sears her ears, lashes the long coat between her legs. She must be crazy, she decides, to be out tonight without a hat or gloves . . . to be out tonight at all. The next gust draws tears.

For as long as she can stand it, she lets the wind scour away all thought. Finally, feeling hollowed, almost weightless, she turns her shivering back to the wind and paces along the water's edge, her boots crunching dully across pebbles.

Like shattered bones through the flesh of the earth, boulders break the surf, and spent waves pulse over the stones at her feet. Some of the rocks resemble emerging bodies, hunched and fetal, inchoate, and she steps onto the first boulder, hugging herself against the chill. A sudden trace of mist blurs her vision. The sea is liquid darkness.

Ragged clouds surge apart, and moonlight bursts in the swells, rolling silver lines across the beach. Suddenly looming, an obelisk startles her. So close, yet she hadn't seen it. A drowned lighthouse—decades abandoned probably and half sunk in the tide. Now she can even make out the chain link fence surrounding it in the water. From somewhere, a foghorn groans mournfully. Again, the wind whips her coat as the clang of a buoy drifts to the rocks.

Enough, she decides. But she lingers an instant longer, freezing and letting the wind buffet her. Then she steps off the rocks onto the softer earth. Taking her hands out of her pockets, she blows on them, rubbing at her numbed face as she hurries back toward the car.

It envelops her: a stench that makes her think of sewage lines and decomposing animals. She covers her mouth and nose.

On the rocks behind her, pebbles rattle.

She jerks around.

A shadow bulges. ". . . pretty . . ." Something like a voice hisses.

Panic jets, battering in her chest as she stumbles back. The heel of her boot slips, and she tumbles, sharp stones grinding into her palms.

A skittering noise rains down from the boulders.

"Who is that?" She scrambles backward on all fours. "What do you want?" She struggles to her feet.

It slams into her back, ripping hotly through the coat, pitching her forward. "Stop!" Terror burbles in her throat as she staggers for the car. "No!" Cries drip from her in small cascades. "Somebody, help me!" Yanking the door open, she tumbles in, jamming down the lock. Beyond the windows, blackness pulsates.

"Oh Christ oh my God." Writhing into the seat, she fumbles at the key. It feels slippery in her fingers. "Oh sweet Jesus." Both her hands feel wet. They look black, and warmth trickles at her back.

With a crackling hiss, the window on the driver's side goes white.

"No!" She twists the key, and the engine sputters. "I'll run you the fuck over. I swear to God!" Shrieking, she pounds on the horn and flips on the high beams, but only mist rushes forward, claiming the light.

As the car lurches, she wrenches the wheel, trying to swing around in a wide circle. Fog swirls everywhere. "Where's the road?" The sea yawns before her.

Cold grips her. She peers up at a moon-cloven sky, as something like a hand gropes through the torn roof. Fingers tangle in her hair, and another hand grips her coat. The steering wheel tears from her arms. Her legs plunge and kick.

Like the cries of some night-flying seabird, her gurgling screams mingle with the surf. The empty car rolls to the rocks. Glass tinkles, and darkness presses around.

Waves gush against the rocks, and nothing moans but the wind.

I

In splintered shadows beneath the pier, waves caressed the pylons, sliding between them in a plunging, receding rhythm. Wind rippled the surface, and light sank in pillared striations, while from the timbers above, susurrations resounded.

On the beach, wind grated across sparse dunes and rattled dead grasses, and a damp chill settled from a dull white sky. Gulls hung motionlessly above sand the color of wet straw.

The rusted mouth of a huge drainage pipe yawned jaggedly at the surf. A man crouched within. Winds hissed, mauling him, and he drew back, his breath clouding. Pulling off his gloves, he blew on his hands and rubbed them together, shivering. He barely had enough room to stand in the pipe, and again he leaned past the lip of the metal tunnel, letting his gaze drift to the far end of the beach: scrub pines straggled near the rocks. Perhaps a century earlier, those boulders had been plowed from the sand. Now they formed a rough wall that crashed deep into the surf. Even from here, he could see spray lash up. The gulls rose.

Still nothing. And the light almost gone. The thought of returning here at night stabbed an icy chill deep into him, and he risked another glance toward the pier. Clouded waves lapped the pilings.

As the wind died away, he drew his head back. Tugging the gloves on, he stuffed his hands into the pockets of his bomber jacket. Straight ahead, the ocean heaved smoothly, silken weights rolling beneath the surface. Languid hills rode each other, until endless repetition, maddeningly torpid, stirred him to twitching somnolence. As the sand crunched softly, he shifted his weight, clumped gravel scratching the soles of his shoes. Soon, he thought. The one he waited for would come soon. He shuddered, his very heartbeat seeming to fuse with the pulse and rhythm of the tide. Between waves, the hush grew so quiet he imagined he could hear things moving beneath the sand, hidden things, secret things.

At the mouth of the pipe, a vein of black splayed through the wet sand. Broken boulders littered the shore, and waves gouged through crevices in granite . . . like slow acid.

A sound drifted across the beach—the softly grating hiss of footsteps.

He stiffened.

The sound grew louder, and he crouched, breath stalled in his throat, fingers curling within the leather gloves. Warily, he peered through a corroded hole in the metal.

On the granulating mud beneath the pier, foam glinted in an oily sheen, sliding ever back into the water. With a backpack slung over his shoulder, a boy emerged from the dimness. He looked about fourteen. Perhaps a bit older. He wore a brimmed cap, tugged down over his ears, and his cheeks had flushed a deep pink as though wind had scoured away layers of skin. The boy took large strides. Straddling the dry rim of sand, he would pass within a few feet of the pipe.

A ripple of sensation spurted across the man's hands, a warming pain, like the twitch of a long-dead nerve. Just a little closer . . .

Tongues of wind rasped along the beach, and waves curled over the rocks like talons.

The boy shielded his eyes from the blowing grit and tried to push back the pale hair that trailed from beneath his cap. Even with two sweaters under the denim jacket, he felt the cold flow right through, and his thin shoulders trembled as he shifted the backpack. Almost against his will, his gaze skimmed out over the sea. He stopped walking.

A gull shrieked.

The sun had not really come up at all today. Swells tumbled sluggishly, and shades of gray blurred together where the horizon should have been. With a jerk of his head, he forced his attention from the bleak seascape to resume his scrutiny of the beach. Beyond the sewage pipe, a boulder protruded from the sand, then another farther on and another until a rock barrier ended the gravelly strip. Either he would have to go back or cut straight across the beach, here at its widest point, a risk he hated taking.

The wind soughed, and a brutal gust scorched his face. Lowering his head, he trudged on, kicking at broken shells. Bird tracks, webbed and hooked like the spoor of tiny dinosaurs, splayed everywhere, and lumps and whorls in the damp sand seemed to mirror the choppy pattern of the surf.

The boy saw only a blur of movement from the pipe. He pivoted. Big hands grazed his back, groping for a hold. Lips pulled taut, the boy's mouth opened in a silent cry as he leapt. His sneakers slipped on white pebbles, but he kept his footing, running hard.

He raced along the edge of the water, straining for the rocks. Footsteps slapped across the mud behind him, louder than his, faster than his. Outstretched hands clutched.

He sprinted with all his strength. Ahead lay the rock wall, and already his pursuer edged to cut him off from the beach.

The boy whirled, sliding toward the water. Surprised, the man passed him, cursing, and the boy glimpsed the pale snarl of his face, the fair hair. "You!" Dread trembled in his legs as he darted back, angling across the beach. "It's you!" His speed seemed to leach away as his sneakers pounded, and sand rose at his feet in slow spurts.

On the dunes, he heard only his own panting. Splinters of icy air gouged his lungs, and he began to think he had escaped. Then he heard a snorting gasp. So close. His sneakers dug deep into the sand.

The man grunted victoriously, lunging. A gloved hand tangled in the long hair at the boy's neck. With a gasp of pain, the boy ducked under his arm. The man rammed into him, butting him backward, then caught him solidly by the shoulders.

The boy flailed, realization twisting his face. "You ain't my . . . !" Strong hands closed like a trap on his neck. As they grappled, the boy's jacket and shirttails pulled up, exposing flesh whiter than the frozen beach.

Gravel shaled down the slope as the man's shoes slipped. He toppled, clutching the straps to the backpack. Snagged, the boy shrugged it off, diving for a dark spot beneath the boardwalk. The man fell with a grunt, plunged at the boy's legs. He caught a sneaker. The boy kicked, slipping under the boards.

With a coughing snarl, the man scrambled to his knees and thrust his arm deep into the opening, groping until his shoulder scraped wood. He dug frantically, enlarging the hole. Sand crept up his sleeves and burned like powdered ice. Then he threw himself on his stomach and shoved forward.

Freezing blackness closed on him. The tight cavern smelled of damp wood, and he twisted around. An ovoid of thin daylight leaked from above, and he threshed farther in, grinding his hip against the underside of the boards. He could hardly move his arms, could barely turn his head. Sand gritted between his teeth, and the boards squeezed down on him. He felt empty space with his right hand and tried to writhe forward, but softer earth sucked at him. Twisting in the other direction, he slipped into darkness.

Glowing in a fine seepage of light, a plume of sand trickled down on him.

He was alone now. He knew it. Wind moaned through the cracks, and haze brightened in his vision as he managed to get his feet beneath him in the trench. The boy was gone. Despair coursed through him.

Icy sand filled his gloves as he clambered heavily up the incline. His shoes felt weighted with lead, and at the top, he struck his head against a beam. When he squeezed toward the opening, his belt snagged on a nail, and he squirmed, one arm pinned beneath him, his legs kicking at nothing. Wedged in, he thrashed back and forth, making his way by inches, until the wind tore at his face, and he crawled out. At last, he lay on the open sand, cold grit in his mouth. *So close.* For several minutes, he listened to the labored pounding of his heart, to the tumbling hush of the sea. Spitting dirt, he rolled onto his back and stared at the sky.

He tugged his gloves off with his teeth, rubbed at his beard-stubbled face. *So close.* Finally, the breath stopped whistling in his chest, and he heaved to his feet. He reached for the boy's discarded backpack. Heavy. No tags. He unzipped it, turned it over. A rolled towel dropped out like a stone.

Red wetness sopped through the terry cloth, and he prodded the towel with his foot. Lifting it gingerly by a corner, he let the things wrapped within clatter down. Sand caked on the dampness. His eyes moved first to the chisel, then to the small saw and the clotted hammer. Two carving knives lay darkly encrusted, and the center of the towel still glistened.

Fluids hung heavy and gelid in his stomach. Gulls slid across the sky.

The wind rasped myriad sounds over the low sand hills: the distant clatter of the pines, the hushed roar of the waves. The dull whisper held hissing cries that broke, pleading in his ears. Turning away, he leaned one bare hand against the boardwalk, and the frost bled into him. He began to sob, the wind dissipating the sound until he himself could barely hear it.

A stream of sand slithered into the tunnel at his feet, and all around him loose grit wound across the beach in stray currents of air. "No!" He jerked his face up. "You don't get away from me again!" Running for the boardwalk stairs, he shouted at the sky. "I don't let you get away."

He pounded up the steps. "Do you hear me?" He sprinted across the deserted planks. "I'll find you!" Empty shops stood silent and shuttered.

On the other side, he bolted down a ramp to a ragged field. "I'll stop you!" But he moved with a jerky stiffness now, and under his tread, flat stones slid and crunched, slowing him even further. The sparse streets beyond the field looked as deserted as a moonscape.

Halfway down the first block, he halted, shoes scuffing heavily on the sidewalk. Empty dwellings have a distinctive look, like dead trees. Not one of the summery curtains twitched, and some of these cottages even had boarded windows. Leaning against a pole, he coughed and wiped at the grit that clung to his damp face. He tasted brine, felt sand between his teeth. At last, the coughing fit subsided.

The sidewalk curved back in the direction of the beach, and his footsteps scraped a hollow noise from the concrete. Dead grasses rattled at a fence where sand leaked between slats. *My one chance.* Dry leaves and yellowed newspapers clumped and drifted. *He'll go to ground now.* In a puddle by the curb, oil shimmered like a rainbow. *I'll never find him.* A creaking chorus filled the wind. Quaintly lettered ROOMS TO LET signs swayed in unison while SALE signs tilted from several of the tiny lawns. He saw only one car, an old gray Plymouth with flat tires near the end of the block. Even from here, the windshield looked opaque with grime.

Right now, he's running. Hooks of guilt dug into his flesh. *And I can't stop him.* He felt his feverish thoughts teem.

never stop him my fault never catch him in the open like that again so close my fault

He stumbled across the cracked ground. With a shuddering exhalation, he jogged to the end of the block. *Never catch him.* Around the corner, another boardwalk ramp rose. He halted, listening to the dull roar of the beach while broken sections of pavement slid underfoot, crunching.

The knives. His breath plumed. *Got to go back for the knives.* As though throwing off a dream, he shook his head and began to climb the ramp.

Beneath the incline, gusts moaned, and tangled in the shadows, debris shuffled rhythmically, as though stirred by the sigh of a sleeping beast.

II

Cracked by sun and wind, the flesh on the backs of his hands resembled drying mud flats. As he struggled to close the padlock, he exhaled heavily so that cigar smoke shrouded him. With his cane hooked over one arm, and the cigar tightly gripped between his lips, the old man grappled with arthritic fingers until at last he managed to jam the door shut. When the padlock on the shed clicked, he turned to face out over the bay.

Waves gurgled and sloshed, the pier swaying stiffly. He stared a long time. Nearly twenty years had passed with grinding tedium since last he'd gone to sea; still he came each morning, never dawdling over the short walk, to fix his Spartan breakfast over a coal stove. By the light of each dawn, he monitored the disintegration of his nets and inspected the progression of the rot that had long since claimed his boat.

A frosty breeze stretched across the bay to tousle the few whitish strands on his head, and still his gaze tracked across the water. Terns wheeled. Buildings on the mainland appeared feathery and vague, while pillars of smoke flattened into haze. Edgeharbor clung to a narrow strip of land that branched southward from the coast, but on foggy mornings, he could imagine with desperate longing that he lived upon an island . . . an island in another time. He scratched a wiry eyebrow with his thumb, and let his gaze sweep farther out to sea.

Clouds hung motionless, fissured with a milky light that seemed to leak away even as he watched. Today no ships marred the frozen horizon. The wind slapped up small waves, and the few tarp-covered boats bucked, furled sails shivering in place.

Decades earlier, the fishing boats had ceased to venture out—he remembered their decks heaped with fish of all descriptions and covered with dead squid like mounds of empty gloves. Long before the births of his grandchildren, the cannery had closed its doors, and now the brick structure brooded dismally at the edge of the larger dock. Its muddy reflection quivered.

While the wind stung at his unflinching face, he stretched and grunted. His compact body had remained lean throughout the years, his arms much harder, he knew, than the arms of many a younger man. He found satisfaction in the thought, but still his vision tracked along the horizon, searching. After a lifetime as a fisherman, he harbored no romantic illusions about the sea, but if it stirred no poetry in his soul, neither did it evoke the superstitious awe harbored by so many of the old men he'd known as a boy. If anything, he sported a faintly hostile, even grudgingly proprietary attitude, regarding it. Behind him, the corrugated roof of the shed rattled, and he shuffled away against the wind, not bothering to turn up his collar. Above all, he was a methodical man, practical, and often the futility of this daily ritual of inspection vaguely troubled him, but he shrugged it off, instinctively dreading the alternative. Better to rise at dawn and hurry to his dilapidated hut than to sit in his daughter's house and listen to the television and the vacuum cleaner and his daughter's blurring telephone chatter. Here at least—brewing coffee and playing solitaire—he retained some memory of purpose.

As he crossed the weathered dock, he savored the sound of the waves. His daughter might lament his advancing deafness, but the sea never fell silent for him. Even on days like this, so still, could he hear it slide against itself, coiling to hump against the pier, while all around him boats plodded up and down in their shifting places, refracted lights dancing on their hulls like memories of vanished summers. He shook his head. Smoke billowed away from him, and he tossed the chewed nub of his cigar in the water.

Something pale shimmered in the swells.

He squinted. Even on such an overcast day, the trembling surface glittered. The object bobbed between two of the old boats. Stooping, he strained to make it out. Some odd sort of fish, belly-up among the sodden pilings? Squidlike, the thing wavered down, now visible, now gone. He crouched at the edge of the rotting wood.

The surface stirred as a swell approached, sloughing sideways like an aquatic serpent. He bent to prod the thing with his cane, to bring it closer, but with the perversity of things in water, it twisted the other way, and he shivered, leaning farther.

Something watched him from the water.

A clammy heat climbed his back. Fear dropped through the tight knot of his stomach, and he gripped the post, struggling to maintain his balance. Memories welled, all the evil tales flooding back. In the old country, his grandfather and the other men of the village had often spoken of *la sirena*, drowned women who devoured men with small sharp teeth in wet and secret places, and dreams of such creatures had terrorized his childhood. He blinked. Small waves slapped fitfully at the broken pilings.

Black tresses smoking around it, the face in the water turned away, one eye, white and yellow, emerging. The head rolled again, bobbed against a floating bottle.

Something pushed against the cane.

Numbly, he regarded the thing that first had attracted his attention. The digits, stiffened and outstretched, did resemble tentacles, and the knob of bone trailed filaments like a lure into the murk. Other things also floated among the pilings—he regarded them clearly now. Clutching at the warped and swollen post, he jerked to his feet and slapped fitfully at his coat as though beating away cinders.

Stumbling across the dock, he limped stiffly away from the peaceful lapping noises. He tried to hurry, but agony thundered in his chest, and pain sparked in his knees. Wheezing in the chill, and leaning heavily on the stick, he hobbled into the streets of the town.

Overhead, seabirds laughed like harpies.

The boy ran until pain slashed his lungs, until reeling with exhaustion, he staggered and caught himself against a fence. Gasping raggedly, he looked back.

No one followed. He hung there, chest heaving, while surge after surge of relief beat through his heart. After a moment, he tried to run again, still panting hoarsely, and sand rained from his clothes to the sidewalk with every jolt. Almost immediately a cramp seized his side. Slowing, he tried to maintain a normal gait, though his legs trembled. Appearing "normal" was so important, the most important thing of all—this had been drummed into his head all his life.

The sky had dulled, and the squeal of a gull echoed above the street.

Leaves eddied along the sidewalk, and his longish hair blew loosely around his collar as he hurried past the church. With quavering hands, he fished a ball of tissue out of his pocket and wiped at his nose. For just a moment, he thought he'd lost his gloves again, but then he remembered he'd had to bury them because they'd gotten all sticky. He crammed his hands into his pockets and let the wind push him along. His cap almost blew free, but he caught it, tugged it down over his ears. Freezing, he blew on his hands. Around the corner, glacial cold struck at his face, and he marched along with his head down, staring at the sidewalk through sudden tears.

Crossing Chandler Street in front of the library always seemed the worst part of the trek. Bracing himself, he bolted for the dark scar of an alleyway on the other side. The narrow channel cut through the wall beside an abandoned restaurant, and he plunged in, hurrying until brick walls blocked out the world completely. Deep within the alley, he stopped running and peered back at the entrance.

A street lamp winked on.

He trudged ahead. The alley trailed behind the restaurant, frozen garbage blistering the concrete at his feet. Wind whistled.

A scream scalded his ears. With a savage movement, the creature rose, swelling to the top of a wall, then over.

The boy's knees unlocked. Just a cat. Heart hammering, he leaned against the frigid bricks and after a moment shuffled forward again. He knew there couldn't be much left around here for the poor animal to eat, and he thought tomorrow he might bring some food for it. Slowly, the convulsive throbbing of his blood diminished, and a moment later, the alley emptied into a deserted parking lot. Raw boards covered doors and windows along the rear of a warehouse.

Leaping a low dividing wall, he sprinted across a narrow street and darted blindly into another alley. Home turf now. The backs of buildings crowded together and blocked the lowering sky as the passage narrowed. Scraping the shoulder of his jacket, he squeezed around a pile of crates, careful of where he put his feet.

A door rattled—claws scrabbled loudly at wood, and a broad black nose rutted through a gap.

He ran. The alley broadened into a canyon of basement doors. In the airshaft above his head, gray clothesline twisted, webbing the fire escapes that tangled up the walls like vines, and wind throbbed through the clothesline as he scurried for the tallest building.

As always, he jumped for the fire escape and as always missed the lowest rung by inches. Dragging over a dented metal trash can, he stood on it, pulling himself up hand over hand, grunting until his thrashing feet found the bottom rung. The freezing metal scorched his palms, and he decided he'd need new gloves fast.

When he reached the first landing, he hugged his hands deep into his stomach, warming them. Then he leaned over the rail. He knew he'd messed up bad today. Empty windows overlooked the courtyard in every direction, and over the roof of the lowest building, he could observe a slice of empty street beyond. He'd been so scared, he'd even raced across that last stretch without checking first. Anyone might have seen. Plus he'd forgotten about that dog again. Eventually, someone would hear it bark. They would have to move again . . . soon. But it would be harder now—things had gotten so much worse. Thinking about the man on the beach, he trembled as the courtyard below him sank deeper into gloom. "I don't want to die," he whispered. "Not now."

Wind lashed the side of the building. He couldn't die now—she needed him. Something rattled below, and the dog barked randomly.

Finally satisfied that no one had followed, he charged up the metal stairs to the top floor. The window was open a crack, and while cold sucked around his neck and shoulders, he slipped his fingers under and strained. It always made too much noise. He shoved it up more slowly, shivering. At last, pushing through the sheer summer curtains, he slipped over the sill.

He slid the window down and locked it, pulled the shade. Still in the dark, he tugged off his hat and started unbuttoning his jacket; then he pried the edge of the shade and peered into the evening shadows. At last, he switched on the kitchen light and tossed his hat on the table. He stripped off his coat, peeling the top sweater along with it so that, inside out, they slid in a lump across the back of a chair. He smoothed the other sweater across his taut stomach, then rubbed his palms above the red coil of a space heater, pain flushing into his fingers with the sudden warmth. When he twisted the knob all the way, the heater hummed. It almost drowned out the whimpering behind him.

Weeks earlier, he'd clumsily screwed a heavy latch into the wood of the closet door. As he unhooked it now, he heard a shuffling sound within, and when the closet door swung open, the pale mask of her face hovered low. He yanked on a length of chain, and the lightbulb swung shadows at him.

Her hair shone softly. She groaned, huddled on the floor, her back pushed hard against the far wall. At the sight of him, her eyes squeezed shut, rolling wildly beneath the lids, and she thrashed her body from side to side with a soft rustle, like the sounds made by a sleeping child. Her elbow struck the wall. Somehow she'd gotten her hands around in front of her, though heavy nylon cord bound them. A strip of adhesive tape still covered her mouth.

"I'm back." He pushed into the closet and knelt beside her, shoving a long woman's coat out of the way. She began to choke. Above them, hangers jangled.

"I told you I was gonna come back." Slowly, he reached for the tape, but she jerked her head with a moan. "You always get nervous." Falling to her side, she drummed her feet against the floor.

Gently, his fingers stroked her throat. "Don't worry." The flesh felt moist and hot, and he could feel the rapid pulse.

Her eyes became glittering slits.

"I'm home now. See?"

As tears coursed down her cheeks, she tried to roll her face away.

"Don't be like that. You know I won't never do nothing to hurt you." He stroked the long tresses, savoring the pale softness. "It'll be all right. You know I love you." He stared hard at her face, knowing that in the sealed cavern of her mouth, she screamed. "I do. You know I do." He slid down next to her, and his thin arms slipped around her waist. "Don't be afraid. You got to trust me. Everything I do is for you."

She trembled convulsively.

"Were you trying to get this off, or what? Good thing I come home when I did." The caressing flutter of his touch strayed to the tape on her lips; then he stroked the ropes. "Don't look at me like that. You know why I got to do this—it's 'cause you don't believe me. You'd try to run away if I left you untied. You know you would. And they'd get you. I know you don't believe me, but they're out there. Hunting us. I mean it. That's why we got to hide." His fingers silked through her hair again. "Or else you'd yell until they found us. Yes, you would. And they'd kill us. Please try to understand. Why can't you believe me? You and me might be the only real people left in the whole town. All the rest are monsters."

III

Beneath the ramp, a rasp echoed. Coughing damply, the fat man lumbered out into the daylight. His parka, which gleamed a dirty orange, distorted his girth and rendered him almost shapeless. He approved. Blinking through wire-frame glasses at the dingy sky, he held up the prizes he clutched: three lengths of thin rope. Stiff with brown stains, they dangled from his fists. Behind him, the contents of a plastic trash bag lay scattered on the sand.

He understood what the ropes meant, and he brought them closer to his face. The girl still lived.

The boy had her.

His gaze raked across the buildings before him, probing empty windows. He would find them. His fists clenched with a spasm of anger. He would. No one else.

Scanning broken glass and eroded porticoes, he turned his scrutiny to the largest structure in the area. The dulled contours of The Abbey Hotel towered above the neighborhood. Terraces scoured by the wind, facade flaking away, the hotel faced the sea. The color of sand, it might almost have been a natural outcropping, a cliff pocked with caves. Even at this distance, he fancied he could hear wind whistle through boarded windows. He knew that sound only too well: it never stopped. For weeks now, he'd been living like a rat in the Abbey's deserted halls. So many windows—the huge old building had provided an excellent lookout, but now the winter had grown more intense, forcing him to move a few blocks inland.

One thought drove him on. No one else must be

allowed to get them, not now when he drew so close. The day before, he'd witnessed the stranger almost take the boy down, and thoughts of it still whipped fury through his bulk. He'd searched and searched, and there remained only so many places where they could be hiding.

Wind billowed suddenly, swamping him in dust, and pale oily tendrils of hair danced free of the parka's hood to flutter over his forehead like the legs of a frantic spider. He needed just a bit more time. He lowered his face, teeth grinding, and retreated to the relative shelter of the ramp.

Beneath the boardwalk, the wind stirred a low moan, like the closing note of a solemn hymn.

Above the cottage roofs, a husk of moon glimmered in the afternoon sky. Before each dwelling, naked trees swayed, gnarled by salt wind, shadows stringing the lawns.

Even with the seat pushed back as far as it would go, his long legs felt cramped in the Volkswagen. As he sipped coffee, he warmed his hands on the Styrofoam cup. The dead streets seemed slightly wider here, the houses larger, but still no noise intruded, and he found it increasingly difficult to imagine these blocks had ever echoed with the normal sounds of human life. Footsteps? Voices? Laughter? Grinning sourly, he decided he knew little enough about normality to be passing judgment. He turned up the heater. Since chasing the boy on the beach the day before, he hadn't been feeling right and had been making an effort to keep warm. Using one of the leather gloves from the seat beside him, he wiped at the mist on the side window.

Still no children in sight. He could wait.

Slumped, he stared glumly through the windshield. Weeks ago, raindrops had dried in jagged splatters on the glass, crusting into a translucent pattern that resembled heaps of tiny leaves. He fiddled with the radio again but soon gave up. *Piece of junk*. He hated everything about this car.

Checking his watch, he resumed his surveillance of the street. Between each cottage lay a space wide enough for an automobile. Wooden fences broke up the monotony at random intervals but none offered anything like sufficient cover, especially not in winter with the trees whip-bare. On the other hand, there were no street lamps, and in full dark it might be safe enough, unless a porch light suddenly went on. He studied the yards, mapping out paths to rear doors and lower windows, a routine mental exercise. On the nearest lawn, a birdlike effigy tilted on stiff wire legs; beyond it, a plastic windmill spun, audibly hissing. On the other side of the street, some inventive gardener had bedded only plastic blooms, sun bleached now to a waxy gray, and everywhere small pine trees straggled like ragweed. *The wildness creeps in*. From many evenings of watching, he knew that jackrabbits frequented these streets at dusk, and twice he'd seen forays of raccoons. Once he'd spotted something like a furred reptile, only afterward realizing it must have been a possum.

As the school bus swayed ponderously around the corner, he slid farther down in his seat and stayed down until the door hissed. Crouching, he could just see the bus in the side mirror. A girl hopped out, maybe twelve years old, dragging a smaller version of herself along, both of them all scarves and curls. Three boys bounced down after them, pummeling each other with their books while the bus groaned off, exhaust bulging from its tailpipe. The boys jostled through the intersection, as the girls headed down the block.

Yesterday, he'd trailed the boys. Today, he waited until the girls got halfway to the corner, then jammed the ancient Volkswagen into gear. It shuddered forward, muffler sputtering. *Lousy wreck*. A cloud of smoke swirled up. *Noisier than the damn bus*. They'd promised to provide him with a "serviceable" vehicle for this assignment. He'd al-most laughed when he'd seen the black beetle. *How the hell am I supposed to stalk anybody in this?* The clumsy paint job, smudged and clotted, made the car resemble a blob of ink. *Like a hearse for clowns.* The passenger seat bulged where broken springs pressed the splitting vinyl, and something thumped persistently in the floor. *Like Edgar Allan Poe's car. Could be. Practically old enough.* He snorted. *Serviceable.* The cell phone they'd given him stayed in the glove com-partment. Permanently. It never worked in any of the places they sent him.

The boys had vanished. The smaller girl wore a red overcoat, easy to follow, as she swung her schoolbag and marched along behind her sister. *I manage though.* He cruised slowly after them. Passing the girls, the dirty black car turned the corner, gaining speed once out of sight. A crumpled fender sang briefly against a tire, and he scanned each desolate side street he passed. Unten-anted dwellings had a look he knew too well. *So why can't I shake the feeling I'm the one being watched?* He circled the block. *Ever since I found this town.* There seemed to be a strangely methodical quality to the cottages. Clearly they'd been constructed in clusters, laid out as irregu-larly as the streets themselves, somehow both monoto-nous and random. He adjusted the rearview mirror.

An antiseptic-looking church on the corner seemed scarcely larger than the neighboring houses. Just ahead, the girls swung into view again. As they started across the intersection, he eased down slightly on the gas pedal.

The gulls wheeled, their silhouettes like sickles, the erratic spatter of their sharpest screams glancing off the surface of the bay. Earlier they had feasted, descend-ing in droves to the banquet. Now, driven from their roosts by vans and cars and flashing lights, they circled, shrilling.

All day, men in uniforms had milled along the old dock, and whenever a gull settled, drawn by morsels still drifting along the surface, the men threw stones or bits of shell. Once, a shot had been fired, and birds had thundered away to hover and swoop in the frozen sky.

Drifting on currents of air now, they pivoted, wailing in the twilight, awaiting their chance to glean whatever scraps the nets and hooks would miss.

The chill quickened his step. He'd left the Volks on a side street and had followed the children on foot to a playground. The older girl had watched the boys toss a football until encroaching dusk had forced them away to nearby homes. These were the only children he'd seen in the entire town, this tiny group. He'd observed carefully, but they'd met no one else, spoken to no one else.

In the fading light, the scratchy planks of the boardwalk seemed a natural barrier between sea and town, sand lapsing into dun wood, then into a granulating wedge of concrete. From the town side, a hotel pressed up against the boards, its tattered banner rustling overhead. He turned away. *So close*. Pain thundered in his head. Above the beach, gulls slowly spun, suspended in the vaporous twilight.

Tide's in. Choppy shadows flickered in the waves, but the roar he heard was in his head, in his chest. He walked on, trying to think.

At last, vision blurring with exhaustion, face blazing from the cold, he crossed the boards and headed down the ramp. Patches of ice pocked the sidewalk with the same dull hue as the sky.

Down the block, a lamp winked through the drapes of the house the little girls had entered. No lights showed in any of the other houses, and no curtains parted. Yet the sensation of being watched intensified as he headed into the center of town.

Hiking past darkened storefronts, he peered constantly back over his shoulder. A fleeting shape trailed always just beyond his sight—he felt sure of it. Another sepulchral hotel glowered, boarded as tightly as the one on the boardwalk, and starlings cycloned above its roof. A few street lamps glimmered to life.

With a growl, a jeep bounced past him down the street. Traces of metallic green bled through the white paint around the word POLICE, and he glimpsed a pale, sharp face through the windshield. The jeep slowed at the corner, and he studied it with his peripheral vision. Pretty amateurish, he decided. The revolving light on the hood looked like the sort that attached magnetically. He sauntered past, hands crammed deep in his pockets.

Hunching his shoulders, he turned onto a small residential street, then hurried past shriveled hedges. The jeep didn't follow. He smelled smoke from a wood fire, and his breath spiraled in mist as dead leaves rasped and scuttled across the sidewalk. Keeping his face down, he studied the sidewalk. Past winters had wracked the terrain. Cracks in the street had heaved a foot above the roadbed, as though from an earthquake. *He's holed up here.* A skin of ice on a puddle crunched beneath his shoe, and his cough felt like a hook in his chest. *I know it.*

I can feel it. He should get the car, he told himself, begin patrolling the roads that led to the highway. Even now, the boy might be sneaking away, and he would have to begin his search again, going from town to town, looking for . . .

No, he's gone to ground here. Yesterday, he'd gotten lucky . . . and blown it. *So now he knows I'm after him.* A trembling rage convulsed him as debris spun about his head. A dried leaf lifted from the ground and rushed against his chest, held there by the wind. He tried to brush it away, but it clung with brittle tenacity, edges curling sharply, scrabbling at his coat.

Where the hell did I leave the damn car? He crumbled the leaf between his fingers and let the pieces drift away.

Dusk charred the facade of The Edgeharbor Arms, and the light in the window smoldered, glinting off a brass plaque by the entrance. As the lead glass doors to the foyer swung shut behind him, winter rattled at the panes, and tasseled drapes swayed in the draft. Just to be out of the wind felt luxurious.

The room seemed steeped in decades of tobacco and musty dirt. A single lamp by the desk—its yellowing shade depicting a turn-of-the-century boardwalk scene—left most of the lobby in deep gloom, and shadows bulged behind the ripely ammoniac old sofas. At first, he savored the thawing warmth, but as blood trickled back to his hands and feet an aching weariness swept through him.

The door behind the registry desk stood slightly ajar, and beyond it an infant squalled while a man and woman squabbled in a language he didn't speak, the cacophony rendered even less intelligible by the din of a television. The wet smell of boiling pasta engulfed him. Suddenly, the voices ceased, and the television roar dropped to a mutter.

So they know I'm back. Only the baby's wails continued. Abruptly, the door slammed, and the chandelier jangled. Reflexively, he glanced up at the trembling crystal daggers. Then he peered around the lobby, inspecting every corner.

From the moment he'd spied the padlocked doors of the elevator, he'd understood them to be permanently sealed and not merely shut for the season. This applied to much else here in Edgeharbor. Already the Arms seemed wretchedly familiar, like the setting for a recurrent dream, though he'd only been in town just over a week. With a sigh, he lumbered up the stairs.

Patches of carpet had worn down to bare boards. At

the second-floor landing only an unshaded bulb in a ceiling fixture diluted the gloom. *Need to lie down.* Pressure swelled in his head, and it hurt to move his legs. *Now.*

When he'd checked in, the proprietor's wife had been furious about his demanding a room above the second floor, and she'd wailed in broken English about all the climbing she would have to do. But she'd relented when he paid two weeks in advance and threw in an extra twenty. Being the sole guest carried advantages, and he had his reasons for insisting on an upper level. Anything lower would have been useless for observation . . . and the windows would have been far too accessible from the ground.

Before he started down the freezing hallway, he contemplated the darkness. A draft fluttered at the back of his neck.

As he turned the key, he listened. Cautiously easing the door open, he groped for the light switch. The threadbare carpet exuded a clammy miasma of suntan lotion and sweat, seeming to emanate even from the few cheerless furnishings. He locked the door behind him, slapped out the light. In the dark, he strode across the room and parted the curtains.

Moisture beaded the glass like black perspiration, and a damp lattice of frost feathered the edges of the pane. Scarcely five o'clock, but darkness rose like floodwaters below. He touched the glass, his fingertips slipping through the haze of moisture, leaving marks like snail tracks. Turning away, he unzipped his leather jacket. Dingy gloom seeped through the curtains, and wind shivered the windowpane. He fumbled with a switch at the back of a sconce until it flickered, barely revealing the room.

The single chair had been painted white so thickly that strands of wicker seemed molded into a single lump. He sat heavily and checked his watch. The numerals gleamed faintly. *Can't call for hours yet.* Silence pooled in the low corners, stagnant and chilly.

Wearily, he got up again, pacing, his movements about the room growing disjointed, purposeless. *Is this all there is now?* Twice he opened and closed the same drawer; then he wandered into the bathroom. The clumsily rigged shower resembled a trap in which the claw-footed tub had been snared. *So this is my life?* He looked behind the shower curtain, then returned to the bedroom and checked the tight closet. It felt as though every cell in his body craved rest. *Should do some work.* He swayed for a moment before falling back into the chair as though shoved. He picked at knotted laces with dead fingers, then kicked off a shoe and watched it roll toward the bed. Pulling himself up with a grunt, he heaved himself onto the mattress just as the wall sconce buzzed and went out. *Swell.*

The bedside lamp had been manufactured to resemble something roughly crafted from a jug. He switched it on, even that slight movement causing the bedsprings to protest like angry crickets. The lamplight made a perfect circle on the ceiling where the dust-thickened remnant of a cobweb trailed. *Have to stay awake.* Again he scrutinized the room. Both the wooden nightstand and the dresser had been painted white too many summers ago, and even in this light, wide swathes of glossy red still showed through. He examined the only picture, a seascape with gulls that sailed stiffly over greenish waters. It squarely missed obscuring a stain on the wall. The lumpish waves and the wings of the birds achieved crude symmetry, and despite the mediocrity of execution, something threatening seemed to lurk in the swirling tide. *Letting my imagination work overtime.* With a shiver, he turned away. *Don't need to invent monsters.*

He still felt dizzy. *Can't come down with something now.* He covered his face with his hands and felt heat throb beneath his eyelids. *Damn.* Only gradually did something like warmth seep back into his arms and legs. *Can't get sick. Not now.* A cough shuddered though him. *But it never gets warm in here.* The day he'd arrived with his suitcases, D'Amato, the proprietor, had bled air from the radiator for over an hour, running up and down the stairs and shouting to his wife, who'd clanged on a pipe somewhere below. The siphoned-off end product had been a pint of evil-looking fluid that smelled like liquid dust. Fetid and catlike, the smell lingered still. *Never warm.* Tonight, his body ached for a hot shower, but he didn't feel up to enduring the pounding whistle of the pipes. *Maybe I'll take a bath later.* Generally, that involved slightly less racket.

He closed his eyes. *Don't.* He leaned his head back against the wall. *Don't sleep now.* Pulling his legs onto the bed, he stretched. *Get the work out.*

After a moment, he felt under the bed. *Go on.* Straightening with a grunt, he shifted his legs and set the case on the bed before him. *Get on with it.* Solemnly, he tapped on the lid, then fished a key out of his wallet.

In a clear plastic bag, the boy's backpack nearly filled the suitcase, but other things had been crammed in around it. Next to his camera case lay a stack of Polaroids, bound with a rubber band, and beneath them bulged two cardboard folders. He pulled out the thicker folder and adjusted the lamp shade so that light spilled onto the bed.

Opening the folder, he glanced at the first newspaper clipping. . . . *torso found* . . . He set it aside, extracted another. . . . *evidence of sexual mutilation* . . . He examined each yellowed clipping as though he'd never seen it before. . . . *police sources say they have no information regarding* . . . Searching for any detail he might have missed, he scanned the words, feeling the muscles of his face stiffen and grow numb—an old and familiar sensation. He fumbled for his notepad. On the first page, the name "Stella" had been underlined twice.

If anything happens to me, so long as they find this, somebody else could take up the search. He found the notion oddly comforting. Leaning back against the wall, he paged through lists of names and dates, many crossed out or with check marks beside them. Some pages began with the names of towns in block letters at the top. *Rock Harbor, Wildcrest, Leed's Point.* Many towns he could barely remember, the names blurring together in his mind.

It seemed he'd spent his life in this realm, perhaps the strangest and most unnatural-seeming terrain ever to exist. The countless white sand trails of the Pine Barrens had at last given way to "construction." In just a few years, most of the old shanty towns had vanished, a whole way of life disappearing as residents packed up and headed south, some to settle in the Appalachians, others to join the migrant labor force. And the landscape of parking lots and strip malls verged always closer, merging one into the other, desperately drab, broken only by the dismally uniform "developments," encroaching on both the sad, shabby resort towns and on the affluent private beaches, on the ghettoed horror of Asbury Park to the north and on the ghettoed horror of Atlantic City to the south. A bizarre world. Different time lines seemed to overlap in this landscape, blanketing one another. He'd seen it everywhere—roadside stands sold homegrown produce beneath buzzing neon.

At last, he turned to a fresh page and, gripping the pen, carefully printed EDGEHARBOR. He stared at it a long time, then began scribbling in an erratic combination of print and script. *Strange, even for this part of shore. Old. Turn-of-century buildings, but falling apart. Some sort ruined factory-type (?) structure near water. Cordoned off, near abandoned dock. Cannery? And tenement buildings middle of town, probably for workers. Empty now.* He paused and read over his words. *Marina other side of peninsula. Deserted pretty much. Looks like tried convert tourism. Too small for resort. No easy access from highway. Some cottages by sea. Small board-walk but almost no beach. And the woods creep into the streets.*

Snapping the notebook shut, he replaced all the wrinkled clippings, then tossed the folder aside and dug into the suitcase again. Articles in the thinner file had been drawn from much less reputable sources—supermarket tabloids, digest-size publications with titles like *Strange Facts* and *Psychic Phenomenon*—but even the underscored passages in these dog-eared pages he studied. *Teenager Stirs Up Poltergeist Panic. Maryland's Bog Monster Unmasked.* Finally, these too he put aside, suppressing a yawn.

From the bottom of the suitcase, he scooped up sheets of paper torn from a legal pad and gave a cursory glance to the rough charts. Feeling around in his jacket, he drew out a road map and hunched forward, spreading it across the bed and trying to smooth down the bunching wrinkles. The paper rattled loudly in his trembling hands. The map depicted most of south central New Jersey and part of the shoreline. Circles and X's in red ink pocked the pinelands region, clustering where the woods encroached on the shore. *Edgeharbor.* He studied the tapering wedge of the peninsula until his vision blurred. *Enough.* Laboriously, he refolded the map and tossed it on top of the papers. *Won't find him on any map.* He stacked the folders, carefully replacing everything in the case before shoving it back under the bed.

Just rest my eyes. Stagnant air lulled him. *Just a little.* The drowsy chill made him yearn to pull up the blankets, and he considered switching off the lamp, then threw one arm across his face and let a sudden flush of weariness take him. *I miss her so much.*

Wind rattled the window with a sound like ice cracking on a frozen river.

A brick wall blocked the street lamp, sinking the alley in darkness. Like a garish phantom, black and gray and orange, one ear tufted with white, the brute of a cat flicked in and out of the light. It stalked along the fence toward a spot where a snarl of dead weeds sprouted like straw through the concrete. Suddenly, the beast froze into taut stillness, only the tip of the tail twitching.

A grimy knot of life scuttled across the alley.

The cat trembled then burst forward, ripping into the tiny creature, lifting it and hurling it against the wall.

The mouse lay motionless. Already its life sapped away in agony. The cat inched closer, crouching, even the whipping of the tail stilled.

In a gray streak, the tiny rodent darted for the pile of debris. It left a mottled trail.

Leaping, the cat landed on the other side of the trash pile and halted again, ears flattened in consternation. The prey had vanished. A cardboard container lay on its side, slightly open at one end. The cat lowered its head quickly, but nothing moved. One paw struck loudly. Inside the container, something skittered. Then the claws began to dig in unison, shredding at the cardboard.

. . . car . . . soft roof . . . pretty . . .

The cat jerked its head up toward the wall.

. . . red dripping on the sand . . .

Instantly, the cat swelled, emitting a needle-toothed hiss. In terror, it fled for a hole in the fence.

It seemed he'd lain awake a long time, trying to recall the dream. Now, he moved his arm away and blinked without comprehension at a ceiling where amorphous shapes and vague colors swam. Across the room, the curtains had drifted apart: fathomless darkness rippled beyond the window. He sat up with a jerk that nearly sent him over the edge of the bed.

He checked his watch. *Damn.* Groping for the phone on the night table, he heaved to a sitting position. *Almost missed it.* Holding the phone in his lap, he stared intently at his watch as the second hand swung. Then he dialed a number, letting it ring twice. He hung up, waited a few seconds and then dialed again.

"I'm sure now." Breath clogged in his throat, and he spoke in a rush, without preamble. "We've got another one."

IV

Night boomed hollowly in the black spaces beneath the house. Propped on stilts like all the properties at the edge of the bay, the duplex faced out over the water, and years of salt spray had encrusted the support beams until they glistened like mica in the moonlight. The wooden slats of the stairs also glittered, as did the rail on the landing. Darkness filled the lower row of windows, but slivers of light pierced the curtains of the upper floor.

Inside, Kit grunted, twisting vigorously and listening to the wind. *Just what is the temperature out there?* The Franklin stove, which took up an entire side of her living room, gave off only sporadic warmth, and even above the sonata that poured from the CD player, she could still hear the windowpanes rattle. *Would it be so awful if I stayed inside just one night?* Illumination from a squat lamp glinted from the moisture beading the pane. *Would I be fat by tomorrow or something?* Bending far forward, she stretched. *Sometimes I think I must be out of my mind.*

Whatever. She stretched to the other side. *No excuses.* The glass doors behind her made up most of the living room wall, and she checked her form in the reflection. The night, dimly striped by the caps of waves, stirred beyond the small balcony, and the moaning wind created an eerie counterpoint to the music. She owned only classical CDs—Beethoven, Chopin, Mozart—a small collection, mostly piano sonatas, and although (to her continuing chagrin) she could barely tell most of them apart, she could almost always lose herself in their melodies.

She crouched, extending her thigh muscles, then the calves, trying not to let her vision stray to the glass doors. In the cramped apartment, any momentary lapse of concentration could result in seriously barked shins, even with the coffee table shoved up against the sofa and the ottoman pushed to one side so she could exercise. This was as cleared as the room ever got. Far too many heavy pieces of furniture, any single one of which was probably too large for the space, had been jammed into the apartment. *Now go for it.* Gritting her teeth, she tried for maximum extension in one leg, then the other.

A clammy dread closed on her.

. . . something watching . . .

Slowly, she straightened and turned to the balcony. Something massive moved out there, some hulking nightmare.

. . . no . . .

A gaze glittered at her from seven feet above the balcony. One of the eyes moved, became a fat droplet that slid down the door, glistening.

What's wrong with me? She stepped closer to the glass. Rolling blots marked the edges of the sea. *There's nothing there.* Often, she had considered that this view made her life endurable, but this winter the hushed whisper of the surf seemed only to intensify her constant unease. *All of a sudden, I'm scared of reflections?* She pulled a cord, and the drapes swung closed, leaving only a wedge of darkness at the center. *Who did I think was that big anyway?*

The central heat rushed on with a grunting exhalation, as though some beast hulked below the grill on the floor. She stepped over the barbells on the carpet, got her running jacket from the closet, pulling up the tight hood of the jogging suit. Tucking her short red curls in all around, she rummaged on the closet shelf for leg warmers and a hat. *Where did I . . . ?* She opened a bureau drawer to a snarl of scarves, and her attention settled irresistibly on the pistol that nestled among them. For a moment, her hand hovered. Then she slid it out of the holster and almost tenderly hefted it before returning it to the leather pouch and smoothing a scarf around it. No one knew about the gun. She'd had it since Boston. The force here didn't even carry them.

I'm just jumpy. Perhaps the run would help. *Who wouldn't be jumpy after today?* The run would have to help: she would not resume the tranquilizers, refused even to consider it. No, she was through with all that.

Grabbing her keys from the small kitchen table, she let the door slam behind her. This stairwell always looked unfinished to her, as though the glaring white paint had been intended as an undercoat. Months earlier, her first-floor neighbors had moved away; yet halfway down she paused, listening. Wind soughed through the foundations. Near the entrance, dank, heavy musk clung to the carpet, something no amount of airing had ever more than temporarily diminished, and an arctic night seemed to bulge at the front door. Squaring her shoulders, she flung it open and stepped out onto the landing.

The chill shocked her. A swath of light rippled briefly; then the door banged shut behind her. Slowly adjusting to the dark, she let her gaze drift out over the bay. She could just make out pinpoints of light on the mainland, faint as distant stars.

Here goes. Freezing air drilled into her chest as she ran in place for a moment, swinging her arms. Then she launched herself down the stairs and into the bottomless night.

Monsters.

He'd hung up the phone, feeling bitterly wretched. They couldn't seem to talk about anything else anymore. He stopped pacing and peered out the window. Had there ever been a time when they could? The endless

hunt had consumed both their lives, crowding out everything else. He knew what he had to do now. But what if
nothing could draw the boy out of hiding? What if all
the months spent tracking him here ended in failure?
How could he face her again?

He poked the curtains aside. At the end of the block
below, a car swung onto the street, and the glacial glow
of its headlights somehow made him feel even more isolated. It was time to make his sweep of the streets.

Shrugging into his jacket, he eased open the door, and
light swung out across the faded hall carpet. He stared
into the brown gloom. Unable to bring himself to switch
off the lamp, he closed the door on it instead, then felt
his way along the hall, letting his hand ride the gritty
banister as he descended into vague brightness. The
stairs creaked in agonized whispers.

The lamp on the desk still glimmered. Barely. Twenty
watts? Nice of them to make that concession to his presence, he thought. *They're probably asleep.* He crept across
the lobby, the damp chill penetrating his clothes before
he reached the foyer. The inner doors groaned softly. In
the vestibule, murky illumination quivered through a
design on the leaded glass. He put his shoulder to the
outer door.

Lord. As the wind struck, he swayed on the doorstep.
Feel sort of wobbly all of a sudden. He looked around. Only a
blue van shared the small lot with his Volkswagen. *Better
eat something.* An empty can rattled across the ground.

The boy could be anywhere by now. The muted rush of
surf seemed to drift in the wind, to drone from the sky,
to reverberate from the wall behind him. *Around any
corner.* He unlocked the car and checked the backseat
before getting in. The engine stuttered to life, but the
headlights barely penetrated the night. The heater would
kick in once he got started, he told himself, letting the
motor idle. By the light of the dashboard, he examined

his hands. *So they're shaking. So what?* The green flicker made them look like the hands of some alien creature.

Usually he drove to a diner a few miles along the highway, but tonight . . .

I need to watch the streets. The wind yowled like a dying wolf. Earlier, he'd spotted a shabby luncheonette but knew it would be closed at this hour, and other establishments he'd seen—variety store, pharmacy—had apparently closed forever. But he recalled a convenience store where he'd bought some coffee and figured they would have sandwiches at least. As he eased the car out of the lot, his teeth began to chatter.

He headed away from the beach, the Volks shivering through the deserted streets. *Could've sworn it was just down the block here.* The oil light blinked red, a permanent feature, and the speedometer glimmered too faintly to make out. No hint of warmth rose from below the dash. By the time he spotted the glare of the convenience store, his head throbbed from the cold.

A pickup truck without wheels angled at one corner of the lot, an oil spot spreading beneath it. Stepping out of the car, he turned up his collar. A decal on the glass door read PULL, so he tugged several times before pushing inside.

He blinked at the sheer brightness. "How you doin'?" He coughed. "Bad out there tonight." The clerk never looked up from a tabloid on the counter, but something like a sneer flickered on his lips. "Do you make sandwiches?" The clerk jerked his head at a hand-lettered sign that read DELI CLOSED. "Oh." The deli apparently consisted of half an unlit case of packaged luncheon meats.

I'll find something. He wandered the tight aisles, but items on the shelves wouldn't stay in focus. *No, I can't get sick now.* And his vision seemed to blur. *I'm just hungry. That's why I feel weak.* Under the fluorescent lights, all the packaged foods gleamed in queasy, garish shades.

Maybe I should try to talk to this guy again. Empty-handed, he returned to the front of the store and leaned against the counter. *You never know who might tell you something useful.*

Flakes of skin curled in the folds of the clerk's face. "Yeah?" The protuberant eyes moved constantly, at first conveying an impression of active mental processes, then merely of habitual agitation.

"So how are you tonight?"

No response.

"Uh . . . do you have pipe tobacco?"

The man made a rude noise and reached behind him without looking. The packet he tossed on the counter was clearly labeled with a price more than double what it should have been.

He paid, disgusted with himself. "Uh . . . thanks." A few months ago he'd have spoken with this man, possibly managing to draw from him some fact about the background or circumstances of the town, something that could have helped in his search, but now the energy seemed to have dried within him. He could barely force himself to talk, couldn't shake this marrow-deep fatigue or the dizziness and the feeling of . . .

A form darted at the edge of the lot: he glimpsed it through the glass wall. *Don't look.* He jerked his head down, trying to track the movement peripherally. *Behind the pickup truck . . . somebody crouching?* He pocketed his change. "Thanks again."

Leaving the store quickly, he moved along the strip of sidewalk, casually strolling away from his car. *So now he's stalking me.* The wind thrust at his back. *So let him.* Frost stung his ears. *Let him catch me even.* He quickened his pace. *Might be the only way.*

Darkness thickened with every step as he plunged into a side street. *I'm invisible here.* But the driveway he picked his way across seemed to be graveled with shell particles that shone like freshly fallen snow, and his every tread crunched loudly.

He halted. Approaching, a noise like no human footstep grew louder until a paper bag blew past, scratching and scooping loudly along the sidewalk.

Shaking, he laughed aloud. *Christ, man.* He scanned the block behind him. *You're losing it.* The houses here seemed smaller, closer together than most others he'd seen. *What am I doing out here in this wind?* He hurried back toward his car, deciding to drive out to the highway after all. *Find a diner. Then get some rest.* It had been days—he couldn't remember how many—since he'd slept more than fitfully. *Got to be able to think straight tomorrow.* Confusion now could be fatal, he knew.

But where the hell am I? He rushed to the corner. *Christ.* Nothing looked right in either direction. How could he get lost so fast? *Leave it to me to get turned around in such a small town.* He huddled onward. *I could get frostbite or something, wandering around out here.* The wind numbed his face, and it seemed the streets altered before him, became a maze of corridors. From every direction came the roar of the surf. *Maybe I've finally snapped.* Steam rose from a sewer grating to swirl like fog. *Maybe this is the end of the line for me.*

Mist streaked as a blaze of cold struck at his face, and he clamped his hands over his ears. A few doors away, a thick gleam bulged at a mottled window, flickering: no frills, just BAR with specks crawling in the neon. Salvation.

Wet heat enveloped him the instant he opened the door, and he stood blinking. The lights, though precariously dimmed, still revealed more people gathered inside than he'd so far seen in all of Edgeharbor, and they all stared back at him.

Each stride drummed against the boards. Her toes ached in the running shoes, and despite the temperature, her chest and stomach grew damp with perspiration. *Damn, this wind.* She adjusted the earmuffs under her hood. *I've got to get off the boardwalk while I still have skin left.* Catching hold of the rail, she spun onto the stairs and quick-stepped down to a landing. *Some nights, it dies away down lower.* She leapt the rest of the way to the beach, landing lightly in a crouch, then plodded across dense, choppy sand to the harder soil by the water. *Hell, this is no good either.* The chill drove her back like a whip. *I can't believe it got so terrible so fast. Just last week I could still make it all the way to the cannery.* Turning her back to the sea, she sprinted. *If I cut under the boards here . . .*

She came to a dead halt and stared into the dark as the feelings of dread she had been fighting for weeks engulfed her. For an instant, it seemed she had become part of the night somehow, part of an inky cloud that swirled up from the sea to threaten the town and the scattered human beings left in it. *I've got to keep moving.* Fighting off morbid fancies was a skill she had worked hard at acquiring. *Or I'll cramp up.* She stepped closer to the boardwalk, and the hand she held out vanished as though chopped off.

No way I'm going under there. Breathing hard, she jogged in place a moment and started back to the stairs.

Her leg muscles ached as she climbed. *I must be out of my mind.* She dashed diagonally across the walkway and down the opposite ramp. *Running out here on the worst night of the year. If this isn't obsessive-compulsive behavior, I don't know what is.* But she understood all too well why she had to run tonight, knew exactly what she was compensating for. She'd been allowed no active role in today's events, not even marginal participation, and her frustration and humiliation demanded an outlet. *First big case to hit this town ever, and what am I doing? Zip.*

Faint blue moonlight flooded the empty lot. *This is my town, damn it!* She had to stop thinking about it, had to concentrate on the run. Crossing the lot almost soundlessly, she turned the first corner to escape the wind, then cut over to an alternate route along a smaller street. *My time stinks tonight. Maybe I can make it up on the home stretch.* Her heart pounded. *I'm still jumpy as hell. Maybe I'll cheat and take the shortcut out past the amusement park.* As she wove in and out of divots of light beneath random street lamps, every noise, every gusting motion made her gasp. *Got to get my nerves under control.*

Empty crates, bundled newspapers and other flotsam of the streets lay scattered around a yawning trash can. Dense shadows loomed. As she dodged past, her foot slipped on a patch of garbage and she felt a pulling burn in her leg. *Shit!* She limped on. *Probably not so bad.*

The pain balled hotly in her calf. *Just hurts like a . . .*

With a mewling choke, she whirled, both hands raised to protect her face. Something squirmed, and a small gray form blurred away from her on the ground. Wind spun an unearthly whine into the night.

What . . . ? Shivering with more than the cold, she hobbled closer.

V

As a frigid wave of air swept in, the barmaid looked up
with a reflexive smile. Yes, she thought, checking out the
newcomer, that was the same pinched, bitter look she'd
seen on the face of each patron to stumble in tonight.
But this one had something else to offer.

Maybe everything else.

Tall. Good shoulders under the leather jacket. Thick
hair. Blond? She couldn't tell in this light, but it hung wild
in his face, and she liked that too. The door swung shut
behind him as he stalked through a winking band of light.
Even watery from the cold, those sharp blue eyes cut at
her from across the room. She watched him saunter up to
the bar and try to look nonchalant with everybody staring
at him. He moved smoothly for such a big guy, and she
caught herself actually licking her lips.

With an elaborately casual glance around, he planted
himself on a bar stool and pulled off his gloves to blow
on his hands.

He looked mean, she decided, or maybe not "mean"
exactly, maybe just a little dangerous. Definitely her
type. "What'll it be, hon?"

He looked up. The barmaid wasn't as pretty as she'd
seemed from the doorway. The straw-colored hairdo had
been sprayed to brittle stiffness, and the makeup had been
applied too heavily. He opened his mouth to speak but
no words came.

"You really look frostbitten." She gave a throaty giggle. "Can I do something to warm you up?"

A sting of burned tobacco tinctured the air, making his eyes water until the room seemed to melt, and the heavy scent of food made him reel. The woman leaned on the bar and smiled full in his face while she talked, her gaze overbright. Even in this dimness, he could see the tight lines that crosshatched her lips. He had difficulty concentrating on her words, but he said something back to her—he wasn't sure what—and as he peered around the room, a couple at the nearest table looked away. The man's collar had twisted, and his companion, an elderly woman with hair the color of iodine, reached to adjust it. Their table wobbled when she moved.

One long multicolored fingernail tapped commandingly against the bar's surface. "Something to eat? Before I turn this off?" Indicating a Crock-Pot with a wave of her hand, the barmaid blew smoke to the side, dropping the unfiltered cigarette into a clamshell. "You all right?" She waved politely at the cloud, then used her nails to daintily peel a fleck of tobacco off the tip of her tongue. "I roll my own."

"Sorry." He nodded. "Give me a minute to catch my breath." But when he asked for a draft beer, she just looked annoyed.

"Bottles only. One brand. Did you say you wanted a sandwich, hon?" She plucked a match from a box on the counter. "So what brings you to Edgeharbor?"

Good—let her do all the talking. But he thought she seemed to be watching him too closely, smiling over at him while she fixed a hot roast beef sandwich. The fatty odor made his head swim. *Can't seem to manage anymore.* She chatted on, raising her voice above the television set that no one appeared to be watching, most of the patrons preferring to keep their attention on him. He tried to look around without seeming to, attempting to draw individual features from the pervasive gloom. Across the bar, a lighter flickered, and a man's face became a goblin mask, then receded.

Various attempts had apparently been made to decorate the bar. A fake ship's wheel hung against the paneled wall, but he could detect no other evidence of a nautical motif. Covered with cowgirl decals, an unlit jukebox stood silent, a Styrofoam snowman perched atop it. Plastic garland twisted around sections of the bar, and on a shelf, pink lights blinked from a tiny white tree effigy, the branches of which resembled bottlebrushes.

"I always get so depressed when I have to take it down." She shrugged, noticing his stare. "Maybe this year, I'll just leave it up permanent. What do you think?" Her husky laugh might have been sexy if she hadn't started coughing. "So what did you say brings you here? Business? You don't look like you're from anywheres around here."

He started to thank her but caught himself and just smiled instead. *Okay, she likes that.* There'd been a time when people had often complimented his smile. *Keep working it.* With a faint, detached amazement, he watched the flush rise in her cheeks. *At least I can still do something right. Sort of.* She smoothed her sweater, pulling it tight over her breasts. *Shy little thing.* He grinned appreciatively, feeling nothing but disgust with himself. This could be a break though, and he needed one: somebody had to answer his questions. "Pretty quiet tonight," he began.

"Off-season." She shrugged vaguely. "You need a glass?"

Off-season—he'd heard that up and down the coast, in every little shore town he'd been through, as though these people lived only for the few months of pounding sun, the rest of the year declining into a kind of stupor. The barmaid clicked away on incredibly high heels, and he noticed that, behind the row of bottles, a greasy fog had settled on what might once have been a tinted mirror. Between a fifth of Jack Daniel's and a bottle of something with a bat on the label, he recognized the smear of his own reflection.

My Lord. Of all the transformations, of all the damaged and aching spots within, nothing showed. It seemed shockingly wrong. He looked the same, exactly the same.

Without quite intending to, he lifted the beer in a silent toast, and his teeth clenched. *Doesn't he look natural?* Between yellowing blotches on the mirror, a handsome man raised his glass, and he studied the image. *A lie.* It sickened him. *Even my appearance.* As he wondered if anything about him had ever been honest, his grip tightened on the beer.

Here I am, alone. As usual. Gradually, he began to peer about more openly. *Funny, how nothing ever changes.* He found he envied even this muttering crowd their dreary camaraderie. At the far end of the bar, the barmaid looked almost glamorous, and the customers in the dimness might be lively, congenial. Who could tell? Sipping his beer, he returned his attention to the mirror, and the handsome image began to melt. The ears stood out red as blood, and the unshaven cheeks bristled. He downed the beer in uneven gulps. Years ago, in another lifetime it seemed, hadn't women liked his eyes?

They looked frozen now. Like filthy ice at the bottom of a well.

Flanks trembling, the cat tried to slink back under the fence but crumpled before it reached the hole. A cardboard box with a burst bottom lay on its side nearby, amid the jars and cans.

"It's all right." Kit approached cautiously. "Don't be afraid." She reached out her hand. "No, no, don't move." The cat dragged dark smears behind it on the concrete. "Ssh. Have you been in a fight or something, huh? Poor little guy." Actually, the cat struck her as unusually large.

I don't even like cats much. In the past few minutes, the animal had twice followed her out onto the sidewalk, circling her while making that terrible noise, then had dragged itself back into the alley.

"You tangle with a dog, kitty?" At the sound of her voice, the wounded feline crept closer, only to twist unsteadily away. "You're a size all right. I'd hate to see the other fellow. There now, cat. It's all right." Its legs tremored.

What the heck color is it anyway? Scant illumination floated into the alley, and she leaned closer. *Great.* Orange tail, one white ear, gray face: it looked as though it had been stitched together from parts of other animals. *Frankenstein's cat.*

The next time the animal fell on its side, it failed to get up. Gingerly, she stroked the fur, but the beast didn't twitch. Four streaks of blood glistened on its flank.

Suddenly, the broad head tilted, straining in her direction. Then the green glimmer of the eyes sealed shut again, and the head dropped.

Oh hell. It just died. She pulled off her glove and touched the cat's ribs with her fingertips. The fur felt like frost, but underneath warmth throbbed. *Anyway, it'll be dead soon on a night like this, that's for sure.* Suddenly, green gleamed up at her again, and the mouth opened in a silent bleat.

Great. She put her glove back on and tried to lift the creature without hurting it or getting blood on herself. *Now, what am I doing? Am I nuts?* Stiffening, the cat arched and bristled, hissing like a ruptured steam pipe. She almost dropped it as claws dug frantically into the arm of her jacket. "Hey, cut that out!"

The cat went limp. *Oh hell, I killed it.* But it squirmed feebly as the wind keened around her. *Now what? Hell hell hell hell hell.*

* * *

"Is one of these going to be enough, hon?"

One eye in the mirror, he watched his own smile erode . . . then rebuilt it, grain by grain. When he considered the image convincing, he turned to find the barmaid studying him, her lips slightly parted, a sharp line creasing her forehead. Nodding at the mirror, he made a show of raking his fingers at the windblown mess of his hair.

". . . have noticed if you'd been in before." She watched him gulp the messy sandwich. "Guess you were hungry." Dragging delicately at her lipstick-smeared cigarette, she plucked it from her mouth and dropped it back in the clamshell. "This bother you while you're eating?"

"Sorry?" The food actually tasted of nicotine. "I mean, no. Fine."

"The way you downed that—you sure one's enough?"

Nodding, he wiped at his face with the paper napkin. "So, you from here?"

"Who me?" She practically gurgled. "I lived here all my life. This place was my dad's, but I run it myself, since me and my husband split." She blew smoke out of her mouth and sucked it back in through her nostrils, an action that made her look bizarre, dragonish. "Bar's about the only business that makes money in this town, especially in winter. What did you say you were doing here?"

He gave her the new name and the story about being a real estate appraiser. ". . . several properties to inspect in the area. Might take a few days. You never know." She accepted this without comment, and he nodded at his reflection. *So easy for me to fool them anymore.* The hollow mask in the mirror watched him. *Lying takes hardly any effort.*

"Sal? Could you get the phone, hon?" Shaking another cigarette out of the pack, she felt around in her apron pocket. "You don't smoke? Barry, is it?" The box of matches still lay on the counter, and she leaned forward so he could light her cigarette.

"I tried a pipe once. Kept dumping it on myself. Got sick of finding scorch marks on all my shirts."

"Yeah?" She raised an eyebrow. "You don't strike me as clumsy."

"I . . . was drinking a lot then."

"Can't picture that neither." She winked at him. "You strike me as the kind of guy who's in control. What? Did I say something? You sure you're all right? I guess there must be a lot of work in this area for you then. What with every house on the peninsula up for sale, just about. Not that there's any buyers anywheres."

"Why's that?"

An old man in a fur hat with earflaps stumbled over from one of the tables, and she handed him a glass. "Here you go, Slick," she said. "Oh, thank you, honey. Did you hear about all that commotion by the bay? State troopers and everything. Some kind of accident, I heard." She counted change. "So did you decide whether you want another one before I put this stuff away or what? Barry?"

Have to keep her talking, find out about the town . . . about them. But have to be subtle, have to . . .

Inexorably, the beer he'd tried only to sip uncoiled a knot of weariness deep within him, and he felt it spring through every limb. Helpless to stop himself, he realized that he was about to say something disastrously reckless. "When I was driving into town, I practically had an accident." He strained to control the stream of words. "Some kid came tearing out of the woods right in front of my car. I think maybe I might've clipped him. But he took off. Maybe you know the kid? About fifteen or so—pale looking, skinny. Ring any bells? Long sort of blondish hair sticking out from under one of those caps. Any ideas?"

She actually took a step back.

Damn. Immediately, he knew he'd screwed up again. *Big-time.* If only he'd been patient, played her along. "I just wanted to be sure the kid was all right, know what I mean?"

She gnawed her lipstick, darkening the edges of her front teeth. "Uh huh." She turned to slice a roll with a long knife. "Where'd you say you was from?" She looked up, scrutinizing him.

"Trenton, originally." He'd have to talk fast now. "These days I pretty much live where they send me. Suitcase in the car mostly. One motel after another. So this kid doesn't sound like anybody from around here?"

"Don't sound like nobody I know." She pursed her lips. "Maybe you ought to check with the cops."

She knows him. He nodded, a pulse thundering in his ears. "Yeah."

"Practically no teenagers left anyways."

"Why's that?"

"Runaways. We had a real problem with that. Something awful. You can't blame them really. Nothing much to hold them here no mores. If you're in real estate, how come you don't know about this town?"

"Uh huh." Meticulously, he prodded the corner of the beer label with his thumbnail. "I'm not in the sales end of things," he explained as foil peeled smoothly from the damp bottle. "I just examine the structures, the land." He replaced the label, upside down, smoothing out the wrinkles. "So, what's it like living here?" Pouring the last of the beer into his glass, he smiled hard.

She got him another bottle. "Oh, you know, like anywheres else, except now it's so empty. But I'll tell you one thing, I wouldn't want to live nowheres where I couldn't hear the ocean." She rinsed a couple of glasses, set them to drain.

Nodding and smiling for the next twenty minutes, he tried to draw her out about the town but could elicit nothing beyond vague generalizations, which seemed to reflect her genuinely vague outlook. Finally her mental fuzziness proved infectious: he couldn't even remember her name. Margie? Tracie? He watched the ashes from her cigarette spill across the bar. After his third beer, their conversation lapsed, and she turned her attention to the other patrons.

"I didn't have to get involved, you know." Three people sat at one of the nearer tables, two men sipping drinks with a woman who kept stirring ice in a glass. "I could of very easily just continued on." The woman wore rollers, which had been covered with some sort of sparkling mesh scarf, as if for emphasis. "I'm telling you." Her eye makeup reminded him of the album jackets of the opera recordings his wife had loved . . . of how he'd used to tease her about all the fat ladies done up like love goddesses. *Can't get lost in the past now. Have to stay alert.* He could actually feel the fever surging within him. *Might learn something.* He shook his head, tried to concentrate. *You never know.* One of the three at the table would speak, then stop, then another would say something, though not apparently in response, more as if they'd suddenly recalled some forgotten detail. "Is that what you want? To wind up like Atlantic City?"

"I'm telling you."

He struggled to find the thread of their conversation, but the loudest one, a gaunt man in a toupee, seemed to be engaged in a different discussion altogether.

"Slums by the sea?"

"You know who found it? Dolly's father. Yeah, the old man. Pieces floating. I hear he's been in bed ever since."

"That's so bad when they get like that at that age. Probably never get up again."

"No," she agreed. "It ain't."

"Homeless people pissing under the boardwalk? Is that what you want?"

"I'm telling you, we will never have gambling here.

Don't be ridiculous." She banged the bottom of her empty glass on the table for emphasis, but the rollers on her head never so much as vibrated.

He strained to listen. It seemed they'd paired off differently now, two still conversing and one continuing to speak exclusively in non sequiturs. "The town council would never allow it." Suddenly, the woman's stare angled in his direction, so he fixed his eyes on his beer and let their words blur around him. A thin drift of laughter reached him from across the bar, and he had the feeling he'd missed something, that someone had at last uttered something crucial, and he leaned his head on his hands and struggled to listen, concentrating first on the nearest table, then on another farther away, but now each remark had developed a chanted, mumbled quality that made his head throb. Everyone around him seemed to be drinking boilermakers, even the dim little couple at the far end of the bar, so when Margie/Tracie returned, he ordered one too. Again, she raised an eyebrow, something he knew she practiced in front of a mirror. He gulped the shot and swigged from the beer, feeling the sweat bead out on his forehead. *God, how do they stand these?* He watched a highly rouged woman drop the whole shot glass into the beer, raise it carefully and take an enormous gulp without blinking.

"No," the guy with the toupee loudly insisted. "The real problem is still the gambling and the whores and the fast-food joints." He waited for one of them to nod in agreement. When no one did, he drained his glass as though vindicated. "Am I right?"

"I'm telling you."

Christ, I need sleep. He realized that he and the barmaid were speaking again, though he had no idea what they'd been saying.

". . . welfare, a lot of them, I guess." She shrugged a bony shoulder. "I don't really know."

"I guess"—he started to cough—"there's not much else to do winter nights besides drink."

"Well, they do enough of that." Abruptly, she teetered away.

Not doing too well here, am I? Haven't done too well in a long time. He shivered, and the faces in the bar rose like apparitions, thin and anxious, bathed in the light from the television, a light as dingy as dirty water. *Probably it's time they sent somebody else.* But who? His glass chattered against his teeth. *Steady.* Then he realized they'd all stirred. Suddenly, they sat up or leaned forward in their seats, staring above his head. Trying to comprehend, he put down his glass.

"Stacey, put the sound up."

"Yeah, turn it up."

On the picture tube, people crowded around a few tethered boats. With a start, he recognized Edgeharbor. ". . . has not yet been identified but police say . . ." His hand gripped the mug to keep from shaking, and he caught a glimpse of milling uniforms before the shot changed to a wet-suited diver. ". . . that of a woman, twenty-five to thirty years . . ." State troopers in heavy coats scooped the water with nets as coast guard cutters chugged past. "Local authorities are asking anyone with information . . ." He felt the glass crunch, stared at the blood in his palm.

"Mob hit," someone declared.

"You think?"

The barmaid hurried over with a rag. "You okay, hon?"

"No. Yes." He pressed a paper napkin into the cut. "I'm all right."

"Why the hell don't they stay in Atlantic City?"

As the newscast dissolved into the swirling colors of a commercial, people erupted with sudden animation all around the bar.

"Oh my God."

"Would you believe that? Right here."

"Oh my God. On the news and everything."

"Thanks." Nodding, he felt the food lump inertly in his gut. "Stacey." He threw some money on the bar, then staggered across the room and out the door without even zipping his jacket.

"Come again," she called, watching the door swing shut on the night. As she glanced up at the television, a line creased her forehead, and after a moment, she clicked to the end of the bar and picked up the phone.

VI

On the private beach, sand clung to the earth in frozen mounds and patches. Boulders, scaled with broken shells and furred green, angled steeply to moonlit surf.

The old house appeared empty, and a ship on the weathervane slued inland as the current that carried it shrilled across the chimney. The house seemed to lean against the wind, and a shutter banged at a gabled dormer. Front windows boldly faced the sea, but thick draperies hung behind the shutters so that no lights showed at all.

In the front parlor, a deeper shadow swayed. One shaking hand clutched at the curtain. "I have seen you," the old woman whispered dryly. "And I know you wait there still." She stared down the beach to where the black sea writhed. "By the rocks at night, I have seen you."

All her life, she'd hated the sea. Bit by bit, it had taken from her everything she had ever cared for. She lived by it now in a state of conscious challenge and had come to believe without hesitation that it was equally aware of her. Sometimes she felt their enmity was all that remained of her life, all that animated her.

"And I know what you are." An acute sense of absurdity floated through her dread. She envisioned herself with clarity, alone in an old dark house, whispering to the windowpane and watching for a dead thing to heave from the waves. "But not yet. You won't rise yet." She wished she could laugh at her own madness. "I'm not quite crazy. I have seen. And I know."

Sea winds surged against the walls, and the beams of the house creaked like the timbers of an ancient ship.

. . . and I did nothing.

His hands shook as he hurried from the bar. *Young woman . . . ripped apart.* The words snarled in his brain. *Right here. In this town. While I . . .*

When his chest began to ache, he realized his jacket still hung open. *Pneumonia won't help.* Fumbling with the zipper, he hurried down the street. He'd have to lay low— the police would be here in full force now. Nothing must interfere. He had to get to the boy before they did.

Cold stabbed into his lungs, and an old knotted scar along his ribs throbbed, but he used the pain, forcing himself onward through the wind. The empty bungalows no longer looked sad to him. They looked ominous, corrupt. *Can't let the cops get onto me.* The maze of streets untangled. The lights in the convenience store still blared, though a placard in the window now read CLOSED, and he fished out his keys and slid into the front seat of the Volks. *My gloves.* He stared at his hands on the steering wheel. *Must have left them at the bar.*

Slowly, his breathing eased, and the engine growled. *Torn to pieces.*

All the way back to the hotel, he fought the impulse to take the first road out of town, to speed on until the pinelands lay far behind him, until even these past years of his life dwindled in the distance. *What life would that be?* So many times before, he'd struggled with the impulse to run. *Sometimes I think I've been dead all these years. Dead and just too stupid to fall over.*

He parked and hurried to the door. *Don't make me have to ring. I don't think I could deal with any more suspicions tonight.* But the hotel door swung easily at his shove, and he released a steaming sigh. The small lamp still glowed in the deep gloom by the desk. *If I can just lie down for a while, I'll be all right.* Closing the door softly, he shivered in the entrance, waiting for his vision to adjust.

"Pardon me, but do you mind if I ask you a few questions?"

Brown shadows slid one into another as someone rose from the lobby sofa. He blinked rapidly and his mouth dropped open. Before he could speak, the door behind the desk flew open, and the hotelkeeper shuffled forward, holding his bathrobe closed. Mrs. D'Amato trailed him aggressively, and as she gestured and muttered in Italian, the sleeves of her housedress flapped to reveal angular glimpses of bony arms. He knew not a word of the language, but her tone of voice he understood perfectly. "You startled me." Turning back to his visitor, he tried to smile with numbed facial muscles. "Is anything wrong?" He'd grown sufficiently accustomed to the light to make out the insignia on her coat.

"Officer Lonigan," she told him. "I'm with the Edgeharbor Police Department." Somehow she made it sound like a question. "Mr. D'Amato, could we get a little more light in here, please?" Her voice held a cajoling quality.

The chandelier flared. A coating of dust blazed on the crystals, and discolored bands of brightness striped the faded wallpaper. Blinking rapidly, he looked down at the old stains that pooled across the carpet.

"We had some trouble here in town earlier. Perhaps you heard about it? Mr. . . . Hobbes, is it?"

"Yes, I . . ." His voice cracked. "Yes."

"We're just doing some routine checking on people, finding out about any strangers that might be in town." As she studied his face, her expression hardened. "Nothing to be nervous about."

He succeeded in making his features relax. "Of course." He spread his hands open as though attempting to conjure invisible forces from the air.

"Thank you, folks." She turned her head slightly, holding him in her peripheral vision. "That'll be all for now. I'll call you if I need you," she added, iron courtesy in her voice. "I mean it, folks. You can leave us alone. Thank you. I'll put the lights out when we're through."

So close. He felt himself sink, mired in the glare from the chandelier. *I got so close.* A torrent of thoughts surged through his brain, all of them desperate. *Can't let them stop me.* The top of the policewoman's head barely reached his chin, and her honey-colored hair glinted in the light. *Not now.* Her hair had been cut unbecomingly short, brushed severely behind the ears, the effect a touch too insistent in its attempt to minimize her femininity. And the face looked young, too young really. *Are those freckles?* The tension in his shoulders relaxed, and suddenly, he smiled. "Anything I can do to help, Officer."

"Won't you sit, please?" She remained standing.

Good. He nodded approvingly. *Basic stuff—maintain the psychological advantage.* He kept smiling. *Right out of a textbook.* Though her stance and tone of voice suggested confidence, the details of the performance didn't bear up under scrutiny. When he held her stare, she shifted her weight and wiped her palms on her pants, and her left leg seemed to tremble slightly. *Well, why shouldn't she be nervous? I might be a killer after all.* He even thought he detected a trace of lipstick. *Total amateur.* Apparently about to speak, she fumbled in her coat pocket for a notebook. *What in hell is she doing here alone?* This nervous woman had waited alone for a suspect? And suddenly he placed her as the type who, though nearly paralyzed with fear, inevitably pushed themselves into dangerous situations. *Just what I don't need.* It was just this quality that always rendered rookie cops a hazard—that need to prove themselves.

"Could I have your full name, please?"

She had the voice of a little girl, he realized, and the officious tone she tried to maintain made him want to laugh. "Funny, you seemed to know it a minute ago."

"I mean, just for the record." She pretended to write something down.

His nerves must be even worse than he'd thought—such a flimsy routine, and for a moment he'd actually been worried. "Barry Hobbes," he told her. "I'm an appraiser, doing on-site inspections for an Atlantic City developer." It amused him to see her tense up as he dug for his wallet. "This is my company's card. Would you mind sitting down too? It's been an exhausting day, and you're making me crane my neck. This weather. Everything aches." He sank back into the sofa and immediately sneezed as a cloud of dust engulfed him.

She perched on the arm of the facing sofa. "Did you hurt your hand?"

He unzipped the jacket. "I stopped in at one of your local taverns, yes. I'm afraid I broke a glass." He smiled fiercely, forcing his posture to slacken.

"That would be The Pine Inn," she continued, struggling to retain an authoritative manner. "It's the only one that's open. Awfully brisk night to be out, isn't it?" She seemed surprised to find herself sitting, and for just an instant, her glance lingered on the way his jacket bunched across his shoulders.

Good Lord, she likes me. It made him uncomfortable again, and he twisted a button on the front of his shirt, trying to conceal one hand beneath the other. She asked something else, but now the ardent voice maddened him. *Run away from me, you little idiot.* Suddenly, he wanted to shake her. *This isn't a game, little girl, with your toy badge. You could wind up dead.* He stared past her, forcing her to follow his gaze. *Didn't your parents teach you not to talk to strangers? You'll never see anybody stranger than me.*

"Folks, why don't you turn in now? Like I asked. Mr. Hobbes and I have a few things to discuss." Her voice betrayed annoyance at finding the D'Amatos still hesitating in the doorway, and with an exchange of worried looks, the couple retreated to their apartment. "We've had some trouble as I said, Mr. Hobbes. Have you heard about it?"

Slowly, his hand rose to brush at his forehead. "Saw something about it on the news." Seemingly of their own volition, his fingers returned to the loose button. "Terrible thing. Really terrible." The muscles of his upper arms and shoulders bunched like a boa constrictor as he fidgeted. "Was she a local woman?"

Her eyes narrowed. The words sounded right, but there was something about his manner, as though the facial expression lagged a beat behind his voice, the effect oddly mechanical. "They haven't released the identity of the body yet."

The button came away in his hand, and he held it in his palm. "But can't you give me some idea?" A smile of impressive voltage lit his face.

"We found a car," she responded. "It's registered to a dealer at one of the casinos. We don't know much yet, but it looks like she may have been involved in some pretty shady stuff." Biting the inside of her lip, she tried to look away from him. "Kept company with some real high rollers."

"That's very interesting. And the body? Is it still here in town?"

"They took it . . . took her . . . what they could find of . . . away to the lab in A.C. They'll do all the . . ."

"And her car?"

"Still at the . . . they'll send a tow truck to . . . get it." Her face clouded, and she seemed to shake herself. "Well, thank you for speaking with me. If I . . . if we have any other questions, how much longer will you be staying in Edgeharbor?"

Not bad-looking. He allowed himself to admire the way the glow caught in the stray curls around her face. *But such an odd bird.* As with so many redheads, her skin held its pallor deeply, showing none of the latent tan sported by most of the town's residents. *What the hell can she be doing here?* Edgeharbor couldn't have more than a handful of cops on payroll. It seemed unlikely she'd seen cases involving much besides summer vandalism. He knew enough about small-town police to guess the layer of professionalism in which she cloaked herself must have been acquired elsewhere, and he wondered how old she could be. Twenty-five? Twenty-six? He squinted, trying to make out the color of her eyes, but they glinted red in the glare. "Until my work is finished." He rose abruptly, dismissing her. "A few more days probably."

The sudden sympathy in his smile startled her even more than the way he'd taken control of the interview. "I guess," she said, a flush creeping up her neck, "that'll be all for the time being." She snapped the notebook shut.

He barely responded as she thanked him for his time. The door closed behind her, and he listened to her footsteps going down the steps, then heard the muted growl of an engine. The front window lit for an instant, and the noise faded. *Cops—last thing I need now.* Shaking his head, he turned away, and the weariness claimed him. He almost staggered. Halfway up the stairs, he heard the office door creak open, and a woman's voice lanced out, shrieking in Italian.

I need time. Her screams scalded his back as he climbed. *I'm so close. Can't let anything stop me now.*

Stupid, stupid fool! Only when her stomach muscles finally unclenched did she realize how tense she'd been. *Idiot!* She pounded her hands on the steering wheel. *What's wrong with me?* The tires heaved over cracked asphalt, and the jeep's worn shocks creaked like mattress springs. *I let him do all the questioning!*

An icy wind prowled the streets, rattling windows and doors and rustling through evergreen hedges. The town seemed truly dead.

She'd gotten nothing from him. The jeep swerved through an intersection. *Nothing!* He had controlled the interview from start to finish. Except for those first few seconds when he'd looked startled.

She fiddled with dials and knobs, trying to get some heat into the frigid vehicle. How could she have allowed herself to be interrogated that way? Just because he looked like that and smiled at her a little? *Pathetic!* With a screech of brakes, she pulled the jeep over by the darkened church. *Who is he that he can do this to me?* Fighting to get herself under control, she adjusted the rearview mirror until she could see herself. *What's the big deal though?* Even an alley cat had gotten over on her this evening, assuming the damn thing was still alive. She almost laughed at herself.

Switching on the overhead light, she examined the business card Hobbes had given her, held it closer to the dim illumination. It looked legitimate enough, but every instinct told her otherwise. *All right, you won the first round, Mr. Hobbes, or whatever your name is. But I'm after you now, and I mean to find out who you are and what you're doing in my town.* She gunned the engine, but the jeep only grunted and fell silent. She cursed and twisted the key. *So be careful, mister.* This time the engine sputtered to chattering life, the stick vibrating like the controls of a mechanical bull. *Be real careful.*

The scream flowered in the night.

It coiled its tendrils about the fire escape, twining over broken gutters and antennas. A lonely cry, like the howl of something lost and afraid, it seemed to change directions in the air, an ember of noise, drifting across the roofs, above the streets. It circled on the wind, at times bestial, at times almost a sob, until at last, it settled into a gurgle of pain—a final shuddering burst of ecstatic agony.

From far below, a few dogs barked, then lapsed into terrified silence.

Finally, only the wind moaned in the empty streets, sweeping the mournful sound of the sea through the town.

Night wind stirred through a tangle of evergreens, and between the firs, sparse white sand shimmered faintly. This strip of ground lay far inland, nearly at the center of the peninsula, as far from the water as it was possible to get in Edgeharbor. Yet the wind still carried with it the distant howl of waves, like the muted wail of a drowning child.

He listened for a long time without moving. From his hiding place among the scrub growth off the road, he cautiously surveyed the fenced lot.

The brown lace of branches twined overhead. Pine shadows, slender and indistinct in the moonlight, mottled the ground, and branches rattled and whispered. Beneath each tree, a mat of dried needles crunched underfoot like dead insects, and skeletal fingers seemed to tear at his sleeves as he pressed through.

He launched himself at the fence, his fingers hooking through the wide links, his shoes scrabbling for purchase. Near the top, a cramp seized him, and hanging by one hand, he clutched his side. Slowly, the deep green scent of the forest filled his lungs, and he eased his legs over the wire.

He dropped to the other side. In the distance, a dog barked.

The wind stung his ears so hard they began to feel warm, and he took the tiny flashlight from his pocket and swung it around. Shapes flared, lurching. Before dissolving in the woods beyond the fence, the circular glow traveled across a metal sign that identified this as a county impoundment lot. Sand and bird droppings powdered the closer vehicles. One of the cars had been stripped, eviscerated even of doors and seats, naked wheel rims jutting like knobs of bone. He jerked the light back. The roof of the convertible by the gate had been shredded in wide strips, and behind it, a dented van listed on rusted rims.

The wind died away, and all around him the night stilled. Solemnly, he approached the convertible. The beam yoked the tattered roof, then quivered to the scrapes on the side of the door.

"Dear Jesus." Despite the intense cold, he felt a film of moisture slide between his shoulder blades. *Claw marks.* A radiant impact had burst across the windshield, its center snowy in the pencil beam, fraying into crystal webbing at the edges. He paced to the other side, the beam slicing ahead. The door had been torn from the frame, and jagged bits of metal still protruded. As he leaned in, a splinter of glass caught at his sleeve, and the beam slid across dark stains on the seat.

Switching off the flashlight, he pulled back from the car. As he gazed imploringly up at the stars, the fierce yapping of the wind surrounded him.

VII

Easing his legs over the sill, the boy slipped into the night as smoothly as into frigid water. Then he slid the window down behind him, leaving it open a crack.

Somehow the moon made the cold seem even worse, and he turned his collar up as he hurried down the fire escape, treading on smears of moonlight around the worn paint. He listened for a long moment before going over the side and down the ladder to the drop.

Landing on all fours, he paused, still in a crouch, his fearful gaze stabbing the night in all directions. Then he scrambled down the alley.

Near the street, he slowed and peered out cautiously; hunching his shoulders, he hurried straight into the wind. At this hour, the sidewalks belonged to him, and he barely felt afraid at all. Besides, he had to go out tonight. No choice. They needed things . . . and he had an important errand. Nothing would happen. Mouthing the words, he hurried down the street. *Nothing. I'll be safe.*

The freedom of the night streets always made him feel drunk, and he sprinted as though the wind had picked him up. He took a different route tonight. Mindful of the near-ambush of the day before, he kept to the back streets with their dead lawns and skeletal trees, fragile light at random windows only intensifying his sense of isolation.

He stopped, his feet frozen in place. *Wha—?* Something with an impossibly broad face squatted on a tiny porch. He took another step. The bulky plastic snowman grinned innocently, and he remembered seeing it lighted many times over the years. He wondered why these people hadn't taken down their decorations yet, but a further look confirmed the answer already forming in his mind. The small house had an abandoned look. Another one gone.

Abruptly, the street ended at a veritable tunnel. Glancing around, he darted up the ramp above it, feeling the temperature drop with every step.

On the boardwalk, the wind made his face flame. Weaving like a kite, he rushed for the rail, grabbed it. Darkness here held a thicker texture, and he inched along, staring out to where moonlight flickered on the breakers. This had to be the place. Clutching the rail, he stepped on the lowest rung and leaned far over. The sand glimmered, stony areas gaping like holes.

He saw no sign of his backpack . . . and again found himself watching the surf.

Stars glinted sharply between wispy clouds. Low and fast, gray shapes scurried at the water's edge where shadows solidified into a barrier of mud—night-prowling seabirds or rats from the drainage pipe. He shuddered. *Don't let it be rats.* Moonlight left white tracks on the water, and he shivered again, feeling exposed as he hopped off the rail.

He started down. As his soles gritted on the wooden steps, the sea rushed louder. Pacing through scrub grass, he stayed beside the boardwalk, searching. He remembered the knapsack had come off just as he'd started under the boards, and the spot where he'd crawled through had to be right about . . .

The opening gaped. Sand sparkled around his sneakers, around tufts of inky dead grass. Stooping, he thrust his hand into the hole and felt around.

The wood groaned. Yanking his arm away, he recoiled.

Above him, someone leaned over the rail. A web of moonlight cauled the man's face. It was huge, bloated.

Him!

The shape lumbered back out of sight.

It's him. Blood thundered in the boy's ears. *This time it really is.* As he tried to run, paralysis gripped his legs. *Him!* He sank toward the hole, but a gray thing squeezed along the edge of the sand, dragging a naked tail. *No!* Spinning, he sprinted for the sea.

It seemed he moved very slowly across the softness, his feet grating with each tread, his breath coming in ragged gulps—he could hear nothing else. Finally reaching the water, he raced along the hardened mud. His sneakers gripped the ground wetly, and with every few paces he slipped.

His chest ached, and a stitch ripped his side as he turned to look back. Nothing stirred on the beach, and no hulking shapes hobbled across the boardwalk. Agony snapping in his lungs, he tried to remember exactly what he'd seen. Blood-dark parka. The glint of the eyeglasses.

Wind pierced his back, and he stumbled on.

Moonlight frothed in black water, and each dying wave shimmered almost to his feet. Something flapped away from a jutting rock, and he groaned, running a few steps more. Boulders, protruding from the shale like broken teeth, stopped him. Beyond the rocks, a cyclone fence leaned into deeper swells, and between the links the moon trembled in water. He couldn't get across this way; he'd have to go back up the beach.

Long arms on the ground reached for him. Only when he recognized his own shadow on the mud did he realize he must be silhouetted against the glittering waves. *He can see me!* His teeth chattered. *That's how come he didn't already chase me. He knows I got to come back, and he can just wait.* All feeling bled from his arms and legs. He had to get away. But where? If he could make it to where the salt marsh began at the other end of the beach, he might . . .

No. Wind sliced through him. *Too cold.* Waves hissed, lapping at a ridge of stones. He would die in the swamp. He had to make it back to town. The hollows of the beach gaped before him. Somehow he had to make it back past the boardwalk. Trotting forward, he dodged erratically before dropping to a crouch.

Wind zipped through beach grass around him, and he began to shake. He scuttled sideways to a deeper depression, freezing air lashing the back of his neck. Scrambling behind a larger dune, he halted, let ragged folds of darkness wrap about him while he listened to the tumbling whisper of the waves.

Finally, he inched forward. On aching knees and hands, he reached the boardwalk at a point where it reared high above the sand. Staring hard, he made out the shape of a concrete pillar, and he edged closer until at last he huddled behind it. Heavy boots clacked above his head.

He darted straight down the center of the passage. Tripping over something embedded in invisible sand, he sprawled, pain flashing in his foot, then stumbled up.

Coming out the other side, he dashed through an opening between two abandoned restaurants. Foot throbbing, he limped into a side street as empty as a graveyard, then cut through a garden.

At the entrance to the playground, a length of chain looped around a pole. As he squeezed through, the gate shifted slightly. He squirmed, briefly stuck, bruising his hips and shoulder as he shoved his way through.

Something struck the ground with a metallic thump. The seesaw banged down again, one end rising a few feet in the wind, then crashing rhythmically. *Did he see? Did he follow?* Clouds churned. A strike of moonlight caught him, and he hobbled for the darkness beyond the slide.

My foot. Jeez. He limped heavily now, and the chains for the swings chimed against metal poles with a sound like buoys. *Maybe my ankle.* He clambered through a concrete tube and hunkered for a long moment, panting. The playground was very near the beach. On the other side of the next fence lay the old amusement park, permanently shut now—he could hide there. He'd done it before, though he found the empty rides and boarded kiosks a little scary. *No, I got to try and get back.*

He crawled out and headed away from the park. His ankle throbbed and his sneakers slipped on the links, but he topped the fence. Clouds flowed across the sky, and great blotches slid over the yards and houses. Agony stabbed through his foot when he dropped to the other side. Frost easily penetrated the jacket and both sweaters, and his muscles twitched, quivering like small animals beneath his clothes.

So tired of running.

Wanting to scream, she gritted her teeth against the itch. Even when she bent as far forward as she could in the heavy chair, her right hand still strained inches from her cheek. Frantically, she swung her head from side to side. Strips of rope cut into her arms, and she felt a trickling on her wrists.

In the frigid stillness, her muscles had stiffened from hours of anguished waiting and now felt heavy, dead. Why didn't someone help her? Surely someone must be looking for her. She stared at the wall, until she saw faces in the rough and lumpy paint, malevolent leers and grimaces that eroded her control until panic overwhelmed her, and the walls reeled. Her body arched, only the straps holding her down. If someone didn't find her soon . . .

Her fingers dug convulsively into the arms of the chair, and the cloth gag twisted in her mouth as tears and saliva slicked one side of her face. She'd seen blood on his hands. *Dear God*, she prayed silently, *don't let me die like this!*

In the blustery shadows, hedges lurked. When a trash can lid clattered, the boy ducked behind a tree, and the shades of thin branches whipped through the fleeting moonlight at his feet.

Grayness flickered at the back window of one of the bungalows, and laughter filtered through the wind, so faint it seemed to emanate from some assembly of phantoms. In the garden, he crept closer, stumbling over roots that knuckled through hard ground. Laughter fluttered again, and bright blurs oscillated through the curtain. *Somebody watching television.* It seemed so normal, he couldn't understand why it made him feel so sad. *I didn't think nobody lived on this block in wintertime.* He wondered who might be inside, wondered if they knew what it meant to be freezing or frightened. Or desperate. Overhead, branches creaked, and he stumbled again, his feet snared in a net of shadows.

While the television murmured, he felt his knee. His jeans had torn when he'd fallen under the boardwalk, and the skin still oozed. He couldn't walk around like this. *I got to look normal.* He could almost hear his father's voice: *You know what they'll do to you if they find out?*

Constantly brushing sand from himself, he hurried on, this time keeping to the sidewalk, as far as possible from the evergreens that crowded the bungalows. Normally, he detoured a block around The Pine Inn, but tonight, already so weary, he hurried right by it.

Don't nobody come out.

Don't nobody open the door. He looked straight ahead as he passed the neon sign. *Just let me get to the corner.* Once beyond the spill of light, he tried to run but pain flared in his foot and knee. *Just a little farther.* Two blocks away, the only other open business in town blazed, and he rushed for it, his hands thrust deep in his pockets.

Trying to look casual, he strolled through the entrance as the cashier looked up and snorted. The boy immediately sought escape down the farthest aisle and, cupping his hands over his ears, peeked at the covers of wrestling magazines and horoscope booklets. Tentatively, he took one hand away from his ears, half expecting to see blood; then he dug through packages of flavored chips, aware of the clerk's derisive stare in the fish-eye mirror. Ghoulishly pale under the fluorescent lights, his own reflection floated in the glass of the refrigerator case. He looked like something out of a zombie movie. He grabbed some hot dogs and a tube of grape concentrate, then found rolls and doughnuts before returning to the front of the store, his arms full. As he dumped his groceries on the counter, his eyes tracked to the glass wall. *Anyone could see me.*

"That it?"

"Uh . . . yeah."

The man snorted again and pawed disdainfully through the items as he rang them up. Sleepy-eyed, the boy fumbled at his jacket pockets. He shucked a bill off the top, remembering to keep his hands low so the clerk wouldn't see the lump of twenties.

"You hurt your leg?"

He started to nod.

"So how's your old man?"

"Okay, fine," he got out through clenched teeth. "Real chilly out." He rubbed his hands together and forced a grin.

"Yeah? So how come I ain't seen him in here?" The clerk stared at the crumpled bill.

The boy's heart pounded, clouding his vision with a bright pulse. "Oh, and a pack of Camels."

"He still smoking them? So how come . . . ?"

"You know." The boy shrugged, his gaze swerving to the door. "He's been busy."

"Yeah, he's a real worker all right. You learn from him, kid. He worked hard all his life for his money. I knew him since we was both kids with nothing, no shoes even, running around in the street. Nobody never gave neither one of us nothing. You hearing me?"

"No." He shook his head in urgent confusion. "I know."

"Yeah, well, just so's you do know." He held out the change, but the boy jerked his hand away. "You tell him I says hi." He slapped the money down on the counter. "Tell him I says stop in sometime." His fingernails hooked, and hairs curled at the edge of his cuffs.

"I will."

"What's he too high and mighty to speak to his old buddies?"

"No . . . just . . ."

"You turning into a hippie?"

"Huh?" He backed away. "Oh, no, I just . . . forgot to get a haircut." He pressed his palm to the door.

"Yeah, you forgot your change too."

"Oh." He scooped up the money and fled while the clerk sneered after him.

Putting his head down, he hurried along the block, the chill soughing through the hole in his jeans. *The cold feels even worse now.* Halfway down the block, he suddenly became afraid; he'd been in such a hurry, he'd rushed right through the lights of the parking lot. *Anybody could of seen.* Now he stopped and peered about, but the fluorescent lights had blanked his night vision. *Was it really him this time? Up there on the boardwalk?* Arms outstretched, he plunged into deeper blackness. *Could of been anybody really.*

But he knew.

Halfway down the alley, he remembered the cat and paused, listening to the wind moan above his head. The handles to the plastic bag had wound tightly around his fingers, but he fumbled out the package of hot dogs. Biting off one end of the wrapper, he peeled out a frank, broke it in pieces, leaving one here on the ground, another by the wall, even tossing a piece over the fence. *So's he can find it.*

Then he let the wind blow him down the alley like a bit of refuse.

We've been here too long already. As he stood on the trash can and reached for the ladder, the thought he'd been avoiding for days caught up with him. *Somebody might of noticed something by now.* Other thoughts engulfed him, unwelcome memories that left him gasping: the woman's long mane and the way the blood had flown up this last time, worse than before, the sticking clamminess of it, spurting on his face when he'd used the saw; the noise of the hammer when it hit bone.

Too long. He clambered up the sharp grid of the fire escape. *Too long in one place.*

With a stiff, metallic grind, the window slid up. Even as he climbed over the sill, he could feel her stare. He'd left her tied in the big chair this time, bound with nylon cord from the basement, two blankets wrapped around her. Somehow she'd managed to knock one away completely, while the other hung loosely. "You warm enough?" He closed the window. "Boy, it's bad tonight."

She watched him rub his hands over the electric heater. His waxen flesh had been scoured by frost until now his cheekbones flared, and his hair—even more blond than her own—held the light with a melting shimmer: he might have been an angel. She turned her face away.

After dumping the groceries on the kitchen table, he crouched beside her and yanked away the remaining blanket to inspect the knots. "Shit," he muttered. Her struggles had abraded her wrists, and one of the cords dripped darkly. "How come you keep doing that?" With one finger, he picked at the adhesive strips that held the chewed gag in place. He yanked. A wounded groan throbbed from her, and he recoiled. "Don't yell or nothing, all right?" Trembling, he wadded the gag and gently stuck it back in her mouth. "You know I can't let you start in screaming."

Everything in the room—the ironing board in the corner, the crumbled newspapers on the small table—shimmered in her vision.

"If I take it out, do you promise to be good?" With the back of his hand, he stroked her cheek.

She moaned, felt the glimmer in her eyes break and roll down her face.

"Just be good." He fondled her ear, then the nape of her neck.

When he pulled out the gag, she jerked her head away, panting gutturally through swollen lips. "Please, let me go. Please, Perry?" Her shoulders heaved. "I won't tell anybody. I won't tell about anything. I swear." She gulped air. "Oh God, please! Somebody, help me!"

"Keep it down, or I got to get the tape again. I mean it. You don't want that, do you?" His voice seemed almost pleading. "Huh?"

Biting her lip, she shook her head. She could taste blood, and the muscles in her neck throbbed beyond endurance.

"You thirsty?" He strode to the sink and filled a glass.

Again, she twisted her face away, but he stood behind her, gripping her head with one hand, prying the rim of the glass between her lips. She gagged, and water spattered her sweatshirt. "That's better," he said. "You hungry or what?" While she coughed, he wiped at her mouth with his sleeve. "All right? Dinner won't be long. Tell you what—I'll move the TV in here so we can both watch, and you can keep me company while I cook. Would you like that?"

When he left the room, she struggled in frenzy against

the ropes. He would hurt her again tonight—she could tell. The tears stung her cheeks, and she could feel a fresh trickle on her wrists. He would hurt her—he had that look. She gritted her teeth, knowing she couldn't afford to lose control. She had to get him talking, calm him down. At moments like this, her thoughts grew so dispassionately logical they shocked her, but such moments never lasted. Seconds later, the savage panic slashed her. Her numbed fingers still couldn't find the knots, and she felt her arms begin to shake. "Oh God," she whispered. She pressed her eyelids shut and rocked back and forth as much as the ropes permitted. "I don't want to die like this."

"You say something? Here we go." He set the portable television on the kitchen table, raveling the cord to the counter. Pulling plugs out of tangled extension cords, he rearranged them experimentally, stringing the hotplate off to the side. "Got to be careful with this." The electric heater buzzed loudly. "We don't want to blow a fuse again." The squat refrigerator cycled with a lumbering grunt. "I wish I could think of a way to get some more oil. Shame it takes so long to heat up water for the tub. I'm starting to smell. Next time we move, I got to find us a place with oil still in the tank. Maybe next winter . . ." His voice faded as he turned to the window.

"Please," she murmured. "Please, God."

"What did you say, Stell?"

She fought, dragging herself back from the fog of despair that lay always ready to envelop her. No one would help. If she were ever to get away from him, she'd have to do it herself. She had to keep him talking, buy time, wait for a chance. It was all she could do for now. She searched his face. The pale mask stared back at her, a face so young, so unreadably soft as to be almost blank. She could detect no human feeling in that unformed countenance. She could no more reason with him than with the ropes that bound her. Again, terror stirred like a small animal within her chest; in seconds, it had her writhing against the chair.

Averting his eyes, he got out a frying pan and started heating the oil, while the television set flickered noiselessly. "Always takes a few minutes for the sound to come on," he muttered. "You like yours burned a little, right?" He rattled things in the kitchen drawer. "See, I remember. I even got the cheese."

She mustn't cry anymore. The rancid odor of frying meat wafted around her, causing a ripple of nausea deep in her gut. She had to get him talking. Sound drifted from the television. She drew a deep breath. "You've grown another inch. Those jeans are too short." She paused, then forced herself to continue. "And you're so skinny. They're practically hanging off you."

Bemused, he fingered the fraying belt loops, then used the heel of his hand to shove the bangs off his forehead.

"You need a haircut too. I could trim it for you. Are there scissors?"

"I'll do it myself." He shuffled his weight from foot to foot, his hip jutting sharply as he turned away. But her gasp fixed his attention on the newscast.

". . . dismembered body has been positively identified as . . ."

He dropped the fork and slowly, as though it required immense effort, he stepped closer to the blaring television. A photograph of a young woman flashed on the screen: a mass of curls and a pretty face caught with just a trace of a grin. Then a man in a suit answered questions while lights flashed.

He turned down the sound. "While this is frying, I'll bandage your wrists for you." The channel dial clicked rapidly. "Maybe I can find some cartoons or something. I wish you'd stop doing that to yourself, Stell. No reason to hurt yourself."

He had killed her, that woman on the screen. She knew it. Terror paralyzed her brain. All thoughts of resistance faded, all plans for escape, however inchoate, melting. Tears blurred her vision so that for a moment he resembled a small, leering gargoyle, reaching for her with one clawed hand.

VIII

Along the edge of the salt marsh, night winds howled like angry ghosts. The fat man's footsteps grated, a mushy whisper, solemn as death, and the reek of the bay nearly choked him. Just ahead, partially hidden behind a bank of withered reeds, a mound of sand seemed to phosphoresce slightly as he approached it.

After studying it a moment, he nodded slightly to himself. He'd been sure he would find this if he just kept looking.

The blade bit deeply into the pile, the first stroke jarring something brittle underneath so that, with a dry snap, the whole mound shifted stiffly. Dropping the shovel, he used his hands to brush away the loose soil. Within seconds, he had the first of them uncovered. He whistled through his teeth as he again picked up the shovel: the boy had been busy.

The darker pile grew, sand and harder things, as the shovel blade broke pieces away from what had been hidden. Many had been there a long time, collapsed and pressed together by the earth, and flattened skulls seemed to shriek silently. Grunting, he leaned on the handle. Wind hissed through the barred teeth at his feet, and again he nodded, satisfied with this discovery.

After a moment, he smiled and began to cover them up again.

"You hear it as well? I suspected as much."

Kit edged closer to the window. "Hear what, Charlotte?"

Outside, a high-pitched moan soughed through the rocks, like the whine of a demented dog. "The wind?"

"I can tell you hear it." Twisted fingers brushed away a strand of gray hair. "It dies away just when you listen hardest . . . as though it knows somehow."

"Don't start with your ghost stories tonight, all right? It gets dark way too early as it is. Besides, we both know what you're hearing."

"And what would that be, dear?"

Kit tried to laugh. "The ghost of the town clanking its chains," she said in her best spooky voice. "Am I right?"

"Ah. This again."

"For one thing, half the shops on our poor excuse for a boardwalk didn't even bother to open last summer. You'd know that if you'd only let me take you out of here once in a while."

"Those days are over. At my age, what need I see beyond this house? Listen. There it is again."

"Charlotte . . ."

After a moment, the older woman turned her face from the window. "You've had one of your premonitions again, haven't you, dear? I can always tell."

"I don't know what you're talking about."

"I suspect you do, Katherine. I suspect you know perfectly well. If you'd only stop suppressing that entire side of your nature this way."

"Stop, please."

"But you do hear it. Truly. You know you do. Of course, one becomes accustomed to hearing things in a shore town. Ask yourself—what does the ocean sound like from a block away? Voices, murmuring in the next room. Ask anyone who ever lived by the sea. Voices whispering continually, so that one can't quite make out the words. It's worse off-season somehow." Her voice trailed away. "More personal."

Kit sighed. "This town is dead."

"You came back. You stay."

Kit contemplated her friend's features. Wrinkles draped the delicate bones, but the intensity in that face had never dimmed. "And every year, storms take more of the beach," Kit went on. "How much did the government spend trying to replace it? Just two years ago? And you can hardly find a trace of sand now." She sighed again. "All right, so I came back. Why can't I ever win an argument with you?"

"Do we argue, my dear? I never noticed."

"It doesn't prove anything. That I came back, I mean. Except that I'm crazy. When you grow up in a place . . . oh, I don't know. Shit."

"I wish I could swear like that, dear. I never could. It just doesn't sound right somehow, coming from me."

"My memories of Edgeharbor had a . . . a kind of halo. I thought it would be—must be—some little island of sanity."

"Peninsula, dear."

"Whatever. No crackheads. No gangs. I thought I could mean something here," she almost whispered, "make a difference." With a sudden gesture, she drew the curtains wide and laughed. "You really ought to start charging me for these therapy sessions."

"I never help you. Sometimes I suspect you only talk to me in order to hear what you're truly thinking."

"Charlotte . . ."

"For my part, I'm simply pleased you have a reason to come. It would be terrible if you received nothing back from our friendship."

Kit held up a hand to stop her. "I get plenty."

"Are you going to tell me now?"

"Tell you what?"

"My dear, you should see your face. Do you think I could know you all this time and not be able to tell when something's troubling you? Has something happened?" Charlotte blinked. "Or have you been dwelling on thoughts of that young man again?"

"Thoughts of . . . ? Oh. No. Not really." She considered how much to tell her. Her friend didn't own a television, never listened to the radio, and in a real sense, Kit provided her sole link to the outside world. "There was a killing. But I don't want you to worry."

"How terrible. Someone local?"

"No. They . . . we think maybe the body was just dumped here, but I think it's a good idea if I come and stay with you for a few days."

"I know you mean well, dear, and I do appreciate your consideration. Truly. But I'm afraid I can't accept that offer. Please. Don't press. I can't explain just now. It's simply important I be alone here. More so now than ever. But is there something you're not telling me? Is there some danger?"

"There's no reason to think that."

"Then I'll be fine. Is this what you wanted to talk about?"

"Of course." Kit looked away.

"I sometimes suspect that young man's suicide affected you more than you let yourself realize."

"You make too much of it, Charlotte. Besides, it was a long time ago."

"Not so long."

"And anyway it wasn't my fault."

"Of course not."

"That has nothing to do with anything." She chuckled. "What do you say we talk about your life? Just for a change, I mean."

"My life ended long ago. Now don't argue. And I don't refer to this wheelchair." Charlotte's attention flickered to a small silver frame on the mantel. "It's all behind me—everything of importance, everything that's ever going to happen. Except one thing perhaps. At times I suspect senility might be a kind of blessing. Don't you agree? Though perhaps I won't think so when it finally comes. If it hasn't already. What good does mental alacrity do me? My eyes won't let me read anymore. I simply dream and wait . . ."

"I only hope when I'm your age—"

"You're a good girl, Katherine." Charlotte interrupted her with a smile. "Nurturing. Almost despite yourself."

"The hell I am. I'm a cop." A damp draft lapped against her, and she returned her attention to the gently swaying curtains. Wintry shadows seemed to drift around the casement, and naked vines veined the window glass. Outside, beneath a clustering tangle of ivy, gray stone crumbled. In summers past, she'd seen vacationers stop and blink up at this house in disbelief. The Victorian gloom seemed so out of place, so out of time. Little remained of the once impressive cloak of ivy. Now, the scant leaves curled brown, clogging the slumped gutters of the gabled roof, and dirt and grit hailed down to scratch at the windows with every gust of wind. In front of the worn porch, the front garden had gone, leaving only a smear of pocked earth. Kit's jeep looked so incongruous parked there. Chunks of fallen slate formed a spurious path around it.

"So intractable, even as a child when your parents brought you to visit. Yet you spend all your free time keeping an elderly invalid company?"

Beyond the grounds, mounded shadows on the beach humped toward flashes of gray. "You know," said Kit, "that's because you happen to be the only interesting person in town."

"And now you've taken in an injured cat?"

"Which I loathe." Kit tugged the curtains shut and stepped back into the warmth from the fireplace.

"Whatever you say, my dear. So much resistance. You affect to hate my lovely darkness, and my little folktales, and you try so hard to be flippant. Don't you ever wonder what sort of life you'd have if ever you stopped denying the romance in your soul?"

"You never give up, do you?" Kit smiled at her. So frail in the antique wheelchair—how was it possible the old woman could radiate such strength? "So how are you fixed for firewood?"

"All my needs are well met." Charlotte smiled. "As usual. Now, tell me again about this cat. Oh, forgive my manners. Would you care for a glass of sherry?"

Kit shuddered at the suggestion—a habitual joke between them—which always seemed to delight her hostess. "Nothing to tell really." She shrugged. "It's probably dead by now, wedged behind the china cabinet most likely." She paced through a wave of warmth in front of the fireplace, then back into the chill by the corner.

Charlotte clicked her tongue.

"I mean, here I knock myself out rescuing it," continued Kit, "get blood all over my best jacket, and the whole time it's like this lump, but the minute I get it home under the kitchen light and try to get a good look at the wounds—what a scene!"

"The poor creature was frightened."

"Hell, I was frightened. For one thing, the damned cat is huge. I could've used a tranquilizer gun. And it's ugly as sin. You should have seen me chasing it while it's yowling its head off. Like one of those nature shows. First it's behind the refrigerator, next it's under the sink. Did you know that vet on Decatur Road moved away?"

"Everyone moves away."

"Anyway, I finally got hold of this vet out by Deadhook, but by then I couldn't find the damn cat. Spent half the night moving furniture."

"Perhaps it simply got out again?"

"I don't see how. I keep leaving food for it, but so far

nothing's been touched. Just what I needed, right? I'll probably find it when I smell it. Speaking of moved furniture, how . . . I mean, this stool by the window . . . ?"

Charlotte looked away too quickly. Her fingers went to her lips, then slipped away. "Lately, I've been looking out." At last, she folded her hands in her lap.

"Okay, but it's freezing by this window. Why . . . ?" Then she noticed her friend's unfocused expression. Around the room, firelight glimmered from the antique frames that crowded among the volumes of collected folklore on the shelves and end tables. The immediate impression was that several generations of a family had been chronicled, all the men showing a strong clan resemblance, from adolescent to grandfather. One of the old photographs, tinted with unnatural hues, depicted a thin, unsmiling young man who posed proudly but awkwardly in an absurdly old-fashioned sailor suit. Across the room, the largest of the frames showed an older man, unsmiling still, in an officer's cap. This portrait stood guard beside a thick, leather-bound book, the gold embossed title of which remained just visible in the gloom: *Legends of the New Jersey Coast* by Charlotte Otis Taylor. "Wasn't it about this time of year that your husband passed away?"

"Yes, perhaps that's all it is." Sudden tension flitted across her face. "The time of year. Forgive me. I know you're not accustomed to seeing me like this."

"Charlotte, I'm so sorry."

"Perhaps I'm only getting even older—though it's difficult to imagine—entering some final dimming stage."

"Never."

"It comes for all of us. No matter how you overestimate me—and you know I adore that you do—sometimes I am just an old woman alone here. Mourning can become a sort of habit, a shield from life. I saw so many women, my contemporaries, retreat into propriety, removed from any real pain, from any passionate sense of loss." Her voice rose sharply. "I swore I'd never be reduced to such hypocrisy." With a slow grip, she wheeled herself forward, then carefully folded back the fire screen and poked at the embers. She did this with reasonable efficiency, despite being barely strong enough to wield the poker. "Forgive me, my dear friend, this wasn't a good time for you to come—I hate to have you witness my gloom. It's simply that . . ." Winded by the slight exertion, she let the poker clatter back into its place. "I've seen something. No, I won't tell you what. Not yet. Not this evening when you must already suspect my mind to be going. No? Then perhaps you should. I sit here some nights, and I listen to the sea. I always told my Nathan that he built this house too close to the water." She paused. "Perhaps I knew even then that I would wind up like this . . . alone and listening for voices in the waves, hearing their words much too clearly. Forgive me. I know you hate it when I talk like this."

"I just . . ."

"You're such a mass of contradictions, my dear. It's one of your most attractive qualities—a dreamer who tries to be a cynic, a skeptic in a landscape of ghosts. Are you familiar with the legend of the widow on the beach? It's one of my favorites. I always meant to do a book on it. You see, she waits for her husband's ship."

"Charlotte, don't."

"They say on stormy nights one can still see her, walking by the rocks near the lighthouse, her white tresses blowing behind her like a bridal veil. Can't you feel how close the dead are to us here?"

"Are you going to be all right tonight?" Kit watched flame spurt blue from the end of a log. "I hate leaving you like this. You won't change your mind about letting me sleep here?"

"On quiet nights like this . . ."

"I want to be sure this door is kept locked. Do you

understand? And I really don't like your sitting by that drafty window all night."

The old woman seemed to surface from a great depth. "What is all this, Katherine?"

"If you call me, I'll come over right away."

"Of course. I've kept you far too long as it is. You told me you could only stop a moment."

"Well, it's just that I'm working."

"Old people become such gluttons for attention."

"I'll come by later, if you want. Is there anything else you need, before I make my rounds? Are you sure? I hate to think of you all alone here at night."

IX

Icy and urgent, a secret tide lifted through the room, swirling the murky desolation that clouded his sleep into a deeper tumult. It seemed he stumbled on a bank of frozen mud. Heavy with the fecund reek of the marsh, sour winds sprang from the water, wafting the sad stench of death around him. He stared down. A pinkish film spread thinly across the surface while men with hooks dragged things dripping from the depths. Gulls skimmed the turbid bay, and their reflections wheeled with squealing cries, their cruel wings curved like hooks . . .

"No." He woke in darkness to the sound of his own voice.

He lay soaked against the sheets, listening. Such silence. He found it difficult to believe a town slept below the windows of this hotel. Even blocks away, he thought he could still hear waves rise against the sand, a constant sigh, though scarcely more audible than his heartbeat. The sound eluded him entirely when he tried to focus on it, but the moment his attention drifted, the ebbing hush swept back.

Something tapped at his window, and his fists clenched. As the gentle pattering grew more rapid, he groped on the nightstand for his watch. He held the luminous dial near his face. Only a little past ten thirty. He had time. *And God knows I need the rest.* He gave himself over to the lulling drum against the pane, and sleep washed over him again.

What began as soporific, the somnolent brush of rain

across the glass, became something wild, distressing. Again, he woke in alarmed confusion.

Where . . . ? Switching on the light, he blinked at the room. Rain glittered across the windowpane. He grabbed his watch and cursed, lurching up and into the bathroom to splash water on his face. *Have to get my thoughts clear.*

When the second hand on his watch touched midnight, he rang the number once before hanging up, then dialed again. *What would happen if some night that phone just kept ringing?* He envisioned the lonely stretch of highway. *What if no one ever answered?*

What would his life become?

It rang twice. With a tremor of something like pain, he shut his eyes when he heard her voice. "It's starting again," he muttered. "Yeah, I'm sure now."

He exhaled loudly. Sleet chipped at the window. "What does it matter how I am?" Listening to her words, he rubbed at his face before responding, despising himself for the petulance in his voice. "Sorry." He pressed the phone hard against his ear, the receiver slippery in his palm. "I . . . think I'm coming down with something. I just . . . sometimes . . . wonder if we're doing the right thing anymore. No, I'm all right, I guess. Don't worry. Yeah. I'm on top of this. Most likely. I'll call tomorrow." He hung up quickly and clenched his teeth until the shivering stopped.

I wonder if I really am sick. He pressed his shoulders against the headboard. *Really sick, I mean.* Gradually, the noise of the storm faded, until he could detect only the faintest tap of rain. *No, probably just a touch of flu, something like that.* He got up, hunting for his shoes. His coat was draped over the chair.

He shut the door softly behind him. At the end of the corridor, a narrow alcove opened to the well of the back stairs. Near the bottom, he paused, and silence settled like dust. Stealthily, he groped along with both hands until he felt the sliding doors. Casters rolled with a low, chattering hum. Weird shapes jutted: tables with chairs on top of them, he guessed. As he crept through the dining room, floorboards barely sighed. A draft found his face, and he located the alcove. Straight ahead must lie the kitchen, and somewhere along here, he knew, a rear entrance led to the family's apartment. With a deft movement, he snicked open a small knife.

Before his probing fingers located it, frigid dampness revealed the service entrance. He sank to his knees, felt cold whittle in through the jamb. Clicking on the tiny flashlight, he held it in his mouth while he tested the lock with the blade. He took a small can of household oil from his pocket and went to work on the hinges. At last, the door eased open almost soundlessly, and he stepped out into the parking lot. Thin drizzle continued to settle, visible under the streetlight. His Volks was next to the old van that always seemed to be in the same place. As usual, there were no other cars.

He released the brake and let the beetle roll into the street before hitting the ignition. *Makes so damn much racket.* On the sidewalk and in the gutters, slimy film glistened. *Enough noise to wake the dead.* Gray patches had already iced over, and at the first corner, the car skidded. He cursed, pumping the brakes, and tires scraped asphalt.

The streets crawled past, empty and slick, until at last some heat leaked up from the grill. For over an hour, he cruised, constantly circling, trying first a main street, then a back road near the edge of town.

Rain pebbled the windshield. Near an intersection, he let the engine idle and switched off the lights to watch for any sign of movement.

. . . the dream . . .

He switched the headlights back on and eased the car forward.

. . . the bay . . .

Deciding to take the long way around, he quickly left the streets and houses behind him. As though barring the way, a tangle of evergreens seemed to leap at his windshield. This secondary road led to the mainland, and with each curve his high beams sheered into the trees.

The forest sank into salt marsh. Even with the windows rolled tight, he could smell it. *Just off the road.* He drove past a shack, then another. Headlights lanced over cedar shingles, across broken windows mended with tar paper.

Near the dilapidated docks, the road ended at police barricades. He stopped the car and got out, left it steaming off the side of the road. On foot, he slipped between the barriers.

Pointless. The roots of an elm had mounded beneath the sidewalk, and he paused on the small rise. *Wandering the docks in the dead of night.* Darkness had solidified, and he peered downward into a blank flatness where the bay must be. *Never stop the killing this way. Why did I think something would be waiting here?* Wind stirred wetly. *Because I dreamed it? Pathetic.* A fecund stench of brine rolled over him: for a moment his mind drifted irresistibly on seaside memories of his childhood . . . until the odor thickened into a putrid miasma. *Dear Lord, is that just the bay?* Breathing shallowly, he edged closer to the water, forcing himself through a stench like that of the decomposing carcass of some huge sea creature. *What must this smell be like in summer?*

The shore road ended abruptly at a low fence, and the earth dropped steeply to frosted silt. *Just as well I didn't try to drive this at night.* Scruffy dunes hemmed the marsh, and he struggled up a hillock to gaze down on a debris-choked channel. *One wrong turn . . .*

Cold seared his flesh. Icy leaves crunched underfoot, and his shoes scuffed quietly as he clambered onto a boulder. *So close.* On one side of the road, the docks. On the other . . .

The bay whispered. He felt another tremor begin in his shoulders.

Hovering over moon-burnished whorls of water, coldness became a vaporous presence. It surrounded him, icing his lungs. Gradually, he made out the docks below, and the wobbling slabs of small boats. *How many pieces was she in when they fished her out?* Just below the road, the ground appeared firm, but he knew the marsh swirled through reeds and grasses, knew the narrow channels that cut the vegetation into islands marked only deeper places.

Even this far away, he could hear waves lapping at the docks, though it sounded strangely hushed, as though the tides had died away forever. The noise of a passing car faded around him, and he quickly stepped aside. His shoe sank, and he pulled his foot up with a loud suck of water. He waited, squinting against the wind. *Not a bad view from here.* The opposite shore seemed as featureless as a storm cloud. Even after all these years, the fear rasped within him. *I can feel them.* With a long sigh, his dread seemed to spread along the surface of the water, and he felt muddied with the sediment of years of sadness. *Out there.* A dull wind snapped, and the cold cracked in his knees. *The creatures.* It tore around him, a sea wind seamed with the thin scent of rot. *Waiting.*

Blind as the eye of a dead fish, the moon hung over the water.

He decided against heading down to the dock where the body had been found—he'd taken enough chances lately. What would the nets and gulls have left anyway? And, even on a night like this, anyone might be watching. Instead, he picked his way down the slope and strolled past the foot of the pier, as though heading for one of the houses just beyond. Dampness penetrated him. One circle of the area, he decided, not sure what he was looking for. *Then back to the car.* He followed the road away from the glittering water and strained to make out some detail of the dwellings he approached. *It's like a cemetery.* Even at this hour, he thought it odd that no lights showed at all.

That's it for tonight. May as well start back. He couldn't risk letting this paralyzing depression swell in him again, not with so much at stake. *Go out again in the morning and . . .*

A snarl ripped at him, and claws skittered fiercely on the ice.

"Down, Queenie, you be good now."

He stumbled backward on the slick sidewalk, clutched at a tree trunk.

"Behave, Queenie." Fear clouding her face, a woman dragged the fat little dog away. The animal strained at its leash with moronic malevolence, and they disappeared around the side of the nearest house.

He hung on the tree for a long time, one arm held up to shield his throat.

X

"Perry, please, why are you doing this to me?" The fabric of the chair chafed stiffly through her clothes. "Answer me. You can untie me. I promise."

"Shut up. I mean it."

"We'll always stay together." Though she knew the penalty for making him angry, her voice wheedled. "That's what you want, isn't it? Perry? Talk to me, please."

At first, it seemed he wouldn't answer. With a frayed kitchen towel, he methodically wiped the knife in his hand. "If I untie you, you'll try to run away and stuff."

"I promise I . . ."

"You know what happened the last time I let you loose. Quit talking about it."

Her chest heaved deeply, and she pressed her head back against the chair to keep from shaking. ". . . want to be somewhere . . ." With a flush of something like relief, she felt her sanity crack a little. ". . . anywhere else . . . I . . ." She shut her eyes hard, until she seemed to feel the chair fall away beneath her, then the floor, then the room, as she imagined herself floating to the window and . . .

"Stell?"

Her eyes snapped open.

He stood before her. "What's wrong with you?"

"You're getting just like him." The words came out of their own volition, as though she had no power to stop them. "Just like Ramsey."

"You shut up!"

She throttled the sobs down inside herself, felt them burst in silence. "You're getting just like he got before he killed her."

The knife shook in his fist. "Don't you never say that!" His face clotted darkly. "Don't you never say that to me!"

"Don't! Oh please. No! I'm sorry. I didn't mean it!" She bowed her head, trying to double over against the ropes. "Help me, somebody." It came out like a prayer, and her shoulders quivered. "Please."

He slammed the knife on the counter and stalked to the window, grabbing his jacket from the chair as he passed. Trembling, he shoved the window up and clambered onto the fire escape. The wind growled in his ears. As he stabbed an arm into the sleeve of his jacket, he stamped up the metal stairs until they narrowed and became a sort of ladder. At last, the tar and tin of the roof crackled underfoot.

Faint ripples of sound drifted up the airshaft: a passing car, a distant boat horn. Behind him, a hinge creaked, and a metal door banged in the wind. He'd have to remember to fix that door soon. But now the wind buoyed him like a tide, until he seemed to float. The whole town glittered beneath him, jagged and flattened, and he sucked the evening chill in deeply and wondered if he'd ever feel warm again.

Last summer had become a dream, a dissipating ghost of sunlight and breezes that grated hotter until the blood throbbed in his temples. Would he live to see another summer? Would either of them? He remembered his face wet in the heat and his hands sticky, clotted grayness on his shirt. The fever always came worse in summer. Now, the winter encased them, hid them, kept them safe.

The wind pierced him, and he fumbled at his jacket pockets. His hands shook so badly he could barely open the cigarette pack, and the first few matches went out instantly. Finally, cupped by his palms, one gave off a bead of warmth, diminishing his vision to just the bright cave of his fingers. Before he'd taken his second drag, his ears stung. Already, the familiar, jangled feelings had settled in his stomach again, and in vain, he tried to recapture that sensation of soaring on the night wind, above the hunt, above the terrible change that . . .

Pacing to the edge of the roof, he imagined he could make out words in the whispering hiss of the wind. Below, a few streetlights fought back the night. Nothing moved. But their enemies were out there somewhere in the night, he knew, searching, hunting . . . for them. It made him think of one of his brother's old books, especially the one about the only person left alive on a planet full of vampires. He surveyed the streets as he paced the perimeter, cigarette slanting from his lips. Blowing smoke through his nose, he started to choke and wheeze. At last he stood still, allowing his vision to glide across the antennas and roofs and wires, until he stared straight into the sea, an undulating blackness that encircled his world.

So he's started smoking, has he? On the roof across the courtyard, a red dot brightened, and the man in the window watched, smiling. *Naughty boy.* Up on the roof on a night like this—something only a dumb kid would do. He'd never tried smoking himself, perhaps because he'd not been allowed matches after having tried to burn the house down at the age of nine. Nine had been an especially rough year—he remembered it vividly . . . and his fingers strayed to the pale line of scars across his forehead.

Naked except for the parka around his shoulders, the big man trembled. *And the dear boy is growing careless as well.* In the apartment across the way, all the lights were lit and chintz curtains trailed through the open window.

It must be getting terribly chilly in there, and anyone might see. He didn't worry about being observed himself: he'd painted the windowpane black except for a roughly circular area over which he'd taped a sheet of newspaper. Holding the paper in one hand, he leaned his face to this porthole and strained to catch a glimpse of her, but flapping curtains revealed only fragments of the kitchen. *Only let me see you, my love.* He lifted the paper higher. *Show me you're still alive in there.*

Beside him on the wall, his own shadow bowed grotesquely. *If he's hurt you . . .*

The candle on the cold radiator guttered, swinging shadows up from the floor until they merged with a greater darkness near the skylight. *No, I mustn't even consider that possibility. That's why I'm here.* Objects in the room, the wooden crate that served both as stool and table, and the sleeping bag, bunched in the corner with some clothing, seemed to sway in unison with the candle flame, as icy air trickled up his legs. *To protect her. To rescue her from him.* Shivering again, he pulled the parka closer. He'd taken it from a man who'd bought him dinner at a truck stop, and it fit him perfectly, as though the man had simply been delivering it. Certainly, his need had been greater. In addition, there'd been enough cash in the man's wallet for the few purchases he'd needed to make in order to ensure that he looked like the rest of them. Or close enough at any rate. He ran his fingers across the leather toiletry kit he'd taken from the man's luggage. Wouldn't do to attract attention. Not now.

Night rattled at the painted glass, getting in around the frame, and the newspaper fluttered between his fingers. *So close.* Glittering dimly, the hairs on his legs stood straight, while his testicles, shriveled from the chill, pulled close beneath his overhanging stomach. The air in the room circled, a faint echo of the wind outside, and his breath steamed the clear oval of glass that candlelight coated with a filmy gloss. The damp patch spread, trickled, a single drop rolling down the pane. As the candle sputtered, his doppelganger capered on the wall. Shuddering at his post, he felt that he knew every molecule of this window: the dust clot in the corner, the plaster crumbs on the fallen strands of cobweb.

Across the way, the red point of the cigarette rose, brightening.

He slapped the sheet of paper down as a sudden draft made the candlelight in the room swell. *Mustn't let him see me.* The flame swayed tenderly, and the shrinking tongue trembled. *No, that would never do.* He took his glasses off and rubbed at the bridge of his nose. When he stared too closely at the flame, the rest of the room blurred into rough shapes, ever more indistinct, until at last the world became a deep brown cave, this hot point its center. His chattering teeth sounded like the rattle of the glass, and again, he felt the chill stir harshly up his legs. Yanking a blanket from the pile of bedding on the floor, he wrapped it about his waist, then snapped up the parka's hood.

He brought the heel of his hand down on the candle, and blackness fell from the skylight. Tearing aside the paper, he leaned to the glass. Even through the paint, the freezing pane burned his palm. *Ah, the nick of time, as they say.* Arcing from the roof, the cigarette scattered embers as it plunged along the lattice. He watched a dim form pitch recklessly down the fire escape; then the curtains thrashed briefly. He could see nothing more, barely any hint of light now, and another shudder sluiced through him, a damp tremor that seemed to begin in the floor beneath his feet. *She was smoking too, the morning I killed her.* He let his vision drift out of focus, while the memory curled around him.

Where had everyone gone that morning? *Oh yes.* An-

other excursion. Some dull museum perhaps, or a mati-
nee concert, another thinly disguised reward for placid
behavior. But he hadn't been allowed to go with them
that day. Dr. Leland had requested he stay behind for an
interview—an unscheduled interview—and any break
with routine alarmed him then.

"Mr. Chandler, do come in. You don't mind if I call you
Ramsey? You didn't really mind not accompanying the
others today, did you? No, I shouldn't think you would.
You don't really enjoy these outings the way the others
do. That's been evident for some time, to me at least. Of
course, you feign a certain enthusiasm, but then you
feign a great many things, do you not?" She sucked on
the cigarette, her eyes glinting like those of a shrewd
rodent. "Is that not the case?" She exhaled an impressive
cloud of smoke and leaned into it.

Even then, he tried to smile, nodding affably and shuffling his big feet.

"And you can stop that playacting, Ramsey. At least, I
assume you can. Correct me if I'm mistaken." A prideful
fascination lay behind her stare, as though she'd discovered some new and astonishing germ beneath her micro-
scope. "And don't simply lean there in the doorway. Take
a seat." She stubbed her cigarette out in a marble bowl,
immediately lighting another. "Does the smoke bother
you? No, that's right, you never complain about anything, do you? The perfect patient. So cooperative." She
smiled thinly. "Small wonder your treatment has pro-
gressed so remarkably."

He kept his face blank while he studied her expression
for clues as to how this scene should progress. Her features bore their customary expression of brittle intellect
and slight malice, but a new line etched the flesh around
her mouth, as if those muscles strained to suppress a
smirk.

"I asked to see you here, away from my office"—she gestured vaguely at the bay window—"because I thought you might be more comfortable on your own home ground, so to speak." She waited for him to meet her gaze, but his eyes had followed her gesture, straying to the window, then to the main building on the hill. "I'd hoped that, here, you might feel more inclined to, shall we say, a certain candor." She emphasized the last word with a wave of the cigarette, and ashes dribbled. "I realize you've a battery of behavioral tricks upon which to fall back, answers you've trained yourself to give. Amazing"—she nodded—"all this time, you've been getting away with that. Truly amazing. It must have involved a tremendous amount of study on our part, did it not? I wonder how much of it was observation and how much reading and research." Her tone of voice might have been appropriate to a lecture hall. "Hmm? Still we can't expect explanations for everything right away, can we? We have time. A great deal of time in fact. And you're a great deal more intelligent than you've ever let anyone realize, isn't that so?" Despite the smile, her voice held only speculation, edged with just a touch of eagerness.

Outside, the trees swayed, flaming with color in the autumnal sunlight: flashes of gold, a surge of red on the gray hospital grounds.

". . . for your own good. Don't you agree?"

"I beg your pardon, Dr. Leland. I'm afraid I was admiring the trees. What were you saying?"

The soft rustle of his voice startled her, as it often startled people, emerging from his immense bulk as though some hapless child he had swallowed suddenly spoke. She sat back. "You do see that, do you not?" she repeated with a visible attempt at patience. "You've not really helped yourself through these pretexts, have you?" She tapped a cigarette pack gently against the arm of the chair. "What you've in fact accomplished is precisely the opposite—the evasion of help. But we're going to correct that situation now, are we not? I intend having you transferred out of this residence and back into the main wing, where you'll be under my direct supervision. I believe that's best. We'll meet daily. And I believe we will make significant accomplishments. Don't you agree?" She paused, as though counting off the seconds. "Ramsey? I asked you how you felt about this."

He turned from the window, his attention fixed on a massive and ornate mirror that covered most of the sunroom wall behind her. "Ridiculous name, sunroom."

"I beg your pardon?"

He examined himself in the mirror. The smile, taut on his lips, added a far from reassuring note to his otherwise harmless visage. He adjusted it, nodded at the results. "Yes, that's much better."

"I'm not sure I follow you."

He continued to assess his reflection dispassionately. "Yes." The blond hair had receded so evenly from his forehead that his unlined face appeared disproportionately large, gaining an infantile quality, bland and cheery. "Hardly prepossessing." His shoulders slumped, almost perfectly rounded, and after years of starchy hospital food, his stomach had grown too soft to stay properly in his pants. "Who could be afraid?" He smiled harder, showing his teeth, revealing just a hint of the ferocity that his padding cushioned from the world.

". . . nothing to be gained by refusing to cooperate. I'd hoped you'd be more . . ."

"Dr. Leland, I hope you won't mind my asking you a question."

She waved her cigarette dismissively. "I'm glad to see you've joined me."

He nodded an acknowledgment of her little joke. "For eight years, I've been a model patient here. What in my behavior first triggered your suspicion that all was not—

so to speak—as it seemed?" The thin pitch deepened abruptly. "My motives in asking this, you understand, are purely academic."

Never before had she heard his true voice, and shock rippled across her features. He also seemed taller suddenly—as though through some internal adjustment—and she stiffened in her seat. "Well, if you must know, something in the way you've responded to therapy has been troubling me for some time now and I—"

"No, Doctor. I fear you're dissembling. Your suspicions are of fairly recent origin. Since the day you took up your position at this institution, your attitude has been as condescending and patronizing as those of your predecessors, those other good doctors whom I've allowed to believe were helping me." He laughed—a damp hiss—and her hand twitched toward the phone table beside her.

"You do seem awfully sure of that." She attempted a supercilious smile. "Interesting. Whatever could have given you the impression that the staff here were unaware of your true mental condition?" She shrugged with graceful disdain, as though reluctant to mention something petty and distasteful. "After all, you did kill your mother."

"Shock tactics, Doctor?" He blinked. "Hardly up to your usual standards of subtlety. Not that I can't comprehend your enthusiasm. Believe me, I do. You came into this room convinced you'd discovered the case history destined to establish your reputation. Surely you're expecting to get at least one book out of this?" He showed his teeth again. "No, I'll tell you when you noticed. A little over a month ago, was it not? Things changed then. You see, I've been involved in a little project."

"This hardly seems—"

"That's when I stopped putting all my energy into deception, you see. Though I must admit, you've demonstrated yourself more perceptive than I would have credited. I don't believe any of the others here have noticed a thing. Have they?" His smile crinkled kindly. "Such arrogance, Doctor, seeing me alone. Such foolish arrogance."

"Yes, well, we can discuss this further another time." Reaching for the phone, she succeeded in keeping most of the quaver from her voice. "Two of the orderlies will be here in a moment to help you move your things. Perhaps you'd like to get started with your packing?"

"The expression on your face . . . how shall I put this? It seems quite independent of your words."

He moved so quickly, she had no time to react. He jumped into her lap, crushing the air out of her, toppling the chair backward. The impact jarred a shattering pain through her skull.

On the floor, he sat on her chest, pinning her arms. "I don't believe you're being entirely truthful about those orderlies, Doctor. I believe you intended this as some sort of test to prove your theory, which of course you won't have mentioned to anyone else as yet. Wouldn't do to be wrong, would it? Yes, I believe you're just that egotistical. Luckily, for me. Yes, I believe you've only just now found sense enough to be afraid."

She hissed something against his weight. Beneath the fat, his muscles felt heavy as iron.

"Whether you're lying or not, dear Doctor, I can't afford to take the chance. You see nothing must be allowed to interfere with, well, with that project I mentioned." She writhed beneath him, twisting her torso, kicking at nothing. Her eyes began to bulge. "And, no, I'm afraid we won't be discussing it at a later date, because in a moment you will have ceased to exist." She opened her mouth wide.

He reached behind him, brought down the end table, and the crash dried the unspent cry within her. "Don't be afraid." He picked up the phone. "I won't hurt you," he cooed as though to a small child. "You know Daddy would never hurt you." With an indulgent smile, he removed his glasses and slid them carefully into his shirt pocket. "I loved my mother very much, Dr. Leland. Did I ever mention that?"

Tenderly, he began to twist the phone cord around her bulging windpipe.

He clutched the window frame. The circle of glass had steamed over again, and he wiped it clear with his forearm. Across the way, light had dimmed. How much longer did he need to wait? All the months of hiding and searching—even now the boy could be doing things to her that . . .

But he had to time this perfectly, because he knew how dangerous it could be. For her most of all.

Wrapping the blanket around his legs more tightly, he dragged the crate closer and resumed his post by the window.

XI

From the swirling chaos of his thoughts, one memory hardened into clarity: he recalled trying to reach the chair. Soaked with sweat, the boy twitched on the floor. His head thudded; muscles clenched in his throat, crushing his windpipe in anguished bulges. Slowly, the paroxysm ebbed, and the boy lay trembling, the chair an impossible distance across the room.

Tears and spittle streaked his face. He found he could barely move his fingers.

Time passed; he maintained some awareness of most of it. The linoleum felt lumpy on his back, and the stiffness in his shoulder finally forced him to twitch. Pain sang in his neck. As he writhed, a loud hum seemed to fill the room, vibrating across the ceiling. Sweat slicked his forehead, clammy, then hot as acid. Agony hollowed him.

The room went gray. He found himself in the chair.

He'd been on his way out—he remembered that much. His jacket still lay by the closet door, and he stared at it. Overhead light filled the kitchen cruelly, revealing the crusted dirt on the linoleum, the furring of dust on every surface.

got to clean

Stiffly, he rose, swaying.

never let them see

He almost fell back into the chair. *I better check on her.* With a grunt, he pulled himself erect and shuffled into the next room. *She had a bad day.* As he opened the door, the oblong of light swung across the mattress, unbalancing the room so that it seemed to tilt. Untied, she lay in the bed, clearly too exhausted to try anything, her mouth twitching in phantom grimaces. No moonlight penetrated the boarded window, but brightness from the doorway spilled across the jumble of laundry and blankets. Yellow locks stuck to her damp face, and through this tangled screen he saw the bruises that smeared her cheeks. *Makes her look old.* She'd cried so much the night before. Why couldn't she understand? *Everything I do is for her.* He listened to the flutter of her breath.

Perry felt a clenching pain in his stomach. *Everything.* Shutting the door on her whimpered sigh, he wandered back into the kitchen and found a gray rag under the sink, left by some summer tenant. He wet it, wiped down the table, then the counter. *So much dirt.* Shivering, he had to lean against the counter until the dizziness passed.

Groceries. He remembered why he'd been going out. They had nothing left in the apartment. *And she always wakes up hungry in the morning.* He threw the rag on the floor, thinking it would remind him to clean the room later, and grunting, stooped to retrieve his jacket. Her best blouse lay beside it on the floor, and he held it to his face, imbibing her scent. Still bending, he felt the second seizure begin.

He grabbed the door frame as fire spouted from his groin, smoking into the cavity of his chest. He tried to shout, but his head filled with the throb of water, with the drum of giant wings. Dimming, the room revolved. Pain flared through his legs, and he crumpled. As he plummeted into swirling nausea, it seemed his head circled away from his body. Terror spurted the blood through him in a wave of misery, and he whimpered as a fountain of flame sprayed up within him. He kicked once, and a thin shriek spiraled through.

Something cracked loudly.

He floated on thickening murk. It receded, draining away down his legs, gurgling behind his ears.

He opened his eyes. A tiny, hopeless cry fluttered. For an instant, his hand had looked like . . . like something else.

When he saw what he'd done to the woodwork of the door, he gritted his teeth on a moan. Unable to stop shuddering, he threw his arms around his face and tried to muffle the sobs.

In time, the horror passed, as it always did. Standing straight again, he struggled with his jacket, but the buttons resisted his fingers.

got to get

He decided not to risk waking her by strapping her down, settled for just locking the bedroom door. Just this once. He wouldn't be long. He fumbled with the window, then stumbled over the sill, but the chill seemed to wake only the outer parts of him, only the surface of his flesh.

we need

Feeling thick and stuporous, he made his way down the fire escape, grasping at the paint-blistered rail and trying to recall the purpose of his errand. At the bottom, he dropped as usual, but the fall seemed endless, as though he'd plunged into a well. *Am I flying?* His heart hammered. Cement drummed against the soles of his sneakers, and pain erupted in his ankle.

He put one foot ahead of the other. *Got to be careful.* Tonight, the alley offered scant shelter from the wind, seemed instead to funnel the blast directly into his face. *Can't make a sound.* Even in the darkest places, he imagined he could feel them watching him. Too many of them lurked about for him to venture out during the day now, so he moved only in the dubious shelter of nighttime, and then only when they needed supplies . . . or when the madness came, and he needed to do other things. *Not my fault.* His thoughts reeled away from bloody memories. *I can't stop it.* He emerged from the alley with his collar turned up and his shoulders hunched.

And I know they don't feel it when I do it. He hurried around the corner. *Besides, I got to.* The wind moaned past him, and a DEAD END sign beat against a pole with a hollow, repetitive clatter.

I got to.

"If memory serves, it's that very quality about good-looking men that gets to one, I suspect—that type anyway. Sad and earnest." Charlotte broke off for a moment and seemed to brood. "They're quite like boys, so full of impossible longings, like my husband. For my part, I always wanted to help them somehow, to satisfy that terrible innocence. But truly such people are deadly."

"You sound like such an expert," Kit observed, smiling.

"I? Hardly. Only old and observant."

"As though you were so ancient."

Charlotte shook her head very slightly. "I've known only one love. And what has it done to me? He's been dead longer than you, my dear, have been alive . . . and I still am hostage to our marriage. How many years since I've seen even the upper floors of my prison?"

"Charlotte."

"Above our heads, the rooms stand shut, the furniture covered. Jade. Ivory. All those beautiful old things, screens and carvings, the framed scrolls. Alone with the dust." She contemplated the fireplace. "Forgive me if I try my memoirs out on you. Truly, it's just as well I can't get upstairs now. All those years, I never grew accustomed to sleeping in that big bed alone . . . though I'd had ample experience of it even while he lived."

"He was at sea that often?" Her friend didn't answer, only listened to the crackle of the fire, and finally, Kit spoke softly. "Sometimes, just at dawn, it's like I wake up in a different life or something. For just a second, anything seems possible. Then I remember who I am."

"Katherine . . ."

"You're always telling me what a romantic I am. But you're the one. The way you go on about my old boyfriend. If you could have met him, you'd know how silly that is. He'd have bored you into a coma in five minutes flat."

"I can't recall whether I've asked you this before, my dear, but was this young man also a police officer?"

"Hell, no. Sorry. All day long, I hung out with rookies and hoods who spent all their free time pressing weights. All of them on the make all the time. All of them convinced they were God's gift. Maybe the contrast had something to do with it. I mean, he did nothing all day but work on his philosophy dissertation. Or pretend to. And he hated himself, so of course he had nothing but contempt for anyone who loved him, which is where it gets funny, because I'm pretty sure I never did really. Not really. Besides, you can't make somebody happy against their will."

"I'm glad you see that at least."

"It's just his killing himself that makes it seem like such a big deal." Resolutely, she kept her back turned.

"And who am I to lecture you on love, dear?" Her laugh sounded like fluttering cloth. "I'm the original widow on the beach, waiting for her dead husband. After a lifetime spent studying our local folktales, I've turned into one."

"You still have the best view of the lighthouse from here." Shadows drifted like rent silk across the dunes. "Waiting for her dead husband." At last, Kit let the curtains fall. "Do you say things like that just to give me goose bumps?"

Brooding, he slid down lower in the front seat, and the shoulders of his coat bunched around his ears. For hours, he'd cruised, searching, parking on one dead street after another, waiting, watching. *Pointless.* He switched on the radio, spattering through choppy static to a news broadcast. *Never find him again.*

Something darted beyond his windshield.

For just an instant, he froze. Then his trembling hand shifted the car into drive.

From the end of the block, someone approached, hurrying along the sidewalk. The face remained a pale blur, getting closer, like a corpse drifting toward the surface. *Wait.* Now he saw the slim figure clearly, and his chest tightened. Slouching behind the dashboard, he eased up on the brake. *Don't spook him.* Peering back over his shoulder, the boy never seemed to glance toward the car. Did he limp slightly? *Just keep coming, kid.*

The Volkswagen rolled forward. *Don't even look this way.* Gunning the engine, he jerked the wheel, and the car lurched up onto the sidewalk.

The boy spun away.

Rear tires lodged, skidding along the curb, and a cloud of exhaust flooded the street. The Volks bucked forward.

The boy dodged, circling across the street behind the car. As the car surged backward, he ducked behind the trunk of a maple tree.

The man leapt from the still-rolling car. "Damn!" Behind the tree, an alleyway sliced between houses, he now saw. Arms outstretched to feel the walls on either side of him, the man plunged in. No sound drifted back to him. He might have been chasing a cat. The passage twisted once and abruptly emptied onto a back street.

No! Naked trees twitched around a single street lamp, their shadows struggling on the ground. *You won't get away again!* As he raced for the end of the block, wind swept away the noise of his footsteps.

Around the corner, he glimpsed a dim form, already

disappearing halfway down the next block. He began to run.

He is limping! How close could he get before the boy heard him? He kept to a patch of hardened mud along the curb, muffling his footfalls. *I've got him this time!*

His shoes struck a particle of glass that rattled invisibly across the sidewalk, and the boy twisted with a bleating cry. The man lunged.

The boy's thin body tensed like a whip, changing direction in quick jerks. Darting for the street, he leapt a low fence.

The man labored after him. Taunted by the boy's back, he cleared the picket fence. For a moment, their footfalls matched, beating across the asphalt in rapid tandem. The boy angled into a garden, then swerved toward a row of rooming houses across the street, porches stacked to the sky.

Can't let him reach it! He saw it clearly in the dim cast of the street lamp—a wedge of emptiness between the buildings.

Too late, he dove into the mouth of the alleyway seconds behind the boy. But he could hear him this time, just ahead, and he pounded after him. Crumbling walls leaned into the center of the rutted passage, and desiccated grapevines twisted along the tops of wooden fences that reeked of mold and rot. Just ahead, the footfalls ceased abruptly, and he heard a grunt of despair.

Glinting in the faint moonlight, an expanse of new chain link connected the weathered fences of the yards on either side, completely blocking the alley. The boy reeled blindly, crashing back into the fence. He hung on it, shaking.

"Okay now." His own voice sounded so calm it astonished him. "Don't be afraid."

The boy's back pressed against the fence. Feral despair lit his face, and the fence made a chittering sound.

"Take it easy." Chest heaving, he stepped closer, his shoulders brushing the rough wood on either side. "I won't hurt you." He held his hands open in front of him. "Just want to talk to you."

Damp breath warmed the back of his neck.

For an instant, terror flared, turning his guts to molten slag; then blood exploded behind his ear. As he slumped, agony burst through him, and the high-pitched screams of a child filled the alley. Even with his face pressing the ground, he could feel the furious shaking of the fence.

Frigid darkness oozed into his body. Something leapt over him, some dull and bloated form that rattled the chain link as it climbed after the boy with ungainly speed.

His thoughts slurred into a dwindling hum as night closed around him, and the side of his face iced against the fading ground. *Failed . . . failed them all . . .*

Finally, only one thought stirred his fading consciousness.

Who killed me?

XII

"Lie still."

Warmth trickled agonizingly into his legs. A hammer blow of pain stopped his rising.

"Whoa, boy."

The voice sounded farther away this time, and he heard something clatter.

"Don't move till I get this ice pack on you."

He felt fingertips probe the muscles at the base of his skull. There seemed to be a snarl of barbed wire beneath his flesh, and a spasm lanced through his skull. Features hovering before him refused to focus. "Who . . . ?" The fog dissipated slightly. "How did I . . . ?" An aching misery washed over him, and his senses returned, slowly, as from some remote shore, spent.

"You're kidding? You really don't remember?" She handed him the ice pack. "Don't just hold that—put it on your head." Her red hair glinted. "Is this lamp too bright for you?"

Haltingly this time, he shifted his position on the sofa, twisting his head to observe a small room clogged with heavy furniture. "Where . . . ?"

"Don't sit up yet." She frowned. "Maybe I should take you out to the med center after all."

"No, no hospital." He shook his head and instantly regretted it.

"Keep that blanket on. Do you feel like you're going to be sick?"

He started to shake his head again, then stopped himself with both hands.

"You sure?" she asked.

Not answering, he bent forward, as though about to pitch from the sofa.

She stared at the mat of his hair, at the broad fingers cradling his skull. "You want to tell me what happened?"

"First . . . how did you get me?" Razor blue eyes flicked up at her. "Sorry, I forget your name."

"Kit." She blinked. "Officer Lonigan." She pointed at the ice pack in his hand. "You better put that where you need it, like I said."

He pressed the ice pack behind his ear but at once removed it and gingerly explored the area with his fingers. The size of the lump made the air hiss out of his lungs.

"You're not going to faint on me or something, are you?"

"How did you . . . ?"

"We got a complaint about somebody screaming. I pulled up just in time to catch you staggering out of an alley. You practically collapsed right into the jeep." She sank back onto an armchair. "You really don't remember? You talked about some pretty strange stuff."

"I said something?" The ice pack slipped from his fingers to the carpet. "Tell me."

"Whoa—not so fast. Let's see. It sounded like 'I'm it' or something." She studied his face. "Yes, something like that. 'I'm it now.' I couldn't make out the rest. That mean something to you?"

For a moment, he seemed to suppress a shudder. "What made you bring me here? This is your home, isn't it?"

"For one thing, I figured it was time we had a talk." She rose to retrieve the ice pack, placing it in his hand. "Listen, are you sure you're all right? Yes? Then you'd better tell me what's going on now."

The room and what he could see of the kitchen beyond contained several isolated areas of intense disarray: the top of a bookshelf, the kitchen table, the windowsills. But the spaces between seemed vigorously organized, as though larger tributaries of disorder had been dammed at their sources. "Nice place. Do I hear the ocean?" Finally, he sighed and rubbed at his mouth. "Damn." He pulled himself farther upright with a grunt. "Can't talk with you standing over me that way."

"All right." She returned to her seat.

"To begin with . . . I used to be a cop." Excruciatingly, he swiveled his head. "You don't look surprised."

"Should I be? After the way you pumped me the other night? For information, I mean."

"But there's more, right?" He still steadied his head with his hands, but his voice grated determinedly. "What else do you know?"

"You're smarter than you look." She pursed her lips.

"And you don't seem so suspicious of me anymore either. Why is that?"

She folded her arms across her chest. "Because I know who killed those people."

"People?" Something moved in his face.

"Two others in the past six months"—she nodded—"both in towns not far from here. Don't try to act surprised. That's what brought you here, right?" She coughed once. "Look, if you want to know what I've found out, you're going to have to level with me. I mean it." Rising, she paced into the kitchen. "After all, we're talking about three murders here."

"More."

She turned back.

"There will have been others." His voice faded. "The missing teenagers, the ones supposed to be runaways—did you know any of them?"

Silence beat like a drum. "You can't mean . . ."

"At the hotel . . . how did you get onto me that first night?"

"Stacey called me from the bar. She said she'd had a strange customer, acting weird, and what with the body being found and all." She shrugged. "It just took me a few phone calls to find out where you were staying." A damp hissing in the kitchen grew shrill. "Tell me what you meant about . . ."

His jaw clenched. Speech seemed to require determined effort. "Stacey often give you tips like that?"

"You're pumping me again."

"Sorry." He swayed slightly on the sofa.

"Are you going to talk to me or what?"

He pressed the ice pack harder against his head. The pitch of the whistle intensified, becoming a prolonged scream, and finally, she stalked away. The noise faded into a moaning sputter. Briefly, things rattled and chimed together; a moment later, she returned with two mugs and set them on the low table. "How's your stomach?"

"My head," he muttered.

"No nausea? Try to drink some of this. Do you take honey?"

Unsteadily, he lifted the cup, then just held it.

"We used to be close, Stacey and me." Talking to fill the silence, she stirred her tea. "But we've got nothing in common anymore. Sometimes I think she's on something." She watched the steam. "She works nights, maybe she needs it."

On the balcony, dead plants rattled in the wind.

With a visible effort, he made himself take a sip of the tea. "Interesting flavor. Dirt?"

"Ginseng. It's good for you."

"Would have to be." Gently, he swirled the pale liquid in his mug. "You work nights too."

"Different." She shrugged.

He set the tea down. "You remind me of . . . damn."

"Bad?"

"Be all right in a second." His face tightened. "I notice I'm not under arrest."

"So far."

"Okay." He sank back against the sofa. "So what do you want from me?"

"It's your turn to talk, that's all."

"Might be. Might be time to . . . tell somebody. Not that you'd believe me. But you're right about why I'm here. I want to stop it. Finally. If I can." Softly, he repeated the words. "Stop it finally."

"It?"

"The killings."

" 'Others,' you said."

Stiffly, he nodded. The surface of the tea shimmered.

"Then why haven't I heard . . . ?"

"Because mostly they get reported as disappearances." He looked up at her. "Kit, is it? Kit, if you've got any ideas that might help . . ."

"Are you sure you don't need . . . ?"

"Just a twinge. I'm okay."

"Your color's a bit better." Frowning, she continued. "Ramsey Chandler. That name mean anything to you?"

"Should it?"

"Isn't he the reason you're here?"

He blinked. "Go on."

"He used to live here in Edgeharbor." She folded her arms. "Son of Clinton Chandler, big developer who just about built this town. Our richest citizen, even back when the town was booming. These days, I doubt he has much competition."

"And?"

"When I was a kid, nobody wanted to talk about them much. I can't even picture the father really. All I remember is he always talks in a whisper."

"What about the son?"

"I only met Ramsey once, when I was maybe eight years old, but he gave me the serious creeps. I don't think he touched me exactly, but I remember my parents pulling me away fast. They never stopped smiling though. Wouldn't do to offend the Chandlers. Right through my teens, those smiles showed up in all my worst nightmares."

Something thumped in the other room.

"Just the cat," she assured him.

The sudden tension in his body eased. "I thought cats were supposed to be sneaky?"

"It may not actually be a cat, more like some kind of mutant raccoon, and anyhow it's not mine. I found it hurt and . . ."

"You make a habit of that?"

"But I can stop whenever I want." She peered into the kitchen.

"So this Ramsey guy, how old . . . ?"

"He looked very grown up to me then. What?"

"So he'd be late middle-aged now?"

"Maybe not. You know how kids see things. He could have been a teenager. He just looked big to me."

"What happened to him?"

Grinning, she played her trump card. "A couple of years after my family moved away, he killed his mother with a carving knife. Worst thing that ever happened in this town. Absolutely the worst. Very few people really talk about it though, even now. Just shows you how much clout the Chandlers had. Of course, it's all different these days."

"How different?"

"The father has been a recluse for years. Since the killing really, I suppose. Retired from business. Retired from society."

"And the son?"

"For the past twelve years, he's been a patient in a private psychiatric facility."

"Tell me the rest of it, before you burst."

"He ran away." She exhaled, finally. "A month ago. Killed some doctor getting out. And no one knows where he is." She watched a cord quaver in his neck. "Except for us."

"No, doesn't make sense." Tension knotted his features. "This is the first place they'd look. Good Lord, is that your cat?"

"I told you it was ugly."

"Has it got too many toes or something?"

She leaned closer. "Nobody would look for Ramsey if they thought he was dead."

He held out his unsteady hand to stroke the cat, but the animal flinched away and jumped onto her chair.

"That's strange. It won't usually come near me." The cat tried to squeeze behind her. "Just follows me from room to room." Suddenly, the cat planted itself and raised its back in a jerky undulation. "Would you look at this? Making a liar out of me." She stroked it tentatively, and then her fingers explored the scabbed area on its rib cage.

"What the hell made those?"

"Fight, I guess."

"With a lion?"

"I managed to get some antiseptic cream on them that first night."

The cat's ears flattened, and it gave a throaty growl, digging into the arm of the chair as it tried to launch itself at the floor.

"Hold still." She tightened her grip. "Healing pretty good."

"Tell me the rest," he said.

"They found his body a week after he escaped." Hissing, the cat struck at her. "Shit." She pulled her hand away as the beast jumped down with a wobbling movement and glided behind the sofa. "One more scratch and I'll need transfusions," she muttered. "Apparently, he'd been sleeping under a highway overpass and somehow rolled under a truck."

"How'd they ID him?"

"Hospital clothes."

"Yeah?"

"Do you actually buy any of that?" she asked.

"I take it you don't."

"You are quick, aren't you?"

"Hey, whatever your name is . . . Kit . . . I don't want to fight. I got my brains half beat in tonight and I'm probably sick on top of it." His voice trailed off. "Okay, you've got a theory. Let's hear it."

"I think he met someone, maybe someone with the same general build and coloring. I think he killed this guy and switched clothes with him, then pushed the body . . ."

"I get the picture." Sipping the tea, he grimaced.

"He's here, isn't he?" She jerked to her feet again. "You tangled with him tonight. You saw him, right?"

From behind the Franklin stove now, the cat watched them. Its tail twitched once, curling around its front paws.

"There must be more," he said. "What are you holding back?"

"A few things. Somebody killed a dog last month. A hundred-and-five-pound rottweiler. Broke its neck, ripped its belly open. An obscene mess. Like that woman in the bay."

The cat's eyes pressed shut then opened wider, glinting like emeralds, like green flames, flickering toward the slightest movements of her hands.

"Just last week a store on the inlet got broken into, but all they took was one jogging suit and one pair of sneakers. Then the drugstore window got smashed. Place has been closed for years. Who would steal old bandages, iodine, stuff like that?"

"Regular crime wave. You have documentation for all this? When can I see it?"

"You haven't told me anything. Not a thing."

Weariness seemed to engulf his voice. "Where do you stand here?"

"I don't get you."

"Don't be dense. With the case. Officially."

"An investigative team from the state police is pursuing a theory about a mob hit that . . ."

"And you don't like that, do you?" His exhaustion, even the gray tint of his flesh, conveyed an odd authority to his words. "It's a real slap in the face, isn't it?"

She frowned. "Don't be so sure you can manipulate me so easy."

"It does make you mad, doesn't it? Being treated like some little nothing? You want to do something about it, show them how wrong they are? Isn't that why I'm here?"

"You're good at this."

"I've had to be." A twitch of something like sorrow flickered across his face; then he focused on her again. "How many on the force here?"

She hesitated. "A few. All right," she sighed, "don't give me that look. I'm it, just about, except for the chief. He's sixty-three with a heart condition. And one part-timer. He'll go to full-time in the summer. Probably. Maybe."

"Except you don't think so."

She picked up her cup. "The town owes me six weeks back pay as it is."

He nodded thoughtfully. "So you won't be going to anybody else about this in a hurry."

"Don't be so . . ."

"The stateys haven't got a clue. You know that."

"I . . ."

"You know that or you wouldn't be talking to me. You're hungry—I knew that the first time I saw you. How long you been in this job?"

"Just over a year. I take it you're feeling a bit better. Are you going to tell me what happened to you tonight?"

"Where you from?"

"Here. At least I mostly grew up here. We moved to New Hampshire in my teens. Then I went to law school." She held up a hand to forestall his next question. "Being a lawyer just wasn't it for me. Then I tried like crazy to find myself, even ran with an EM service for a while. What?"

"Nothing. I . . . like I said, you remind me of somebody."

"I wound up at the police academy in Boston."

"So? You want to talk about it?"

"I couldn't take it, okay? No big deal. I burned out. Had a breakdown. Is that what you want to hear?" She crossed her arms defensively. "Why am I telling you this?"

"Maybe because you trust me."

"Then I should have my head examined." She gulped a mouthful of tepid tea. "Again."

The cat moved in front of the sofa, and he dropped his hand. Quick as a cobra, the animal sank its fangs into the base of his thumb before darting away. "Jesus." He brought his hand to his lips.

"You all right?"

He took his thumb out of his mouth. "It's not rabid, is it?"

From beneath the sideboard came a low snarl.

"I don't think so."

"Let me know if it develops symptoms."

"For heaven sakes, it's just a little bite. Here, there's some peroxide left."

"You have any other cute pets around the place? Snakes? Scorpions?"

"Don't be such a wuss. Gimme."

Sucking on his thumb again, he mumbled something.

"What?"

"Divorced?"

"I said you were good."

"Just assuming. You know—cops."

"Anyway, not exactly. We lived together for three years."

"Another cop?"

"Graduate student. Philosophy. He ended up cutting his throat with a razor blade." She drew her hand across her windpipe. "Or, no, like this actually. He was a south-paw." She switched hands and made the gesture again. "Punishing me, I guess."

"Tough."

"That card you gave me—I haven't been able to track it down. There's no such company, is there?"

"How did you end up back here?"

"You just don't stop, do you? All right. My family had some connections here still. When one of the old-timers quit to do security work in A.C., they found out about the job." She sighed. "When I . . . when I got out of the hos-pital, you know, after the breakdown, I needed the work, and my parents still owned a house. At first, I thought I'd live there, but then I saw the condition of the place. They hadn't even been able to rent it in years." She gestured about vaguely. "A lot of the furniture was salvageable though. Too much of it probably. Are you through with this?" Abruptly, she gathered up the mugs and spoons and marched into the kitchen. When she returned a mo-ment later, his position hadn't changed. "All right—that's not the reason I came back. I thought maybe a small town like this, maybe I could do something real, maybe the ugliness wouldn't overwhelm me. Are we finished with this topic now?"

"And you found the town dying?"

"I never was much of a beach person anyway. Burn too easy. It's a redhead thing." Shrugging, she paced into the kitchen again and began to rinse out cups. Behind her, a floorboard creaked. "Should you be up? Watch out for the barbells on the floor."

"Damn!"

"You okay?"

"Yeah. Broke my foot is all. You work out with these?"

"You're going to say it looks like a guy lives here, right?" Nervously, she stacked the mugs on a small drain board, then grabbed a can of cat food and began rooting through a drawer. "Where's that can opener?"

"How do you have room to move?" A spasm of dizziness took him, and he pulled up a wooden chair.

"I'd get you some more aspirin, but you should probably put something solid in your stomach first. Do you think you could eat?" Her voice trailed off. The cat leapt, clicking softly across the countertop to the food. "Get down from there." She set the food on the floor, then glanced up. He had slumped forward. His hair gleamed a thick, dull gold under the kitchen light, and she reached out to stroke it.

"What?"

"Nothing." She flinched. "Sorry."

"I mean . . ."

"No, it's all right." She leaned against the sink. "It's just you've got to be about the best-looking man I've ever seen." She smiled at the confusion on his face. "A lot of women must see that as a challenge."

Unsteadily, he got to his feet. "Not much of one." He stared: the open button on her blouse exposed a pale cloud of freckles. "Have you thought about what I said . . . about not telling the state police because ... ?" He stepped closer. "You're so skinny."

"Watch that, you."

"You run, don't you?" Suddenly, he slid his hand along the curve of her hip.

"Now I know you're feeling better."

He ran his hand along the fabric of her blouse, smoothing it absently, as though he wasn't aware of doing it. "You should throw me out of here." He grunted softly. "I mean it. Don't let me do this to you." The veins in his forehead swelled. "You don't know what I'm like."

Gently, she pushed against him. His breath grew heavy and uneven, and she felt its heat on her cheek. His beard stubble scratched her.

A sigh rose from him, husky with weariness, and he clutched her tightly, too tightly, as if trying to break through a barrier of flesh. His hands spread on her hips, slid down the back of her legs. Groaning, he pulled her up against him.

She caught sight of his face, blinked. "Oh. Look, we don't have to do this, you know." She tried to back away. "If you're not feeling up to ..."

He made her stop talking. Her mouth was wet, soft. He felt the little teeth behind her lips.

She pulled her face away. "What?"

"You remind me ..."

"You keep saying that." She attempted a smile, played her fingers along his chest. "I take it you work out."

"Not in years."

"So? We did mine. What about your stats? Divorced?"

Something clouded his eyes.

"What? She died?" Again, she tried to pull away. "I remind you of her?"

"No. Somebody else."

"What happened with that one?" When he didn't an-swer, she added, "Another man? She must be nuts."

"Worse." He shook his head. "A cause."

"Oh." She stopped stroking him. "And you still love her, right?"

He barely nodded.

"I suppose I knew that." Another thought hit her. "She's mixed up in this somehow?"

He considered it a long time. "You could say that. You could say that's why I'm here."

"I don't understand."

"It's the only way for us. Right now." He tried to pay attention to what her hands were doing, but a bloody fog seemed to fill his head. "Only way I can be of use." His voice snagged on the final word, tearing like cloth on a nail. "My head. Don't feel too well. Don't think I can . . ."

"Shut up. There's no obligation, you know."

"Sorry . . ."

"Shut up, I said." Moving away from him, she twitched aside the kitchen curtains and peered out at the night. Frost cobwebbed the glass. "So what do you live on?"

"What?"

"While you're chasing a killer? That's what you do, isn't it? It sounds pretty nuts. You're not independently wealthy or something, are you? Is she?"

"There's someone who takes care of . . . hard to ex-plain. Other people are interested." His gaze sought hers, soft, insistent. "My needs are met."

A tiny crumb of paper clung to the sleeve of her sweater, and she stiffened as he picked it off. "You mean, you've got some sort of patron or something?"

"I told you there were things I couldn't talk about."

She turned back to the window. "Right."

"Quite a view."

"Used to be the marina," she muttered distantly.

"Could I . . . ?"

"What?"

"See your notes?"

"They're on the desk. In the other room. The rolltop in the corner." Not moving from the window, she stared down at the empty dock. She heard his footsteps, then the sliding rattle of the desk. The cat finished eating and jumped to the windowsill and settled. Without thinking, she reached to stroke it, and instantly, the cat flipped onto its back, wrapping both front paws around her hand. "Oww! Oww! Stop that!" The claws just lanced her flesh without really digging in, holding her so she couldn't pull away. The tongue startled her—it felt like hot, wet sandpaper. "All right, fine, I like you too, now let go of me, all right? Oww!" The cat flipped back around with a snakelike movement and huddled against the pane.

"It's no good."

She followed his voice into the living room.

"No good," he repeated, perched uncomfortably at her cluttered desk. "You haven't done much actual investigative work, have you? Check out the dates. Your man escaped from this halfway house or whatever late in September. The first corpse turned up in a pond almost a week before that. In pieces. Never even identified. All we know for sure is her first name was Stella."

"How do you know that? That's not in there, is it?"

"I forget. Maybe a tattoo?"

"Don't be creepy."

"It's right here in your notes. See the date?"

"And don't patronize me." She snatched the notebook. "I checked with the hospital administrator, the new one. Patients in that part of the facility are monitored, not—how did he put it?—'unduly restricted.' Look. Clay Mills is approximately an hour's drive from that pond. Just suppose he got hold of a car and . . ."

"How far is that pond from Edgeharbor?"

She started to answer, caught herself. "You know how far it is."

"About twenty minutes. Straight inland. If you're on foot, takes about . . ." Suddenly, he pushed the rest of the file away. "My head. Damn. You're close, but that's not it."

"What are you talking about?"

He tapped the papers. "This Chandler, the father, what does he have to say about his son's disappearance?"

"I haven't been able to contact him."

He turned completely around in the chair to face her.

"There's been no answer at his office or his home," she explained, straightening the papers. "I'm not sure what I'd say anyhow. Why do you look so interested all of a sudden?"

"There must be court records about the killing of his wife."

She nodded.

"Could you get them?"

"I don't think I could remove them from . . ."

"Could you take me to them, let me read them?"

"They're in the old courthouse."

"But you could get in?"

"I . . . no, I'm not taking you there." She held his gaze. "There are limits."

After a moment, his shoulders sagged. "Could you maybe look the file over, and tell me what's in it?"

"I could do that, yes."

"Could you do it now?"

XIII

Fog pressed up the dark beach, damply flattening the saw grass. On a bluff, the abandoned summer cottages clustered, facing the sea, one a little apart from the others. Mist enveloped it. Moisture slicked the green and white trim, and the front window shimmered faintly. Drapes hung closed at the side windows, but light pooled thinly in the small yard.

The back door wasn't closed all the way. "It's got to stop." Crouched on the kitchen floor, Perry whimpered. "It's got to." He waited for the trembling in his shoulders to abate. Clutching a scrub brush, he wiped the back of a wet rubber glove across his nose, then plunged the brush back into a bucket. Reddish water turned the gloves orange. "Got to stop." The boy slopped more water over the caking filth on the linoleum and scrubbed at it, making a brown swirl in which tiny bubbles hissed. Wet, it smelled like blood again. "Not my fault."

A dull ache circled up his knees with each sob, and his shoulders began to stiffen, but he scrubbed on, pushing the pail ahead of him, while the cold pierced through the open crack of the door, and a trace of fog ghosted into the kitchen.

The mist spun halos around her headlights, and her grip slid damply on the steering wheel. Heading down Decatur Road, she glimpsed movement at the end of the block. *Must be high tide.* Water glittered in sharp, vanishing segments. Then she turned onto Chandler Street.

Another halo hovered above the street lamp, a jagged nimbus that glistened and changed shape in the floating vapor. A freezing glow shivered across the front of the courthouse, bleaching the granite steps, and shadows wavered like gargoyle wings.

She parked the jeep across the street from the courthouse but didn't move. Branches clicked against the lamppost, and icons of civilization—phone booth, mailbox, hydrant—clustered in the desolate funnel of brightness. *Well, I do seem to be here.* Getting out of the jeep as quietly as she could, she marched straight through the light. *I probably should have gone around back.* Across the park, darkness buried the houses. *Anyone might see.*

She headed up the stairs. *He's got me feeling like a crook now.* The cold of the doorknob stung through her gloves. *But I suppose I should have thought of that before I swiped these keys from the chief's desk.* Metal ticked against metal as the key scraped the lock.

A slap of wind pushed the door, but she grabbed it before it could bang open. She looked back once. Mist winked across the street lamp. Then she eased her way in. With an icy crack of hinges, the door sucked shut behind her, snuffing the light. *Nothing to be nervous about, right?* Her fingers searched along the wall. *I've been here hundreds of times.* She located the switch but didn't turn the lights on.

Just never at night.

The hesitant click of her footsteps resonated down the hall, fading reverberations fusing into a dissonant hum. The lump of keys in her hand rattled, and she stumbled as though drowsy. A damp smell hung in the air. *Can't see a thing.* When she judged she'd gone far enough from the draped front windows, she switched on the flashlight, swinging the beam past a glass case commemorating the town's war dead. One side of the building housed an auditorium, long unused, and she played the light across office doors on the other side of the corridor: county clerk, registry.

A door stood open. The beam rippled across letters reversed on frosted glass, then planed over surfaces within. Above a row of file cabinets, window shades blocked the night. *I suppose I can chance a bit more light now.* Stepping into the office, she closed the door quietly behind her. *I am the law after all.* Instead of flicking on the overheads, she groped her way to a desk and switched on a gooseneck lamp, twisting it to face the wall.

The cabinets loomed like gray sentinels. She tugged the first drawer—it made a low grinding, suggestive of metal teeth, but didn't budge. However, a desk drawer slid open smoothly, revealing pens, index cards, and a tray full of keys marked with letters on bits of tape. A moment later, she clanked open the A–G drawer.

Inside lay a mass of crushed papers, and she pawed hastily through them. Only the Chandler file sported a typed tab, and she hefted it to the desk, swiveling the lamp so that light pooled on the blotter.

She paged through arrest records, but the snapshots shocked her so that she had to lean against the desk until the trembling stopped. The woman had been slashed apart. Pudding seemed to seep from the tatters of her dress. She turned the photos facedown and flipped open a small notebook. As the pen scratched loudly, the shadow of her own hand flowed massively across the page.

Finally, she returned to the photographs.

Raising her head, she confronted the dark.

After a moment, she moved to the next desk and switched on that lamp as well, and a second bright puddle gave shape to the shadows.

He answered on the first ring. Her voice sounded faint, far away.

"No, I'm all right," she told him. "Just a little rattled.

I've been looking at Polaroids of the crime scene. Yes. About what you'd expect. Not much here we didn't already know. The initial report is sealed."

He perched on the bed. She had dropped him at his hotel before going on to the courthouse. "Sealed?"

"By court order."

"Can't you open it, Kit?"

At first there was silence on the other end of the line. "You don't understand. It's probably in a safe somewhere. There's just a card here referencing it."

"Why would it be sealed?"

"Courtesy probably. I told you. Influential local family. All I've got here is some incidental information filed by the officers who went to the house. Doesn't tell us much. She was a teacher apparently. There's something weird though."

"What?" His own voice grated in his ears.

"Mrs. Chandler's maiden name. It's the same. Chandler. According to this anyway. Could be a mistake. Did you say something?"

"Never mind. What else?"

"A business address I didn't know about and . . ."

"Any other family?"

"I'm not sure."

"Could you check?" he snapped. After a pause, he added, "Please."

"Just a minute."

He heard the phone clack down on the desk. Hollow footsteps faded; then he heard the muffled clang of a file drawer.

"Hello?" Soft rustlings accompanied her voice. "Yes, it's here." Loudly, she rifled pages. "Another boy and a girl."

"How old?" Tension twisted deep in his stomach.

"Uh, the girl, let's see, she'd be . . . seventeen."

He forced himself to inhale calmly. "And the boy?"

"I guess he'd be about . . . thirteen or so."

His lungs emptied out, purging him.

"Barry? Are you there?"

He could hear her voice, but bright spots pulsed around him.

"Barry?"

"Yeah." Light-headed, he breathed again.

"What's wrong?"

"Nothing. I . . . I'll tell you about it when I see you. Get out of there now. I'm . . . not feeling too well. My head."

"Of course."

"We need to plan our next step. Come over and . . ."

"You need to rest. I'll pick you up in the morning, and we'll go get your car."

"Come now."

"Quit giving me orders."

"You have to . . ."

"I have to take these keys back now."

The line went dead in his ear.

At least I can still hang up on him. She slumped back in the chair. *A bit of light burglary, some mild illegal entry. Throw in "withholding information pertinent to a criminal investigation." Not bad for one night.* She scooped the contents of the file back into the folder. *What else would I do if he asked?*

The phone rang.

"Look, I told you—I have to take these keys back. We can start looking for Ramsey in the morning and . . ."

She stopped talking. She knew.

"No need to look further, dear woman." The words pushed through with a mushy quality. "She will die. Can your limited mentality comprehend this? If the boy spots anyone around, if he so much as suspects the police are after him, he will take her life." The voice slurred and choked. "You cannot imagine what he is." Groaning wind all but drowned out his words. "And for my part, I cannot let you endanger her with your meddling. Do you understand? I cannot allow it."

She leaned over the phone, as though sucked in by his words, and she gripped the receiver so tightly her fingers ached. "If you have any information regarding this . . ."

Branches rattled in a sudden gust; then the dial tone rose loudly.

"Hello?" Panic settled on her. *Get him back on the line. Try star sixty-nine.* Her numbed fingers stabbed at the buttons. *Get him talking, get him to say something useful. Act like a cop for once.*

In the distance, she could hear a phone ringing. Not over the instrument, but faintly through the windows behind her. She replaced the receiver, and the ringing ceased.

The phone booth outside.

She pressed the back of her hand to her mouth. *Don't scream.* She bit down, hard. *Don't make a sound.*

I'm unarmed. She had to will her numbed fingers to move, to pick up the phone again, to punch out the number of Barry's hotel, but panic boiled through her. *three and then eight and then* She more felt than heard it, a strumming vibration, a change in the quality of silence, almost in the air pressure. *Did I lock the main door behind me?*

Faintly, the floor beneath her feet vibrated, and she knew the heavy front door had just closed.

She put the phone down. With painful slowness, she inched closer to the doorway. Almost imperceptibly, the glass panel rattled. Feeling along the wood of the door, she found a small latch. She twisted it, backed into the light. Her hands traveled to the desk drawer. Rubber bands and paper clips scattered under her fingers, and she lunged to the other desk. A side compartment squealed open.

A heavy pair of scissors lay on a pad of paper.

Clutching the scissors, she fumbled with the lamps until darkness thrummed around her, and papers slithered from the desk to the floor. For an eternity, she listened.

The shuffling of cloth drifted in the air, and the sliding of soft footfalls scuffed to a halt.

A whisper seeped through the cracks. ". . . never hurt you . . ." The doorknob rattled. "Don't be afraid."

"I have a gun! I'll shoot if I have to!"

Expecting him to come right through the glass, she backed into a file cabinet. Terror crept along her veins like smoke.

Nothing. No sound. No movement.

Then she felt the change in pressure, heard the muted vibration of the front door closing again, and she leaned against a desk until the roaring darkness quieted.

The ringing roused him, not from true sleep, but from some miserable condition beyond the edge of consciousness. Fully clothed, he sat on the bed still, his shoulder to the wall. *his name I know his name have to* He started at the next ring, almost pitching forward, then grabbed the phone before it screamed again. "Who . . . ?" His tongue felt thick, and he had difficulty forming words. "Kit, is that . . . ?"

"He's been watching us."

He knew fear too well not to recognize it in her voice. It brought him fully awake. "Are you all right?"

"There's something else."

"Where are you?"

"Something we didn't know about. I think he has a hostage."

XIV

At least the sun's out today. A pale slab of light pressed the concrete. *First time in weeks.* Slamming the car door, she surveyed the empty sidewalk. *Not that it feels any warmer.* Once this neighborhood had been the business hub of Edgeharbor, and she still remembered it seething with activity. A sheet of newspaper clutched at her ankles, then ghosted away down the street. Solemn gusts clutched at the bit of paper in her hand.

Scanning addresses, she peered at a shop window. A hand-lettered placard proclaimed USED BOOKS, and the whitened covers of comics curled amid a clutter of souvenir pennants and plastic fish, tiny dolls with bulging foreheads. Farther down the street, a sign swayed above what had once been a candy shop. The doctor's office beside it, she knew, still opened for a few hours each week during the summer months, the doctor—well into his eighties now—dispensing little beyond tetanus shots and bandages.

She paused to peer at each storefront. Few of the doorways sported legible numbers. Checking the slip of paper again, she crossed the street.

A square of raw wood patched the grimy door of what apparently had once been a real estate office. The window had been soaped, and sharp angles of light splintered against the translucent film, bright patches sliding rectangles of grime down the far wall. She found a clear crevice but could make out only bailed papers within. Dimly reflected, the whole of the desolate street floated behind her, and a plastic bag drifted along the sidewalk like a jellyfish.

Remnants of cellophane tape still clung to the row of buttons, and she tried each of the silent buzzers in turn. A second door, hung with venetian blinds, angled into the frame. Cupping her hands, she squinted through a gap. Gradually, stairs coalesced from the gloom. Behind the stairs, at the far end of a hallway, daylight pried around the frame of another door: a rear entrance.

Well . . . here goes. If someone spots me, I stick to my story— I'm checking out a report of a break-in. Strolling around the side of the building, she tried to look somehow both casual and official. *Not that I expect anyone to see me. This has got to be the most deserted part of town these days.*

The empty lot could have accommodated half a dozen cars, and her shoes scuffed at the gravel. *Hell.* Crushed stones bounced, clattering. *So much for sneaking up.* No windows interrupted the blankness of the stucco. *At least, no one in there can look out.* At the back, a gate swung, the rusted padlock uselessly clasped through a link in the fence.

As she stepped into the shade behind the building, dried leaves skated up against a row of metal trash cans from which painted addresses flaked away. It wouldn't be the first time a cop jimmied open a door, she reasoned, but the knob turned easily, the hinge whistling. Only as the door grated inward did she notice the cracks. Half the lock dangled from a broken wood screw.

Allowing dim light to stream in around her, she took a cautious step. The break-in could have occurred long ago, she told herself. She unzipped her jacket, and her hand moved to her holster. *No reason to get nervous.* She wore the gun all the time now.

Behind her, the door tapped the wall, and venetian blinds clanked at the other end of the corridor as a faint gust stirred up the musty smell of the carpet. Cautiously, she crept forward and checked a door beneath the stairs. Locked—broom closet or stairs to the cellar, she guessed, moving on.

Stepping on a smear of light, she peered out through the blinds of the front door. Across the street, a thin layer of sunshine coated the jeep, still the only vehicle in sight. If anyone did notice it, at least the broken door would enhance the credibility of her story, she decided. *Still, I'd better be quick.*

Letting the blinds click back into place, she turned to the stairs. "Police," she called, flicking reflexively at a useless light switch. "Is anyone there?" The first step groaned softly beneath her tread. "Did you know your back door was open?" Linoleum had worn through to pine planks, and paint splintered from the wobbling banister at her touch. "Can anyone hear me?"

The tracery of age mapped the plaster walls, and a dank chill filled the stairwell. *First, I sneak into the courthouse.* The unseen strands of a spider's web melted across her lower lip, and she rubbed her knuckles against the withered taste. *Now, I'm breaking into an office.* Through thickening haze, she ascended, thoughts scurrying in her skull like mice. *Who would have believed it could get so much easier so fast?*

A thin smear of dust coated her teeth, and she took her hand from the banister to rub her gritty palm on her jacket. *Why would Chandler have an office in a dump like this?* She became aware of the barest tickling of a pulse in her throat, and by the time she reached the upper hall, she'd grown accustomed to the muddy dimness. A wan gleam illuminated curtains that appeared to be made of vinyl, and she could smell old rain. Concentric blurs on the carpet marked where puddles had dried around the grime-matted radiator.

One of the doors sported a stained card that read

CHANDLER PROPERTIES. She knocked, then felt the furred ledge above the jam. *Doesn't look too solid—I could probably break it down.* But this door also swung open, the faint illumination from the hall shaping a phantom arch on the opposite wall. *Hell, if someone catches me searching the guy's office, nothing I tell them is going to matter anyway.*

A sigh stirred behind her, a rustling cough of wind in the curtains.

So I'd better be quick. Closing the door behind her, she just stood for a moment in near darkness, then groped for the outline of a window shade. She banged her knee on something. "Shit!" Her outstretched hand touched a stiffly yielding and scratchy mass, and she knelt on it to reach the window. At first the shade resisted her tugging, then it hissed and rustled to the floor.

Sunlight flooded the office, and dust motes ignited. Dry as a leaf, a dead moth spiraled to the carpet. The sofa she crouched on all but filled the cramped space, wedged between a pair of gray file cabinets and an old wooden desk, lumpish with disordered paperwork. *This is Chandler's office?* No trophies or civic awards. No pictures on the dingy green walls, no framed photographs on the desk. She noticed faded rectangles on the walls, however, as though things had been removed.

I'd better put this back up, just in case. Clambering onto the back of the sofa, she hooked the shade, lowered it partway. As she did so her glance settled on the empty street below. Only the gritty wind stirred.

The shade hung crookedly above an ugly orange sofa. Cheap-looking, it seemed to be the sort that folded down flat to form a kind of lumpy cot, and she noticed stains on the ugly fabric that seemed to radiate musty dampness.

Hell, it's freezing in here. I can practically see my breath. One of the cabinet drawers stood open and empty. She moved to the desk, feeling the thin carpet slide and crumble beneath her feet. Stacks of canceled checks had been strewn with old insurance documents and leases, and they mounded on the desk, cascading to the floor behind it. Examining papers at random, she lifted a sheet of torn notebook paper. Numbers covered it, columns of figures penciled so precisely they might have been typeset.

Wind clanked at the window, shifting dust. Strands of cobweb that threaded the ceiling waved like tentacles.

The middle desk drawer snarled open, empty save for a single frayed and wrinkled envelope. Even before she fumbled the flap open, her fingers had identified the contents as snapshots. She slid them into the open drawer, expecting to find photos of various properties.

She blinked. One hand covered her mouth.

Polaroids. Thirty or so. Yellowed. Images fuzzy and poorly lit. In some, the children wore T-shirts or socks, the brown sediment of the shadows seeming to engulf their pale bodies. But in others . . .

Many different children. Often bound. She blinked again. No. Not different children. The same three over and over, at different ages. In some, the little girl seemed scarcely more than an infant. In the last few, the biggest boy was already old enough to . . .

Stop shaking. She covered the photos with her hands. *Get hold of yourself. Be a cop.*

She forced herself to look at them again, this time slowly. Different rooms appeared in the backgrounds; nothing remarkable except that in several the predominant color seemed to be an unusual blue. She froze. In one, the corner of a mirror had captured the photographer himself. The flash obscured his face, but his chest could be made out through the glare, the body hair so thick he might have been covered with fur. Several shots of the little girl looked different from the others. She was photographed alone, deeply asleep. Or drugged.

With a start, she recognized the sofa on which the child lay as the one by the window. Fighting nausea, she flipped back to the last photograph. The oldest boy covered one of the other children, impossible to tell which one. The older one's body had already thickened into fat. She felt dizzy.

Evidence. Sickened, she slammed the drawer. *I'll have to take them with me.* But she wondered if she could even force herself to open that drawer again.

Wanting to put her fist through something, she looked about wildly.

Something hung above the file cabinets: rows of empty hooks studded the Peg-Board, each hook bearing a number on a bit of tape, all in that same perfect script. Glancing down at the strewn pages, she began to spread them. A three-digit number caught her eye, and she glanced up at the board. *Yes.* She sorted through more papers. The number repeated—a lease from four summers ago. An electric bill from last year. She pawed through more documents. Dozens of different addresses appeared over and over, sometimes with different units referenced, and a labeled hook corresponded to each number. *An actual clue.* She carried a handful of papers closer to the light of the window.

Face pressed to the scratchy fabric, the boy lay on the sofa, a blanket twisted around him like a cocoon. Even asleep, he tensed, listening for the droning hiss of her breath from the next room. Daylight bled in around the shade, and he shivered, his eyelids twitching.

The sound that had awakened him scratched in the air again. Kicking free, he stumbled up from the sofa, nearly tripping on the blanket as he shuffled into the bedroom. The floor felt like ice through his socks.

Even in the sealed room, some sunlight filtered in, and a streak of it touched her face. She twisted in hot, fitful sleep, her corn silk hair writhing on the pillow, coils of it igniting with the faint radiance. As he watched, she kept trying to twist over on her side, but cloth bandages bound her wrists to the headboard. Through pain-clenched lips, she groaned. Her eyes looked puffy. The dusty dimness played tricks—her lashes looked longer and darker, and rosy welts stood out angrily where she'd some-how managed to scratch her cheek. Or had he been hit-ting her last night? He couldn't remember, but he wished she wouldn't make him hurt her.

The pressure in his bladder demanded release, but he kept the bathroom door open so he could hear her if she stirred. After the splashing stopped, he listened again. Si-lence in the next room. Running water in the sink, he flinched from the sight of himself in the mirror—the puny arms, the hairless chest. His sweatpants hung loosely. Tensing his shoulders, he tried to bulge out his muscles, tried it a number of different ways, but still looked emaci-ated and pale as a worm, his ribs actually showing. Some stud, he thought, and wanted to laugh, but his eyes looked charred, dead, and he backed away from the mirror.

One of his socks had fallen past his ankle and flapped over his foot with every step. The bedroom rug felt rough through the cloth. He bent to stare at her, draw-ing in the faint warm smell of her soft neck.

Wrenching her head from side to side, she whined softly.

Thinking she might be cold, he returned to the living room. When he tugged at it, the thinner of the blankets scraped across the rough fabric of the couch. He wrapped it around his shivering shoulders, then found the one he'd kicked to the floor and padded back to the bed, care-fully draping it over her. As he yanked a corner down, she murmured.

Dumping soiled clothing out of it, he dragged a wicker chair up alongside the bed and pulled the blanket tighter about himself. The wicker creaked while he curled into the chair to watch the slow heave of her breasts. One of his hands strayed toward her, but after a moment, drowsiness began to claim him.

XV

The sky had tarnished to the color of old silver.

Pardon me, sir, but is your homicidal son by any chance hiding in the attic? The imposing house seemed to glare down at her. *Don't you think I should check, sir?* She coasted the jeep into the driveway and just sat, gazing into the early twilight and wondering what she'd say to whomever answered her knock. *And by any chance could you explain that weird office you keep in town? Yes, sir, I did break in. No, sir, I don't have a warrant. Or an attorney.* Across the paved road, only one other home faced her. Farther down the lane, another house peeked above a slight rise. The lawns looked brown and dead, and a frozen unfriendliness seemed to emanate even from the height of the evergreen hedges.

When she cracked the jeep door, the chill washed in. *Maybe I had better call the state cops.* Gravel crunched underfoot as she started up the walk. *Or at least wait to talk to Barry.*

The lawn had grayed with frost in wide swathes, and close to the house, the corpses of flowers lay brown and rigid. Small pines bristled, and sharp yellow leaves flared among the curled rhododendrons that screened the porch.

Her shoes drummed up the stairs, and desiccated fronds rattled in a breeze. Along the wall, dead plants cleaved to clay pots, and yellowed circulars littered the porch floor.

The heavy drapes appeared tightly drawn. She checked

her reflection in the glass of the storm door. *So I look nervous. So what?* She pressed the bell. Nothing happened. When she opened the outer door, a small avalanche of catalogs and circulars tumbled and slid. *No one has been here in quite a while.* She stacked them on the floor before trying the brass knocker. Finally, she pounded with her fist. *And now?* When she let go of it, the storm door hissed shut.

She regarded the row of evergreens. *Maybe the neighbors can tell me something.* As she moved to the stairs, wood throbbed faintly behind her.

Someone is in there. She waited until she heard it again. *Don't look around.* Faintly, a hinge creaked. *Someone is watching. Go down the walk. Pretend to leave.*

Between the house and the hedge lay a crude path of worn earth. The tiny pines had gone dry, dead at the marrow, and brittle needles lanced her hands as she inched along the wall. She ducked as she passed a draped window, almost crawled. Flickering shade mottled the hard earth, and the bushes rattled like beetles.

Behind the house, a yard stretched in perfect flatness, as devoid of any semblance of occupancy as the rear of a movie set. No trellised vines. No covered pool. No sailboat beneath a tarp. Nothing.

The back door gaped brokenly, glass dangling in shards from the frame. *He's here.* She touched her jacket, felt the gun beneath. *I should call for backup.* As she pried the door open farther, a fragment of pane dropped. *I should call.* She stepped up. On the single concrete step, a layer of dust coated the points of glass.

Unzipping her jacket, she reached for the holster. With a soft rush of air, dim sunlight swung in with her, and she panned the revolver across a large kitchen. A thick stench of spoiled meat hung in the air, making her grateful for the draft. Her heel scraped sharply on the tile. Blinking rapidly, she scanned every corner. Copper pots and utensils glinted on hooks beneath white cabinets and above a white counter. One drawer stood open.

Edging forward, she looked inside. Carving knives nestled in a rack. One empty slot. A large one.

Go back out to the jeep and call. Her heart tripped raggedly. *Do it now.*

Her gaze swung toward the next room. Beyond the doorway, the light held a viscous quality, stained blue through thick draperies. *But who would come?* She inched forward, steadying the gun. *The chief? Wouldn't he just call the state cops?* In the next room, a floorboard creaked, muffled by carpet.

Right. Talons of panic tore her. *This is it.* She edged along the kitchen wall. *Now!* As she launched herself through the doorway, something thudded near her head.

"Kit!"

"Barry!" The gun shook. "I almost shot you!"

"Lord, you scared me."

"I almost . . . !" Her voice quavered.

"Quit pointing that thing at me."

"What the hell are you doing here?"

"Same as you probably."

"You tried to . . ." She couldn't look away from the deep wedge that splintered from the door frame.

"Don't be an idiot." He hefted a crowbar. "I thought you were him."

She blinked. "This is breaking and entering. I should run you in."

A pine branch rasped against the window.

Trembling, she holstered the gun. "Couldn't you see it was me?" she demanded. She had a hard time forcing her fist to unclench, then a wave of relief pounded through each aching finger, sweeping up her arm in a numbing current.

". . . didn't break in. I swear it. The door already . . ." He looked down at the crowbar. "Okay, I'll admit I came here intending to do whatever I had to. But somebody beat me to it."

She opened her mouth to object but fell silent, remembering the dust on the broken glass.

He flexed his arms. "Anyway, before you arrest me, wouldn't you like to know what smells like that?"

"Isn't it . . . ?" She gestured back at the kitchen.

"No, that refrigerator's empty. And take a look at this."

"Where are you going?" Whispering fiercely, she followed him through a dining room lined with glass shelves. "Come back here." Chairs were lined up at the table with military precision.

"Relax. The electricity's off. Nobody's here. May as well check it out."

"We shouldn't be here either. If anyone . . ."

"Relax, I said. Nobody saw—those bushes outside were planted to keep anybody from seeing the house." A heap of mail had mounded beneath the slot in the front door. "This is what I tripped over when I heard you at the door. Except I didn't know it was you." Light that filtered through turquoise curtains sank into an azure carpet. "There's a family room sort of thing down that way, big circular fireplace and a wet bar. But no bottles. No glasses even. Then a bathroom and a door to the garage through there."

The miasma of rotten meat seemed to permeate the walls of the parlor, clinging to drapes stiff with dust. She stepped farther in, feeling that she didn't walk through the subaqueous gloom so much as float. Her gaze veered about wildly—transparent vinyl encased bulky aqua loveseats grouped around a teal sofa. Sectional pieces hemmed a glass coffee table. "What makes this room so . . . odd?

Besides the colors, I mean." Everything increased her edginess. She turned completely around, her gaze shifting across plastic flowers in a ceramic vase, across throw pillows and a framed clown print. She found herself unable to imagine people who would have chosen this combination of items for their home. "It's not . . . not . . ."

"Convincing?"

"Right. Why is that?"

"Don't know," he answered softly. "But I had the same feeling in the other room. No books. No magazines. No television set. Like nobody really lives here."

"The kitchen looks the same way." She nodded. "Like a store display." Her words trailed away. "The blue room in the photos. This must be it." She edged closer to him. The vinyl runner on the floor made a shuffling crack, and air hissed beneath it.

She stood close enough to see a vein throb in his neck, then followed his intent gaze to the stairs. Dark matter had lumped and dribbled down two of the steps, and the same crust swirled thinly on the vinyl.

"What is that? Barry?"

"Did you hear something just then?"

"What?"

Ignoring her, he peered upward into the gloom, and a tic began to tremble his right eyelid.

"No. I didn't hear anything. Barry? Don't do anything. Please. We need help." She moved away to pick up a baby blue phone. "Dead. Of course."

Behind her, a stair squeaked.

"Please, Barry," she spoke without turning. "Don't go up there." It felt like the beginning of an old, familiar nightmare. They would go upstairs, she knew. Nothing could stop them now. And nothing would ever be the same.

Barely aware of what she was doing, she followed him.

Her feet moved, and the stairs croaked sluggishly. Her damp palm squealed on the banister, a thin treble.

"There's more of it." He gestured with the back of his hand, indicating a dark patch on the baseboard. The plastic runner ended at the top; so did the faint light. He stepped soundlessly onto thick carpeting.

She followed, straining her eyes in the dimness. Closed doors lined the hall. She swung her service revolver around like a flashlight.

"Stay behind me," he whispered, brandishing the crowbar.

At the end of the hall, he swung open a door, and hinges shrilled. She followed him in, then paused, amazed.

Skirted dolls ranged along a window seat, and ashen light soaked through the curtains, turning the whole room a deep pink that matched the ruffled bed canopy. He yanked open the closet door, then knelt to peer under the bed. "Watch your back," he told her.

He pushed past her back into the hall and paused at the next door as though steeling himself, then jerked it open. Hanging from the ceiling, a model plane tilted in the sudden breeze. Squeezing in behind him, she saw pennants on the walls, a neat stack of baseball cards on a shelf above a small desk. Again, she watched him give the room a cursory search. "It's trying too hard," she prompted. "Same as the others. Like somebody's idea of how a boy's room should look."

"I said, watch your back. This isn't a game."

She gritted her teeth and followed as he returned to the hall.

Faint illumination from the two open doorways fought back the shadows. In the huge bathroom, she glimpsed a glass-walled shower and a double sink, the floor padded with thick carpeting even here. As he checked the shower, she twisted a knob on one of the sinks, and the faucet hissed to silence. "Water's off too," she muttered. "I don't get the feeling anyone's ever planning on coming back here. Do you? Barry?" She wandered back into the hall. "Where'd you go?"

He stood at the next door, his shoulder pressed against the wood, and he pounded with his fist against the top of the frame.

"What is it? I can't make it out. Oh." Metal spikes angled deep into the wood. "Why would anyone nail a door shut?" In the shadows, she could barely see his face. "Barry?"

At the end of the hall, the remaining door sank in deepening murk.

"What time is it now?" Her voice broke. "I think we should leave." She caught his sleeve as he moved toward it. "Look." At their feet, smears on the carpet broadened and disappeared beneath the door. "You know what happened here, don't you? Answer me."

As he twisted the doorknob, he looked down to find her hand on his arm, small but surprisingly strong.

Fiercely, she whispered up at him. "Why won't you tell me?"

The door swung open. Within lay madness. A dim blue glow suffused the room, but in the corners, shadows spread like mold. The massive headboard lay in splinters, strewn with hunks of mattress. A shattered bureau—drawers tilting crazily—oozed clotted garments across the carpet. Crusted palm prints splayed desperately up the speckled wallpaper, and she blinked at the brown imprints of spread fingers. A stain spread across the ceiling, and she stared up at the blur until she seemed to discern a shape.

"Worse than I thought." His voice had become a hoarse creak.

She kept staring upward.

"Further along than I realized," he continued. "There'll be no collecting him. Have to be put down."

"The shape." She kept shaking her head and pointing at the ceiling. "It must be because the light's so bad, right? I mean, nothing could throw someone to the ceiling like that, could it? Not even an ape or something, right?"

"Don't look at it." Taking her by the shoulder, he marched her out of the room, slamming the door behind them.

Even in the dark hallway, she could see that his face had gone terribly white. "Tell me what's going on." She held on to his jacket.

"I want you to go outside and wait in the jeep. Do you understand?" His eyes tracked to the nailed door. "There's not much light left. I have to check that last room. If he comes back . . ."

"No."

"I want you to . . ."

"No." She broke away from him. "Whatever it is, you do it while I'm here."

He only paused a moment. "It's getting late." Now almost no light filtered through the open doors at the end of the hall.

She watched him. The hollow blows echoed. Grunting, he struggled with the crowbar. A nail squealed out, plopped softly to the carpet, then another, and at last he hurled his weight against the frame. With a splintering crash, it burst.

"Wait! It's too dark in there! Where are you?" Her footsteps clicked loudly as she followed him. "How can it be so black?" Gradually, she made out a mattress in the middle of a bare wooden floor. "Barry? Look—the windows are boarded up. And I think the glass is painted over."

Across the room, a flashlight clicked on, and light rushed along the walls, the ceiling, the floor. Rafters had been crudely exposed, the wood blotched with plaster, and large hooks protruded from the beams. Near the mattress, clothing spilled out of a cardboard carton.

By the light of the flashlight, he examined the contents of a tight closet, and she watched him paw through huge sweatshirts and pants so broad in the seat as to appear comical.

Completely rigid, he stared at something on the back of the closet door.

"What is it?"

A worn-looking leather belt swayed on a nail. When she reached past him for it, he caught her wrist. She pulled her hand away but didn't try to touch the strap again. Alongside it dangled four pieces of rough cord.

"Hold this," he said. Passing her the flashlight, he unhooked a piece of the rawhide cord and tested its strength.

"Barry?"

He knelt by the mattress.

She moved the beam. Even in this dimness, she could see the stains . . . and the metal hook in the floor. She realized that other hooks had been screwed into the boards. The two at the bottom of the mattress had an extension cord twisted around them.

"This is the only room in the house that's honest, isn't it?" she asked him softly. The light played across a complicated knot.

The piece of rawhide still dangled from his hand. Abruptly, he wrapped it around one of the hooks and yanked.

"What are you doing?" Sudden perspiration crawled coldly at the roots of her hair.

He tugged harder. With a groan, he strained against the cord, the muscles of his arm and neck bulging visibly.

"Please? You're scaring me."

When he let go of the cord, it raveled harmlessly on the floor.

"What is it?" She trained the beam on his face. His flesh had gone a leaden gray, and moisture stood out like pellets on his forehead. "Have you been here before?" She let the light slide past him and play along the wall. On the crude shelves of raw pine, objects had been spaced evenly—a candle, oddly molded at the base, a long-necked wine bottle, smeared with something oily, a box of fireplace matches, a length of rope—the spacing and arrangement seemed strangely formal, almost ritualistic.

"This room." His voice startled her. "I know . . . what it . . . I've seen . . ."

A miserable heat suffused him, and she felt it radiate from his face, from his glittering stare. She watched him stumble away to grip the door frame, and the light flitted after him. The bones of his knuckles stood out white, and she saw a tensing shock tremble through him. After a moment, he turned to her.

"You don't have to tell me now." She reached out, stalling his tremor with a brush of her hand. "Come on, we're leaving." She pulled him toward the door. "Here, hold the flashlight." She led him into the hall. "What?"

His lips writhed silently.

"Tell me later," she said. "Take it. Hold the light steady." She guided him down the creaking stairs.

Shadows blanketed the walls now, enfolding the parlor in sliding layers that overlapped and deepened on the floor. "No, not the front," she said. "Let's go back out the way we came in." The light moved ahead of them, uselessly picking out the dust on the glass coffee table, the fur of grime on the petals of the plastic blossoms.

"Listen," he hissed.

They stopped moving, and the sound filtered to her—a softly grating slither. It came from beneath their feet.

"The basement," she whispered. The damp noise rasped like broken glass against her flesh. "We never checked the basement."

He touched her wrist. Though he moved as cautiously as a soldier in a minefield, a floorboard groaned beneath him.

She couldn't make her feet move, and she held one hand across her mouth as he drifted away from her. The room seemed to stir, and the rustling noise drifted up from beneath her feet with a soft rush. Finally, she lurched forward.

"Kit!" He caught at her as she pushed past him into the kitchen.

Gloom had settled through the jagged glass, and the basement door stood in the deepest corner. She gripped the revolver with both hands now.

He kept one hand on her shoulder. "We don't mean to hurt you."

Her spine went rigid. For a terrible moment, she thought he spoke to her; then she realized the soft clamor below had ceased.

"We want to help." He called through the basement door. "Do you understand? I know what you are."

"Jesus." Suddenly, the revolver weighed too much for her to hold it steady.

"We saw the room upstairs." In front of her now, he edged closer to the door. "Can you hear me? I know what they did to you, and I understand why." Gently, he pressed the palm of his hand to the wood. "Let me help you." His voice splintered, went ragged. "Let it be over. There's a place I can take you."

Behind them, wind hissed through broken glass.

"Don't open that door, Barry."

"Can you hear me?"

"I'm warning you. I'll shoot anything that moves."

"Do you understand me?" As he twisted the door-knob, a scrambling noise receded. "I'm coming down now."

"No!" Her revolver trembled wildly.

"Don't be afraid."

The hinge shrieked. The corrupt damp of rotting timbers seeped into the kitchen, slowly at first. Then it poured upward, a geyser of stench, unpurified by frost, issuing up from the pit.

"This is the real house, isn't it?" Her voice became almost inaudible. "Like that room upstairs."

"I'm coming now." He angled the flashlight downward, but the faint oblong only spilled across the first few steps, revealing corroded wood and crumbling plaster walls. At the bottom, filthy darkness writhed.

Her face had hardened into a numb mask, and she seemed to have lost all feeling in her arms and legs. No sound reached her ears save a tiny scrabbling. It climbed, growing louder, a terrible murmur that struggled toward clarity, and she knew she'd been hearing it all along, ever since she'd entered this house, aware of it only on the edges of her consciousness.

The steps sagged softly beneath his tread. In the beam, tiny creatures seethed and darted, soft, bloated bodies hopping off the stairs as the light found them. The boldest one stood its ground on the bottom step, its quivering snout smeared with foulness. Dainty paws dug at the feast.

The pistol hung uselessly at her side. "Oh dear Jesus." She was conscious of making a wheezing sound, of blood circulating in the veins of her scalp.

He pounded his fist on the wall until the squirming gray mass receded, exposing the thing they'd gorged upon.

Over his shoulder, she glimpsed it: the snarling teeth,

the blackened talons held up as though it were still trying to defend itself. Rigid darkness looped through the exposed ribs.

And Kit began to scream.

XVI

"I always wondered how I'd handle a real crisis." Pacing into the wind, she sipped coffee through a hole in the plastic lid. "Now I know."

Below them, a pipe cut across the narrow beach into the surf, and receding waves revealed a slime trail in the mud.

"You did okay."

"I froze."

"You're not the type that freezes. You're more dangerous than that."

"Well, I'm freezing now." Shivering in the early morning light, she tried to laugh.

"Charging in that way. Typical rookie maneuver." He shook his head. "Trying to prove something. Good way to get killed."

"I . . ."

"Think about it. Why did you go to that house alone?"

"Why did you?" She grinned. "Exactly. It's my job too. The difference is I don't do mine very well."

"You did okay." By now his words had become a comforting litany, having been repeated over and over since the previous evening. After their grisly discovery in the Chandler basement, she'd seemed to go numb, calmly allowing him to lead her back outside. She'd even surprised him by insisting—in a faint monotone—that they pay a call on the closest neighboring house. He'd thought it best not to argue. After a flash of Kit's badge, an elderly woman had peered nervously into the twilight. The woman told them she'd seen no one entering or leaving the Chandler house in months but had indicated she found nothing unusual in this. "They mostly come and go at night, and, Officer, the sounds from that house, the noises." Then she'd clapped a hand over her mouth.

Kit sipped her coffee, and the wind stung at her from across the boardwalk. "We haven't any choice now."

"We've been all through this." He stalked around her. "You said it yourself. He's got a hostage. He'll kill her if he sees uniforms. How many more times can I say it?"

Her voice rose sharply. "But the body . . ."

"Could have been anyone, Kit. Even Ramsey himself."

"No—he called me."

"How much could you really tell about whoever called you?"

"It was him. It had to be." Her fingers went to her temples, as though she could push away the headache. The previous night came back in vividly chaotic flashes: she could remember the sudden rush of cold when he'd gotten out to retrieve his own car from its hiding place off a side road; then blankness settled. She recalled nothing of the drive home, except perhaps for his headlights, icy and remote in the mirror. Reflexes alone must have guided her. By the time they'd reached the duplex, the shaking had started, and she remembered his arm around her shoulder, helping her up the stairs. She'd barely resisted when he made her take the last of the Xanax he found in her medicine cabinet. He'd spent the night on her sofa. Vaguely, as from a dream, she retained some impression of his making a phone call in the middle of the night. Before dawn, she'd come anxiously awake to find him sitting at her kitchen table with the cat glaring at him from the windowsill. That's when they'd decided to head out to the boardwalk. She couldn't remember why.

"Was it you who broke into Chandler's office?" she

asked. Bleak sunlight glimmered down on them, and despite the chill, she suddenly needed to walk. "Before me, I mean?"

"Somebody broke in?" He met her stare. "No, I swear it wasn't me."

"I don't believe you," she told him simply as she moved to the rail.

"Kit . . ."

"Look at that sky. It's going to be a pretty day. You think it might warm up a little?" She squinted toward the end of the jutting pier. "I can remember watching the old men fishing out there when I was little." Like fragments of mica, sunlight glinted from the water. She sipped more coffee, then tossed the remnants of a doughnut at the scattered pigeons. With a rapid slapping, the birds rose at her movement, then settled back, twitching along the walkway.

He also surveyed the dock and turned his collar up against the wind. "Why does it go so far out?"

Beyond the edge of the dock, gulls wheeled.

"Didn't used to." Shading her eyes, she watched the birds. "It's even low tide now. The sea gains a little ground every year. I used to play right underneath here, right where the water is. Can you believe it? I remember the sand always felt cool, like a slice of winter. And the old men had to fish from the very end." She paced along the rail, the wind blowing the short curls of her hair into a bright tangle. "You've been lying to me all along."

A tern shrieked, and the laughter of gulls echoed from the beach.

"Kit, I . . ." He seemed to concentrate on getting the lid back on his coffee. "Uh . . . why are you looking at me like that?"

"I was just thinking—I've never seen you out in the sun before."

"What's the verdict?"

"Your eyes are almost the same color as the sky. What?"

"Nothing. Just I don't much like this sky."

"Me neither. Don't look at me like that. You're still the prettiest man I've ever seen. It's no particular accomplishment. On the other hand, you're the biggest liar I've ever met. That took some work."

Clutching the rail, he stared downward. At the edges of the mud, the underbellies of dead fish showed white, and farther down the beach, signs warned bathers to avoid the area. Gulls swarmed. "I can't help it." The words seemed to drop away from him, to leave him lighter. "I don't even know if I can explain."

"Try."

He sighed. "This isn't the world we were born for."

"All right."

"You know what I mean."

"Do I?"

He brought his fist down on the rail. "Is it any wonder they . . . ?" His mouth moved silently.

"Get it out." She took hold of his sleeve. "Sooner or later, you're going to have to tell me."

On the beach, several of the gulls lifted until a gust kited them closer. They shrieked with reptilian ferocity. Rage squeezed wheezing cries from their bodies, and two of the largest screamed to a landing, then jabbed their way through the pigeons. Gray and filthy, another lighted on the rail nearby. A wet morsel dangled from its beak.

"Why do I feel like Tippi Hedren all of a sudden?" She turned her back to the wind. "And I'm freezing. Let's get out of here."

But his gaze swept along the sand to where more gulls descended heavily. "There must be someplace we could live, someplace that doesn't make you feel like life is just . . . an infection on the planet."

"Somewhere *we* could live?"

"Some days, nights really, when I can tell the days from the nights, I think about how I have nothing to show for my life, about how easy it would be to just end this. But they're counting on me."

Now terns and gulls swarmed across the sand below. A few slate gray pigeons bobbed amid the horde; then a gull raced forward, wings canted, beak hooking, and the pigeons pattered rapidly away.

"The waves sound so far away," she said. "Like in a shell. Don't stare at the beach like that. You're making me nervous. I didn't report that corpse. All right? I'm in this. I'm in it good now. Don't you think it's time you trusted me?" She watched a muscle twitch below his left eye. "Don't you want to talk about it, Steve?"

It took a minute. "What did you call me?" Heat worked to his face.

As she marched away, the gulls rose, wings slapping like banners.

He caught her arm. "How long have you known? How did you . . . ?"

"Give me some credit. After all, I'm a cop too. Kind of." She shrugged away. "Besides, it wasn't as difficult as all that, not that big a deal." She turned up her collar. "Just took a little digging is all. Barry Hobbes is one of five people known to have been killed by Ernest Leeds three years ago. This morning I made a few phone calls. It seems Officer Hobbes had a partner. Tall, blond, name of Steven Donnelly. Apparently, Officer Donnelly vanished shortly after being exonerated in his partner's death." She released a fractured breath. "How'm I doing?"

They walked slowly. The wind groaned.

"Is that it?" he asked at last.

"One other thing. Ernest Leeds was blown to pieces in full view of over a dozen state troopers. Yet these recent killings bear all the earmarks of the murders attributed to him . . . and now you're here. It can't be a coincidence. Don't you think it's time you told me what the hell is going on?"

"Your lips are practically blue."

The drawer coughed open in a snarl of socks and shirts, one glove, a ski mask.

"What are you looking for? Perry? Answer me."

The boy's glance skimmed in her direction. She still wore the same old sweater she'd had on for days, all stretched out and soft-looking. If she could stand up, it would hang to her knees, but now it had twisted itself around her, the neck pulled so that one pale shoulder poked through. He looked away. "I can't find that jogging suit with the hood, you know, the blue one."

"That's because it's such a mess in here." She forced herself not to tug against the ropes. From where he'd positioned her chair, she could just see a corner of the mirror. She found she couldn't look away from the snarl of her hair, the puffy flesh, the way her complexion took on an almost greenish hue in this light.

"What's the matter?" he demanded. "What? How come you're staring like that?"

She made herself face him. "You've lost more weight. And those pants are too short now."

"So?" His frayed flannel shirt wouldn't stay tucked in. He'd made additional holes in his belt with a nail, and the extra length of it dangled from his belt loop.

"You should let me help you straighten up. Perry, did you hear me?"

He didn't answer, but a moment later he began picking things up off the floor and tossing them into the bathroom, quickly creating a heap of soiled clothing. Then he shoved a different heap into the closet and slammed the door. "I'll straighten up and stuff," he muttered, his eyes slanting to the bed. For a moment, he struggled to smooth it into shape. "I'm so achy." He sprawled on the wrinkled bedspread. "The backs of my legs feel frozen." He turned onto his back and stared down the length of his jeans at her, while he tried to push down the rumpled corner of the bedspread with his foot.

"You were out too long," she told him. "You should let me make the bed."

He peered at her uncertainly, bunching up the sheets with one hand so she wouldn't see the stains.

"You're such a boy. Please, let me. This place needs a good cleaning."

He turned his head as though watching something beyond the walls. She was accustomed to that look, to that strange attention to a world beyond the one she could see. She even knew he might suddenly resume speaking an hour from now as though no pause had taken place. She knew too many things.

He turned over on his stomach and mumbled something into the pillow.

"What? Perry, what?"

He barely lifted his face. "I said it's clean enough."

"You can trust me. Where could I go?" She saw his hand tighten around the bedpost. "You can untie me."

Propping himself on one elbow, he turned and stared, calculating. "Maybe later. I got to wash your hair again. I'll heat up some water."

"It's all right."

"Such long hair."

"Your fingernails are filthy."

"Such a pretty color."

"Don't start anything. Please. Anyway, yours is long too."

"I want you to feel better and stuff. I mean it."

"Why were you out so long today?" She smothered

the panic in her voice. "Perry?" He turned his back to her, but she saw the tension in his shoulders: it made her stomach clench.

"Oh, I almost forgot." Suddenly, he bounded off the bed and lunged into the other room. "Where's my jacket?" He hurried back in. "I brought you all this stuff the other night, but I didn't give it to you 'cause you were . . . you know." He fumbled through the pockets, dumping things on the bed. "See? There's a new comb and perfume and stuff." He stood in front of her, holding up each small item in turn for her to see.

"The perfume is opened." Her voice broke. "Oh God, whose is it? What did you do? Where did you get this?"

"What do you mean? Don't talk about that! Just . . . !"

"No, I'm sorry—I didn't mean it!" Pressing her head back against the chair, she wept. "Don't hit me! Please! Oh please, don't hurt me. Oh God, why doesn't somebody help me?"

"You're so pretty." All the light had drained from Steve's face. "I've never known anybody with eyes like that before," he went on. "Sometimes I think they're blue, sometimes I think . . ."

"They're a muddy green, and now you're really making me nervous." Kit tossed the Styrofoam cup into a trash bin. Slowly, they headed across the boardwalk toward the jeep. "Please don't think you have to handle me every minute, all right? I'm on your side. Would it be so hard to just tell me? Just straight out?" She crammed her hands deep into her jacket pockets.

His gait slowed even further, and he leaned on one of the weathered benches. "I don't expect you to understand this." He sank heavily onto the bench. "Or to believe it. Not at first." The wind stirred, and his hair fluttered heavily across his forehead.

She saw a few gray streaks, and the morning sun revealed lines in his face she'd never noticed. "You know I'll . . ."

"No, don't say anything. Not yet." His shoulders tensed. "Not till I'm finished. It's the only way I'll be able to get it out." Suddenly, his teeth chattered audibly. "You don't know how much I've wanted to tell somebody. Anybody. For years now." The wind seemed to tear his words away, to fling them along the boards. "To begin with, Ernie Leeds was a demented creep who tortured and killed at least six people that I'm aware of, but he didn't kill Barry Hobbes."

"Then who did?"

He watched gulls caught in the upward sweep of the wind. "Me." The cries of the birds scrambled overhead, and the cold stung him to tears.

She wanted to shout at him not to tell her, but her lips formed no words.

"I left him unarmed, stranded in the pines. Knowing what was out there, I left him."

"What do you mean?"

He rubbed a gloved hand across his face. "We got into a fight. I jumped in the car and drove around till I cooled off. Maybe half an hour altogether. When I went back for him, I found his body—didn't even know what it was at first."

She touched his arm, but he didn't seem to notice.

"My fault—as sure as if I'd disemboweled him myself. But Leeds didn't do it. He took the heat to protect someone, a lover probably. At least that's what we think. It fits with his history. And, no, the authorities don't know about it. No reason they should. The real killer's dead too." Suddenly, he got up. "Hell. How do you explain something like this? Without sounding like a raving lunatic?"

"Barry, I mean, Steve . . ."

"No, wait till you've heard it all, then decide if you still trust me so much. The kid, the killer I mean, he had a—how do I say this?—a condition, a genetic condition, like a mutation. Do you follow me?"

Hesitantly, she shook her head.

"No, I don't suppose you do. I'm not sure I do myself half the time. Sometimes I wake up and think we must all be insane. I do know this boy wasn't the only one. Something to do with the gene pool in that part of the barrens. Isolated. Inbred for generations. It—the condition—was rampant." His tone of voice told her he was quoting someone. "We think they brought it with them, the people who settled the area, I mean. Some ancient European affliction. Probably the same thing that started the werewolf legends in Europe all those centuries ago. So maybe there've always been people like this. Every country has legends." His arm swept back inland. "And here. In the pines, I mean. Every generation or so, there'd be another one. It started a different legend."

"You're telling me what? This guy was some kind of a monster?"

He got up and headed down the wooden stairs.

"I'm sorry." She leaned over the rail and called down to him as he reached the beach. "Tell me." She watched him pick his way across the wedge of pebbled sand. "Oh hell, right into the wind again." With a sigh, she followed him. Instantly, cold numbed her flesh, and she plodded unsteadily. Graveled earth looked churned and lumpish, and her exhaustion seemed to make her see every grain too distinctly. The beach hardly existed here. With little more than a single stride, they were at the water's edge. The sand looked black.

They watched waves roll into the shattered lighthouse. Once, the fence had kept the curious away from the dangerous ruins, until the promontory itself had given way. A few yards in, nubs of broken posts protruded in a row, waves sucking around them, and farther out, rust red tentacles broke the water—the ribboned remnants of iron supports. One clutched dried seaweed above the waves like a nest of straw; others twisted coils around hunks of concrete. The top of a cyclone fence protruded from the wash, seaweed and barnacles clogging the links. Spray exploded from a concrete pillar. From along the half-submerged wall of stone, terns rose in a shrieking flurry to float in the sunlight, dipping for the uneven glint.

"Sand dollar," he muttered, stooping. He studied it a moment. "You never see them alive." He held it out to her. "Only after they're dead, after they wash up onshore." His words came out in a rush of sound. "You don't know me." Wind buffeted them, rolled over them, blowing clouds of fine gray sand around their legs. "You only know what's left."

She pulled off her glove. "It's really beautiful, isn't it?" Like a splinter of ice, the sand dollar lay in her palm. Beyond the breakers, birds had settled on the water, mere flashes of white, indistinguishable from the flickering surface. The pale rind of the moon hung above the water.

". . . never really brave." Hoarseness grated in his voice. "It kills in secret—the young, the defenseless."

"It?"

"They. We think they mostly die young themselves. There are convulsions that come with the changes. Or else they're killed by the people around them, family, whatever, unless they just run off to the woods and starve or die of exposure."

A wave collided with the closest rock and droplets sprayed them. "Monsters." She turned and wandered along the edge of the surf. Clumps of vegetation mottled the mud, and she found a stick of driftwood almost buried in sand.

"They can't help what they do. It takes them at puberty, when they're still children practically, and . . ."

She threw the driftwood far out into the shimmering whitecaps, watched it crest a hill of water. "I can't hear you."

". . . like a disease. They need help. But other things go along with it. Gifts. Special abilities. I've seen them do things."

"Them." The word hovered. "I can't believe how cold it is. I can't believe I'm freezing on the beach, talking about what? Mutants? Werewolves? Ever since I met you, I feel like I'm out of my mind. For one thing, I must be crazy just to be out here."

Splinters jutted from the sand at their feet: a short distance away, more shreds of wood seemed to sprout from the gravel. "What the hell's buried under here?"

"A piece of the old dock maybe," she answered. "Don't make conversation. Just tell me. How many?"

"How many?" he repeated.

"Monsters or whatever."

"We've found . . . a few."

The thunderous slap of another wave startled her. "Hell, I'm getting wet. Where do you have them?"

"A house. Far away from anybody who might get hurt. I can tell you that much. And they're well supervised."

"In the barrens, you mean? My God. Just like the stories. Monsters in the woods. Look, just give me a minute here, all right? Let me just make sure I've got it straight. You want me to believe these kids are . . ."

"Demons. Changelings. Whatever you want to call them. She says it can be a gift. I don't know. Sometimes I think she's . . ."

"Delusional? Swell. This is the woman I remind you of, right? Assuming for a moment that you're not a stark raving maniac—and I'm trying to—aren't you, well, apart from everything else, aren't you scared?"

The cloud of his breath dissipated. "Every second of every day."

She touched his arm.

"I've been . . . close to them." The muscles in his face tightened. "She believes they can be helped, that they're the future."

"This woman," she murmured, "that's why you're here. Am I right? You collect monsters for her?" She watched him flinch, watched the thoughts untangle themselves on his face. "I knew you were just using me," she added before he could respond. "I knew it. You don't care about stopping any killer. You couldn't care less about saving any hostage."

"You don't understand. I do want to help the girl . . . if there is a girl . . . if she's alive. That's the biggest part of it. For me. Keeping them from hurting anybody. You don't . . ."

"I don't know if I can believe anything you say."

They had backed away from the water, moving closer to the boardwalk. "I guess I can't blame you."

"It's insane." The wind shifted, and bursts of grit rippled across the beach, tracking each other in silent swells, until the gusts grew stronger and spun themselves into a conch of sand. "What if it's true?" She shielded her eyes. "What if they ever got loose?"

"I thought you didn't believe me?"

"I don't. Look at me. Be honest. I'll know if you're not." She squared her shoulders. "Do you really think . . . ? Do you really believe Ramsey Chandler is one of these . . . ?"

"No." He saw puzzlement twist her expression. "Not him." In the frigid sunlight, the fine veins near her temples were like purple cobwebs, the delicate hollows of her face almost blue. For an instant, he felt as though he confronted some weird child, some seductive elf with smoky red hair and eyes the color of moss. "It's the boy," he told her.

"What?"

"The brother. Don't you see?"

Her mouth opened and closed. "He's only . . . what? Fourteen? Fifteen?"

"That's how I got onto him. That's what I was searching for."

"You were looking for a little boy?" Twisting away from him, she ran. "Oh God." Cold air stabbed into her chest as she pounded over the gravel. "You're crazy." He caught her at the stairs and held on, until they leaned against each other, panting painfully. "Get away from me." But she didn't fight, only jerked her arm away. "What have I done?"

He released her. "Kit?" As he plodded up the stairs behind her, she dodged into a tiny gazebo. "You have to listen, Kit." He found her huddled on a bench. "Please. After the first killing a few months ago . . . the pond where they found the first girl. Remember? I went there myself. On a hunch." The balustrade blocked the worst of the wind. "I hid in the woods. And waited. It paid off. I spotted a boy prowling around. I stayed hidden. He seemed to be searching for something. Kit, I'm good at what I do. I've had to be. There's no way he could've seen me, but all of a sudden, he knew I was there. He just knew. And he took off. Only animals run like that. No way I could move fast enough. I figured I'd blown my one chance at him, never thought I'd get close enough again. But then a second killing made the news a few months later, farther down the coast, and I played another hunch and started checking out the resort towns. Especially small deserted ones, right on the outskirts of the pines." He chuckled grimly, a sound like the crunch of a clamshell underfoot. "It helped that I started hearing about Jersey Devil sightings."

She smiled thinly. "You really are crazy, aren't you?"

"You tell me." He turned to look back at the beach. "I found footprints in the sand. Not every morning. But enough. And I waited."

"I could have made those. I run every night."

"Not these tracks. You see them once, you never forget. Then about a week ago I, well, let's say I caught a glimpse of the boy." Disgust and frustration gritted together in his voice. "That day they found the woman in the bay."

"Spell it out for me. Let me just hear you say the words, just so I know I'm not dreaming this."

"What difference does it make? Whatever you want to call them. There's one of them here in this town, and I'm not going to let him get away." He pulled something out of his coat pocket.

"What is that?"

"A list."

"I can see that much."

"From the cemetery."

"You copied names off headstones?" She leaned away from the bit of paper.

"There are families that show up a lot." A muscle tightened in his face. "I was looking for any kind of lead I could follow. I found Chandlers going back four generations. All over the pines." He squeezed her gloved hand between his fingers. "I'm not crazy. Honest to God, I'm not, Kit. And I need your help. Kit, please, look at me."

"Stop."

"Look at me. I'm a zombie. Going through the motions. And sooner or later, I'll drop. Entropy, it's called. And it won't matter. Not even to me."

"Stop, please."

He didn't seem to hear her. "There's only one door out of this place. If I can finish this, if I can stop this nightmare, then maybe I've got a chance to get my life back. Some kind of life at least."

Stiffly, she pulled her hand away. "I can't do what you're asking." She brushed at her coat, stood.

"Can't you?" He rose beside her.

"I'm a cop."

"A cop who doesn't report homicides?"

Her expression hardened.

"That has to tell you something, Kit. Like it or not, you do trust me. What if he really does have a hostage? You want her death on your hands? Like you said, you're involved in this now. You know what kind of job the troopers will do, don't you? Blundering in like an army? A minute after they pull into town, pieces of that girl will start hitting the water, because you can be sure he's aware of everything that goes on. Can't you feel that? Can't you feel he's watching us all the time?" He scanned the beach. Far off in the haze, a gull dipped languidly. "We're her only chance. If we can find out where the boy's got her . . ."

"It doesn't make sense. It's the other one, Ramsey, who has the hostage. Has to be. But what did he say? Something about . . ." Her voice faded like a receding wave. A stiff wind pushed her, and she staggered against him. "I knew you were good at this." She shuddered with anger. "This is what you wanted, isn't it? To suck me into this. To compromise me. Now I'm stuck. How could I explain my delay in reporting . . . how could I explain that I . . . ?"

"You could always make an anonymous phone call."

She huddled into her coat. "I still might."

"No, you won't."

"Don't be so sure." A pigeon seemed to fall out of the air. It flapped spastically on the boards. "I'm freezing. Can we go now?"

His hands slid beneath her jacket, slipping from her waist to her back, under her sweater. Despite the chill, his palms felt warm against her spine, and she pushed against him, then went slack. Her head barely reached his shoulder.

"Go on. Tell me you're not just using me." Angrily, she tried to pull away. "I'll end up doing whatever you want."

He pressed closer.

She'd never felt anyone's heart pound that way before, dull, rapid blows, as though some animal struggled beneath his jacket. Pulling off a glove, she touched his cheek, felt the heat flare beneath her fingertips, and she kept her hand there as though her touch had the power to silence whatever thundered within him. "Don't look like that." The pale stubble of his beard scratched her palm. "I've never seen anything so sad."

She kissed him back, hard and determinedly, like a stubborn child. She felt him shiver but realized that she herself had stopped shaking.

He pulled her harder against him. Even in the wind, she felt his heat increase. He brought his mouth to hers and forced her teeth apart, sliding in his tongue, as she ground her hips against his.

"Can we get inside now, please?" She jerked her head away. "Before we freeze to death?"

XVII

As dream images lanced her psyche, she twitched: something vaguely human prowled along the swamp, and somehow she knew its pain and sensed the fetid lusts that drove it, even felt the freezing water that sucked around its legs. A thickly veined mixture of mud and stringy weeds dripped from its clawed hands.

No, not mud, she realized.

She sat up in the bed. Bright patches brindled the ceiling and blotted down toward the floor. Beneath the bureau, the cat curled in a wedge of sunlight, just a twist of dusty fur, belly-up to the warmth. Kit lay back, and the movement disturbed Steve so that he slid against her. She listened until his breathing eased again. After a moment, he turned slightly, and his chest, damp against her side, pulled away with a sound like a kiss. She stayed very still, and the drumming of her heart slowed. *Just a dream.* Heat faded from the bed, and a sweetness thickened the air. Molten light still pooled on the windowsills, but a tide of shadows rose along the walls and dimness sloped through the room. *Chilly in here.* Folded, the fireplace screen leaned against the wall. *I have to get more wood.*

Pulling the blanket higher, she tried to examine her feelings of exhaustion and tension . . . and contentment? Faintly, she could hear the wind chimes that had been left behind on the downstairs balcony, and her thoughts wandered to the past. Her mother used to play something for her on their old stereo. What was it? She could almost hear it. Something classical of course—Mozart or Beethoven, she supposed. Always, it had seemed to transform their cottage into something grander. This piece in particular had been her favorite to run about to, dancing and leaping, and always she'd hated to hear the final crescendo, to know that it heralded the return of drab normality. She felt that way now. This was fragile magic. Carefully, she rolled her head on the pillow. The blanket rose evenly with his chest, and she studied the square, flat muscles of his torso. *So strong-looking.* Yet he exhaled haltingly, as though gritting back a continuous onslaught of small pains.

She took in as much of the room as she could without moving. A puddle of amber light dripped across the edge of the carpet, and the cat rolled through it, then shook its head free of dust and sneezed before curling back to sleep. *What have I been doing here?* These past two years, she'd scarcely allowed herself to think about her life, but now, struggling not to twitch, she clenched her fists. *I've got nothing of my own.* How could she still be living like this? *I've done nothing.* All the furniture had come from her parents' house. Even the dishes. Pictures on the walls. Everything. *Like some college student whose adult life never got started.*

In the dusk across the room, his leather jacket sagged over a bench, seeming to radiate some animal heat of its own. *Dressed like a biker and trying to look inconspicuous.* Ruefully, she grinned. *And that awful car.* Then she frowned, searching for the source of a low sound. *I don't believe it.* She blinked at the cat. *The thing snores.* She felt herself sinking back toward sleep. *Now, if I could just teach it to spit, I wouldn't need a man in my life at all.*

Without opening his eyes, Steve stretched across the rumpled bedding to draw a finger along her stomach. ". . . soft . . ."

" . . . "

"Did you say something?" he mumbled.

"... m ..."

"Beg pardon?"

Sprawled in a languid stupor, she rolled and mumbled into his shoulder. "I thought you were asleep." Her knees slid up beneath the sheet, and her legs wrapped around him, slackly.

Murmuring something that sounded like "I am," he molded himself against her.

The blanket slipped down, and she wriggled on her side. Imbibing the musky smell of him, she toyed with the tightly curled hairs at the back of his neck, then languorously stroked the bright dusting of fur on his shoulders, remembering the warmth of his mouth and the taste of his tongue. Honey-colored light streaked his chest, and her fingers traced the muscles that braided his arm, traced the prominent veins. She brought his hand to her mouth, kissed his fingertips. Golden hairs glinted even on the backs of his hands.

He drew her damply into the nook of his arm. "You're a very beautiful lady."

"I was just thinking the same thing."

"And modest too."

"I meant about you, stupid."

"I'm a beautiful lady?" He twitched back the sheet. "If you'll notice ..."

"Shut up, idiot." She smacked playfully at his head. "And I can't believe this hair. Like animal fur."

His limbs wound hot and moist around her. "And you haven't commented on my almost canine sensuality."

"Idiot." Her laugh blurred against his chest.

"Doesn't say much about your judgment, does it? What kind of a cop are you anyway?"

"The world's worst. Haven't you figured that out by now?"

"I think there's some pretty stiff competition for that title just in this bed."

"Stiff what?" She stroked him.

"Stop that. Hussy." In retaliation, his hand slipped silken between her legs.

"Oh." Her words flowed in a warm rush. "This scar on your stomach. It's not from an operation, is it?" Everything had changed from this morning on the beach. Even their voices sounded different, she thought, like the voices of happy strangers, and they couldn't stop touching each other. "So jagged." She leaned forward and tried to kiss it, but he shifted away. "There's another. You're lucky to be alive, my boy." She traced a line beneath his chin and down the side of his throat, until her hand hesitated. "My God." Her voice cracked. "One of them did this to you. This is what you meant, isn't it?"

The bed quaked as he turned away and sat at the edge of the mattress.

"Steve . . . I still can't believe any of this is happening." She watched his back. "Look at me."

"Uh . . . do you have that list of properties here?"

He barely turned his head, but she glimpsed his eyes: dirty ice.

"You have it here? The addresses you found in Chandler's office?"

"I have it." She rolled away.

"We should begin checking them."

"Of course." She reached for the clothes she'd thrown off earlier. "I didn't mean to waste your time. Should we divide them?"

"Wait. I'm sorry. I didn't mean we had to . . ." He tried to pull her toward him, but she continued to dress. It seemed the light clarified every freckle on her pale arms and legs. "Kit, there's no reason for you to be involved in this any further, I'll . . ."

"Don't even try it." Fingers trembling, she zipped her jeans. "We'll take turns watching the apartments."

"No, if you insist on coming with me, we'll . . ."

"Barry, Steve, whoever the hell you are . . ." She squinted at the window. "The only possible excuse for my not having informed the authorities already is for us to be handling this ourselves. We should have moved on it by now, but here we are instead. So tell me again how committed we are to saving lives. Do you want to eat something, before we get started?"

He shuffled through the blankets. "Kit."

Shrugging away from his touch, she tugged her blouse on, then hurried out of the room. As she walked, the cat pressed at her ankle.

What am I doing? She got out a skillet and began to root through the refrigerator. *He's just sitting on the bed, waiting for me to say something.* Her hand went to a package of ground meat, and her fingertips pressed it. Gelid. Grainy. Deep pink dotted with white. At the crinkled bottom of the cellophane, a tiny amount of red fluid had gathered. Swaying, she closed the refrigerator and leaned against the door while the room swayed; then she rushed for the bathroom. An unblinking feline gaze observed her.

Leaning on the sink, she listened to his movements in the next room. *I won't be sick.* She twisted a faucet, and water gushed. She watched it beat against the basin and splash across her blouse; then she adjusted the flow and cupped her hands to bathe her face. It cooled her burning eyes, but when she looked at herself in the mirror, she cringed. She tugged at the sleeves of her blouse. It made her look bony, boyish. Salt spray and the pillow had made a bizarre frizz of her hair, which now curled chaotically in a coppery mesh. The cat scraped at the door. "Can't you leave me alone for five minutes?" She turned the shower on full blast before letting her clothes fall in a heap, as though she couldn't bear to touch them. *They smell of the beach.* She stood under the water a long time. *Everything smells of the beach.*

Afterward she wiped the skin of steam from the mirror and combed her hair straight back before wrapping herself in a white terry cloth robe. *Maybe he's right.* She had to wipe the mirror with a towel again to see herself, the image smeared and blurred around the edges. Wet, her hair looked almost chestnut. *Maybe all I care about is a chance to take the killer down myself. What would that get me anyhow?* She shrugged the thought away. *Out of here? Is that what I want?*

She found him sitting in the armchair, his face buried in her notes, and she walked past without speaking. Finding her slippers, she headed back into the kitchen.

Moments later, cooking odors twined through the warm air. *Or do I just want him?* She'd pulled the curtains aside, and the last of the light pooled in the center of the table where the cat fitfully purred. "Who said you could sleep on the table?" But the cat just lifted its head, squinting at her. The electric clock on the wall whirred softly. It seemed a reassuring noise, so normal, making nonsense of all their talk of monsters. In the next room, a chair scraped, and a few seconds later she heard the shower. Slicing onions and peppers, she prepared an omelet for them, annoyed with herself at the amount of effort she put into it, disgusted with her own transparent need to impress him with her domestic skills.

The cat slid off the edge of the table and leapt to the windowsill. "What do you want from me, cat? This never letting me out of your sight business is getting on my nerves. You're not hungry. You won't let me pet you." She moved to the old china cabinet and got out her best dishes and linen. "So what is it?"

The cat's tail tapped the wall in a restless oval.

"We should start with these cottages on the outskirts of town," he said, his fingers tracing a column of addresses.

"The ones most likely not to attract attention. We need to go back to the Chandler house too—just to check—periodically. See if anybody shows up."

Her hand glided above the table, started for the salt, then the water glass, hesitated and returned to her lap. "This is what it's all about for you."

He poured himself another cup of coffee.

"This search. Everything else . . . just a means to an end."

He chewed mechanically.

"What happened to you? What could make a person like this?"

"I shouldn't have touched you." Finally, he faced her. "Taking warmth from you. I don't have the right." He forced his attention back to his plate. "What? Were you going to say something?" His hand dropped to the table with a thud. A moment later, he tried to smile. "I'm sorry. Was this for the cat?"

"Shut up. It's tofu. It's good for you."

He prodded the omelet with his fork. "No sprouts?"

"Don't try to be funny." She snatched the list off the table. "It scares me worse than anything when you're charming." She studied the page. "You know, these places will all be locked up tight for the winter. How do you intend checking them out?"

He forked another bit of omelet into his mouth.

"Oh." She picked up her coffee mug, almost brought it to her lips, set it down again. "We're going to do some more breaking and entering, right?" Her fingers tightened around the handle of the mug. "Didn't take you long, did it?"

He swallowed glumly. "What?"

"To turn me into an outlaw."

"Like me, you mean?"

Her shoulders pressed back, and her arms stiffened.

"Can't you trust me just a little longer, Kit?" Veins in

his temples bulged, and the muscles under his shirt twitched visibly. "Can't you believe we're doing this for the right reasons?"

"How can I believe anything you say?" She covered her face with her hands. "What's wrong with me? Monsters. Am I crazy too? There aren't any rules for this, no departmental directives."

"You're right about one thing. I can't do this alone, Kit. Help me, please." He stroked her arm. "I've told you everything I can." He stood up. "It's your call. I'll go if you want me to."

"And?"

"And try on my own."

"I don't know what I'm doing," she said. "I'm scared. And I probably am falling in love with you. God help me." Silence thundered in the room. "Did you hear what I said?"

"I haven't even thought words like those in a long time." He stood close beside her, and his hand smoothed the delicate tendrils of hair at the back of her neck. "I'm not sure what they mean anymore."

She pressed her face damply into his shirt.

"C'mon, Kitten." He stroked her back. "We've got work to do."

XVIII

Motion washed over him, and bare trees banded the gray sky. For a moment, it seemed they might be going anywhere at all, away, to safety; then her voice brought him back.

". . . used to be the best section of town." She maneuvered them through the narrow streets. "Did you nod off?" Surreptitiously, she checked herself in the rearview mirror. She'd worn the green scarf in hopes that it would bring out the color of her eyes. It didn't, she decided. "Used to get the highest rents."

He noticed she wore earrings today, the first jewelry he'd seen on her, and the tiny gold circles glinted dimly as she turned her head to peer down the street.

"Stands to reason the Chandlers would own half the properties here," she said as she parked the jeep and zipped her jacket.

They walked briskly down the block, side by side under the trees, neither quite looking at the other. At the top of the bluff, majestic homes commanded an imposing view of the sea.

"Used to?" Wind tore at the flesh of his face.

"What?"

"Used to be the best?"

"When I was a kid," she explained, "these were the summer homes of rich people. After that, they started to rent by the season, but you had to know somebody. These days, the owners are lucky to get tenants at the height of the season. If it wasn't for this wind, I'd walk you down.

Used to be our nicest beach. Nothing but rocks now. And during a storm . . . hell. See that watermark way up there on that porch?"

"Jesus."

"This town's never coming back." She shrugged. "So what am I doing here?"

Withered gardens tightly encircled the first three properties they visited. As they tested doors and peered through windows, she watched him, beginning to comprehend the extent to which he operated by instinct.

"Doesn't look like anybody's been at this one either. Three strikes," he grunted. "Let me see that list." Slowly, they drove back toward the center of town and passed the next place several times before parking on the opposite side of the street. For a moment, they remained in the jeep. The three-story houses had porches on each level, like shelves, empty flower boxes clinging to each of the ornate railings. Identical structures ranged up and down both sides of the street.

"This time, let me go alone." She put a hand on his arm. "Just stay in the jeep. It only makes sense. If somebody spots me, I can say I'm checking out a report of prowlers or something."

"You're out of uniform." A smile whisked across his face. "But you're getting good at this."

She thought he sounded sad. "Anyway, it'll make me feel less like I'm just along for the ride," she told him.

"If you see anything . . ."

"You'll be the first to know," she said.

The door slammed before he could respond, and he watched her stride across the street and study the house. *What have I done to her?* The set of her shoulders struck him as both proud and innocent, suggesting a determined youngster. *Too late to start feeling guilty now.* Suddenly, she headed around the side of the building. *What the hell is she doing?* He opened the door and almost stepped out. With a tearing noise, the wind sliced itself through the branches of a small tree. *All right, so she's checking windows.* After a moment, he pounded his fist on the dash. *Where is she? What's taking so long?*

Swinging her arms like a little girl, she came around the side of the building. Glancing at the jeep, she shook her head before starting for the first porch. He settled back in. He had a perfect view. He saw her finger on the bell, watched her look around before trying the door. She put her face to the front window then turned away. A moment later, she headed farther up the steep, trellised stairs.

Damn, this is no good. Now he could barely see her through the wrought iron grillwork, and she vanished altogether on the next porch. *What if he's there? She could be dead while I sit here.* As he shoved the door open again, he caught a glimpse of her heading for the third level. *Damn it. Stay where I can see you.* A second later, she leaned over the rail, beckoning.

Against the wind, he bounded toward the house and took the stairs two at a time, the dull chill of the metal rail cutting into his flesh.

She looked flushed, guarded excitement tightening her face. "There's a light on inside, way in the back. See?"

He peered through a gap in the curtains: dark forms bunched on the floor.

"That's suspicious all by itself, isn't it?" she asked. "I mean, why wasn't the power turned off? And . . ."

"Quiet." He tried the door.

Behind him, she leaned against a porch swing, which gave a rusted squeal.

"Quiet, I said!"

She steadied it with her hand, but it continued to creak faintly. "Steve?" Thick soot covered the vinyl cushions. "The swings." She strayed to the rail. "On every other building, the swings are down for the winter. But all the porches on this building still have . . ."

His shoulder hit the door, and the lock gave.

Nervously, she glanced around at the other houses. When she turned back, the doorway stood empty. "Steve?" Entering, she stumbled around bags and boxes, toward the light in the back. A heap of bedding covered a battered sofa.

"Freezing in here." His voice drifted from somewhere ahead in the brown murk. "And it stinks of garbage. Take a look at this."

Grease spots glistened like mica on the kitchen wallpaper. Strewn among pizza boxes and fast-food containers, garish magazine covers depicted rock bands and wrestlers, curling pages glued to the counter. Comic books littered the floor around the table.

"You ever seen anything like this?" He waved his arms at the mess.

"Could still have been summer people," she pointed out, hesitantly.

Soda cans and paper plates gathered against one wall like a snowdrift, and a plastic trash bag full of old clothing sagged open. He poked into the clutter and pulled a copy of *Soap Opera Digest* from under a stiffened ice-cream container. "The November issue. They were here." He tossed it aside, and the soles of his shoes crackled over a greenish patch of something sticky on the linoleum.

Beneath the layer of grime, the linoleum appeared to be yellow marbled with purple, like a bruise. The floor curled up in a weird lump at one corner, and she wondered what picture she'd get if she connected the dots of the cigarette burns. "Steve?"

"There's got to be something here." He paced into the next room and began to dig around the sofa cushions. "Some hint of where they went." He dumped out the contents of a drawer, turned over a wastepaper basket and began to sift the contents.

She followed him to a small bedroom where closet doors hung open, bare wire hangers tilting. The stained mattress had been stripped, and bureau drawers lay empty on the floor.

"Looks like they took everything they could use. Steve, there's nothing here." Wandering back into the kitchen, she twisted a knob on the range. "Gas is off."

A twisted paper bag lay atop the dirty dishes in the sink. "Water's on still." He demonstrated. "Check that refrigerator."

She pulled open the door and gagged at the sour stench. "Half a bottle of orange soda. Ketchup." On the bottom shelf, a head of deliquescing lettuce had covered the grate. "And some . . . looks like it used to be onion dip."

"Swell." He shook his head. An almost empty bag of pretzels, an empty pastry carton and three nearly empty boxes of breakfast cereal shared the surface of the kitchen table with a jar of peanut butter, scraped clean. "What's the expiration date on the milk?"

"The twelfth." Her voice dropped. "Of last month."

"I knew it!" He pounded his fist on the table, and the pretzel bag rattled to the floor.

"Do you think he'll come back?"

"Electricity's still on. Water. Yeah, he might."

"But won't he see the door's broken and . . ."

"We'll have to split up." He met her stare. "One of us is going to have to watch this place while the other keeps searching. It's the only way. What?"

"Look at this." She prodded at the trash bag, and stench smoked through the room. With the tip of her shoe, she pushed the opening back, and even in the poor light, they could see the blood that stiffened the denim overalls within.

XIX

In a bizarre assortment of architectural styles and follies, crowded roofs ranged tall in this part of town. Brick chimneys jutted from sloping shingles alongside squared flattops, all at different heights and angles, and wind-driven rain and sleet bounced as though trying to scour them all away.

Sleet chimed against the glistening fire escape. From the streets below, the barking of dogs rose, keening thinly against the wind. Then a deep rumble reverberated, and the dogs fell silent. Again, the hellish cry razored the night, unwinding like a pulsing wire of noise. Mingling bitter grief with raging hopelessness, it surged and echoed over the deserted streets, then whimpered to silence.

Sleet gave way to soft raindrops that spattered the metal stairs. Through the open window, the sodden fabric of summer curtains trailed and billowed in a damp gust. The scream spurted once more, shrilled into a mewling shriek.

He doesn't sound terribly happy this evening.

The screech faded into a pathetic groan. Then the pounding began, vibrating clearly even at this distance, as if great fists rammed against the walls in that room across the courtyard.

Ah, it's begun.

Lenses clicked against the pane. At his window, Ramsey Chandler twisted the knob on the binoculars. His focus swept the mouth of the alleyway, then jerked up a wall, across a low rooftop, scouring the brick canyon in nervous swoops. He could hear the wind moan below, battering windows as it passed.

Somehow, the tables had been turned. No longer did he stalk his prey unseen. Now someone hunted him, and he fought to control his trembling. *I should have taken the time to kill him in the alley.* But to have been so close to the boy! To see recognition kindle in that face. In those eyes. So like hers. Luminous. Knowing. To have it all so close to a final resolution—a quick twist of that slender neck! It had been too much, and in that moment, he'd forgotten all else. *But I should have made sure the stranger was dead.* Instead, he'd left the man unconscious and pursued the boy. Foolishly, stupidly, with no real chance of overtaking him on foot, he'd revealed himself. *I lost my head. So uncharacteristic of me.* The boy had scurried into the blackness, and he'd blundered after him. When at last he'd given up and gone back to finish the man, he'd arrived in time to see the redheaded policewoman helping him into her jeep. *No matter.* They'd driven in the direction of the marina. *It is set in motion now, and nothing can stop it, regardless of whom this stranger might be.* It had taken hours of scouring the neighborhood around the docks in that freezing wind before he'd spotted the jeep again.

With a jerk of the binoculars, he wrenched his mind back to the present. *Whoever he is, whatever he is, I cannot allow him to live. And little Perry. He must die as well.* A wave of fear swept through him as he considered the boy. *Difficult that. Problematic. But I almost caught you once, little brother. Vulnerable. Unchanged. I shall find you that way again. And soon. It must be soon.* He twisted the focus. *But first things first.*

Nothing stirred in the alley. Yet his pursuer lurked out there, he knew. Somewhere.

Eventually, he sighed and swung the binoculars back toward the apartment.

The window! It was open wide now. He slapped his palm against the pane too hard, cracking it. *No!* Frantically, he scanned back and forth across the fire escape, the alley, the . . .

He caught just a glimpse of the boy's cap vanishing down the alley. Tossing the binoculars on the bedding, he grabbed for his parka. The door thudded against the wall as he pounded into the hallway and down the well of the stairs.

In the empty room, the candle flickered feebly, and tendrils of smoke twined up to the ceiling. As the door drifted shut, sleet began to tap at the cracked windowpane.

"Oh, so you're still around."

"Nice little town you have here."

The barmaid swiveled a look to someone at a nearby table, and one of the patrons shook his head.

"Stacey, isn't it?" Steve ordered a beer, then spent ten minutes trying to draw her into conversation. "I was in Cape May last month, stayed at a couple of the famous haunted hotels." He grinned. "You interested in that sort of thing?"

Wiping a glass, she barely looked at him.

"Psychic phenomenon is sort of a hobby of mine."

"Uh huh." She went on to the next glass.

"Ghosts and poltergeists, that sort of thing." He raised his voice, watching the other patrons in the mirror. "You know, things moving around by themselves. Anything like that ever happen around here?"

He heard somebody mutter, "What in hell's he talking about?"

"I mean, are there any old legends about the town? You know, haunted beaches . . . or strange families. That kind of thing?"

The white-haired man on the next bar stool cast him a

look of utter disgust. "People here ain't no stranger than anywheres else," the man grumbled as he picked up his beer and moved away. "Leastwise we mind our own business."

"Here, give me another." Steve put a twenty on the bar and forced a smile.

"Uh huh." Stacey shook her head. "You're different all right. I'll give you that much." Under the makeup, she looked tired. "You ought to meet Tully."

"Who?"

"Besides, if you really want to know about the town, he's the only one's gonna talk to you." Smirking, she looked as though she might say something else but wiped the counter instead.

"Why's that?"

With one long fingernail, she scraped at a spot on the bar. "Everybody else has gotten pretty leery of strangers since last week. Cops and reporters. Pestering everybody. Just the kind of publicity this town don't need."

"You expecting this Tully character tonight?"

"Hey, Tull, come over here," she called. "Man wants to buy you a drink."

Steve blinked. A young man rose from a table near the wall. No one could have appeared more out of place, and he watched him smile in habitual apology as he squeezed around a table. The sheepskin jacket and cable-knit sweater looked expensive, and brown curly hair hung to his shoulders, slightly exaggerating a suggestion of weakness in his features.

Cigarette scissored between two fingers, Stacey said, "Now tell him what you was telling me about." Folding her arms, she observed them through the smoke.

While Steve repeated his comments about psychic phenomenon, Stacey poured drinks. "Oh," the newcomer interrupted with a chuckle, "so that's why she wanted us to meet. Sorry, but she thinks you're weird too." His hands twitched. "Am I right, Stace?" All his gestures seemed jerky, barely controlled and at odds with his polished appearance, as though he constantly reined in some violent reaction. "They all think I'm a little crazy here."

She smiled with her lips closed.

"Tully, is it?"

"Nickname. Long story. Real name's Jason. Jason Lonzo."

"I take it you're not from around here?" Steve leaned forward. At the closest table, a laugh cut off suddenly.

"I am. Sort of. My folks have a place here, and I've been here every summer since I was born just about."

Steve patted the sleeve of his own leather jacket. "Strange time of year for the beach, isn't it?"

"Hmm? Oh, you mean why am I here now? I more or less dropped out of grad school a couple months ago. The situation got a little tense at home, so I've been staying at the shore house, you know, trying to figure myself out." He shrugged. "Maybe do a little painting."

"You paint?"

"Hope so. I don't really know yet."

Steve nodded. His third beer had settled on an empty stomach, and his companion's last remark suddenly struck him as both eloquent and poignant. "Yeah," he expounded.

"You think less of me for that? For quitting?" He searched Steve's face as though this stranger's opinion suddenly mattered intensely.

"Well, uh," Steve cleared his throat.

"Hey, Charlie, how you doing?" The long hair swayed in front of Tully's face as he nodded at one of the regulars hurrying past. "I'm too sensitive, that's all. I'm sorry, but it's a little weird. Sometimes I know what people are going to say. You know? What they're thinking even. Sometimes I think they can tell, and they resent it. Is that crazy?"

"You tell me." They kept talking and drinking, though the blurry discourse in which they indulged barely qualified as conversation. Tully's whole demeanor changed whenever he addressed one of the other patrons, his vocabulary and tone of voice altering with a spurious attempted to affect a jocular coarseness of character. Always the locals turned from him with barely concealed sneers. *He should give it up.* Steve shook his head, feeling a surge of compassion for this young man, so desperate for acceptance. Oblivious, Tully prattled on about some philosopher whose work he found "strangely meaningful," while Steve ordered more beer. *Hell, why am I sitting here? I don't have time to waste. The boy could be anywhere. He could sneak out of town, and I'd lose him and never find him, and he'd kill and kill and never stop.* But a luxuriating paralysis seemed to spread through his body, preventing his muscles from tensing when he willed himself to rise. What next, he wondered? *Wander back outside? Into that terrible cold? Kit can only watch the apartment another hour; then she goes on duty. I'll be there to take over.* Besides, he found himself liking his tense and melancholy new acquaintance. *I'll be there. No rush.*

"Toxic dumping for one thing. Did you get a whiff of the bay?"

He interrupted the younger man to order food, and they moved to a table.

"You've met Kit? Really? That's somebody else I always thought was out of place here. Hard to believe she's a cop."

Steve just watched and listened. While the barmaid wiped the table, he noticed the way she looked at Tully, the way she moved with an exaggerated twitch of the hips. An indulgent smile played across Tully's face as Stacey leaned far over him to swab out the ashtray with a damp cloth.

Good for you, kid. Steve told himself he wasn't just wasting time here, that mingling with the locals constituted part of the investigative process. *Okay, so we'll talk a while, and maybe I'll learn something about the town.* Except they didn't seem to be discussing the town. What was the guy going on about now? Renaissance architecture? The beer created a haze in his vision, but he made an effort to focus. "This town," he interrupted. "It's sort of laid out strange for a seaside resort, isn't it? Doesn't look much like the rest of the towns around here."

"It's older than most. Except for the boardwalk. That only got built about fifty years ago, before the beaches started to go." Tully nodded enthusiastically, switching conversational tracks without noticeable effort. "The earliest residents were mostly English and German, then a big wave of Italians. Lots of fishermen. They built the center of town—you know, brickwork and alleyways. But they're mostly gone now." He sipped his drink. "Like all the people I knew as a kid."

"I've been meaning to ask somebody—how come the beach is black?"

"Iron ore. There's a mine in the barrens the town buys sand from."

Cigarette smoke seemed to create a fog around the lights, and Steve couldn't concentrate on the words he heard. The younger man was telling him about how off-shore dumping had changed the coastline and destroyed the beaches or something like that. He could smell a cigar, and suddenly the bar felt cool and damp. He became acutely aware of hostile glares from the corners. *Enough.* In a moment, he knew he'd find the strength to leave.

For hours, Charlotte had perused the photographs in the old album, turning the yellowed pages so that light from the fireplace slid across them, illuminating now a face, now a background figure, vivid, then faded . . . and sometimes strangely unfamiliar, as though they belonged in the memories of another person, some stranger who'd begun telling her a long story full of bewildering details. Then an image would resonate and remembrance would flood back, buoy her a moment, then ebb, leaving her stranded with her sense of loss. Yet she couldn't stop turning the pages, the surge of feeling worth the pang it left. Her husband's face looked back at her from every page, and when she glanced up, she found him in every corner of the room, framed on the wall, encased in silver on shelves and end tables, large images and miniatures. Gradually, the firelight faded into bright shadows, and she began to feel the chill. *I should put on more wood. What would Katherine say if she saw me shivering here?* Gingerly, she placed the album on a delicate table, then wheeled herself to the fireplace. *I refuse to become one of those old persons who suffer through self-neglect.* Her hand tightened about the wheel rim, and a trace of pain gnawed at her wrist.

A noise trebled below the squeal of the chair.

It's here. Flames hissed softly. *It's here again.* She twisted her body to the curtained windows, listening to the night.

The voice of the sea drifted on a low wind, grunting through the window, like the noise a wolf might make in its sleep.

"Where are you, poor dead thing? Are you right outside?"

The drapes swayed slightly in the draft, and she reached quickly for the phone on the table, but only let her hand rest upon it. *No, I won't disturb Katherine with this.* Laboriously, she turned the chair around, while the floorboards sang out their sad, ritual creaking. *I will not bother her again so soon.*

Guttural panting rattled the glass.

But the dead don't breathe. And surely they are silent.

Straining, she guided the chair adroitly to the windowed alcoves, until the wheels struck the single stair. She felt for the lock on the wheel, then braced herself with the heels of her hands.

Pain radiated through her. The delicate muscle cords of her arms quivered as, with a thin groan, she levered herself from the chair. But her legs didn't tremble, and she stood like a statue. In seconds, a film of sweat slicked her neck. Her foot faltered at the step. She swayed upward until her hands clutched at the curtain cord, and she hung on it for balance. Then she pulled weakly with numbed fingers, and the heavy drapes slid open.

Firelight glinted from the pane. Bulging eyes glared at her from the outer darkness.

The curtain cord whipped from her fingers, and she stumbled back. The room reeled.

. . . something deep . . . soft . . .

She lay on the carpet.

The fire had grown dimmer, plunging the parlor into gloom, the shadow beneath the coffee table as black as the sea. *I saw it.* A brittle soreness sputtered through one side of her body, and her right hand groped for the chair. *And it looked right at me.* With a moan, she caught at the spokes of a wheel, pulled herself to her knees. *How did it get so dark? Was I unconscious? How long . . . ?* She shivered. *Is the thing still there?* Her vision twisted to the windowpane. A leafless china apple tree danced and skittered in the wind, and beyond the dead garden, whitecaps flickered around the rocks: silent, numinous explosions.

Above her head, wood creaked.

Her heart hammered painfully, and dying flames whispered. All around the room, windows shivered in their frames. At last, she sat heavily.

The board creaked again.

"So you're here." Faintly, her words rasped. "In the

house." Her head sank forward as though in prayer. "Finally." The axles squeaked shrilly as she wheeled herself toward the doorway. "You've come back to me."

Firelight barely shimmered into the hall, but it danced the shadow of the banister high across the wall.

Her own shadow loomed, slumped and brittle. To her left, another doorway opened into a smaller sitting room, long since converted into the bedroom she'd despised for years. "I've waited such a long time." Her voice rose with tremulous indignity. "At first, I was afraid. You know how foolish I can be. I didn't understand. But I know what you are now." Her voice cracked. "Forgive me, that's not right. I know who you are."

Phantom movement flurried at the top of the stairs, like veils in the wind, and she stared upward, straining until she could just make out the window on the landing. Sheer curtains danced frantically. At first, she heard only the creak of a stair, so soft she could almost have believed she imagined it, but there followed the distinct thump of a footfall.

"Yes," she chanted. "Yes, dead thing, I'm here. Dear dead thing." She stared into nothingness. "Come down to me."

Another footstep creaked on the staircase, and Charlotte groped blindly for the light switch too far above her on the wall. She edged closer. Darkness spiraled up the steps. She reached out, her fingers waving like an anemone. Was there a form? Some shape motionless on the stairs? A tingling sensation crawled across her face. "What's that?"

A squeaking burble seemed to tumble down the steps, barely audible.

"What, dear? Are you speaking?"

She saw the hand first, the way it dug into the banister, sliding into the faint gloom. Then the stench poured over her. "I've gone mad. I always knew . . . knew this would happen. Alone in the dark and I've gone mad in the end, howling by myself in an empty house, imagining something has come to me."

It growled.

Why is it making that sound? Like an animal. It should be calm. Stately. Sad.

Like heat from a furnace, stench came at her in waves now.

It stepped down into the dim spill of light.

"No! No! Henry, help me!" The pain in her chest struck like a sickle, and a pool sprang up around her.

The parlor surfaced through swirling colors. *Such a nightmare I've had.* Somehow she must have fallen asleep by the fireplace. *But I was in the hall. I'm sure I was. How did I get here?*

Then she saw it.

It stood quite close, turned away from her, and she watched the way its naked shoulders bunched. She saw it lift one of the photographs from its place on the mantel, and her fingers closed instinctively over the poker. "No! That's mine! Get away from there! Monster! Put it down!"

The creature turned to her as though in astonishment, and she lashed out with the poker.

One hand struck like the paw of a great cat, ripped through her, sent her hurdling from the chair. She struck the wall. She felt things crack and snap within her, but still her voice stuttered. ". . . mine . . . leave them alone . . . you can't . . ."

A clawing hand lifted her by the hair, and taloned fingers buried themselves deep in her soft, old face.

XX

"The world gets more and more like science fiction every year." Tully tilted his chair back. "It's weird. Some nights I lie there in a sweat just thinking about it."

Ignoring him, Steve strained to discern the newscaster's words above the electronic buzz of the television set. Around the bar, a dozen patrons squinted up at the weather report.

"Three inches, they said," Stacey reported, setting down the plates.

"What?"

"Snow. Didn't ya hear?"

"You're kidding?" Steve flinched. Around him, the patrons buzzed in outrage.

"Did you hear what he said about the hurricane?" asked the younger man.

"What?"

"And snow tonight maybe," Tully continued while gazing into his empty glass. "Doubt it though. Too cold. My father used to say that. Too cold for snow. But there's a bad storm heading up the coast, not a hurricane exactly but . . ."

"Unusual time of year for something like that, isn't it?" Steve coughed. "I thought . . . I thought . . ."

"Never," a man at the bar called over. "Never happen." The tavern had suddenly grown raucous. "Never after the first snow."

"It's like the seasons are so weird anymore." Tully shook his head. "Like somebody shuffled the calendar pages or something. I never took a science course I didn't get an 'Incomplete' in, but storms have something to do with a mass of cold air meeting a warm front and . . ."

"Warm front where?" demanded a guy at the next table. "What warm front? It's frigging freezing."

"He must mean Stacey. Hey, did you hear me? He said warm front and . . ."

"Oh you," the old lady with the eye patch giggled. "You're terrible." She turned to someone else. "Did you hear what John said?"

The woman with the operatic makeup still sat rigidly at the bar, her hairdo—the color of a wasp carapace—unveiled for the evening. "Ever since they put a man on the moon," she enunciated carefully. "The weather ain't been right." She pursed her lips and nodded with an air of profundity, her necklace glittering. "I'm telling you."

Steve looked around the bar. He'd never imagined these people so animated.

"It'll miss us probably," Tully continued. "Usually does. Though we had to evacuate a couple times when I was a kid."

Above their heads, a view of the Edgeharbor bay flashed on the screen, followed by a glimpse of the newscaster. Milling policemen flickered, succeeded in turn by an aerial view of Atlantic City. Although no one in the bar appeared to be watching, conversation drifted to the killing, and Steve sat up straighter. For whatever reason—news of the approaching storm or simply because he'd sat here so long this evening—the patrons had finally begun to relax and forget his presence.

"And this body in the damn bay. What do you think that's gonna do to us?"

"People won't remember that come summertime."

"The hell they won't. You wait and see how many cancellations we get by Memorial Day, every damn one of us."

It quickly passed, and soon they appeared to talk slower and to say less, until only a companionable silence remained, broken by occasional, fragmentary comments, emphasized by aimless nods or vague gestures. Only Tully kept talking, and as the flurry of his words drifted around him, Steve shook his head wearily, his thoughts growing muddled. ". . . been outside of everything . . . so long . . ." He tried to phrase an appropriate response to whatever Tully was saying but stumbled on his own strange words. ". . . just looking in I . . ." He tried again, then gave up and only savored the warmth of the room. Beyond the door, he knew, icy winds savaged the streets. He blinked at the glass bricks: they flickered with pink neon, and for a moment, it appeared that a swarm of insects had been drawn to the light. "Snowing," he announced. He couldn't remember their leaving the table or going to stand in the doorway, but the snowflakes swirled in glorious profusion, filling the night while they gawked and laughed like children.

"What are youse, crazy?"

"Would you close that goddamn door already? Freezing in here."

The younger man wrapped a red mohair scarf several times around his head, and Steve turned back to the doorway through which patrons glowered in unanimous umbrage. "Come on now, guys," the barmaid called. "Close the door already." Disgusted patience crackled through the cigarette husk of her voice.

He took a few steps, and it made him sadder to realize that, no matter how carefully he struggled to maintain his balance, he still wobbled. So he was back to this—he could feel the alcohol beading through his flesh, simmering in his brain, dissolving the jagged edges of his thoughts. The door hissed shut on the television drone, snuffing the throb, and snow swirled. Through the flurry, he glimpsed Tully's raw face, cigarette smoke unwreathing in the air with his words. Then he swayed alone, realizing that Tully must have said "good night," and he minded suddenly, because it seemed he'd meant to say something important (though he couldn't recall precisely what) and there might not be time later.

Snow fell with a sudden hush.

The door fought him, and he staggered back into the damp-smelling tavern. As he groped to the table, the tobacco stench closed on his throat. Looking at no one, he struggled into his coat—gave up on the zipper—and threw down some money, having no idea how much, before stumbling back out to the welcoming snow.

Naked trees glistened with ice, and white patches already gathered in the crooks of twisted limbs. Where was the car? He'd scarcely gone a block before the cold settled on him and the pleasant dizziness jelled into a damp blockage in his head. He'd thought it was right here. What was he doing on this street? His neck ached from keeping his shoulders hunched, and he realized he'd walked in the wrong direction. "Great," he muttered. As he started back, the sweat that slicked his chest made the wind feel even more cutting.

It flurried thickly now, and he could barely see to the end of the block. The sidewalk turned velvety, and the chill razored his forehead. Frozen branches rattled like wind chimes, and he drew his breath carefully, nurturing the ache in his chest.

A monster shuffled in the night. He blinked. A black hedge writhed in syncopation with his inebriated pulse, and skeletal branches crosshatched a sky through which demons hurtled. Just ahead in the blur, something made a chopping movement. His shoulders clenched, squeezing pain through his back, but he forced himself to walk steadily. An elderly man alternately swept and shoveled in front of one of the cottages, sculpting a narrow slice on the walkway despite the swirling flakes that filled in another faint layer while he worked. Steve nodded curtly as he passed, and the shovel rang out, grating against the sidewalk. Near the corner, he glanced back, already scarcely able to see the man. It seemed so earnestly futile an endeavor. Was the old guy so desperate for something to do? Did nothing wait for him within that cottage? He hurried on, suddenly feeling a wave of sympathy. Were they so different? After all, what waited for him? Another stakeout in a freezing car? Around him, snow already banked softly on doorsteps and windowsills.

Turning up his collar, he walked faster, nearly lost his footing, unable to tell whether it was ice or rock salt that crunched underfoot. Silence drifted down, and the swift, simple patterns of the snow began to tangle.

A wail reverberated. The wind battered at the noise, swirling it into ripples of sound along the boardwalk. Sometimes it gusted out over the sea. Sometimes it seemed to contract itself into a dense mass that rolled along the boards. Rapid dots of white glittered through the headlights, steadily increasing as she guided the jeep up the ramp. The screaming alarm faded erratically. At the end of a cluster of shops, she pulled over next to a novelty store. Leaving the headlights on, the keys in the ignition, she got out, and snowflakes stung her cheeks.

The boards felt slick underfoot as she strode to the side door of the stall. Snow settled on her collar while she examined the padlock by the headlight's glare. *Probably nothing.* The lock seemed intact. Flakes whipped across her face. *These old alarms are always going on the fritz.* She headed around the front of the shop, straight into the wind.

Snow flooded around her, streaming almost horizontally, and sand rippled across the boards at her feet, advancing on low currents of air. *Great. All of a sudden, it's a blizzard.* Melting flakes struck her hands and clung sharply to her face. Bracing herself, she swung around the corner.

Shadows surged. Already, the snowfall had transformed

the tawdry stalls, conveying a sudden glamour. Carried by the sea wind, snow winged past her face, circling and rising, to flow steadily up and over the shedlike structure. She slid the nightstick out of her belt as wind hollowed through the front of the shop. A window grate lay in splinters, shards of glass littering the display platform.

Beneath the broken glass lay a severed arm. And a leg. She made out another limb and several naked torsos in violent confusion. Hovering flakes reversed themselves, spinning upward to float, settling on stumps. The alarm kept screaming.

She blinked. Dismembered mannequins sprawled along the front of the T-shirt shop. Two of the mannequins boasted smooth doll breasts, while a third had been muscled like an action figure. In places, the flesh-colored surface had been gouged away to chalky whiteness, and a plaster hand pointed up, white stubs where the fingers should have been. On the boards at her feet, a blank head bled chalk.

She played her flashlight deep into the store. "All right, come out of there." Where the light swung, darkness melted. "I said, come out." She put her foot up on the window ledge. Something glinted, and a triangle of glass flashed past her face to bell at her feet. She tilted the light up to where a larger curving section wobbled. "Don't make me come in there." She took her foot down, angling the light. It reflected from gusting snowflakes.

Thick blackness filled the back of the shop. *No reason to get spooked.* Already, whiteness dusted the mannequins. *Whoever did this is gone.* Everywhere, it spiraled and glided in graceful chaos. *Probably.* She stepped back, heart still pounding. *I suppose I'd better get that alarm turned off.*

She barely saw it. At the edge of the boardwalk, something solid moved. She turned toward it.

A hellish vision coagulated: one clawed hand, reaching up from below to grip the crossbar.

What . . . ? She blinked. *It can't . . .*

Horned fingers dug into the wood, and the arm muscles bunched.

Fat as bees, flakes hovered in front of her face, then swooped on countless varied courses. Through them, the malevolent face leered. A rope of saliva glistened from the mouth.

Demon. Melting darts struck her eyelids, clung to her lashes. *Monster.* Steve's words skittered through her mind. *Whatever you want to call them.* A wet shiver rippled up her spine and throbbed behind her face. *I don't see this. Not really.* With a practiced motion, she slid the nightstick back into her belt and drew the gun.

Blood hammered at the base of her spine. *Nothing there.* Snow swirled where the face had been, but the afterimage blazed in her mind: eyes bulging with rage, lips snarled back from dripping teeth. *A mask?* Did they sell masks in that shop? *It must have been a mask.* And those rubber hands kids bought at Halloween. *Of course.* They sold all kinds of crazy things in boardwalk novelty shops. *Whoever broke in took a mask and . . .*

Her fingers clenched hard around the butt of the pistol, and she shivered, the blue jacket suddenly binding around her shoulders. *I saw . . . thought I saw . . . a monster.*

A slow minute passed while snow settled. *I really must be losing my mind.* Forcing one foot ahead of the other, she crossed to the railing, and the revolver trembled in her grip.

She peered down. The roar of the surf smothered the shriek of the alarm. Snow lumped over whitening hillocks, caking on gravel. It frosted the tufts of beach grass, but even in the diffused light, she could see the footprints below. They had been made by bare feet. And what was wrong with them? She leaned over the rail. Did they look too broad? Did the toes hook crookedly?

She leaned there until a cramp trembled her leg. With one hand on the rail, she pulled herself to the stairs. All around her, gusts whirled one into the other, maddening, dizzying.

As she descended into the hush of the surf, sand and ice gritted on the wooden stairs beneath her boots. Whoever it was, he had to be hiding down here. She played the light through the gaps between the slats of the stairs. But what if he scuttled under the boards and came up on the other side? He could come down at her from above and . . .

The thought flickered too late.

Stench coiled around her like a draft from an open sewer. Behind her, a growl rumbled. A fist like a knob of bone struck her between the shoulder blades, and her head snapped back. She tumbled over the rail, arms flailing.

For an instant, she became part of the blizzard.

Thudding in the sand, she tasted red, and pain buzzed in her skull.

With a moan, she raised her face from the sand and fumbled for the gun. *Where is it?* Crystals glinted, and she felt a shudder as something heavy landed near her.

Flinging a handful of grit and snow, she rolled. The growl ripped closer, and she lashed out with her foot. Her boot connected, and she heard a grunting snarl as she slid over the edge of the dune.

Scrambling to her feet, she stumbled, agony flaring in her hip and shoulder. The ground seemed wildly uneven, vanishing beneath her and suddenly reappearing as a soft ridge that left her boots scuffing at empty air. Icy sand mushed underfoot. She fled blindly, hoping to lose herself in twisting flurries. Splinters of pain sliced into the moist tissues of her lungs, and her chest crackled as she whirled around. *Run! Get off the beach!* Banners of white snapped. *Where's the boardwalk?* Chaos sifted down steadily, striping the air. *What direction?*

Something hissed at her ankles. A spent wave sputtered across her shoes, plunging over the mud. Black foam seethed, and the sea wind circled at her back, sighing right through her heavy jacket.

Her teeth clicked together, and it seemed her brain began to work again: she became conscious of the muted grumble of the surf, of the grainy texture of the freezing mud into which her boots sank, of the way the wind would groan away, allowing snow to sink in shifting forays. She stared. A mosaic of movement—pillars of white seemed to topple as the creature emerged through veils of motion.

No! She absorbed a fleeting impression of nakedness and hulking deformity. *Nothing can look like that.*

It lurched across the beach.

She stepped back into the water, and the wind slashed. *Nothing!* Snow flew horizontally, blasting endlessly from sea and sky. With numb fingers, she brandished the nightstick.

Swirls of sudden crimson pulsed in airborne layers. In a smear of light and noise, the dunes blazed, and the bright splotch of the spotlight altered like an amoeba as it rushed across the beach, pursued by the blurring humps of the high beams. The horn blared steadily. The siren wailed.

"Kit!"

Light struck her. The club dropped from her numbed fingers, and she lashed with both hands.

"Hey, no!" He caught her. "It's okay, Kit, it's okay, babe, I've got you, it's okay."

"Run!" Her eyes tracked wildly as she shivered. "Get back in the jeep!" She flinched violently when his arm encircled her back. "It's here! It's right . . . !"

Waves of snow rolled over them as he guided her to the jeep. Remnants of beach fence dangled from the fender. He opened the passenger door for her, and she clung to him when he tried to let go. ". . . coming . . . saw it . . ."

"You're okay now. Lock the door. Do you hear me? Lock it." He pried her hands away and slammed the door.

She covered her face.

Moments later, he got in the other side, his shoulders heavily dusted with white. "I don't see any sign of it." She didn't appear to be listening, just sat very still while her teeth chattered viciously. "What's in here?" He reached for a thermos on the floor. "Coffee?"

After a moment, she trembled, barely getting the word out. "Cocoa."

He poured some into the lid. "Here." She shook her head with a jerky motion. "Come on." He steadied her hands while she gulped it.

"How . . . ?" She choked a little. "How did you get here?"

Taking the lid from her, he set it down. "I heard the alarm, found the jeep with the motor running. I just went tearing up and down the beach." He rubbed her hands briskly, then poured more chocolate into the lid. "So you've seen it."

She gulped hungrily at the cocoa. "A mask . . . some kind of costume." By the interior light, she studied his face. He reached for her shoulder, then held something up, and she took it from him, wondering. "My jacket." Between two fingers, she held a strip of shredded cloth.

"Are you hurt?"

"I don't think so." She shook. "Nothing broken."

"Why are you sitting like that? Where does it hurt? This side? Let's get you home so I can look at your shoulder."

"I can drive."

"No, you just . . ." He shifted into first and swung the

headlights toward the boardwalk. The jeep bounced. Snow completely layered the beach, and the tires spun.

"Slow down." She leaned forward. "Can you see anything?"

"Kit?"

"Do you see any footprints?"

"You really are a cop, aren't you?" He grunted with a sort of sad admiration, and the tires crunched slower.

"Are the wipers on high? Damn, I can't see. What's that over there?" She caught at his arm. "On the left. Can you . . . ?"

"I can't tell. It's coming down so hard. Might be tracks."

"They go over that way. No, the other . . . that's it. Under the boards."

"This isn't such a hot idea. If we get stuck . . ." The jeep jerked over a mound. "I think I came through the fence right about here." He eased them into a blot of shadow. Pillars leapt and dodged in the rushing glow, a row of cement columns vaulting. Almost no snow had found its way beneath the boardwalk, but a hill of sand rose steeply before them.

"What in hell . . . ?" He hit the brakes. The headlights poured up the hill, its mountainous shadow concealing everything behind it. "This wasn't here. I could swear it."

"I lost my weapon," she said quietly. "Do you have a gun?"

He nodded, staring straight ahead at the mound. "Who could have done this?"

"We have to check." She unlocked her door.

He grabbed at her. "Kit!"

The door hung open, and she waded into the flood of the headlights, her shadow washing across the mound.

"Kit, get back." He clambered out. "You're hurt." Around them, in the light's periphery, a curtain of snow defined the edges of the boardwalk.

The mound heaved.

"Get away from it!" Sand cascaded down the sides, and he leveled the revolver. "Kit!" Near the bottom, something squirmed.

She stepped closer, and a shout clogged in her chest.

A black hand scratched up out of the dirt; crusted fingers clutched, fluttering.

"Lord." He shoved the gun under his coat then threw himself at the hill. Sand flew, as he furiously dug.

"I don't understand." She began to help him. "What kind of dream is this?" It felt like digging in powdered ice. "What kind of nightmare?"

The arm moved, then a torso wobbled beneath them. Darkened sand clumped thickly on the naked chest, crevices of white flesh showing through black rivulets. The throat gulped, headlights turning the smears of blood a deep purple.

With a fierce tug, Steve yanked the slender body up out of the dirt and into a sitting position. Mist swirled around clotted flesh.

"Is it on fire?"

He stooped, hefting the body up against his chest. "Steam from the wounds." He grunted as he rose. "Get the car door."

"Where are his clothes?" Liquid still oozed black from the head, mingling with the grit that clung to the neck, streaking down the chest to the rib cage. "I . . . don't . . . understand. How did he . . . ?" Legs dangled. Splotches caked on the calves, completely covering one foot.

"Kit! Move!"

She threw the doors open and shoved the seat back, then clambered in and pulled the body in by the shoulder. The white legs looked so long, but the body weighed surprisingly little. Darkness still leaked from gashes on the shoulder and the chest, and clots of sand rained from the sticky mass of the hair and face.

He squeezed in behind them. "My God."

"You know him?" she asked. Through the clinging thickness, the sheen of brown curls resembled bubbles in a pool of oil.

"Where's the nearest hospital?" They secured him with bungee cords, one across his chest and the other around his legs. "Can you stop the bleeding on his head? Is there a blanket?" He tore off his coat and threw it over the pale form, then scrambled behind the wheel.

The tires whined, but the jeep didn't move. He gunned it again, until it lunged forward. She steadied herself against the roll bar, and he jerked the steering wheel sharply, plowing through a fence. She gasped as they plunged down a steep embankment, bouncing onto a narrow street.

"That way! No! Go right! Just follow it out to the highway."

He leaned forward, twisted the heat up as far as it would go. "He's in shock. We've got to get him warm."

"Straight ahead here." She coughed, pain and cold seizing her chest. "Who is he? How did he get there?"

For a long moment, he didn't answer, just concentrated on driving. "You know how he got there," he said at last. Jerking at the wheel, he floored the gas pedal, and the jeep veered through highway slush.

"Look out!" They swerved into the far lane. "His pulse is so weak I can barely . . ."

No other lights moved. The engine droned, and the wipers squealed, and only a few thick flakes plunged straight down, heavy and wet. In a quiet monotone, she directed him to the medical center two towns away. "Oh my God," she whispered. "It's the Lonzo kid, isn't it? You can barely see his face under all the blood. Dear God." They seemed to crawl, yet the jeep slipped at every turn, the tires spinning with a sharp whir.

Wind whistled at the gaps in the windows, and the

steering wheel fought him. "Like an animal burying its meat," he muttered.

"Don't."

"You saw it."

"Please." They seemed to catch up with the retreating blizzard now, and their headlights glinted from the flurry, creating a heavy curtain that billowed around them. Windshield wipers left a curving trail of frost on the glass.

Icicles made the highway overpass look like some fanged maw. On the highway ahead, a behemoth growled, and the snowplow lumbered past them, the orbs of its headlights gleaming with malevolence.

XXI

The fluorescent glare reflected off wired glass; beyond the window lay blank fog. "But I thought you were going home today?" Steve tried to smile, his attention wandering uneasily around the room. "No?" Rapid tapping began at the hospital window, and suddenly raindrops the size of quarters splattered on the glass. "Well, you look a lot better than you did yesterday."

"He sure does." Kit stared at her leather boots, mottled with slush. "Got some color coming back and everything. I mean, that night in the jeep, I didn't even recognize you. Oh, listen, here are the clothes you wanted. Steve, uh, I mean, Barry went and picked them up at your place. Was there anything else you needed?"

From the bed, Tully stared vacantly. A broad bandage hid his forehead. "I'm sorry," he said at last, trembling. "I know you want me to remember." Purplish bruises bloomed from his left temple to his jaw, accentuating both the pallor and the blotches beneath his eyes.

"It's the concussion," Kit began. "I'm sure in a few days . . ."

He shook his head—a barely perceptible motion—then grimaced. "A thing. That's all I remember. The thing I always knew was there. When I was a little kid. In the closet. Under the bed."

"How did you know?" Steve leaned forward.

"Steve, don't."

"You're with the police now?" Tully looked him over with dull curiosity. "And you have a different name." His face seemed dead flesh pulled taut. All his gawky charm had been stripped away, and his body seemed entirely composed of fragile points. "It picked me up. Like a doll."

She edged closer, pressed his hand. "It's all right."

Slowly, painfully, he pulled his hand away. "It carried me." His stare pivoted from her to the wet dimness beyond the window. "I fought." The eyes alone seemed alive as they twitched with wild suffering. "I kicked, screamed."

"Listen," Steve began, "you don't have to . . ."

"I knew . . . what it wanted was worse than anything . . . any nightmare." The noise in his chest might have been the ghost of a laugh. "I guess monsters are like that." He held a bandaged hand over his face. "What do I do now?" A sob shook him. "Knowing it's real? You tell me. How do I go on?"

Havoc unfurled in the sky. They stared through the glass walls of the hospital lobby, and Steve gave a bewildered grunt.

"Some storm." Grimly, she shook her head. "It's funny. He's someone else I used to be friends with. But I haven't seen him at all since I came back. Never called him. Nothing. He does seem a bit better, doesn't he?" They watched rain beat the fog to the ground. "Don't you think so?" Without turning, she examined the reflection of his face in the glimmering glass.

"They say he's well enough to leave," he told her, haltingly. "Doesn't want to go . . . talks about signing himself into the psych ward." He pushed at the door, and damp wind stirred his hair. "Might be the best thing."

Fog still drifted low near the entrance.

"You don't believe that," she said, following him out. The snow had begun to melt, then freeze again: it was like walking on wet glass. As they slipped through the parking lot, rain settled heavily. Brittle tracings of snow still crusted the canvas roof of the jeep. "What do you think, should we put the top down?" The steam from her mouth mingled with the mist as she clambered in the passenger side. "That was a joke," she explained. Behind them, the hospital entrance deliquesced into a smear of light, and the snow on the ground looked soaked and dangerous. "God, I'm freezing."

"Yeah?" Droplets beaded his leather jacket. "It's warmer than it's been in weeks." He revved the engine, then let it idle while the windshield defogged.

"That's not saying much." Turning one glove inside out, she wiped it across her window. "You sure you don't mind driving?" She peered through the clear spot at the growing puddles. "My shoulder's still bothering me a little."

He clicked on the headlights, backed into a river of slush.

"You're silent again." She bit her lip, combed fingers through her damp hair. The box on the backseat held the new revolver she'd bought that morning, and an awareness of its presence obsessed her, seemed to fill the jeep. "We're not doing too well, are we?" Billowing rain swept around them as the jeep pulled out, and the headlights sifted through alternating layers of vapor and water. "I mean, there's been no sign of anyone at the apartment. No sign of them period." Mist clung thickly to the ground and the splattering water mingled with it, but soon rain slashed down and broke it into drifting fragments that settled into the streams at the edge of the road. "Maybe it's time we call the authorities, don't you think?" she asked. "Maybe it's time. He could get away if we don't. Couldn't he?"

"It."

"What?"

"It could. Get away."

The jeep swayed slowly, and water sheeted up behind them. As the engine thrummed, she fancied they were falling, plummeting back to Edgeharbor. Usually, she expected some sense of release whenever she left the town limits behind her, but today she'd experienced no lightening of tension, and it occurred to her that perhaps such respite no longer existed for her. Tires crunched over a crust of ice in the dirt-scaled snow. Patches of rubber from the tires of some passing eighteen-wheeler littered the road like the fallen scales of a dinosaur.

Ahead of them, other tires had rutted the wet snow, but gray ice already filled the curving furrows, making their slow progress even more arduous. Isolated objects stood out in the haze. A boulder. A call box. Then a bank of trees pressed close, coalescing into a single mass. A mini-van growled by, and gouts of slush hit their salt-streaked windshield. Cursing, Steve braked as the roads merged. They waited for an opening, listening to the slush-clogged sounds of traffic. It would have been a natural moment for him to look at her.

Particles of ice clotted on the windshield, and he stared through them at smudges of light, swirls of motion. Finally, they shot forward. "Turn here," she said.

"I see it." Melting snow clogged the old highway, and mottled water lashed up at the windows. Suddenly, the rain sluiced down in blinding sheets, and the windshield wipers splashed ineffectually. "Going to have to pull over."

Water hissed up from the tires. An expanse of gray spread onto a field, submerging the rest area. This pool bled into an ocean that seemed to roll from the surrounding pines, smeared with green and carrying a primeval scent of moss and mud and twisted roots. "Christ." They passed other cars on the shoulder, and he chose a spot, braked. The leaden swirl soaked rapidly through snow at the side of the road, until beer cans and other debris bloomed. Slush hung heavily in the nearer trees, meshed in the webbing of needles, bowing the branches, a diamond casing of ice on the boughs. The windshield wipers slapped loudly, and the interior of the vehicle began to seem like a small cave.

"Have you ever seen fog on the beach?" she asked him softly. "It looks like the end of the world. Especially at night. You can't tell where the land ends and the sea begins."

After a time, the downpour slowed to a drizzle, and a car passed, then another. Without speaking, he started the jeep.

She bit her lip. "When we get back to town . . ." The jeep surged to one side. "If we get back to town . . ."

"No cracks about my driving." Finally, his glance veered to her, and he tried to smile. "You're going to tell the authorities finally, right? You've been threatening to all day. Go ahead, if you feel you need to. But do you really think it's such a good idea?"

"I've seen it now." The glittering curve of their headlights preceded them along the road. "Whatever it is. It's not a game anymore."

"Nobody was ever playing games, Kit." He turned to her, fully taking in her appearance: the soaked ringlets, clinging to her skull like a cap, the tense intelligence of her eyes. "Nobody." He returned his full attention to the road. "Besides, I thought you'd decided it was just some guy in a mask?" A casino bus swerved at them, spraying water on all sides, and she gasped as he jerked the wheel. "Try to relax," he said.

"Just shut up and drive." The tires hummed wetly over the asphalt. "So this is what it feels like to want something again," she said. "All right. I want something. I want to hope for something and work for something, and

I hadn't even realized I'd let go of all that. Until I met you."

Rain shuddered on the roof.

"Steve, please? We need to talk." Suddenly, she couldn't look at him. Rivulets snaked across the glass, and she forced herself to watch the drowned forest. "I hate this." Pines sagged, bunching together against the freezing drizzle, the thinner branches vibrating until the trees seemed to shiver, the whole forest twitching. Moments later, the woods thinned, and the first drab buildings rose. "What are we going to do?"

The slick road ranged into town without apparent strategy. Sometimes it swerved to avoid rocky outcroppings; sometimes it plowed straight through boulders that reared like ancient sentinels. From the first steep rise, she glimpsed the gray hump of the sea; then the streets of Edgeharbor engulfed them. The road climbed so that they seemed to be level with the upper stories of the houses they passed, and the windows of those houses reflected the stony havoc of the sky. "Steve, I'm scared." The clouds looked solid, mountainous, like the contours of some frost-covered shore they had no hope of reaching. "I've never been so scared. I think something awful is about to happen, and there's nothing I can do to stop it."

"You could have been killed." He spoke with considered finality, turning onto the road to the marina.

"Steve . . ."

"No more." The jeep slowed. All around them, gulls screamed and wheeled, their bodies the color of the winter sky. They settled on rooftops and posts, until shrieking in outrage, they simply raised their wings to the wind and lifted again.

He pulled into the carport, close beside the Volkswagen, and they hurried to the stairs through a chilling veil of drizzle. A sudden gust slapped hard at her, and she clutched the rail as he caught her about the waist. For an instant, she turned toward the sea. "Jesus."

Foam rolled across the edge of the dock.

Above them at the kitchen windows, the cat stared through wavering glass.

XXII

"I can't get an answer at Charlotte's. I'm worried. Storms always hit worse on that side of the inlet." She hung up but kept her hand on the phone. "The lines could be out in places, I suppose. And she never picks up after she's gone to bed."

He could see how nervous she was becoming. Sitting stiffly on the sofa, he cradled his head in his hands.

Twice the lights flickered, until finally she lit candles. The effect was hardly romantic, actually seeming to accentuate the shabby, claustrophobic aspects of the duplex. Eventually, she threw together a meal, but neither of them really touched it, and though she tried repeatedly to begin a conversation, he couldn't seem to bring himself to respond. After dinner, he sank back on the sofa, still silent.

Outside, rain billowed at the windows with a sound like cracking glass. A moment later, he kicked off his shoes and shifted a cushion. He saw her turn away quickly when she realized that he meant to sleep right there.

She left the room.

After a moment, he heaved himself up and followed. She had her back to him. Perched on the kitchen windowsill, the cat tentatively allowed the stroke of her fingertips. Rivulets snaked across the glass, and wind struck again. With an explosive hiss, the cat backed across the sideboard, knocking over a ceramic vase. "It's okay, cat. Don't be afraid. Just a little storm." Stooping, she began to gather the shards of the vase. "Hell, that was my mother's."

"You need help?"

She whirled around, not having heard him enter the room. Before she could respond, the ringing of the phone made her jump. "Could you grab that?" She dropped the fragments. "It might be Charlotte."

He'd already picked up the receiver.

"Who is it?" she asked. "Steve? Is it . . . ?"

He turned away, cradling the phone. "It's for me," he answered in a flat voice.

"Oh." She dropped the pieces into a wicker wastepaper basket. "Who knows you're here?"

"Yes," he muttered into the phone, pacing back into the living room, as far from her as the cord would allow. At first, all he heard was a dissonant hum; then the voice on the phone reached his brain like the twitch of a nerve.

"Shall we not play games? Good. You know who I am," the voice grated. "Is your little policewoman in the room? Simply say 'yes' again in a normal tone."

He pushed the phone so hard into his ear that it ached like an old wound. "Yes."

"Well done. You'll want to memorize this address. Six thirteen Decatur. Fourth floor rear. I assume you do understand why I'm contacting you. Am I correct in this assumption? Yes? He'll move soon now. He's been searching for a new place for days." The words broke apart on a raking cough. "Just remember—leave the girl alone! Can you comprehend that instruction?"

"Yes."

"Pardon me if I get personal for a moment, but I've been observing you for quite some time now. You seem, if you don't mind my saying so, passionately involved in your pursuit. Is that correct? What precisely is your stake in all this? Did the boy take the life of someone you loved? Not that I object to such a motive, you understand. This merely represents, shall we say, academic curiosity on my part."

A dead voice issued from his throat. "Something like that."

"I thought as much. How virtuous of you. Virtuous in the old sense—an eye for an eye and all that. Moralizing, however, is hardly my line, and—as I said—it scarcely matters so long as you take his life."

Even after the line went dead, he kept the receiver pressed to his ear, as though seeking somehow to gain control of it. "Monsters," he whispered.

"What did you say? Steve?"

He kept looking at the phone as though expecting the instrument itself to reveal some secret. Finally, he returned to the kitchen and hung up, then stood staring out at the teeming rain. A moment later, she followed him in.

"Who was that?"

He watched her reflection in the window, saw the imploring way she stared at his back, the way the palm of her hand wiped invisible dust from the tabletop. "It has to end," he said at last.

Outside, the storm wailed, and an atmosphere of leaden exhaustion seemed to fill the apartment. She cleared away the dishes, and he wandered back into the parlor. Later, she brought him a blanket, but neither of them spoke as she retired to the bedroom and closed the door.

He lay on the sofa and listened to the wind. The rain droned, and he could hear the cat padding around the kitchen. He would have no choice now. He knew it, and the thought filled him with dread. Very soon, he would have to kill.

"You're not going to tell me, are you?"

"Tell you what?"

Kit wrestled with the steering wheel. "What's different? What's changed you?"

"Nothing's different." Rain sloshed at the vinyl windows.

"Right," she said through clenched teeth.

"So dark." With a sharp movement, he turned to face her, and she almost flinched. "More like ten at night than ten in the morning."

She sighed. "Are you going to stake out the apartment tonight?"

"Look at it come down." He stared at the rain again.

"Steve?"

"Like it's never going to stop."

"Answer me. Do you want me along or don't you?"

Shaking his head, he stared through the windshield. "I'm tired."

She pulled the jeep up in front of the hotel. "You sure you're all right?" The light held a thick, dull quality that made the bricks of the hotel seem luminous.

"I need to rest for a while." He leaned toward her. "Rest and think." He tried to make his voice warmer, less distant, and the effort cost him. "How's your shoulder, Kitten? Will you be okay?" As he spoke, his hand slipped to her arm, then to her shoulder, kneading. "You're exhausted too."

"Right." She stared straight ahead.

The noise of the rain intensified as he pushed the door open.

"What are you planning, Steve?"

He paused, rain drumming on his back. "Nothing." As he turned away, the rain shot in at her almost horizontally.

"Right. Call me." She gunned the engine to keep from saying anything further, to keep from demanding or pleading.

He slammed the door, and the tires splashed away along the shiny asphalt. He watched the red glimmer of the taillights disappear. She was too smart, and she'd guessed too much, he knew. There had to be a way to keep her out of it now. The wind struck, raw and wet, and falling water drove against him in steady waves. Streaks of ice glittered on the bricks of the hotel. Slush sheeted off the roof, most of it blowing away down the street, and in gurgling puddles at the curb clots of snow floated like miniature icebergs. Hunching against a sodden gust, he pushed up the few steps, water shimmering copiously around him. Rain smoked down in rolling clouds now, and it blurred the light in the hotel window, hammered at his face to slide dripping fingers down the nape of his neck. Another gust struck just as he reached the top of the stairs, and for an instant, he could barely move against it.

The wet doorknob yanked out of his hand, and the door slammed in his face. He clutched at it again. His jacket slapping around him, he yanked the door with both hands. A sudden billow drenched the foyer, pushing after him. The inner door also flew open, and he caught the street door before it could pound the wall again. As the turbulent downpour slanted through, he struggled with the door, finally slamming his shoulder against it. At last, he stood, gasping and dripping on the carpet.

"Sir?" In his bathrobe, D'Amato quavered behind the desk. He beckoned, looking worried.

The rain stirred along the beach like a pulsing liquid entity. Lightning mottled the sky, and the rocks glittered.

Every particle of the sea heaved. A single strip of foam lashed continually across the surface, and thick currents undulated like gigantic snakes.

Fierce wind gnawed at the land. The beach vanished in flying plumes, and debris gorged the air. Freezing water scoured the rooftops of the beach houses, wave after wave shattering down as though the sea had left its bed in great convulsions. Cataracts spouted from the boardwalk.

Blocks from the beach, teeming pools already shivered between the houses, spreading, merging in the streets, until streams swirled into intersections and surged over curbs to engulf the sidewalks. Frothy currents gushed, lapping at cars, trees, houses.

Behind Decatur Street, rain lanced and ricocheted into the courtyard, and thunder rattled the windows along the back of the apartment building. Steady torrents cascaded from the fire escape, plunging from ruptured drainpipes as the cellar stairwell filled.

The infant made terrible noises, the small angry face clenching like a fist.

Near the crib, photographs and plastic religious figures crowded the low shelves, and Steve hovered uncomfortably, his clothing dark with damp in long ovals down his arms and legs. He gasped at the steamy warmth of the room, and for an instant, D'Amato looked embarrassed: apparently, the landlord's family never suffered from the lack of heat. Flashing movement dragged Steve's attention back to the picture tube. "That's farther down the coast, isn't it?" he asked, edging closer.

Film clips of devastated towns rolled behind the commentator. Tensely, D'Amato muttered something in Italian, clearly urging his wife to hush the baby so he could hear, and Steve glanced at her. She'd pulled a coat on over her long nightgown but still looked mortified at his presence. Lifting the infant from the crib, she crooned almost inaudibly while making a slight jiggling movement, but she never stopped staring at the set.

Still more photographs of dark-complexioned smiling faces covered the top of the television; beneath them the storm raged. Steve glimpsed houses twisting in the flood, bedraggled people snatched from rooftops, a brief shot of children pulled from a bogged car. "Cresthaven, Blackwater," the voice droned on, "Ebb Cove and . . ."

"Eh? Near here?" She stopped rocking the baby, her face and lips the color of one of the sheets she'd been folding when he'd entered. "Eh?"

"Mrs. D'Amato, please, sit down."

"We got to," her husband murmured.

"Did they say it?"

". . . Stone Harbor, Rock Shore, Edge Water . . ."

"Did they say?"

"Got to."

Could waves be that high? Steve watched, paralyzed. Static and glimpses of gray violence pulverized his nerves. "What?" At once, they all realized that the desk phone had been ringing. D'Amato teetered vaguely into the doorway, but the baby began to wail, and he paused, his glance flicking back to the television as Steve squeezed around him.

"Steve? Is that you?" Her voice sounded faint, rigid. "I'm at the station. Can you hear me? The connection's bad." An electric burr grated. "Can you get out on your own?"

"What's happening?"

"Didn't you hear? We have to evacuate."

The very concept filled him with dread: months of searching, only to have the town itself ripped away.

"Steve, can you hear me? There are still some older people I have to get. Will you be all right? Is anyone else at the hotel?"

"Just the D'Amatos."

"For crissakes, why are they still there? Tell them to get the hell out now. Go straight to Pinedale. And don't try to use the bridge—they closed it twenty minutes ago. Go straight out the old highway to—"

A faint buzz emanated from the phone.

"Kit? Hello?"

"Ah, *Dio, Dio!*" The woman wailed in panic, and instantly the baby's shrieks intensified. Steve barely had time to put the phone down before D'Amato rushed at him. "They just said! We got to get out!" He dodged back inside, and his voice harmonized with the woman's harsh wails. "What are you do? Get that . . . !" Steve stood with his hand on the phone, listening to them argue in English and Italian, repeating over and over about the property and the National Guard and the evacuation center and the property and insurance, while beneath the cacophony of the baby's shrieks, the television muttered instructions on how to turn off gas and electricity and issued advice about emergency routes and pickup points as well as warnings about downed power lines.

"That van out back is yours, right? Does it run?" Steve peered through the doorway.

"Yes?" The man looked up, puzzled. "Yes, it runs, the van." The woman bit her lip.

"That's it then. Better grab what you need for the baby and run. I'll just get my suitcase." He gave the woman what he hoped resembled an encouraging smile and headed for the stairs.

"Sir? Sir! They say must leave at once."

"Won't be a minute." He bounded up the staircase. Below him, the sounds of rapid movement—of drawers coughing open and the woman's urgent complaints— faded into the thin wails of the infant. Before he reached the top of the stairs, the lights flickered.

The television exploded as it struck the wall. "Now, will you shut up?!"

The girl cringed deep into the chair. "You heard it! We have to get out of here." She gave a small, hiccuping gasp. "Perry, please—we'll die if we stay!"

His hand lashed out, open palmed, again and again,

knocking her face from side to side and battering away her words.

"We'll die," she gritted her teeth, tasting blood as he struck her again. "Stop it! We'll die. You have to listen to me!" She sobbed in terror. "Stop!"

"Shut up!" It burst from him in a roar that racked his throat. "Will you leave me alone? I have to think!"

Rain cracked at the window like a fist.

XXIII

While the sea twisted in countless anguished circuits, a gale howled ashore and dragged the ocean with it. Where beach had been, waves spewed in varied directions, explosions of muddy froth marking lines of collision. Darker currents surged across what choppy, sodden earth remained.

Winds had already gouged away most of the gravel, exposing concrete foundations beneath the boardwalk. *Not one of my better ideas.* A single darkening lump of earth remained beneath the boards, and as Steve watched, dirt flew like smoke. *Hiding till everyone else cleared out.* He huddled behind the wheel of the Volkswagen. *Well, nobody'll see me here, that's for sure.*

It had gotten bad so fast. Finding only static, he switched off the radio, giving his full attention to the liquid shapes that flattened on the windshield. *Coming down even harder, just in the last few seconds.* In random spurts, water struck through gaps in the boards overhead, like hammer blows against the Volks.

The car shivered. *What now?* Vibrations trembled through the steering wheel into his bones, and suddenly he understood. He heard the rumble, felt the ocean pound away at the very shale and bedrock of the peninsula. *My God.* Again, the ground shuddered.

I wonder if these things really are watertight. A gobbet of water hit the side window and he jerked his head away, expecting to see the glass cracked. *Guess I'm about to find out.* He clenched his fists around the steering wheel and willed his shoulders to relax. *Some plan.* It had been an easy thing to help the D'Amatos load the baby carriage into their van, then double back in his own car. *I should give myself the "Suicidal Dope of the Year" award.*

He observed the whirling gray of the horizontal torrent, and his stomach clenched. *Give it another minute.* The sea had undergone some alchemical transformation, become an entirely new element, neither wholly wind nor water, an eruption of foaming vapor that streaked at him. *Are you nuts?* Mist struck the window. *Get out of here!*

Froth flew, and the car rocked. *Shit!* He hoped that only rain drove against the windows, not seawater. The engine sputtered. *Damn it! Come on!* He twisted the key in the ignition again, and the Volks bucked over the mud, then splashed toward the street.

Water surged around the tires, skewing the car as the steering wheel tried to wrestle away from him. He sloughed through a flooded field, splashed across a lawn. Volleys of rain struck like buckshot. Two empty cars angled on the corner, and he twisted the wheel, narrowly sluicing past them as the wind shoved the Volks onto the sidewalk.

When he reached the corner, the gale eased up fractionally, but in the rearview mirror, he caught a glimpse of movement. A white avalanche slid out from beneath the boardwalk, frothing over the cars, burying them and tumbling down the street.

He stomped on the gas pedal as the hissing roar pursued him.

Water streaked on the windows until the world became a streaming gray. *Where the hell am I?* With a thundering slap, the Volks went down a steep curb into a shallow pool. *Christ, the hotel has got to be . . .*

Liquid havoc swirled. Some structure hurtled down the street, plunging end over end, already unidentifiable, splashing and smashing itself into bits that the wind swept away. The dim brick facade of the hotel momentarily surfaced in his vision, and he jerked the wheel, sideswiping a mailbox with a dull clang. The Volks splashed deep into the lot. He stomped on the brake, but the car kept going. Slower. Pushing through the water. The Volks hit the wall with a shattering thud, and he pitched forward against the steering wheel and flung open the door.

The storm shoved him down like a hand, and leaves and dirt filled the air, choking him, as brackish spray swept up from the ground. Head lowered, he clambered toward the back of the hotel, his jacket coruscating with a thousand violent ripples. He clutched the doorknob. A spout of wind pounded him to the wood, and the door burst open. Groping his way in, he snatched away the bit of electrician's tape he'd earlier used to disable the lock.

He threw his weight against the door. It stopped a foot short of closing, wind roaring through. *It's getting stronger.* His shoes slipped on the wet floor as he strained. The door slammed with a soft chop. Gasping, he leaned against it, rivulets running from his clothes. A muffled roar drummed through the wood.

Damn . . . soaked . . . His teeth chattered. *I'm sure as hell not going back out to the car for my suitcase.* He'd thrown his clothes together, just to fool the D'Amatos, but left everything else.

He staggered down the hall. Just ahead of him, a window blew out, and the curtain billowed, glass and water scattering.

He edged around the window, uselessly flicking a light switch as he passed. At the end of the corridor, the lobby windows glimmered, and he stumbled onward. Above his head, the chandelier tinkled softly, then jangled like piano keys. Groping to the foot of the stairs, he mounted slowly, pausing to listen. The storm bellowed against the walls. Another window exploded, but faintly, in another part of the hotel, and his grip tightened on the banister.

He felt his way along the recessed shadows that lined the corridor. A door slammed, nearby this time, and a ripping moan—full of the shattering of glass—grated along the outside of the building. "Just the wind," he said. "The wind." He repeated it louder, then shouted it but still couldn't hear himself.

He could see now, like a diver rising into shallower depths. The windows held a turbid incandescence, and streaming radiance filled the passage as he fumbled his key into the lock.

In his room, light faded. An eruption rattled the floorboards beneath his feet, and the downpour drowned the thunder. *Here it comes.* He groped for the window. *The real thing.* Bits of debris skated past outside, too fast to make out, and the buildings across the street streaked and blurred. Something huge sloughed through the street below. *A car? A tree? A shark?* Then the world beyond the window ceased to exist.

Coruscating patches glimmered.

Something clattered overhead, and the walls buckled with a loud crack. *Like the end of the world.* Twisting around, he felt for the swaybacked chair, dragged it away from the window. As he began to sit, his hand strayed to his wet clothing, and he shivered. Unbuttoning his shirt, he peeled it off and dropped it at his feet. Setting the flashlight on the dresser, he angled the beam into the oval mirror so that the room filled with a rippled gleam, and the reflected light seemed to pool in the dent in the mattress. He perched on the edge of the bed and worked his heavy shoes loose, then kicked them away. Rolling soundlessly in the din, they left a mottled trail.

The door to the hall swung open. In his wet socks he rushed to slam it, threw the bolt. His soaked pants clung as he wrestled them off. Gathering his things, he started into the bathroom.

He stood very still.

The building swayed.

Wind blasted, and the bathroom lit with a sputtering flash. He heard the clatter of something falling in the other room, and again the building moved. Windows popped along this side of the hotel, a steadily tinkling cascade, and he wondered how much more the old bricks could take before they burst from their mortar. No longer even aware of the chill, he dropped his clothes in a sodden heap and stumbled naked to the chair.

A clap of wind rattled the windowpanes. Then the wind veered from another direction, seeming to move slowly around the building, groping for a point of entry.

Winds mounded the water, then chopped at it, shattered it.

Waves slapped into the air. They surged forward, crushing the stairs, splintering across the boardwalk—a row of shops vanished. Power lines sparked and flared, and flame spurted like a tear in the fabric of the storm.

Even in the sheltered bay, rain-slashed waves swamped the few boats and submerged the dock. Storage huts blew into pointed boards as sheet metal crumpled, peeling back from roofs, and metal and wood took flight.

The door exploded open, and she burst into the hall with a swell of rain. Gasping on the floor, she rolled onto her back. "Charlotte!" With both feet, she kicked the massive door shut against the gale. "Charlotte, where are you?" Stumbling, she massaged her shoulder. "Charlotte, I've got the jeep outside. The wind blew it into the porch—we've got to get . . ." She raced, dripping, into the hallway.

The grandfather clock ticked harshly. "Where are your lights? Is your heat off?" She tripped, her flailing hands identifying the object in her path as she caught herself. *No.* The chair lay on its side, and her hand went to the bent wheel. "Oh no, please." She felt around on the floor. "Charlotte, it's me." In the parlor, the smell of damp soot tinged the air.

For a second, she thought the storm had destroyed the room, but when she tugged at the curtain cord, the torrent pounded against intact glass. A flash of lightning made the wreckage lurch with shadows. Only then did she realize that everything around her looked dry, despite the smell of wet ashes from the fireplace. Her glance wandered numbly across the broken knickknacks littering the floor, the torn cushions, overturned table. "Charlotte, can't you hear me? Are you hiding?"

She raced back to the stairs. "Charlotte, it's a hurricane! We have to get out of here!" Above her head, floorboards creaked. "Are you upstairs? How did you get up there?" She put one foot up on the stairs, but solid blackness stopped her. "I'm coming," she whispered. "Wait." Stepping down, she felt her way back toward the kitchen. "I'm coming." Rain slapped at her face when she pushed open the kitchen door. Both windows had gone, and the dripping curtains dangled like knotted ropes. A fiery light in the sky seemed to flare through the broken glass. Yanking open the utility drawer, she felt for a flashlight, then raced back to the hall.

"Charlotte?" The beam slipped up one stair after another, finally dissolving. "Are you there?" She took a step. Somewhere, a shutter banged rhythmically. She climbed.

Behind her, a hinge creaked.

Her head turned in agonized twitches. Below her in the hallway, shadows swirled, filling the house like water. The creak sounded again. Insistent. The door to the cellar swayed slightly in the draft.

She'd look for shelter. As she descended, her feet felt strangely heavy. *It's easier for her to go down than up. And the storm is so loud. That's why she can't hear me.* She pulled the cellar door open wide. "Charlotte! Charlotte, it's me. Are you all right?"

The smell floated like dust.

Oh God, not rats. Not here.

Retreating from the beam, the gloom swung about her. Rotting plaster had crumbled away from the walls, exposing slats furred with cobwebs, and she thrust the flashlight forward like a weapon. Her holster chafed at her side, and the stairs creaked damply beneath her tread. Peering about, she clutched at the dusty banister.

Sheeted furniture loomed like fun house ghosts, and crates blocked the walls. *More of her husband's memorabilia. A whole museum's worth.* From the back, a muddy dimness shimmered back at her.

Just a mirror. She moved closer, choking on the must that hung in the air.

The sheet puddled on the crumbling concrete, dirty water already seeping through, and the beam trembled over the heap in the corner.

No. But she recognized the dress. And she knew death when she saw it.

My fault. She moaned softly at the crooked position of the legs. *I should have been here.* Something sparkled. On the bureau. Dazedly, she tilted the flashlight back: the silver frame flashed softly.

portrait of Charlotte's husband what's it doing down here Charlotte will be so upset she

A dark lump occupied the shelf beside it, and she angled the light farther. It took her a long moment to comprehend.

What remained of the face still bore an expression of outrage.

It made a sound like nothing he'd ever imagined—a hollow, roaring whine that thudded against the walls until the whole building lurched and clattered. It seemed to possess actual shape, this noise, a terrible spinning circularity, constant and without contour. Still the roar grew shriller, and pressure gushed against the walls.

At first, he'd tried to take notes, scribbling incoherently in the flickering dimness, until the notebook dropped from his fingers, the pen rolling. *No heat.* He couldn't feel his arms or legs. *Never any heat in this room.* He'd pulled the blanket from the bed and wrapped it around himself, but the chill sank deep, and the blanket sagged away from his shoulders. He couldn't move to adjust it, could only twitch when the floor rocked, and his mind seemed to drift in a howling void.

The room settled into a deeper layer of gloom. Rain drilled at the glass in random flashes, and he felt a muffled rumble, as of something being dragged across the floor above. Did the room brighten perceptibly? He seemed to feel a tightening in his chest, as though he'd surfaced too quickly from the depths, and ripples of light disturbed the ceiling. No longer solid, the walls seemed to quiver, pulsating like the flesh of some huge, shivering beast. He focused with perfect clarity on a spider that scuttled along the opposite wall. Pale. Nearly translucent. Suffused with the green throb of life. He watched it sink gently into dimness.

The boy has to die. His mind seemed very clear. *It has to end.* The howling tore the world, leaving a hole that sucked him in and spun him down to a familiar nothingness. Memories swirled, slowly engulfing him, and he floundered, desperately trying to grasp at one thought, only one, that might no longer have the power to wound him. He found nothing. The storm drummed in the floor, and in tiny lurches, the painting of the sea beat rhythmically against the wall.

Thunder shuddered the window—it startled him, and a moment passed before he understood why. He'd heard it. He'd heard the glass rattle.

The surging din of the storm had begun to diminish. A resonating groan, like the death agony of a whale, rumbled through the walls, and the pattering of rain flooded the room with noise. He had no idea how much time had passed. Trying to make out his watch, he stood, clutching the blanket, then wobbled to the window, the floor like ice on his bare feet. He pressed his face to the pane, and the glare of lightning froze falling silver that glittered at a rapid angle. A quick look downward made him gasp.

The world glinted in a solid shimmer . . . as though the old hotel had been carried out to sea.

XXIV

Water seethed, mottling the glass. He cracked the door and blinked as daylight flooded the foyer. *Now or never.* A chill whistled in. Small waves rippled over the front step as he pushed the door wider. For a moment, the impression of ubiquitous movement disoriented him. Rain pelted straight down into broad puddles that covered the sidewalk, and spinning rivulets connected those puddles to deeper pools in the street. Streams gurgled around the corner, and a dented stop sign rattled.

He'd already checked the back. The parking lot had become a small lake—no sign of the Volks. *Guess they do float after all.*

Adjusting the hood of the slicker, he pulled the door closed behind him and stood with his back pressing the glass. Beneath the slicker, which he'd found after kicking down the door to the D'Amato apartment, he wore his leather jacket, two sweaters and the heaviest shirt he could find in D'Amato's closet. He could barely move his arms. *At least it's not so cold now.* Shuddering, he snapped the top clasp of the slicker. *Not really.*

A swatch of gelatinous seaweed raveled on the stairs beneath him. The shocking chill of water seeped through the heavy rubber boots—also D'Amato's—and right through the doubled socks. Rain dripped heavily from the slicker. Clutching the rail, he surveyed the flooded block. In the streets, water looked knee-deep, but the pavements on this side seemed only partially submerged.

Across the street, tiny waves lapped at the other hotel, cresting on the stairs. Wind slapped wetly.

Splashing down onto the sidewalk, he tried to keep to the higher patches of concrete as he headed into town. He ducked under doorways, staying as close as he could to the dubious shelter of buildings, grasping at every rail and post. Freezing water trickled into his boots before he'd made it to the corner, and his pants felt like ice at the knees.

Monsters. Like an alien spider, a crab-thing with impossibly long legs splayed across the sidewalk. Nearby, a flattened creature the color of clay sprawled in a puddle: it appeared to have fleshy wings. By the curb, a mass of tentacles bulged. *Everywhere.*

A twisted street lamp tilted above the flow. Jutting with bricks and mortar, a fragment of chimney dominated the center of a shallow pool, and a drainpipe raveled across the pavement. Like some huge ruined umbrella, a television antenna poked from a larger pond, and the corner of a door protruded from the water. He alone prowled the wreckage.

Rain slowed to a saturating mist. He'd hardly started before he needed to rest. Blasts of wind boomed down the block as he climbed the stairs of a building he didn't recognize. *Have to go on.* He sheltered in the doorway, gasping, while the wind seemed to strike in some complicated rhythm, driving chilling wetness in around the edges of the slicker. *The boy will move.* Clutching the rail, he splashed back down and hurried into the deepening gloom, skirting a side street that had become a river. *He'll run now.* The boy would need to be holed up in a new hiding place before the townspeople began to trickle back. *It's what I'd do in his place.* He bent into the wind, scarcely progressing. Just ahead of him, a storm door banged with a constant, furious clatter, until it pulled loose and scraped across the sidewalk. Water slid in patches of brown and green. His hands slipped away from a pole, and the gale danced him across a sodden lawn. Everywhere lay trees, uprooted or shattered, and some of the houses sat at strange new angles—several had moved considerable distances. *Some of these dark spots in the water might be basements.* Struggling toward higher ground, he skirted a car that had wedged tightly against the front door of a cottage on a slight rise. With each gust, wet gravel from the driveway hailed into the side of the car, making a noise like bullets, and he ducked his head, protecting his face with his arms.

The drizzle ceased, and wind sighed to nothing. *Be night soon.* In the sudden silence, he sloshed forward, the muscles in his legs aching with every step. *Got to hurry.*

Before him stretched a swamp. He could see no way through the flooded intersection. *Could go back the way I came, try to find another way around.* But the sky dimmed steadily. *No time.*

Wading in, he tried to feel a curb beneath his feet, some ridge to balance across. A fine mist began to blow, and he stumbled. His boots plunged hard. Instantly, numbing water climbed above his knees. *Shit!* Slowly, he pushed on through the muted hush. The gurgle pouring from a broken pipe had become the loudest sound, almost the only real sound. *Can't stop.* Nearby, an old Chevy tilted against the Seaside Savings & Loan, and the drowned car began to founder. His teeth chattered as he waded deeper, giving it a wide berth. *What the . . . ?* He felt a pull. *It can't be a current.* With a low moan, the wind stirred again, and he struggled to keep his footing, but each gust twisted him, and the water rushed between his legs. He lunged for a handhold on the car, his grasp sliding along the windshield. Sucking waters surged around him.

As he clambered onto the roof, liquid coils tightened, and he felt the vehicle wobble, then begin to lurch away in an angling roll. *The street!* Water moiled, and the Chevy sank deeper, engulfed in a welter of blurring forms. *There's nothing there!* The front end of the car dipped. Whatever sewage line or natural fault had lain beneath the asphalt had given way. A stony grinding shuddered through the roof, through his bones, and the car began to spin. Tipping, it plunged past the entrance to the Savings & Loan. He gathered his legs beneath him and leapt.

With a splash, he caught at a railing, rust and paint chips grinding into his palm. He grunted, twisting his knee on the stairs. Ripples tugged at him, and he tasted salt. Pulling himself to the top of the stairs, he clung to the doorway and shuddered.

The car vanished in a snarl of muck, and water swirled, choked with disgorged effluent. After a moment, he inched his way along the ledge. A fat wave lapped at a window, then dragged the length of the facade without cresting. *Not so deep here . . . maybe.* Edging around the corner, he reached the back of the building.

Staring hard, he waited for the swirling to stop. He braced himself, then slipped one foot into the water, felt for the bottom. Water rose almost to the top of his boot, and the edge of the windowsill slipped from his freezing fingers. He yelped once. But both feet found the uneven ground, and he slogged on, his wake striping the surface behind him. The water reflected a dimming sky.

He balanced precariously along the trunk of a downed tree, then plowed for the corner. Half a block farther on, he splashed through shallow puddles. At the corner, the little library tottered brokenly, glass walls completely gone. The final liquid flickers of light revealed sodden books, floating everywhere, spread in the puddles like the carcasses of broken gulls. Lightning veined the sky; wind wrinkled the puddles. *If the storm comes back, and catches me outdoors . . .*

Thunder detonated across the low rooftops, and he ran,

splashing wildly. With a sudden hiss, rain slanted down, spattering the smooth sheets around him into leaping patterns.

Gargantuan clouds tumbled inland, dense as oily smoke within which splinters of light flickered, still smoldering. He bolted past the church. The ersatz stained glass hung shattered now. Spinning around the corner, he halted.

Halfway down the grimy block, one apartment building towered above the rest.

As Kit approached, the door of The Edgeharbor Arms banged softly. All the glass had gone, and wet slivers glistened on the steps. From inside, a steady tinkling drifted, almost like music.

Cautiously, she edged through the door. A damp blotch spread on the Oriental carpet, and the chandelier chimed, swaying—she gave it a wide berth as she yanked the drapes aside. Sudden dust added to the reek of decay, but a wave of fading twilight swept through the lobby. Stifling a sneeze, she turned to the desk and the dim apartment beyond.

The closets stood open, contents ransacked. As she paced back toward the faint light of the window, she spotted an old registration book on the desk and found only one name on the latest page, only one room number.

Wind resonated around her on the stairs, and the clanking of the chandelier pursued her. Even as she climbed the staircase, she knew nothing living shared this structure with her. Two floors up, one door stood open, casting a patch of paleness on the hall carpet.

"Steve? Are you in there?" She found little to indicate that the room had been recently occupied. But what had she expected? He had trained himself to leave no sign.

The drawer stuck, then gave with a thin howl of wood.

She searched the dresser, then the single tight closet. Finally, with a small grunt of satisfaction, she hauled the two suitcases out from under the bed. Grabbing the flashlight from the dresser, she propped it on the pillow and tried the smaller case, only to find it locked. Briefly, she considered searching for the key; then she struck the clasp with her pistol. A second later, she dumped the folder into the light.

The beam glinted thinly from a snapshot of a mangled face, and her bile rose. She yanked the rubber band off a stack of photographs and tossed them on the bed where they spread like an evil deck of cards. She blinked. How could he have these? She barely noted the newspaper clippings and maps that filled the bottom of the case— her eyes kept returning to the photos. How could he have gotten them?

Numbly, she flipped the catch on the larger case. Stuffed in among the clothes lay several large manila envelopes and an old knapsack. The knapsack felt stiff.

She unzipped it and reached in, then drew back her hand with a sharp gasp—darkness welled in her palm. With her other hand, she angled the flashlight: a slice oozed from the base of her thumb. Holding the flashlight gingerly, she tilted out the contents of the knapsack, and something thudded on the mattress. She tugged away the rolled towel.

A carving knife, a cleaver, wire cutters and a hammer— all clotted and dark—covered the photographs of carnage.

"What have I been helping?" she whispered. "Oh God. What is he?" She thought of the Chandler children, hiding from him, skulking from apartment to apartment because they somehow knew what stalked them. "What have I done?" She backed away from the bed.

Frenzied now, she searched every corner of the room. Where could he have gone? There had to be some clue here. She had to find him. Her foot struck something by the leg of the chair.

Picking it up, she held the notebook to the light: it took a moment for her even to recognize the marks as writing. The insane scrawl made the flesh at the back of her neck tighten, though most of it remained incomprehensible. ". . . changing . . . every day . . . feel it . . . the need pulsing in the veins. No choice now. Must kill the boy." The very bottom of the page was filled by what appeared to be numbers, and she strained to make them out.

Six thirteen Decatur. A glint of silent lightning flickered on numerals above the door. *Perfect lookout.* The tallest building in town—he cursed himself for not having thought of it. *They'll be on the top floor.*

Steady. Trembling with anticipation, he regarded all the darkened windows. Most were shaded, many broken. *This is too easy.* He backed into the nearest doorway. *I didn't come this far just to walk into a trap.* Scraping his hand along the wall, he crept away along the glistening street. *Somewhere around here . . . there must be a . . .*

He felt the opening.

His boots sloshed through unseen puddles as he wandered down the alley. Again, the drizzle had ceased completely, even the wind dying away, though a distant rumble drifted in the sky. *Might as well be blind.* Thick odors of brine drowned the stench of rot, and he stumbled around a corner. The passage broadened into a sort of courtyard, and from the lower corners all around him, sloshing noises echoed faintly.

I'm here.

At last. Dimly, he perceived the rear walls of the buildings that surrounded him: sharp tracings and blocked masses, and the tallest building, just ahead, its fire escape a jagged chevron. *I've got him.* He lurched forward, the shadow at his feet shifting like weighted silk. Deep water filled the courtyard, he realized, and a vicious tremor shook through his body.

Above him, metal rattled.

He's up there!

Something splashed heavily; then gulping and thrashing resonated in the dark closed space.

A gift!

The sky flickered. Faintly, he made out a slender form, wallowing.

You can't get away this time. He reached. *Not this time!*

He groped toward the noise of the foundering boy. *Monster.* His arms began to ache and tremble, his fingers clutching convulsively. *Just a little closer.* The splashing stopped, and he actually heard teeth click together. *Keep coming.* He strained his vision. A foot from his face, two smudges hung. They blinked back at him.

He lunged. The boy fell backward with a splash, then burst like a deer through the flooded courtyard. Steve hurled himself at the sounds of flight, water striking him like a wall. "No, you don't! No!" Plunging into the freezing pool, he pitched forward to cut off escape through the nearest alley.

He saw the boy reel backward, the white face like a night-blooming flower. A trickle of moonlight revealed only part of that face: the mouth open in a black howl. The visage seemed to float, dissolving, and a shrill moan filled the courtyard.

Scuttling clouds dashed more moonlight into the courtyard, revealing cellar stairs that sank behind the boy. The flood crested his knees.

A shroud of liquid around the boy swelled. With a grinding roar, the cellar door behind him opened. Steve echoed the boy's wordless shout, something viscous uncoiling in his stomach. Instantly, the flood churned downward, forcing the door wide with a squeal that sucked deep into the basement.

The boy cried out again—a splintered shriek—as he threw out his arms and clawed into the door frame, bracing himself against the flow. Whirling, he stared down into the pit behind him. A tumbling splash diminished down the stairs, but his groans trembled to rebound from the walls. At last, he scrambled backward up the steps against the thinning cascade.

One of Steve's arms tightened about Perry's shoulders; another circled his stomach, crushing him to his chest. "At last." Steve's breath rasped against the thin neck. "I've got you." The slender body felt soaked and frozen against him. "Monster." His lips pressed close to the boy's ear. "You know what I've got to do now." His grip wound tighter as the boy thrashed convulsively. "Be quiet." He could feel the pulse of the boy's throat against his chin. "It won't hurt." He heard the air go out of the boy's chest. "Don't struggle." He spun Perry around to face him.

Snap the neck. He shook the boy until his head lolled back and forth, then clamped him again in a bear hug. *Do it, damn you!*

A growl echoed in the basement, like a cry from the depths of hell.

Steve froze, his hands on Perry's throat.

Footsteps clomped upward.

Still clutching the boy, Steve inched back. The splashing came closer. He stumbled for the alley, groping for an entrance. As they plunged into the narrow channel of the passage, his shoulder struck a wall. Perry hung limply in his arms.

He dragged the boy around a corner, then slipped, going down on one knee, almost dropping him. Behind them in the dark, their pursuer stomped faster, moaning with sorrowful rage. Steve lurched to his feet, finally staggered out onto the sidewalk.

A blinding light lanced the side of the building. For an instant, he thought lightning had struck.

"Put him down, Steve." She melted out of the shadows. Thrusting the emergency lantern forward like a weapon, she stepped closer. "If you've killed him . . ."

Her other hand gripped the revolver.

The boy sagged like a corpse in his arms. With no breath left to speak, Steve just nodded back down the alley.

"Don't move. It's over. Don't try to run. I'm warning you." She stepped closer. "I know everything. I found the knives in your room."

". . . coming!" He tried to gasp the words out.

"Don't move, I said."

". . . there! It's coming!"

"Please, don't make me shoot you." Wonderingly, she muttered, "You're really scared." Her glance took in the trembling pallor of his grimed face; then her gaze tracked to the alley.

Water dripped loudly, and she trained the lamp into the passageway. Dark pools and floating refuse stood out in the glare, and farther back . . . did something move?

Something hissed explosively—like the snort of a huge beast.

"What is that? What's back there?" The light wobbled, dimming as it probed, and in the faintest periphery, a form tumbled back, then scrambled over a wooden fence to thud wetly on the other side. Splashing noises faded.

"Evidence." His voice cracked. "Those things you found. Evidence. What? Did you think they were souvenirs?"

"Was that Ramsey?" She turned to him, trembling slightly. "Is the boy . . . ?" She played the light across them, and Steve closed his eyes, his face a mask of misery and exhaustion. "I don't understand."

The wind moaned wetly.

Suddenly, the boy clung to him, quivering with terror. "No, Ramsey! Don't!" He flailed with his fists, his blows containing no more strength than those of an infant.

XXV

Dark silence pressed at the grated windows, and the single orb of an emergency light glared above the entrance. "Runs off a battery," she told him. "Hold him while I get the door." Though she struggled to sound calm, tension vibrated in her voice.

Steve took hold of Perry's shoulders, partly to keep him from bolting, partly to prevent his falling. He felt the boy shiver like a colt.

"The bridge is still down. I checked the radio." She fumbled with the key ring. "Lots of beach towns got hit worse than us, I suppose. That's mostly where the rescue efforts are focused—farther down the coast and . . ."

Feeling another tremor in the boy's bony frame, he tightened his grip.

". . . besides, they probably think we all got out. So we're stuck here for . . ."

"You going to open up or what?" He peered through the wires that meshed within the diamond-shaped window.

"Oh. Yes, just . . ." She jerked the key in while his stare probed the structure. A corner property, it might have been any sort of business, except that nesting up against it, blocking the sidewalk and part of the side street, sat a modified trailer on cinder blocks, with heavy grills covering the window vents.

"Holding tank?"

"What? Oh. Right. We don't use it much." The door popped open. "One other thing I heard on the radio that you should know—we're not a peninsula anymore."

His eyebrows went up.

"Right. An island. Temporarily anyway." She seemed to guard the entrance. "So he stays here till help arrives."

As Steve maneuvered him through the doorway, the boy sagged. "Knock it off!" Steve shook him.

Suddenly, the boy wrenched around, scratching.

"Knock it off, I said, or I'll break your arm!"

"Steve!"

"Get out of the way, Kit! Here. Help me with him. Take his other arm."

"I've got him. It's all right. He stopped—ease up, Steve."

At the end of the short corridor, a desk and several folding chairs filled most of a small room. Bleeding away color, a floodlight near the ceiling streaked the cinder block walls and banded a cement floor from which gray paint had mostly worn away. Shielding his eyes against the glare, he looked around for somewhere to deposit the boy.

Catching Perry around the shoulders, she pulled him along like a puppet. His feet moved feebly. "Okay, here." She steered him to a seat, knowing he'd hit the floor if she let go. "Sit down." She shoved him gently. "Stay there."

He coiled back into the chair.

"Don't be afraid," Steve told him.

The boy cringed, his hair matted and dripping, his whole body shuddering.

Steve reached for him. "I won't . . ."

Perry grunted, his stomach and chest beginning to rise and fall convulsively beneath the sodden jacket.

"I'm not . . . not going to . . ."

The boy watched him with eyes the color of pale, polished oak, his terror like a tangible force in the room.

"Here." Kit stepped closer. "Look at me." She'd unzipped her thermal jacket but kept it on. "Your name is

Perry Chandler?" One glimpse had taken in the whip-thin frame, his long legs and bony hips. "Are you hurt, Perry? Why are you holding your arm like that?" Her hand hovered above his shoulder. "You don't like to be touched, do you, Perry?"

He trembled. Without warning, he bolted from the chair and dodged past her.

"No, you don't!" Steve blocked the exit.

Perry plunged backward, flattening himself against the wall.

"No one's going to hurt you." She barely gasped out the words.

Brushing away her touch, he grunted like a wounded animal and molded his body to the corner.

"Get away from him. Don't argue. Now stay behind me." Steve pushed her aside. "Stop that, you. I said, stop it."

The gurgling sob in the boy's chest choked to silence.

"You're safe. No one will touch you. No one but me. You understand? But right now you have to deal with me." He righted the boy's chair and shoved it at him. "First, get out of that damn corner!"

"Steve, you're both shivering. There are some blankets in the lockup. Let me . . ."

A look of feral alertness flashed across the boy's face as quick eyes darted to the door.

"Don't even think about it," Steve told him. "Now, sit down, I said. Time to answer some questions. Where's your sister? Answer me—where is she?"

The boy's lips drew back, exposing his teeth in a desperate grimace, and a swelling rattle began in his throat.

"Stop that!"

"Steve, what's wrong with him?"

Crouching farther into the corner, Perry bashed his

head back against the wall, a yowl gurgling out until Steve grabbed him by the collar.

"Those scars on the back of your hands—how'd you get them?"

"Make him stop!"

"You've never seen the kind of marks that ropes leave, have you, Kit? How about the kind of scars a strap makes?"

"Don't!" She caught at his arm.

"I'll bet if we looked at his back we'd find some really interesting souvenirs." He wrestled the boy into the chair. "They control them that way sometimes. For a while."

"You're terrorizing him."

"Him?"

"He's just a little boy." She stared at the bedraggled hair plastered to the thin face, at the clothing that clung so darkly. "He looks so fragile." The terrible noise had stopped, and he sagged against Steve's large, clutching fists. "I'm going to get the blankets," she said, imagining she could almost hear the boy's heart pounding beneath his shirt. "Did you hear me, Steve?"

Full of terror, the boy's gaze followed her.

"And don't touch him while I'm gone, Steve. Do you hear me? Don't touch him."

Hard knots bit deeply into sore wrists, and sharp pain surged up her arms. Somehow she'd managed to twist her hands around in front of her, and again she threw her weight against the closet door. It felt like the air was almost gone, and she could barely fill her lungs. But the door didn't budge. Again her bound hands rasped at the tape across her mouth, loosening a corner and finally ripping it away. Gasping deeply, she hit the door and rebounded, tripping to strike her head against the wall. *No more, please, no more.* Huddled in the darkest corner, she began to sob. *Let it end.*

A vibration slid in the wall by her head. Faintly, it throbbed again. Pushing as far back as she could, she bit her lip to keep from whimpering.

The doorknob rattled; she tasted blood.

The door jarred. *Perry! Help me!* She slid to her knees in terror, as the door leapt in its frame. *Who is it? What's happening?* At the last instant, she recognized the explosions of noise as hammer blows against the lock. *He was telling the truth, oh God, the truth all along, they're coming to get me, they're here! The monsters!*

The noise stopped. With a soft click, the door swung in, and she blinked. In the trickle of light, a countenance swirled: slowly, it coalesced into the face of all her oldest nightmares.

It smiled.

Ripping from the bottom of her belly, the scream hurt coming out.

The boy sneezed again. Then the man sneezed.

Perry's hair glistened like metal as it dried, falling forward over his face, and he stared fixedly at the floor. A pair of thin blankets around him, he hunched forward, his bony knees jutting bright crimson. Periodically, he mouthed at a paper cup full of water. A slow pattering provided the only real sound in the room as his sopping clothes, wrung out and hung across the back of a nearby chair, dripped onto the newspapers beneath them. Earlier, he'd stiffened when she'd tried to get the clothing off, silently flailing his arms and legs like an infant, but she'd gotten him dried as best she could. When she'd pushed the darkened tangle back from his face, she'd expected him to be hot, but he'd felt cool to the touch, the sharp bones delicate beneath her hands.

"Was it your brother who chased us?"

He still tensed whenever Steve uttered a word. The defiant mask on the boy's face quivered, as though some exhalation disturbed a reflection in a pool . . . or as though something deep below struggled toward the surface.

"Look at me when I'm talking to you!"

"Steve . . ."

"Answer me."

The questions hammered on until the boy's determined stillness began to crumble, first in small flinches—as one hand found the other and clasped it—then in gradual gestures and shifts of posture, as he sank farther into his chair, shoulders bowed. Trying to cover himself, he clutched and pulled at the coarse fabric of the blanket.

"Do you hear what I'm asking you?"

"He hears," she insisted.

Slowly the boy's face tilted, and Kit squirmed before the smoldering delirium of that stare. For a moment, it seemed he might finally speak; then his lips jammed together.

"Damn it." Grappling his own blanket with one hand, Steve perched on the edge of the desk. "You're going to have to answer me sooner or later. What happened to your father?" He leaned forward. "That was him we found in the basement, wasn't it?"

The boy rubbed one bare foot against the other, then yanked both feet back under the blanket.

"He's shivering still. Look, his lips are practically blue."

"Who hid the body in the basement? Did Ramsey do it?"

Again, something seemed to stir beneath the boy's features.

"Perry?" She kept her voice gentle. "You've just been

moving around ever since, right?" She watched emotions drift across his face: cloud reflections on window glass. "Going from apartment to apartment?"

"No, don't look away. Answer her." His hand shot out.

"Steve!"

The slap stopped short of the boy's cheek, and Steve turned to her, sadness in his voice. "Not exactly what we were expecting, is he?"

She got up from her chair. "Let me try again." She knelt by the boy. "You're going to have to trust somebody sooner or later, Perry. Believe me on this." Her face hovered inches from his. "All that blood. Who tried to clean up the house? Did you do that?"

He might have nodded, the movement so slight as to be barely discernible.

With a sudden gesture, she reached out and pushed the tangle of damp hair back from his forehead again, and for once, he didn't pull away. She stared at a face so pale each eyelash stood out darkly. The flesh felt hot now, moist. He shuddered painfully, while his eyes wheeled around the room, shimmering like glass. He made her think of a stuffed fox, frozen in a semblance of futile cunning. "Lashes like these wasted on a boy." She almost stroked his hand, and he jerked reflexively. "And this coloring." The raw entreaty of his stare stunned her.

"Kit. Come away."

Again, she stroked his head, watched primal shadows flutter across his face: panic, rage, and always, just below the surface, hopeless sorrow. And suddenly she knew who he reminded her of. She watched him force his feelings back down, one by one, watched grinding determination return to fill the delicate, sullen features: she'd seen Steve do the same thing countless times. Setting his mouth in a hard line, the boy folded his arms across his chest. "That was quite a workout you gave us before," she continued before their tenuous contact could fade. "You're pretty strong."

Finally, his lips moved feebly. "Sometimes I am."

Behind her, Steve rose.

Her own voice emerged a conspiratorial whisper. "How do you get into the apartments?"

Wide with hurt, his stare probed the room, seeking a rift in the glare. ". . . knew Daddy had keys." He drew a damp, snuffling breath. ". . . took the office key. From his pants . . . after . . . went and got them." The soft rasp grated more rapidly now, as though he'd lost some struggle against the need to talk. "Lights weren't turned off in some of the places, you know, for the winter yet, you know, the electricity, so when the bills came . . . I just copied his signature on the checks." He panted, his mouth twitching.

"You forged his signature? That was pretty clever."

"Used to do it in school anyway. Report cards and stuff. Had to. When I went, I mean." His voice became a thin croak, and he sounded older now, though his expression remained vulnerable, dreamy, unconnected to his words. "Stella never went."

"Never?"

"Went to a special place . . . for a little while." Ashamed, he choked it out. "But Daddy didn't like it."

The floor felt icy on Steve's bare feet. "Special how?"

Perry flinched.

"This is your sister you're speaking of?" She wanted to keep him from going silent again. "No, don't look at him," she prompted gently. "Look at me. How was the school special? Don't you like talking about Stella?"

"Did you kill her, Perry?"

"Steve!"

The boy's chest rose, and the expulsion of air seemed to push him limply back against the chair.

She crouched beside him. "Perry?" For an instant, she thought something flickered in that grimed face, not trust so much as a yearning to trust. "Why couldn't she go to a regular school?"

He turned away, and his hands locked, the fingers working against each other in a deathly clutch. "Didn't use to be smart," he said finally.

"How do you mean?"

The boy shrugged. "Slow."

"Used to be?" The pink bedroom in the Chandler house surfaced in her mind—the frills and dolls—preserved like a museum exhibit. "Is she dead?"

". . . still gets like that sometime. Stupid like."

"Where is she?" Steve barked.

Slow tears glistened on the boy's cheeks, but he didn't cringe.

Lightly, she stroked the back of his hand with her fingertips, admiring the courage of this child. This time, he didn't snatch his hand away, and she clasped his fingers between hers, trying to sooth their tension. They burned, small and damp, and she noticed the scaled-over scratches on the backs, the dirt caked around the fingernails. A killer? This child? What were they thinking?

". . . goes back to the house sometimes." The husking whisper drifted. "Once . . . found her at Daddy's office . . . crying . . . think sometimes he used to bring her there."

"Why would he do that?"

The boy didn't answer.

"Did you kill him? Answer me."

Whatever nebulous feelings had lingered in Perry's expression instantly hardened into hate.

"Steve, maybe we should . . ."

"Okay, okay," he stopped her. "Never mind. We'll chill out a minute. Something's just hitting me, and I can't even believe that . . ." Lowering himself back onto the desk, he seemed to consider his next words very carefully. "Jesus, I'm stupid sometimes. You ever have ghosts in your house, Perry?"

"Steve? What . . . ?"

"Did you?" Suddenly, he loomed above the boy, the blanket slipping down. "Or something like ghosts?" Blood worked to his contorted face. "I can't believe I didn't see it before."

She stared: almost naked, enraged, he towered over Perry . . . and he looked completely deranged. She struggled to sound calm. "Why would you ask him something like that?"

"Because that's part of it! That's how it starts!" His voice rose ecstatically. "They don't control it. It just surges out of them. All that power. Answer me, boy. Did things ever move around your house? Move by themselves?"

The thin frame trembled.

"It happened, didn't it? You know what I'm talking about. I can see you do."

"Stop it." Her voice quavered. "You frightened him."

"Surprised him. It's different."

"Then you frightened me." Anger swelled in her words. "You agreed to let me question him."

"Fine! Then do it. Ask him what he was looking for by the pond that first morning I spotted him—all those months ago. That girl who was torn all to . . ."

"Don't."

"Ask him."

"Okay. Perry?" Gently, she lay a hand on either side of the boy's face, but his shoulders shuddered, and he twisted his head away.

". . . have to . . . let me go. Please . . . don't you understand?" He clawed savagely at the tears that mottled his face. "Not me . . . hid because I knew he'd come. She's all alone." The straining voice roughened. "You have to let me go."

"You know we can't," she told him, but he wouldn't look up. "Tell me. Let us help." She reached out again, laid her palm on the side of his neck. "Oh God. He feels so hot now. Steve? What are you doing?"

"Is there something dry here I could wear?"

"Why?"

"We've wasted enough time. I never had a chance to check the apartment. Caught him outside. Then his big brother put in an appearance." He rubbed his mouth. "If that girl's alive, she'll be there."

She stared at him. "Don't say it."

"I have to go look."

"You know what's out there." She shook her head. "You don't face that alone. I can't let you."

"And him?"

"I . . . we . . ." She hugged herself, her fingers digging painfully into the flesh of her own arms. "How likely do you think it is she's even still alive? We can leave the boy in the holding tank. He won't . . ."

"No!" The boy exploded in fear. "Don't leave me!" The chair crashed to the floor behind him. "He'll come! Please!" Panic knotted his features. "Can't leave me here!"

"Then we'll wait. Steve, it won't be, can't be long before help gets here."

"You said it yourself. If she's alive, God knows how long she'll stay that way . . . if Ramsey finds the building . . . if he's searching now . . ." The words poured out. "We lock the boy in the back, and you keep a weapon and wait here. To guard him. You understand me?"

"Forget it."

"I have a gun. The apartment's not far."

"No."

"That's the way we do it. And the door to this place stays locked until I get back. What choice do we have?"

XXVI

As he stepped into the night, the sound of surf billowed roughly over him. Turning, he nodded at Kit through the diamond pane. As their eyes met, he heard the latch. She smiled wanly, her face etched by a glare that turned her hair a harsh orange.

He started down the slick street. *Don't look back.*

As he rounded the corner, his flashlight caught the gently settling drifts of rain so that bright patches seemed always to hover just ahead of him. He turned up the collar of the slicker, grateful for the dry overalls Kit had found in one of the lockers.

He'd decided to go on foot, in case some emergency came up and she needed the jeep. And progress was much easier now, especially this far from the beach. Suddenly large drops covered the sidewalk. *Hell, not again!* But the squall faded before he'd reached the next corner. Without streetlights or house lights, the sidewalks glittered, and invisible rills gurgled below the curbs. The flashlight beam bounced back at him from the wet concrete and glinted from flickering water. With careful tread, he rounded another corner.

With constant ragged flapping, a rotting canopy rustled above his head. It took a moment to orient himself. All the old brick buildings looked alike, but his flashlight trembled up the facade of the tallest. Shivering, he approached. Another spattering of rain struck, and a dull stain of lightning rippled on the numerals.

The outer door creaked open at his touch, but an inner door held firm, so he angled the beam through a glass panel. Shadows huddled in the alcove. The gleam trickled across a stairway, and peripheral gobbets of light dripped up the tiled walls. He kicked the door. And again. *So much for the element of surprise.* The wooden frame splintered, glass shattering loudly as the door rebounded from the wall.

His boots crunched over the glass. He thundered up the stairs, past the inky stillness of the lower floors. At the top landing, he swung the flashlight, gripping the revolver tightly in his other hand. A fluid glow washed the walls. One door hung partly ajar, scarlet brightness oozing around it to dimly flood the hall. He shouldered it open.

A votive candle flickered on the kitchen table, the red glass sliding ruby shadows around the room. From the hall, wind sighed as soft illumination circled, lilting from corner to ceiling, and crimson pools trembled up the wall. A broken chair lay on its side, and a shattered door leaned askew. Fragments of a wooden table littered the floor.

In the room beyond, the flames of other candles danced along the floor and windowsills. In one corner, a strange substance mounded, white and lumpish like old snow—the stuffing of a gutted mattress that leaned against the wall.

A hinge creaked. The closet door moved. He eased it open and thrust the flashlight deep into soft dimness. On the floor, stained strips of clothesline coiled beside a carving knife.

He got her. He turned away. *Ramsey.* Everywhere the candles quivered, filling the apartment until it resembled a chapel, some shrine to violent dementia, and the smell of hot tallow mingled with a stench of rot. *Must have been some kind of ritual.* Flattening along the wall, he crept toward the bedroom. *She's dead for sure.*

A flimsy lock on the bedroom door had been shattered. Inside, the box spring tilted from its broken frame, and craters marked the plaster between crumbling gouges in the wall. He noted brown smears near the baseboards. Muttering a curse, he checked the bathroom. *Nothing.* As he hurried back through the kitchen, he caught sight of something in the periphery of light.

He tilted the beam to the wall, bringing it closer. In the bright circle, faltering stripes gouged the wood of the door frame.

Claw marks.

A block from the station, he felt his stomach lurch. *Where's the light?* He jolted over the slick sidewalk. *The emergency battery, maybe it just wore down.* But fear roiled in his belly. *Not Kit. Please, not Kit.*

The door swung loosely. The light above it had been smashed, and points of glass crunched like ice under his boots.

Inside, the emergency light still glared, and one of the chairs lay splintered among plaster chips from the wall. The desk had been shoved aside so hard the blotter had slipped to the floor with the phone and lamp still upon it, like the result of some evil conjuring trick.

On the concrete floor, it glistened. A few drops only. Blood. Darkly shining in the light. He crouched and tapped a fingertip to one spot. Already cool. But still mostly fluid. A lump compounded of rage and fear wadded in his windpipe.

Something filtered to his eardrums, nothing so definite as sound, more a faint vibration, a sort of scratching in the air where a sound should have been. His grip on the revolver tightened, and he stalked to the holding tank.

It was still locked. He fumbled the key out of his pocket, and the door swung out, letting the edges of the glare flow in as his shadow bobbed to the ceiling. "Come out."

After a moment, he heard a stifled whimper.

A pale hand fluttered beneath the cot, and then an arm

and shoulder emerged. With awkward, clogged movements, the boy crawled out. Still on all fours, he nervously licked his lips and asked, "Did he take her?"

And his eyes gleamed like candles.

XXVII

Awareness filtered in: it butted against . . . then receded from the pain, and in those first moments, she understood the cellar of the Chandler house to be her punishment. *The rats.* She understood that she lay in the fetid dark while the vermin advanced, scuttling forward then retreating only to ebb closer, and as she squirmed helplessly, they began to nibble with crimson snouts, tiny paws digging delicately into her flesh. *No!* She shuddered into consciousness, and pain flared.

Beyond her eyelids, the world dipped and rolled, then a chair beneath her stiffened. *Where am I?* Something bit deeply into the flesh of her wrists, and a moment later she knew the burn for ropes that pinned her arms behind her. *Not that cellar at least.* Lifting her head, she blinked at the bursting waver of the room. Though the dream of the Chandler house dissipated, the chittering of the rats grew louder, and confusion warred with misery as she coughed, sucking in air thick with the smell of mold and brine. *Where . . . ?* The scuttling slither swelled into a roar.

Fear erupted from her with an ugly snarl. A clinging film seemed to hang in the air, densely redolent of perfume and some underlying rankness. It stung her throat and rose smarting to her eyes, softening her view of the cramped space. But her gaze drilled into the shadows, drawn to the source of soft moans—feeble as the sighs of a dying infant—and discovered random spasms of movement on something like a cot.

In the corner, a form twitched on the bedding. An arm
flailed, and one leg hung over the edge, kicking spas-
modically as though from electric shocks.

"Who is that?" Kit strained against the ropes.

With infinite slowness, heavy-lidded eyes drifted open,
and a slack face turned toward her.

"Are you all right?" Kit could see blood on the blanket, and a large bruise bloomed across the girl's cheek.
She's alive anyway. Is she drugged?

The girl groaned, twisting to the side. ". . . you can't I
don't want you please untie me oh help he's coming have
to get away somebody . . ." Her battered head jerked back
and forth, the broken words chattering out of her.

Kit couldn't make sense out of even what she could hear
above the thunder that filled the room. Shadows and dimness swirled, then coalesced: an agony of brightness
erupted. She closed her eyes until the roar diminished.

The girl spoke clearly, perhaps not for the first time,
for the words somehow seemed an echo. "Does he? Does
he love you too?"

"My head. Something's wrong with my head." Kit
seemed to fall into the rumbling hiss that surrounded her.

". . . that now we were like married."

"What the hell is this place?" The cloud of pain dissipated, and though she could discern more of her sur-
roundings now, she comprehended less. The warped and
darkly colorless boards—this chamber must be part of her
nightmare—sticky black dirt, the stench of the kerosene
heater and the way it threw giant shadows of switches and
mechanisms. These shadows stirred. So did the room. It
swayed, vibrating with the rat noise, and parts of the
dream seemed to liquefy . . . in the corners . . . down near
the floor strewn with broken boards and splinters where
the rushing grew loudest. *Melting.* She tried to force her
mind to clarity. *I'm not crazy. I'm not. I've got to remember
what happened.*

Her thoughts probed back beyond the pain in her skull. The station house. *Yes.* From outside, the explosion of glass and that deep, terrible man's scream. Yelling for Steve, she'd rushed outside, waving her gun. *Like an idiot.* The pain had erupted shatteringly in her skull. *Worst cop in the world.* He must have been crouched on the low roof of the station, poised to jump, and she wondered what he'd hit her with. Points on her ribs still burned. When a shudder passed into her bones from a thrumming deep beneath the floorboards, she raised her head.

From the cot, the girl stared back at her. Different shades of ash, the long and tangled hair clung to the dampness of her forehead. The rough cot had marked the flesh of her face. Her skin looked unwashed, grublike, and a greenish vein pulsed at her temple. She might have been about seventeen, but as with the boy, the feverish pallor made her look older. In other circumstances, she might have been pretty, but the dark blotches and the bruises beneath the dirt made it difficult to imagine. Then her mouth went slack, and her head jerked to the side.

She's in shock. Maybe dying. I've got to help her. The room swam in a deep murk, but isolated details focused. *Damn it, I've got to figure out where I am.* Books on a raw plank shelf had long ago swollen to burst their covers, and paperbacks without covers rotted on the floor around a barrel, around a lumpish roll of decaying carpet. It was mold on the walls, she realized, not gray paint. Again, the edges of the room seemed to liquefy as the sea entered freely through cracks near the floor. *A boat, it must be . . .*

". . . did?" The girl's eyelids fluttered.

"What?" asked Kit. "What did you . . . ?" But the girl slumped out of consciousness again as she watched. The walls seemed to bow inward, and the girl's eyes twitched open. Kit watched her jerk almost into a sitting position, tossing her head with a childlike gesture. "Stella?" Kit forced the words out steadily. "That's your name, isn't it?" She tried for a smile, her face rigid from the pain and the cold. "Are you listening?" She tried to hold the girl's gaze. "No, stay awake. Look at me. Where's your brother, your brother Ramsey? Is he here somewhere?"

With a wobbling movement, the girl slid back down on the cot.

"You're not tied, are you, Stella? Can you stand?"

The girl hunched forward into a fetal posture, and she began to rock with her arms clasped around her knees. It would have looked like a trance if not for the furious rolling motion beneath her eyelids.

"Stella, listen to me. I'm a police officer. I can help you. But first you have to help me. You have to get up. You have to untie these ropes before he comes back." She shuddered as another fragment of memory plummeted into place—a voice at the station house screaming for the keys, the keys that Steve had taken with him. A bellow of frustrated rage as he dumped out the desk drawers. So big, so much stronger, he'd knelt crushingly on her chest, trussing her with the cord he'd ripped from the lamp. He'd taken her gun and gone off to try and reach the boy, and she'd heard shots. Then his kicks exploded on her sides, and he'd crashed something wooden again and again into the wall, until the pounding roar had faded.

The ocean thundered.

"Stella, please, can you hear me?"

The girl writhed.

"You have to . . ."

Wind knifed through the room. "Have you figured out where you are yet?" The moist, gravelly voice seemed to come from all around; then the door banged, and he rose up against the wall like a shadow.

The breath froze inside her. His head seemed to block the light, and for a moment, she thought some dead thing lumbered toward her. All heat left her body as she twisted against the ropes.

The thin, dripping hair slicked down to a glistening forehead, pale as the belly of a shark, and the heavy eyelids lifted slowly to afford her a glimpse of the red-rimmed blaze beneath. With difficulty, she recognized the thick expression as a smile. ". . . such a miracle really, that we should have survived this. Wouldn't you concur? So near the inlet. But the rocks always did protect this section of the boards. Daddy owned these rides, you realize. Strange to think of it, I must admit. He owned the whole amusement park once but sold it off one piece at a time. Now, of course, even the gears are rusted stiff. You see? These particular levers once operated the Ferris wheel." He raised a lantern from the floor and jogged it a little to hear the gurgle of fuel, then peered into the shadows. "Aren't you fascinated by the history of the town?" The lantern rocked, and a gleam swayed up the wall and down.

She couldn't seem to control her breathing. *The monster.* Locks of his pale hair seemed longer than others, possibly the result of a self-administered haircut, giving his head a bizarrely ragged look. *No, not a monster. A man. A killer. I've got to hang on, got to watch him, figure out his weak spots, find a way to . . .*

". . . only appropriate that it should be all that remains intact of the town, though it will do my sentimental old heart good to see it wash away finally. Only the rocks left. Finally clean." Even in the cold, he blinked constantly against the sweat. ". . . keep staring. I know what you're seeing, my dear." His eyes glistened like leeches. "I'm not human anymore, am I? I am aware of that, never fear. As though I've become the ghost of myself here, haunting the settings of my youth." The smile creased his face again. "My youth." He shucked off the parka and let it slump across a spool. "Don't you find that a pleasingly romantic notion?" Muscles bulged under the black sweatshirt, even through the layer of fat, a startling contrast to the weak face with its moist, smallish mouth. ". . . thinking how ugly I am. No, no, don't deny it. No need. Perfectly true. Except for my mouth. Don't you think my mouth is fine? Daddy used to say it was the only thing about me he didn't hate. Charming man, my father. You'd have liked him. Everyone did. Or perhaps you knew him?"

His brimming eyes burned even to look at. She felt this man lived, had lived perhaps for decades, perpetually on the verge of screaming, and it sickened her even more to feel pity mingling with her terror.

". . . realize he's dead. Oh, yes. Or, more to the point, I realize that you also are aware of this."

The rasping gnaw of the surf surrounded them, and she realized that the girl had begun sobbing with guttural, desperate gasps, like a child. Ramsey stumbled toward the cot, and Kit stared at the massive curve of his back. "Don't, Stell." Raising a doughy hand, he let it hang above her face, thick fingers splayed in the air, and the girl sucked a damp shriek deep into her stomach. Gently, he brought the fingers closer; then he hissed between his teeth as he drew back. "Families. So difficult." He looked up at Kit. "You know how it is."

Moving away, he chuckled, pacing into the center of the room. "Some old guy used to run this place." He flapped his arms at the walls. "Mr. Johnson. He used to let me hide here. Sometimes. When I needed to." Sweat trickled down his neck. "Sometimes. He always had so many books. All kinds. Science fiction and romance and murder mysteries. I read them all. That old drunk was the closest thing I ever had to a friend. Do you remember him? I remember you. You were the freckled one who always wanted to play with the boys." He stepped closer. "I always liked your hair."

Her stomach knotted. "Keep your fucking hands off me."

"You always had a mouth too, if I recall." He chuckled.

"How amusing that you became the town's protector. A misfit like you. Not much left to protect now, is there, dear? Impressive job you've done. There there—you shouldn't feel too bad about the town. They all knew. You understand?"

She saw the madness like a flare, a sudden red flowering in his gaze, and she pressed back against the rough chair.

". . . must have heard us . . . must have heard every night . . ."

He moved even closer to her. Fleetingly, the light from the kerosene lamp slanted up on him, revealing an odd, rubbery quality to his flesh, until his features themselves seemed somehow unformed, as though the skull beneath remained too soft to provide sufficient definition. His sparse and ragged hair glinted like spun glass. "Tell me, do you still like to play with the boys?" His touch spidered across her cheek, and a silent scream rattled in her brain. She forced herself to dispassionately observe his subtle facial deformities: something about the eyelids; a distortion to the shape of the upper lip. She began to wonder if they might represent ancient beatings . . . and she recalled the room with the strap.

"And if I'm not human anymore, what am I, you're wondering." His breath felt damp on her neck. "Maybe I'm a vampire. Maybe I'll tear out your jugular with my teeth and suck up your blood."

Her anger rose like balm. "Maybe you're a fucking maniac."

"That temper of yours will get you into trouble, my dear, one day." He chuckled. "Mark my words." His eyes seemed to stretch to unnatural roundness, showing white all around the murky blue, and his fingers trailed to her throat. His fingers slipped into her open jacket, then under her blouse. She felt them slide to her bra, and the calluses on the balls of his fingers scratched her nipples.

The heat of his breath jetted down her neck. With his other hand, he loosened his pants. Suddenly, he began to laugh and pulled away from her. "My dear, you should see your face."

"Knew . . . ?" She croaked out the word. "What did they . . . ?"

He reached out again, his fingers tracing her breasts, and the warmth of his hand made her gasp. "Don't endeavor to engage me in some psychological gamesmanship. You're ill suited for it." His stroke resembled the most casual caress. "That face shows everything. Your best feature really. Very appealing, that raw quality." Her flesh went numb in patches, but she could feel his exhalation on her cheek as he bent over her. "Enticing. Even now. But of course I have Stella now."

Rank with a stench like choked-down vomit, his breath sickened her, and she waited for the meaty hands to tighten around her neck. "The Chandler house, your house, is pretty far from town. How could anyone hear . . . ?"

"I said, don't play games!" The bellow erupted, ending with a giggle. Nothing could have frightened her more— the high-pitched snigger went on and on, repetitive, mechanical. He pushed closer, nothing in his face sharper than paste. It seemed teeth didn't belong in so soft a face, even stubby yellow ones. She tried to look away but couldn't. She bit her lip, using the sharp ache to hold back a groan.

"He'll have returned by now," he said, the grin melting from his lips. "Your gentleman friend, the one who hunted me. Perhaps I should have waited for him after all." His glance tracked across the room to his sister. "Yes, I can see now that I miscalculated by returning here so quickly." His expression stayed dulled, as though whatever passions boiled in his chest failed to reach any higher, but his hands clenched into fists. "I could have shot him." As he paced, his fists began to beat against the upper part of his legs. "I had your gun. I could've gotten the key from his body—then I'd have had Perry too, and it would be over. Finally. None of this trading business." The fists drummed faster against his thighs. "Yes. Hindsight. No need to say it. But he had a gun as well. Mustn't overlook that. And I can't take chances of that magnitude. Not now. Not when I've got Stella. Finally." Brutal shrewdness glinted in his face. "He'll bring the boy here. He'll trade for you. Then I'll take your lives. Nothing personal. You understand? I'll have to. You do see that, don't you? For the sake of the family." The words droned quickly, some furious craving driving them. "And I'll take care of Perry. Finally. The way Daddy would have done. Then it'll be only Stella and myself. Together." His face clenched. "Perry had no right. I'm the eldest. After Daddy came me." Water gurgled all around them as the room rocked. "But Perry must come to me first. No one must know about him. Don't ever let them see—that's the most important rule."

"What rules?" The trembling in her shoulders grew uncontrollable. "Know what about him?"

Within the heater, flame pulsed softly. As the chill closed in, he sat on a crate, his shadow mountainous on the wall. "He always told us that. Draw the curtains. Don't scream so loud. Don't talk to the neighbors. Don't talk to anyone. Ever. Always been like that. And it worked well. When his family came here from the barrens, they were laborers. Now we own the town." After a pause, he added, "What's left of it."

I've got to hold on. Her jaw clenched against nausea as the liquid floor gushed again, and in her vision the freezing room broke into pieces, buzzing like angry flies.

His voice hissed faintly. ". . . consider the possibility that I may really be quite insane after all. Wouldn't that be quite a joke?"

"What . . . ?" She coughed, pain rattling in her chest. "What brought you back to Edgeharbor?"

His chest heaved as he turned to her.

She held his stare, desperate to delay whatever action she sensed he was working himself toward. "I mean, why now?"

"The papers. We do get newspapers, you know, even in lunatic asylums. So sorry. Mental health facilities. It's the one truly great curse of late-twentieth-century man—we know everything that happens and have no idea what any of it means. But when I saw that the killings had begun, I understood." His voice rose in outrage. "My brother had taken my place. Besides . . . he's too pretty, don't you think? Too much like her."

"Who? Who is he like?"

Silence swelled, filling the shack.

"Your mother?" She watched tension bulge beneath his fleshy jaw. "The girl, your sister," she spoke quickly. "She looks sick. She needs . . ."

His face moved with an oblique shifting of shadowed eyes: the sleeping girl's breasts rose and fell. "You think my mother was good, don't you?"

"I . . . you . . ."

His gaze sliced at Kit like a razor. "Everyone did." From his temples to his bulging throat, the sheen of perspiration formed rivulets. "But she never tried to stop him." Sweat beaded his chin. "Do you know what she told me? She told me to pray for strength. And the things he did—she called them punishment." Grunting, he gulped air. "But for what? My fault. Mine. Ugly me." His fist thumped against his chest. "The things he made us do." Then he rubbed his hands together with a dry rasp. "Nothing unique, of course. Quite banal, I'm afraid. I often read about people like him in the hospital library. Not at first, of course, but later, when they trusted me." He made a laughing clack in his throat. "Sometimes, he used to make me watch. When she was just little. And then after, right in front of her, he'd make me . . ." The bone-dry chuckle obliterated his words. "Such a close family." He slammed a big fist into a thick palm. "And—after all that—Perry gets her?"

"You wanted to help her get away from him? I could tell them that. You were just trying to help her. They won't . . ."

"I'm here now." His voice rasped with purpose. "And I'll take Stella away with me. Would you like that, my angel? To finally get away from Edgeharbor?"

Kit peered toward the darkest corner of the room. *This can't be happening.* Agony throbbed in her head. *It's not real.* Fear made her thoughts grow vague. She heard his voice raging on, but the words tumbled faintly into one another, dissipating like a spent wave.

". . . after I've killed them all. Then we'll be happy. You'll see."

XXVIII

The boy crashed against the door.

"Look at it!" Steve grabbed him by his shirt. "Look at it, I said!" He shook him hard.

Bullet holes marred the heavy wood of the door. Long scrapes ran along the frame, the knob, the lock, and the safety glass had been cracked and chipped till only wires held the sections together.

"It was you he wanted!" He shoved the boy's face against the wood. "Now tell me! Tell me where he's got her!"

"I don't know. Don't hit me." Trying to push his face from the jagged glass, Perry gulped air. Blood branched slowly from his nose to his chin.

"Tell me!" Sputtering with rage, he hauled the boy back by the collar. "Or I'll cuff your hands behind you and toss you outside. How far do you think you'll get before your brother finds you? You think I won't do it?"

The sobs raked up from deep within him. "Stell . . ."

His hands circled the back of the boy's neck, and strong fingers clamped down, tightening. "Tell me!" The bones felt fragile and sharp.

Beneath the pressure, Perry bent forward until his head pointed at the floor. "I'm sorry." He choked out the words.

Steve took his hands away, and the boy sank to the concrete. Steve watched his own fingers clench and unclench; then he moved to the window and stared out at the night. Behind him, he heard the boy whimper on the floor, and his fingers dug into the grill over the window. *Killer.* Moisture glimmered on the glass. *Monster.* Wires cut into his flesh, and he felt the sting of blood. *Oh, Kit.* His first gulping sob emerged before he could force it down.

"There's one place."

He whirled around at the sound of shuffling movement.

The boy spoke in short gasps. "One place he might be."

"Please, you have to help me."

On a filthy cot by the heap of moldy newspapers, the girl lay unresponsive, almost inert. Again the shack rocked, one wall shivering violently as muddy water slid across the floor. The girl's head lolled, and white crescents flickered beneath her parting eyelids.

"Get up!" Kit shouted hoarsely. "Before he comes back. Listen to me. You have to help me. You have to get up! He'll kill us both. Do you hear me?"

The girl's head jerked, her gaze glittering like broken glass, and the fingers of her left hand jerked. "Perry . . . he'll get me again . . . no, please . . . don't let him." A rusty edge grated in her voice, as though she were unused to speaking aloud.

Kit's thoughts raced. Clearly, the girl's mind had broken—it was as though she had no will to move. "Perry's gone!" She shouted again. "Are you listening to me? It's Ramsey we have to worry about now. You have to stand up."

"He'll hurt me." One white hand floated up to cover her face.

"No! Stay with me! Keep looking at me. I can protect you from Ramsey. I'm a police officer. Do you understand me? Listen to me—if you'll untie me, I'll take care of . . ."

Softly, the girl began to weep. "I love Ramsey."

"Yes." Kit dropped her voice to a gentle murmur. "Of

course you do. He's your brother. But he's sick. You know he's sick. He hurts people. We have to get help for him. You understand? Before he hurts you."

"You won't let Perry hit me?"

"It's Ramsey . . . you know he'll do something bad to you when he comes back. And to me too. You don't want that to happen, do you? Look at me. I'm your friend, Stella. The only reason I'm here is to help you. You don't want Ramsey to hurt me, do you? Well, then you have to get up now. Do you hurt anywhere? Can you walk? Did he give you something? Make you take something?" Shock waves coruscated through her body. It was hopeless. God only knew what the girl had been through, and she might well be drugged. Despairingly, Kit strained against the ropes that scored her wrists. Slow movement across the room caught her attention.

The girl wobbled to her feet with a strange fluidity. She seemed faintly puzzled as she watched her own arms and legs, and each slow gesture—the trailing of a fingertip to her face, the listening tilt of her head—melted into a profound lassitude that suffused her. ". . . don't know what . . ." As she tottered into the light, her shoulders slumped.

"No, don't collapse! Stay on your feet. Look at me! Here! Come around behind me." A trickle of hope began to course through her. "Get me out of this. Quick!"

The girl's manner still seemed dreamlike, but she stumbled closer. "I know this place."

"Hurry!"

"He hurt you, didn't he?" She staggered. "Your head's bleeding. All red in your hair. Pretty. Where's Perry?"

"Thank you." She swallowed. "You're pretty too." Fighting panic, she forced something like a smile onto her face. Perhaps the girl had been driven as mad as her brothers, or perhaps she was in some kind of shock. When she spoke again, it was as though to a small child. "The ropes. You have to . . ."

"Do you have boyfriends?"

"What? Sure. Why not?" She repressed a hysterical laugh. "Dozens. And a pretty girl like you—you must have a lot of boyfriends too. Now, please . . ."

"No!" The girl's face twisted. "They never let me. Daddy says . . ."

"Please, just listen, untie me before he comes back. I'll get you away from here. I'll take care of you. I promise." She felt her tenuous control slipping: already tears pooled, blurring the room. "Stella?" Footsteps sounded behind her. "What . . . ?" She felt tugging, sharp pressure. "No! No, stop it! That's not the way!"

"I can't." The voice sounded sorrowful, and long tresses brushed Kit's cheek.

"Then find something to cut it with. Hurry! Look over there on that table."

The girl seemed to move a bit more steadily on her feet.

"Do you see anything?" Again, the whole room shook, the door actually bulging on its hinges, while water squirted in at the gaps. "We've got to get out of here. Did you find . . . ?"

"This?"

"Yes, try it! Hurry!"

From the shadows, Stella wobbled forward, holding up a rusted screwdriver. A tiny bead of lamplight gleamed on the tip, and the girl stared at it in wonder, as if she'd never seen anything like it before.

"Is it sharp at all? Stella?"

The girl's features dissolved in dimness, only the glitter of her gaze still bright.

They crouched on the floor, the boy poised like an animal.

"What do you think, kid?" Easing the barrel of his gun

over the edge of the desk, Steve peered at the window grate. "He's your brother."

The first of the bullets had plowed into the outer walls with a sound like hail, and now particles of glass iced the floor.

In the heavy silence, the boy seemed to concentrate. "He went away," he whispered at last.

"What makes you so sure?"

"I . . . just think so."

"Yeah?" Steve watched him. "What else do you think?"

The boy's lips pressed tight.

"Never mind. Don't have another seizure. You said you knew where he took Kit."

"There's a place."

"No bullshit now."

Perry shook his head. "I mean it—I'll take you there, if . . ."

"If what?"

"If you promise to kill him," he said. "If you promise."

"Easy to tell you're brothers." Steve swallowed hard. "Why do you hate each other so much?"

". . . didn't used to. When I was little, he . . . tried to help me, take care of me."

"But you're afraid of him now?"

Perry drew back.

"Just so we understand each other, kid—and so you don't try anything—there's something else you ought to know. He has the girl too. He's got Stella Marie."

"No! No, you're lying!"

"Shut up! Let go of my arm. Stop that, I said. I'm telling you, he's got her. Stop that or I'm gonna deck you, so help me. That's better. I found that apartment of yours. Finally. Place looked like it'd been torn apart by baboons."

The boy trembled violently.

"There's no time for that now. Snap out of it. If you really know where they might be, you'd better talk fast. There's no telling how much time they've got or if they're even alive still. Because you know as well as I do, sooner or later, your brother is gonna do what he does best."

"No, across—use the point. Slash back and forth. That's it. Oww! No, don't stop! Is it cutting?"

The door banged open, and a wave of freezing air flooded the room. The screwdriver fell to the floor, but any sound it might have made faded into the rumble of the surf.

"Ah! Sorry I took so long, ladies." He stomped and splashed into the room, bolting the door behind him. "Stella, dear, stop whatever it is you're doing there at once, and come away from that woman. There's a good girl." The parka dripped copiously as he dumped a duffel bag on the floor. "I experienced quite a difficult time getting back. The waves have commenced coming up over the boards again. We shall have to leave now, Stell." He patted the girl gently on the shoulder, and she whimpered faintly. "I'm afraid I couldn't get to our Perry. But—never fear— we'll find him later." His expression went vacant, as though he'd withdrawn to consider his own words. "See? I've brought some things from your apartment."

As the girl shuffled toward the bag, Ramsey turned to Kit. Carefully, he removed his glasses.

She glimpsed something dark snaked around his hand. "No."

"Don't worry." He unraveled the extension cord. "You know I'd never harm you."

He moved fast, like a big animal. He jumped up, his knees on either side of her, and the chair teetered, groaning. His stomach crushed her, suffocated her, and the rough fabric of his jeans scraped her face. He shifted down. She could barely moan. She'd expected his hands to burn damply on her flesh, but they felt dry as corn husks. With a surprisingly gentle efficiency, he wrapped the cord about her throat.

"No, no, don't move, dear. That's it now. Almost done."

She writhed, twisting against his bulk, as he jerked the cord tight.

The room splintered into clattering fragments. A damp hiss emerged from her mouth, and he smiled tenderly.

"That's it." Saliva stringed his lips as they parted. "Just another moment."

A mumbling shriek shook the room. He jumped up, and Kit gasped brokenly, throat bulging against the cord, as the room throbbed like blood. The cry went on, shatteringly, as though it would never end, a scream of horror and outrage and suffering.

"No, no, Stell, no." Prone on the floor now, he cradled her. "It's all right. I won't let anyone hurt you. Stop. I promise. Oh no, Stell, no, baby, no." He rocked the girl in his arms, while shrieks rattled through her contorted mouth. Her whole clenched body reddened, muscles twitching, as she screamed until at last all the breath poured out of her. It wouldn't stop; the convulsion shook her. The cords of her face and neck swelled, while her fingernails ripped splinters from the soft wooden floor. "Perry used to get like this too." Piteously, he looked up at Kit. "When he was just little." The girl's feet pounded the boards.

Kit jerked her head desperately from side to side, scraping her head against the back of the chair until the cord slackened. She sucked a burning gulp of air and savored the agony of it. Slowly, her vision cleared.

He crouched with the girl in his arms, and tears streaked his face, mingling with beads of sweat. "Can you help her?" With his open hand, he wiped froth from the girl's mouth. "If I untie you, can you . . . ?" His face went white with terror. "What was that? Did you hear it?" His chest heaved. "Who said that? Stop that! Don't! Stop it, I said!"

She attempted to tell him she heard nothing, but her vocal cords wouldn't work.

"No, Perry, not like this!" Ramsey shouted. Behind him, a shuttered window exploded. Shards of glass scattered against the far wall, and a bullet gouged wood from above the door.

"Chandler! Let her go, Chandler!" The voice boomed on the wind. "Let her go now, or you'll never get out of there."

When he dropped his sister, the girl rolled once, then put her hands out and lifted her face from the floor, shaking her head numbly.

"I won't let him," Ramsey yelled. Yanking Kit's revolver from his belt, he rushed to the window. "Not now." He fired twice, fragmenting what remained of the glass.

The explosions obliterated Kit's hearing, and a blue-black cloud singed her lungs.

"He can't hurt us now." He peered between the slats.

The shout seemed to come from a different direction. "I've got the boy, Chandler."

Ramsey jerked around. Beyond the walls, the ocean howled.

"If you want him, I'll trade." The cry sounded nearer. "You hear me, Chandler? Isn't that what you wanted?"

"Lying. Trying to trick me." He mumbled rapidly to himself. "He wants her." And his fingers scraped the side of his face, as though trying to scratch away the sweat. "He wants her for himself." In his hand, the revolver trembled. "Don't worry, Stell. I'm here." He crouched beside her again. "Ramsey's here. I won't let him touch you." Staying low, he scrambled to the far corner of the room, pausing only to push her down again. "No, Stell—stay there." He shoved the ancient card table, sent it collapsing against the wall. "Wait." Frantically, he clawed at the floor.

Kit stared.

Beneath his fingers, a section of flooring pulled up with a squeal of rust. The trap crashed open, and a burst of freezing air filled the shack with a thick, fetid stench of waste and rot and dead things churned from the depths. Grabbing Stella by the hand, he yanked her upright. "It's not very deep." He dragged Stella to it as she struggled feebly, glassy panic in her eyes. "Truly. See, dear? It goes down under the pier."

Softly, the sea rumbled below.

"Ramsey?" Another voice probed, thin, urgent. "Ramsey, it's me, Perry. Don't hurt her. Ramsey, please, don't hurt her. You can do anything you want to me. Okay? Stella, can you hear . . . ?" Wind swept the voice away.

"We'll be all right." Ramsey jumped down, splashing to his knees. "Just stay with me, Stell." He sank to his waist, still tugging at her. "There's just a few steps here. Don't be afraid. I'll take care of you." A wave slapped him, sloshing up into the room, drenching the floor. "Always. I will."

Though the girl pulled back, he steadied himself against the edge of the trap, holding her with one hand and drawing her down. "It's so cold. Hurry." His teeth chattering, he pulled harder until something in her face stopped him.

As though in a trance, she stared down at the water. Her long hair hung motionlessly around her face, and as the wind howled up into the room, her cheeks twisted as though her face were melting. Slowly, she swung one leg forward. Moving like a sleepwalker, she descended into the lapping waves.

"You have to bend down here. Then just keep . . ."

The thunder of the sea claimed them.

Kit sat alone in the shack. She was alive—that thought alone seemed to rattle in her skull. She was alive. A plume of water rose at the lip of the opening. "Steve." She choked out his name and then screamed with all her strength. "Steve!" It felt like an explosion of blood in her throat.

The rusted latch rattled, and the door burst at the hinges before falling inward. Steve waved the gun, water rushing in around his ankles.

"Get me the fuck out of here," she gasped. "I'm freezing to death." She barely recognized her own grating whisper. "Damn you. What took you so long?"

He stepped warily inside. "Where . . . ?" Following her gaze, he rushed to the trapdoor. A thin ripple stretched after him to trickle over the lip of the opening, seawater joining seawater.

"Now. Please." She shook against the ropes. "It hurts."

He flicked his knife open. "I didn't really believe I'd find you." The ropes came away, and as she slipped forward he caught her. Somehow her arms went around him, and he pressed her face to his chest. "I didn't believe."

"They drowned themselves," she whispered and felt his body stiffen. She lifted her head.

From the doorway, Perry stared fixedly at the trapdoor. Beyond him, gray chaos raged.

"The boy didn't run away," Steve said in a wondering voice.

". . . know where they went." Spinning, Perry fled.

"Wait! Wait a minute!" He rushed to the doorway, then whirled back to her.

"Go," she told him. "I'm all right now. Go on. Stop him. Save him."

"No! Come on!" Shaking with urgency, he grabbed at her. "I'm not leaving you here."

"Steve, I can't walk. I . . ."

"Get up!" He yanked her to her feet and wrapped one arm about her waist. "Put your arm over my shoulder."

She stumbled feebly. "My legs don't work."

"That's it." He dragged her through the door. "You're okay."

A wet mist billowed with each lash of wind. When she saw how close the giant waves heaved, she screamed in terror. The world stunned her, blinded her. Gray light filtered from everywhere, from nowhere, and everything glowed, the water more brightly than the sky. No beach remained, and just this one tilting section of boardwalk still stood. A flat, foaming surface rushed beneath the pilings.

He pulled her along. Through the mist, she tried to make out the rest of the boardwalk: rocks and splintered pilings poked from the water. A trail of seaweed and pulverized shell sediment covered the sodden boards they slipped across, and the wind staggered them. "My God," she moaned. Huge waves curled, flinging plumes of foam with each collision. "My God!" A breaker heaved across the dangling rail ahead of her.

He held on to her. "Must have gone this way." He dragged her toward the ramp. "Do you see him anywhere?"

"No! That's the ocean!" Leaning on his shoulder, she tensed as he pulled her down the ramp. "We can't go that way!"

XXIX

The sky churned. Clapping in the wind like a gull, one yellow pennant still trailed from a high cable. Beyond the remnants of the boardwalk, the amusement park sank in a murky tide, and ruined metal structures protruded from the mud like dinosaur bones.

As they splashed into the lot, she leaned heavily against him. "What is this?" A twisted loop of metal blocked the path.

"Used to be a Ferris wheel I think." He pulled her along. "They can't be far."

Something zinged past them; then an explosion echoed faintly. "Get down!" He shouted into the wind, but she heard only a garbled flurry of words. "Stay there!" he barked, shoving her behind a tilting barricade.

She sprawled in the muck. "You jerk!" She spit brackish water and sand.

"Shut up and stay down!"

"Don't tell me what to . . . !" Her anger dissipated into the general haze along with her clouding breath. "Do you see them?" Her wrists still flamed where the blood pounded back.

Crouching beside her, he peered over a sheet metal partition, the other end of which ribboned out of the earth to wave in the wind. "Keep your head down, I said." Beyond the barricade, one of the cars on a broken ride spun continuously in the wind. "What? I can't hear you."

"I used to love the tilt-a-whirl."

"Shut up. You're hysterical. And keep still."

"I know I'm hysterical. And stop telling me to shut up."
A shiver began in her stomach, and what little strength
she'd been able to muster seemed to drain from her limbs.
She let her gaze roam over the ruins of the arcade. Behind
them, a fragment of a carousel sloped into a deep pool:
galloping animals frozen in panicked flight, drowning. A
wooden horse reared, patches of gilt paint still shining,
exposing corroded teeth in a silent scream.

Another shot echoed. It sounded faint, harmless.

"Steve?" She had to shout above the wind. "Can you
tell where it's coming from?" She peered over the edge.

"He's back there," he yelled, pointing to the edge of
the sunken field. Between a pair of concrete outbuild-
ings, a delicate line of white smoke hung briefly in the
air. "Keep your head down."

"Can you see the boy?"

Clutching the gun, Ramsey hazarded a peek around the
corner. He couldn't risk wasting more bullets, but if he
could just hold them there long enough for him to find
Perry . . .

Movement! He saw the man leap behind the carousel,
and something flashed, bright as an acetylene torch. The
bullet spat against the wall by his ear, and particles of concrete lashed his cheek. He cowered. "I don't know who
you are, I must admit," Ramsey called out. "But I know
what you are, what you've become." He pulled the trigger,
and his own gun jerked in his hand, roaring, the stench of
sulfur blazing into his lungs. "You hunt the boy," his voice
murmured, becoming part of the wind. "Would you even
exist without him? Without the hunt? Ask yourself. And
what wasteland do you go to now? Look around you. Does
not this—at long last—resemble a final destination?" He
turned away, staying low. Pressing his bulk against the wall,
he slid around the corner. "They're right out there," he told
her. "We shall have to flee."

One hand on a drainpipe, the girl hid her face in her arms.

"Do not be afraid, my Stell."

She trembled, seawater dribbling from the nightgown that clung to her legs.

"My poor Stell. You might get sick now. You could even die. After all this, I might yet lose you."

She let her arms drop. Her lips had gone blue, and nothing of sanity remained in her expression, as though terror had reduced her to something barely human.

"It will be over soon. I promise." Fury contorted his face as he whirled away. "Come out to me, Perry! I've got Stella here. We will all be together." He panted loudly, like a wounded animal. "It's your fault she's like this! I know where you are. Do not force me to come for you."

Wind slapped wetly along the ground, echoing the pounding rush of the surf, unseen yet all around them. ". . . why . . . ?" An exhausted pleading drifted on the wind. ". . . want to hurt me . . . ?" The wail seemed to fall from the empty sky. ". . . hate me?" The words clapped hollowly against empty buildings.

"Help him, Steve." Beside him, she crouched.

"I think the kid's in that ticket booth," he mouthed into her ear. "I'm going to try to get to him. Promise me you'll stay here."

"I can't move anyway. Ssh. Listen."

The voices swirled.

". . . hate you?"

They soared, disembodied, like the moaning of specters.

". . . know how much I love you? Little Perry, you can't die thinking I don't love you."

She watched Steve crawl away, while the wind howled like demented goblins.

* * *

"You're my brother," Ramsey called softly, inching farther along the wall. "Family is all we have now."

He twisted around the corner to peer through the rough tunnel of a window swept clear of glass and casement. "Why do you run from us?"

The wind floated an answer to him. ". . . want to hurt me?" It came finally in the voice of a child—without toughness or cunning—the voice of a small lost boy, so near.

"Perry? Come to me."

Steve crawled along the base of the tilt-a-whirl, his elbows sinking into the soft ground as he tried to hold the revolver up out of the muck. He got to his feet, and bolted for the ticket booth, trying to gauge the boy's exact position, but the voices veered again.

Cautiously, he peered about. Now the voices seemed to drift from behind the fun house. He turned toward a hint of movement.

The earth undulated.

Beyond the broken derricks and the fallen Ferris wheel, a cloud rolled slowly into the lot. He felt his body go rigid. Solid blankness, the cloud oozed nearer, obliterating everything in its path.

Panic tightened in his chest. If the fog reached them, they would vanish. Steve knew he had to move now.

". . . won't make it hurt, Perry." Fading wind slapped the words away. "I am sorry, but you know I have to do it. And you know why. Trust me—I don't want to. But it's up to me now. My responsibility. You must see that. You're out of control. Soon everyone will see. Everyone will know." The voice grunted with sudden exertion. ". . . know I don't want this. Even when you were only an infant, you were the one I took the beatings for. Always you. You were the reason I let him . . . to keep him off you." The words droned faster, became a searing monotone. ". . . thought you would be the one untouched by it all. But when I read about the killings, I knew. Knew you took after his family—the stories he used to tell us. And I could not allow you to hurt her."

Then the fog swept over them all. Impossibly, it seemed to move against the wind, sliding inexorably between eddies of air. It buried them.

"Hurt her?"

The boy's reply came from somewhere quite near, and Steve crawled blindly.

". . . would never hurt her."

Now the voices seemed to emanate from the same point in the mist, and he headed toward it.

". . . not able to help yourself . . . must know . . . tears my heart out. Don't prolong this, dear boy. If you come now, I'll let you see her one last time. She . . ."

"No! You think . . . ! Stupid! Stupid!" The words sliced shrilly through the whiteness. "Run away! You . . . stupid, you . . . !"

Through a thinner patch—a sort of opaque tunnel—Steve glimpsed sudden movement.

Perry sprang up behind the shattered gate to the fun house. "Run away!" the boy shouted. Behind him, a huge green head tilted, grinning with weathered malevolence, carved teeth yawning cavernously in the wind. "I'm not the one!"

As the mist seemed to solidify around him, Steve froze. Certainty grew in his mind . . . finally . . . like the fragment of a forgotten tune . . . slowly recalled . . . gaining pattern and rhythm with each heartbeat. He plowed forward. He understood now. He could stop this.

Gurgling screams pierced the mist.

"No!" Blundering toward the screams, he made out the dim shape of the boy. "Stay there!" Wraithlike, the form disappeared between the buildings. "No, wait!" It seemed Steve ran against the cries, pumping his legs but unable to progress, while the howls rasped into a wet, hoarse choke of agony, interspersed with loud panting.

Silence settled thickly.

"Get back, Perry!" Spinning around the corner, Steve leveled the gun. Nothing stirred in the muddy field behind the buildings. Then he saw him.

Drenched and bedraggled, Ramsey lay on his back in the gravel, one shoulder propped awkwardly against a wall. His chest heaved, and his twitching legs splayed brokenly. Thick fluid puddled around him on the muddy concrete.

Steve gaped at the red ruin of the man's groin.

Ramsey stared up with lids at half-mast. His mouth hung slackly, his expression full of sadness and pain. He twitched again, a hiss gurgling in his open mouth.

Footsteps grated damply. With a moan of fear, Steve whirled.

Facing into the barrel, Kit braced herself on the wall.

"I told you to stay back."

Her gaze traveled past him.

"Don't look." He tried to block her line of sight. "We can't help him."

"god oh my god oh"

"I said, don't look." He caught at her arm.

"He's still alive." Pulling away, she crouched.

"Come away. Did you see the boy?"

"Why is he still alive? How?"

The mouth writhed as though Ramsey attempted speech, and she leaned closer. But his head had fallen forward on his chest, and she heard only clotted mumblings. Pink saliva beaded on his lower lip, and the hissing in his throat melted into a liquid rasp as thick fluid filled his mouth and spewed down his chin.

"He's dead now. Kit, come away."

"You have the right to remain silent." She began to giggle. "If you refuse that right . . ."

"Kit, for God's sakes."

"It looks like somebody circumcised him with a shovel." A laugh cracked in her throat. "We've got to stop that rabbi."

"Stop it."

"No sense of humor, Stevie-boy, that's your trouble."

"Hang on just a little longer, Kit. Don't fall apart. Get up. Come on. Stay close to me now. There's only one place they can be." Rapidly, he surveyed the walls: brick caves gaped where doors had been. "Take his gun. There on the ground. No, don't look at him."

"A mon . . . a mon . . ." she sputtered, giggling, "a monster got him. A monster."

"Don't look at him, I said."

"I didn't believe you. Oh, Steve."

"Look, we can both go to pieces later—there's no time now. Pick up that gun!"

She found it in a shallow puddle. "Why didn't he shoot?" A single drop of blood trembled on the barrel, as she lifted it to snap open the breach. "There's one bullet left."

"Make it count. No hesitations. No second thoughts. The thing's cornered now."

"Stop, please. No more monsters. Just a boy—an insane boy, chasing a frightened girl."

"No."

"Please, Steve. Don't make me see it. Just get me out of here."

He marched toward the twin doorways. "Stay behind me. You'll be all right." Planting his feet, he raised the revolver, gripping it with both hands. "Perry," he shouted. "Can you hear me?"

The wind. Only the wind, shredding the mist. Then a groan echoed.

"No, Steve, please." A rattling noise seemed to fill her.

A moment passed before she realized her teeth chattered together, that she couldn't make them stop.

"I have a place, Perry," he called. "A place you could go. Somewhere we can help you. Where there are others like you. I swear. A farm, deep in the woods. Hidden. That's why I'm here. The two of you can come with me. You and your sister both." He paced forward slowly. "Perry?"

The groan rumbled. Growing winds tore the mist into trailing patches.

"Wait for me." She stepped up alongside him. "What is that? What's in there?"

The groan became a growl, echoing.

"You know what it is, Kit. You've seen it."

The growl crackled into a snarl.

She caught at his arm. "Make it stop!"

On the low roof, a casement erupted, and chunks of glass rained down amid hunks of wood.

"Damn!" He raced forward.

A bulky form crashed through the ruined skylight. Bellowing, it clattered out onto the slick tile in an explosion of furious movement.

As she stared, Kit felt all her remaining strength bleed away.

It stalked to the edge and glared down. Vapor-laden winds damply thrashed the long yellow hair. A blast of sound—an exultant agony—shredded the remnants of mist as the monster shrieked again.

She felt the revolver slip from her slackening fingers, heard it chime against the muddy concrete at her feet. She could not look away.

Shreds of white cloth still adhered to the swollen form on the roof, and something bulged on its back. Through a widening gap in the mist, she glimpsed the red-smeared body across the creature's shoulder.

She covered her face with her hands. That terrible cry

rang out again, and she heard Steve shout something but couldn't sort out the words. Then his voice faded. Freezing water soaked the left side of her body, and dimly she realized she must have fallen, and only gradually did she understand that what she heard now were running footsteps. She took her hands away.

Nothing paced on the roof. Shreds of fog slid across the ground around her.

"So cold." She groped until she found the gun. "I can't anymore." She wobbled to her feet. "Steve? Where are you?" She took a hesitant step. "Don't leave me here." She broke into a staggering run. "Please."

The world eddied. Isolated objects seemed to float: a single pole, mysteriously still erect; a fragment of wall. Her footsteps thrummed across wood, and she nearly tripped as the surface tilted. Sticking the revolver under her belt, she stumbled up the ramp.

The wind hit. Fog streaked and vanished in a heartbeat, and the sodden planks creaked as she hurried into a blowing mist that made everything blur and glimmer.

"No," she whispered. Her leg muscles cramped, and she steadied herself against a post. "Not out there, please, no."

Somehow, the pilings of the old fishing wharf still tilted from the sea, but the ocean rose almost to the boards. Many of the beams had gone altogether, and others slanted madly into waves that squirted up between sodden logs.

"I don't want to go out there." The churning expanse gapped before her. At the end of the wharf, where the swells slapped straight across, figures seemed to dance.

XXX

Wind shoved her to the edge. Below, a flotilla of debris, mostly timbers torn from the pier, rushed and receded. The cold knifed through her.

A breaker spumed, and she fell, thudding hard against the dock. As she struggled to rise, the retreating water pulled, and she slid, clutching at slime. Suddenly, the dock pitched, and splintered wood jutted over the water.

A single rail bridged the two halves of the broken pier, rusted spikes poking from where crossbeams had been. It was the only way across.

If a wave comes now . . .

With a convulsive shiver, she clutched the rail with both hands and began to crawl, wary of the nails. *Don't look*. She gripped the beam with frozen fingers, squeezing it with her thighs as she inched forward. *Stay focused*. Her jeans snagged, and she tugged, grunting when she felt blood trickle warmly on her knee. *Balance*. Water slapped at her, stinging her stomach, and she crawled faster. *Slow down*. Her hand slipped, and she lurched to the side. Feeling the revolver slide, she grabbed at it but missed.

It vanished silently into the sea. Foam drew patterns on the surface, kaleidoscopic striations that seemed to hint at a bewildering design. She had no name for the color.

The beam vibrated, slanting as she clambered off. "Help me!" On the other side, she pulled herself into a crouch. "Steve!" Again she sprawled, her hands clutching frantically at slick wood as the pier groaned to a violent angle, miniature cascades draining across it. ". . . help . . ." Some-how, she stumbled to her feet.

Just ahead of her, the pier ended abruptly, smashed away. On the jagged point, the creature whirled and screeched, the boy a motionless heap across its shoulder. It shrieked again with a voice like the storm.

She struggled to reach them.

"Listen to me, Stella." He kept the revolver trained on it. "Listen to my voice. Try to understand." His voice held only weary anguish. "Try to hold on to my words."

Kit staggered closer. Spray from the waves battled back a wall of mist. Were those wings that curled from the creature's back or plumes of spray? Tentacles that writhed or lashing froth?

The clenched travesty of a female form shrieked again, and its rage—a gust of sheer fury—billowed at them. Lips rippled away from snarling teeth. Straining muscles twisted as its body swelled with savage dementia, and it hoisted the boy above its head.

"Put him down, Stella. There's no place left to go."

It shivered, breasts glistening with seawater.

"Don't fight the seizure. Let it ride over you. Think. It fades. You know it passes. You'll be all right again, I promise. Then I'll take you someplace, you and Perry. Someplace good. Someplace you'll be safe."

A tremor shook it. Slowly, the creature began to lower the boy.

"You have to trust somebody," his voice pleaded.

Another wave struck, and Kit slipped, clutching at Steve's arm. The creature snarled, seemingly aware of her for the first time. It whirled the boy. For a moment, they seemed to waltz, while the convulsing sea slung plumes of water into a blaring sky.

"Stella! Don't!"

It tossed the boy at them. He hit the wood and rolled limply, like a discarded rag doll.

"Don't make me shoot!"

With a wild shriek, it stomped at them. He fired once into the air. The thing halted its charge, backed away.

"Listen to me," he shouted. "You. Whatever you are. Whatever any of you are. You can't run. It only makes it worse when you try to run."

"Kill it!" She grasped his shoulder. "For God's sakes, shoot it!"

"Get back, Kit!"

"Give me the gun! I'll kill it!" She grappled with him.

"Stella! No!"

The creature rushed to the boy again.

"Get away from him!"

It groped with a gnarled claw, then jerked the boy overhead, clutching the slack body with both hands.

"Put him down! Down, Stella!"

The creature's head swiveled toward the ocean, and the muscles in its arms bunched.

"No!"

Kit let go of Steve's arm and pushed forward. "Stella, don't."

"Get back, damn you, Kit." He grabbed her. They stood close enough to hear the creature's grunting breath. The boy's head lolled in their direction, mouth slack.

Kit saw the breaker first . . . and moaned. With a spitting snarl, the creature clutched the boy to its breasts as the huge swell struck the edge of the pier. Frothing white, it crashed over the creature's head, and the monster screamed once, a very human cry of despair. An instant later, the water struck Steve and Kit, and the cascade staggered them backward, reaching blindly for one another. Bracing himself around a piling, he caught her arm. An instant of wrenching pain then, gasping, they sprawled on the broken dock . . . alone.

There was no sign of Perry, no sign of what had been his sister.

From across the heaving waves drifted the terrified wail of a small boy.

With leaden arms, Steve crawled forward.

". . . no . . ." Kit writhed toward him.

His head jerked in her direction.

". . . don't . . ."

For an instant, hopeless longing clouded his face as he gazed at her. Then he slipped off the edge.

"You can't save him!" She clambered to the shattered brink. "No! Somebody, help me! It doesn't end like this!" Waves seethed, swelled even higher, plunging at her. "I won't let it end like this." She forced the shout through her tortured throat. "Where are you?" Salt stung painfully at her. "Steve, swim to me!" Coughing and sobbing, she grabbed onto an upright post and hung out over the jagged boards. "Come to my voice!"

Angry grayness rushed around her. In the boiling madness, a pale area bulged. A head emerged. Shoulders.

"Here!"

It thrashed wildly.

"Steve! Come . . . !"

The creature faced her from the water.

"No!"

The eyes were full of terror.

Almost before she could think, Kit had stretched out her hand.

The water rolled massively, the satin muscles of the sea protuberant with force. The wave heaved toward the pier.

The mountain of water pounded down.

Trying to wrap herself around the post, Kit felt herself torn away, rolled. Her lungs filled with frigid seawater.

Something stopped her movement. She choked, flailing as the breaker receded into foam. Another wave exploded. The whole pier lurched as rafters cracked, and she squirmed away, tremors of wood rattling through her bones.

She couldn't stand, could barely crawl, but she turned her head toward a hint of movement.

The legs twitched. At the end of a shattered piling, the monster hung, impaled through the chest and abdomen. A long splinter of pointed wood extended through the stomach, and crimson fluid gushed away in the foam. A black cavity spurted where the face had been.

She watched a log lurch in the water, rolling closer on the next wave. It struck, smashed one of the hanging arms to grisly fragments.

Spray pummeled her. She crawled away across the planks. Beneath her, the pier shuddered, groaning loudly, and her teeth rattled in her head.

On all fours, she teetered back across the rocking surface, water sucking at her arms and legs. She started across the gap too quickly.

And dropped.

She hung, a nail spearing her palm. Saltwater and splinters rained from her clothing. Grunting, she pulled herself across the beam. At last, she collapsed on sodden wood.

From this more solid remnant of the pier, she surveyed the world. Black shale glistened where sand had been, and the shattered boulders seemed to roll as waves seethed up around them. Below the boards, thunder murmured. *All gone.* The surf seemed to whisper. *Dead. Drowned.* Waves stretched onto the nearer streets, swamping the ruined cottages, claiming them.

I'm probably in shock. Somehow, she didn't feel cold anymore. *I have to get down from here, out of this. Have to find shelter.*

The sheath of water rushed forward, a sudden rift exposing bedrock until the tear smoothed shut. Something floated.

Suddenly, impossibly, she moved. She dashed along the boards, leapt. The icy splash shocked a hiss from her. Liquid weight dragged at her, and she choked, waves closing above her face as a fluid whirlwind gripped her. Her arms pushed against a current almost black with sediment, and her foot struck something solid. Then her boots found gravel, squirming and shifting, and she climbed a sunken hill until water lapped at her waist. Pushing forward, she shuddered into knee-deep water, stumbled faster as a wave struck from behind, lifting her.

One leg drawn back as though in flight, the man's body bent with the movement of the water, the child's white hands locked about his neck. The boy's head stayed bowed as though in supplication, and both their faces lay beneath the surface.

"No!" She threw herself headlong, twisting them into the air with all her strength. "Not now." She clutched at Steve. "You can't be dead." Another wave tumbled them away from her, but the man's arms somehow stayed around the boy. Frantic, she caught at Steve's jacket with both hands. Dead weight dragged her down, and she rose sputtering. She tugged Steve's hair, his clothes. His head lolled back; limbs flailed stiffly. Sobbing, she towed them through the shallows while the sky went black again. A wave swept her legs, and the wind thrust upward, blowing caps of foam into quills that twisted across the coruscating surface.

Sudden rain whipped them.

The storm! Lightning burst in the choppy water. *Is it coming back for the kill?* Thunder detonated, and the tears on her face mingled with salt spray. She could barely shift their bodies now, and pain screamed in her arms and shoulders. *collapse going to* Somehow, she dragged and shoved them toward the shattered remnants of a concrete pillar beneath the pier. *can't*

Exhausted, she cowered behind it, gasping as the water

rose. A muscle in her back spasmed. A chunk of cement stairway led nowhere but to a broken ledge. *I can't stop shaking*. Step by torturous step, she heaved them upward, groaning while the tide climbed after them, until the boy sprawled limply on a ledge, his eyes closed as though in sleep, and she got both hands beneath the man's arms and dragged him on, scraped him on. Her boots made squishy sounds that echoed under the pilings.

In the water too long. With a sob, she fell upon him. *Both of them*. She shivered hard. *Mouth-to-mouth*. Trembling with exhaustion, she leaned forward. *have to try*

Steve never moved, his mouth hard and cold. She thought she felt a pulse in his neck. Or was it just an echo of the thunder? Something warm slid on her cheek, tears or blood, she couldn't tell.

The boy lay on his back, staring up at her.

XXXI

Milky light rippled across the floor. In an effort to get the place warm, she'd burned everything she could think of, both in the Franklin stove and in the bedroom fireplace, newspapers and paperbacks, even hunks of the banister from the stairwell. The last of her grandmother's old kitchen chairs was smoldering now, and heat wavered from the stove in the living room. She warmed her hands, muttering. Pulling the terry cloth robe closed, she limped haltingly into the kitchen. Under the robe, she wore a wool sweater, and under the slippers she wore two pairs of sweat socks, but the kitchen floor still felt like ice.

For perhaps the thousandth time that morning, she glanced out the window as if trying to convince herself that what she saw was real. Here, on the sheltered side of the peninsula, most structures remained intact, and they'd found her apartment relatively undamaged. The flower-pots and benches had gone from her terrace, and even the wrought iron table had sailed away, taking most of the railing with it. But only one windowpane in the kitchen had been missing, along with a jagged piece of the bathroom skylight. She'd spent half an hour with cardboard and duct tape, patching them as best she could.

An arctic draft knifed through the room, and again she checked the tape around the sill. Below the window, the sea murmured softly to itself, still swamping what remained of the dock. She saw no trace of the little boats.

She returned to the living room with a bottle of vitamin C and zinc tablets. "I want you to take some more of this." She checked the kettle. It wouldn't exactly boil on top of the stove, but after half an hour or so, the water got hot enough to steep a pot of herbal tea. "I put some milk out by the stairs a while ago," she said sadly, "but it's still there." Setting the teapot on the coffee table, she settled herself in the armchair. "I hope the poor thing's all right. I'm not surprised it didn't come back really. It never really was a house pet. But I thought it had gotten sort of attached to me. I mean, it hadn't bitten me in days, and I found that very encouraging." She uncapped the tablets, poured a cup of tea. "Ignore me. I'm babbling. The cat's dead. I know. The cat and Charlotte and the whole town. You don't have to tell me. I know I sound hysterical. And listen to my voice. I'll bet I'm coming down with strep or something worse, and I feel like I've been hit by a bus." She slid the cup across the table. "Can you tell me something? At the Chandler house—the straps in that room, that meant something to you, didn't it? Right then, I mean. You knew something."

"Part of the pattern," his voice husked painfully. "We keep finding it." Wrapped in blankets, he huddled on the sofa. "Not just madness in the family, though we see that too, but that the families develop ways of . . . suppressing." Steve barely shrugged, too exhausted to even hold his head up. "Maybe it works . . . sometimes . . . a little . . . or maybe Ramsey never really was one of them. Probably he never . . . changed . . . the way the girl did." His right arm hung in a makeshift sling, and he lifted the cup carefully with his left hand, steam curling as he sipped. "At least not so much." One side of his face had mottled a deep purple, the bruise spreading down his neck. The flesh around his eyes looked gray with weariness, the bloody rims giving him an unhinged appearance. Also, he hadn't shaved in days.

She thought he looked beautiful. "About the boy, Steve. About his not being . . . one of them."

"I swear . . . when I look at him . . ."

"He's still out." Nervously, she glanced toward the bedroom. "I checked a few minutes ago. He looks so . . . fragile, but I never could have made it back to the jeep if he hadn't come to and helped me."

"I meant to kill him." He followed her gaze.

She nodded. "But you couldn't." Her fingers closed tightly around a bottle of aspirin on the table. "Are you breathing any easier now? You sound better."

He turned away. "The world doesn't need more monsters."

"Maybe he can become something more than that, Steve."

His laugh startled her.

"What?"

"That's what she'd have said."

"Swell." She stirred her tea. "You're not a . . . what was it you called yourself? A phantom? You can still have a life, Steve. Right?" When he didn't respond, her throat tightened. "He should be in the hospital."

"He's not hurt. That in itself tells me something. All he needs is rest, and he's getting that here."

"He could be developing pneumonia right now. So could you."

"Kitten."

"Don't. He had a fever yesterday."

"So you said." Sighing, he ran his good hand through his hair.

She watched him. Through the sheer curtains, dawn light picked out gray threads with merciless clarity.

"Kit, he's been through a shock worse than anything we can imagine." His eyelids, purple with fatigue, drifted closed. "Let's just hope it's over."

"What's that supposed to mean?"

"I always seem to end up on this sofa, don't I?" Sighing, he forced himself to stay focused. "The best thing we can

do for him is to let him be. Maybe try to get some food
into him. And just be here for him. That's all. Who knows
what it would do to him if people started asking questions? Doctors? Cops? Think about it. Dredging up the
mother's death from all those years ago. The father. The
brother. That poor damned sister. How many more times
does he have to be pushed to the edge? Can you honestly
say you don't think he'd wind up in the same hospital
Ramsey broke out of?"

"I . . ."

"And probably for life. When they first sent Ramsey
there, was he much older than Perry is now?" He put the
cup down sharply, flexed his left hand. "All those years of
treatment. Didn't seem to do him much good, did it?"

"But . . ."

"If we took him to a hospital, how could we even begin
to explain?" With a stiff movement, he rubbed his face.
"Have you thought about that?" His words grew faint,
blurred.

"What?"

"The father too. Maybe the father. Maybe something . . . some sadistic ritual . . . maybe it helped him
repress the changes in himself. Maybe that's why
he . . ."

"You should be in the hospital yourself."

". . . fine . . ."

"No, you're not. And you're not making any sense."

". . . maybe it saved him for a while but turned him
into a different kind of monster. The father, I mean."

"Stop it."

"The things he did to those kids. Maybe to the mother
too."

"And it might make it harder for you to get your hands
on Perry?" Her eyes glinted like broken glass. "If he
went to a hospital?"

Wearily, he reached across the table to stroke her arm.

"I know you're tired." She shrugged away. "But these things. What did you call them? Mutations? Tell me more about them. Why is it happening?"

"We don't know why."

"I wish you'd stop saying 'we' like that. You haven't done that since the first time we . . ." She flinched. "I thought it was always boys."

"So did we. Sorry. So did I. She may have been the first. In all the stories, it's always been young males."

"Why now?"

He shook his head.

"But you have some idea."

He turned to the window, and the tension in his neck told her how much the concentration cost him. "Maybe they've always been there," he replied at last. "Maybe the world has finally changed enough for us to see them. Maybe a new world needs . . ."

Something like a laugh caught in her throat. "And these are your new people?" The teacup rattled in her hands. "Mass murderers?"

He didn't turn to face her. "I think that's . . . some sort of . . . phase . . . something they're working through."

"Terrific. Slaughter therapy."

"One of the people we . . . I . . . work with is a psychologist." He stared hard at the table. "I know someone who believes the metamor . . . the changes . . . stem from the effort to repress what's growing in them. This power. Throbbing. Inside them. Scares them. They fight it. The people around them teach them it's evil, so they fight harder. That's what warps them, twists them into monsters. She tries to help them stop being afraid. She tries to help them accept the change and channel it into . . ."

"Them?"

"What?"

"You said, 'them.' How many? No. Don't tell me. I don't think I can handle any more of this right now."

Against her will, a sob burst from her. "Are they all . . . demented? Deformed? What good does it do any of them, this place? Are they all children?"

"I know a little boy." When at last he spoke, his voice seemed to come from a long way off. "A strange little boy everybody used to think was mentally defective." He smiled faintly to himself. "Not so little anymore. And so smart it scares the hell out of me."

"It's hers, isn't it? Her son. That woman you say I remind you of." She forced a shattered grin. "And what about us? Just tell me now so I'll know. I can handle anything, just so I know what's coming." The words tasted like acid in her mouth. "Were you just using me?" She forced herself only to watch as his expression knotted, forced herself not to speak, not to touch him, only to wait for his words. But no response came. Finally, she turned away.

As though released, he leaned forward, and his hand went to her waist.

"Don't." She choked back the words. "You love her." Her fingers flew to her lips.

"I." He spoke the syllable with unconscious finality, forming neither the beginning of a sentence, nor the end of one. "She." He tried again. "They need me to . . ."

"Stop telling me what she needs. What do you need? What do you want? Tell me that for once. Just tell me."

Behind them, a vase hit the floor and shattered.

"No, leave it. The cat's always knocking things over."

"The cat ran away, Kit."

A row of books slid from the bookcase to the floor.

"What's going on? Is the place collapsing? Should we get out?"

"It's the boy," he explained.

"What do you mean? No. Leave it, I said. Just answer me."

His face went blood dark. "I want not to feel all torn up inside." A fleck of saliva flew from his lips. "Can't you feel it?" He rubbed at his forehead. "They do something to us too. Stir something in our brains. Can't you almost touch him in your thoughts?"

"Stop that. You sound even crazier than usual. What is it, Steve? Aren't you allowed to be happy? Do I threaten some kind of bargain you made with yourself?" She looked at the bedroom door. "He belongs in a hospital, and that's where he's going."

"And afterwards?"

"I don't know." Her head twitched.

"The kind of help he needs only I can give him." He stared hard at the door. "I guess I always hated them. Wanted to kill them all. But now . . . when I look at him . . ." He shook his head. "Did you see him lying there? How broken? How helpless?" As though to himself, he whispered, "I'm ready. I can go back now."

"That's where you want to take him? To those people? To her?" She wouldn't look at him. "What? Is he some kind of present? Wouldn't flowers do just as well?" She pressed her eyelids down with her fingertips, felt the moisture begin to leak. "What if you're wrong about him? What if he's not some kind of creature? What if he's just a little boy who's been through hell? What will that do to him?" Abruptly, she rose and crossed to the window. "What if you're wrong about all of them? What if there are no monsters?"

"You saw." Patience rasped in his voice.

"I don't know what I saw. There was fog. The storm."

"Don't do this."

"All right—what if they really are monsters? And you're helping them?" Gazing out at the sea, she kept her back to him. "No. This little boy is in shock, you said it yourself. Who knows what taking him to your crazy friends might do to him? If he's not insane now, he soon would be." She crossed her arms. "No, I can't allow it."

"But you helped me." Behind her, he rose unsteadily. "You believed."

"Just in you. I thought I'd found something, something that reminded me of what I used to believe in . . . about making a difference . . . but all I found was you, and I just did what you wanted. Whatever you wanted. We didn't save the town. I couldn't even save poor Charlotte who trusted me. I'm too weak."

"No, you were weak when I met you. Now look at you. You fought to protect the town."

"Fat lot of good it did."

"And you'd do anything to protect the boy now, wouldn't you?"

Her fingers dug deeply into her own arms, and she rocked back on her heels. Slowly, she turned to face him.

He stared at her, at the way her curls burned like copper wires in the morning light. "I really do love you, Kit." His face had become a mask of stone. "It's important that you know that."

She felt her eyes grow hot and milky, and he blurred in her liquid vision. She blinked to find him coming toward her with an extension cord in his hands, the sling hanging empty about his neck.

"Don't be afraid, Kit. You know I'd never hurt you."

XXXII

"She never knew, did she? Never knew what was happening to her?"

Wintry sunlight flooded over the debris-littered shore, and the gulls wheeled everywhere. Below the road, vines and scrub sloped to clear water that rippled inches above the submerged seawall. Gentle waves rasped and licked against the stones of the hill.

They hiked on. The shore lacked most contours now: coves and hills, pine groves and inlets had all vanished. In places, low waves rolled almost to the roadway.

The sight seemed to fascinate the boy. "Look! There's some beach left." He bolted down a sodden incline that led to the edge of the water. Though energy surged in his voice, he moved stiffly.

"Be careful." Nursing injuries of his own, Steve limped faster. "Stay where I can see you." Mounds of drying sea vegetation strewed the rocks, forming huge hillocks.

Sunlight glinted off the ripples. The man caught up to the boy, and they stood together, staring out. The curving shore blurred into mist, and quiet swells emerged from a haze to slap languidly upon the rocks. The shadow of a gull floated on the water.

The man studied him. With the light on his face and the breeze caressing him, the boy seemed perfect, untroubled, his features ripe with budding strength. Then a cloud passed and the illusion vanished in shadow.

The boy turned from the view, his flesh unnaturally

pallid, dark smears beneath his swollen eyes. ". . . sometimes she was better," he droned in a hiccuping voice,
"and she could walk around like she used to." He thrust
trembling hands deep into his pockets. "And sometimes
I had to feed her. Take care of her. You know? Like a
baby?" A larger wave crashed, and droplets settled on
him like frigid tears.

Steve led the boy gently along the edge of the sea. The
debris resembled bones, and they picked their way across
bleached wood and rocks. A powdering of pulverized
shell particles coated the mud.

". . . because I remember the bad times and want
things to be good for her so we hide at night and sleep
during the day and we move whenever I think we've
been one place too long and . . ."

"It's just a little farther now." They skirted an uprooted pine garlanded with seaweed, still twitching in
the breeze. "Do you need to rest?"

"She don't, doesn't like other girls. Makes her mad to
see them, like on television and stuff, if they show one
kissing a guy she gets all . . . she gets like . . ."

"And she never remembered anything? Afterwards?"
He halted. "Look at me. Does your chest feel better?
You're sure? There's something I want to say to you, and
I want you to listen. About your sister. No, look at me."
He put a hand on the boy's shoulder. "This is important.
On some level, she may have known . . . and fought it.
You have to remember that. She fought it. Because she
didn't want to hurt you. Never forget that."

"She thought I wanted to kill her. She . . ."

"She was scared. Do you understand? I have . . . a
friend . . . who believes that's what causes the . . . the
problem . . . the distortion"—he groped for words—"the
changes you saw. You know what I mean? Her face? Her
body?"

The boy nodded.

"Trying to fight it, I mean. That's what does it. She, my friend, she tries to help people."

"Like my sister?"

"Sometimes they turn out to be very special, to have special abilities." He watched the boy carefully. "They can make things move with their thoughts, though they don't control it. You understand? And sometimes they know what people are thinking. Do you know what I mean?"

The blood had drained from Perry's face. "Where are we going?"

"We'll walk to the ferry. Once we're back on the mainland, I'm going to rent a car. If anyone wants to know, just say I'm your father."

"Will you tell me something?" Perry's whole body seemed to tighten. "I mean, will you tell me the truth?" His thin frame shivered. "Am I one?"

Steve let his gaze swing out over the water again. "So calm today. Doesn't seem possible." Sunlight flickered hypnotically on the surface, and he let himself sigh deeply. "What did you use the knives for?"

The boy made a noise at the back of his throat like a twig snapping. "When she got loose, I could always find her, and . . ."

"How? How could you find her?"

"I . . . just knew where she . . ." He shook his head dazedly, and his hands went to his face. "Like I could hear her."

"Go on."

"And when I found her . . . she would listen to me. Sometimes. She'd come home. Later on, it got harder. But I only have to tie her sometimes," his voice faltered. "Had to. Tie her. Stella." He started to choke. "I had to. Let her out sometimes. Was like she'd die if I didn't. Sometimes." Strangled sobs shook him. "Then . . . other times . . . she just got loose and . . ."

Steve tightened his grip on the bony shoulder until gradually the trembling ceased. "The knives?"

"I had to hide what she did. I couldn't let them see. The scratches. And teeth marks and stuff. I couldn't let them see what she was, and when I did it, they were already pretty much . . . apart. Pretty much. So I could get rid of . . . bury . . . hide . . ."

"Or throw them in the water."

". . . scared . . ."

"Yes."

"Scared they'd take her away. Like Ramsey. Then I'd be alone." From somewhere nearby, they heard an automobile engine. "It's all of us, ain't it? The whole family."

"Are you warm enough in that jacket?" Beneath a sky rinsed clear of clouds, they walked on. "It's getting chilly again." His fingers moved deftly, as though by instinct, to turn up the boy's collar. "We'd better hurry."

Heading for higher ground, they rounded a bend, startling a gull into flight. Wing tips slapped the sand, but still the bird barely rose. Then the wind took it, and it soared, swinging out over the water.

"Perry, that morning at the pond, remember? When I first saw you? What were you searching for?"

"Her gold chain." Shell particles and pebbles rained down the embankment, and the boy stared at his shuffling feet. "Daddy gave it to her. It had a charm with her name. She was gone all night that time. First time she ever got out without my knowing. When I got her home, she didn't have it and if they found . . ."

"You shouldn't have worried. They did find it, but they thought it belonged to the other girl, the one in the pond." He stepped onto the road surface. "Are you ready to tell me what happened to your father? Don't look away. It's all right. I think I know."

"He was going to hurt her again and she called my name and I . . ."

He let his hand settle on the boy's head, then slide down to cup the smooth cheek. "You're safe now. You can trust me. It's going to be all right."

Hallowed by the pale sunlight, the boy held his stare. "I'll take care of you, Perry. Don't be afraid."

EPILOGUE

I won't.

Tears ate at her.

I won't cry anymore.

Her throat constricted from sobbing, she felt her lower lip begin to tremble again. *Oh, Steve.* Her jaw ached, and one leg had gone numb. The feeling had left her hands, and she could barely move her fingers. *How could you?* An aching cramp crept up her arms and across her shoulders. It had taken almost two hours to work free of the knots.

"Forgive me," he'd said. "It's the boy's only chance, and you can't be involved any further." She'd seen tears in his eyes too, just before his fist caught her under the chin.

The worst part is he meant it when he said he loves me. She rubbed at the rope marks on her arms until the blood surged painfully. *I know it.* She hobbled into the bathroom. *Damn him.* Scrubbing her face, she stared at the mirror. *It's been hours. No point in going after them now.* The flesh of her face hung flaccidly, gray as a cadaver. *No point at all.* She grinned mirthlessly at herself: a death's head.

Stumbling back into the living room, she pulled on her coat. *Damn him to hell.* As she shut the outer door behind her, sunlight struck the cord marks on her wrists. She wobbled stiffly into the glare. When she gaped toward the horizon, her mind seemed to hang suspended above the flat and glinting sea. *Time to move on.* Floating gulls dotted the water in the distance.

Suddenly numb and drowsy with the cold, she started

down the stairs, her shadow cascading thinly down the steps ahead of her. Below, everything looked sodden.

Chilling wedges of light fell between the buildings, and she stumbled through them to the jeep. As she fumbled with her keys, a sudden breeze murmured in her ears.

What?

With aching slowness, she turned her head and took a step back toward the duplex. A moment later, she crouched deep in the shadow of the beams beneath the stairs. She listened a moment. Stooping, she squeezed down among the stilts where surf echoed and boomed like the heart of a whale.

"Here. I'm here."

Deep in the rancid darkness, something stirred.

"But you have to come to me."

A faint cry vibrated into the eaves.

"Keep coming. I can't get to you if you don't."

At last, a patch of muck squirmed on the darkness at her feet.

"Come on now." She stepped back into the brittle sunlight, and just for a second, she thought it might be the wrong cat. "Look at you!" Filth clotted the fur, and the beast lifted its face to her, opening its mouth, sharp teeth glinting in a plea pitched too high for human ears. For once, the animal didn't struggle when she gathered it in her arms. Mud smeared the front of her jacket, but the cat purred like an outboard motor. Snapping her jacket open, she huddled the shivering creature to her warmth, and as she carried it back up the stairs, it began to pant like a dog, bright pink tongue curling.

"You go in and get warm." She struggled with the latch, clutching the cat in one arm. "And stay away from that window. I'll feed you when I get back." Putting the cat down just inside the door, she backed out onto the stairs.

The cat screamed.

"No, you have to stay inside." When she tried to pull the door shut, a hooked paw shot out, and the yowl echoed. "What are you doing?" Claws raked the wood. "Stop that." She tried to shove the cat inside with her foot. "All right, never mind. Bad idea. All right. Shut up already. Follow me then. Whatever." She closed the door and started back down the steps, the small beast at her ankle. "Stupid cat. Lucky to be alive."

Her footsteps squished across the mud of the driveway, and the cat pranced lightly ahead. The drive now emptied directly into a broad, shallow pond, and a gust of wind coruscated the surface into advancing lines, each glittering into a gray diamond pattern. The silt around the edges had dried into a reflection of that pattern.

She gunned the engine as the cat sniffed suspiciously around the interior of the jeep. "Another miracle." The jeep started immediately. "You don't get carsick, do you?" As she pulled out, the cat startled her by leaping onto the back of the driver's seat, claws digging in loudly. "Would you settle down, please? Before I drown us both in a ditch?"

Mud hissed at the tires. Everything was water and debris. She steered around the side of the duplex, then had trouble finding a road to stay on. Sounds of activity drifted everywhere. She heard a helicopter and the buzz of a power saw. Around a corner, men in bright yellow hard hats stood in the intersection, and the road crew stared at the police department insignia as she swerved around the barricade. *That's it—just nod and smile at everyone like you know where you're going.* Down the road, a tractor tugged at something large and muddy, and men with electric company jackets yelled as the jeep splashed past. She glimpsed a state trooper. *Just my luck. After all this, I'll probably get shot as a looter.* All the poles tilted in the drowned streets, and houses angled on flooded lawns.

But even the deepest pools lay lifeless and still, all violence drained. *I don't know this place anymore.*

In the center of town, streets had mostly been cleared. *They won't stop a police vehicle so fast.* She steered around obstacles, trying to avoid a truckload of troopers, tires sloughing through soft muck. *This could be the last time I get to use one.* She turned a corner. *Might as well make the most of it.*

At the end of the road, the ocean glowered somnolently, two blocks closer than it should have been. She wondered if the salvage crews knew they had become morticians. Some flicker of life might remain in the town, but fan this drowned ember back into a flame? Never. People would trickle back to rescue what they could, a determined few might even come back to live. But in the long run . . .

The cat bumped its head against her shoulder insistently, and she shifted gears, coasting down a side street. "Yeah, I love you too, Gruesome. Now, settle down." At last, she pulled over.

Not a bad house. Water stains rose only a foot or so up the yellow walls, she noticed, slamming the door behind her. "Settle down in there," she called to the cat as she squelched up the garden path. Near the porch, inchoate purple and white forms butted through sodden soil, lured out by the flood. Too soon. The frost would wither them, she knew, but now the stalks looked pliant and brave.

"I know you're in there." She pounded on the door. "Don't ask me how I know. I just do. Come on, open up." She pounded again. "I'm not going anywhere until I see you." She glanced back at the jeep. Through the window, the cat stared at her, and she saw the mouth open in that silent cry. "No use pretending you're not home." Finally, she heard the metallic sliding of locks.

He peered at her from behind the chain. A mass of curls hung in a tangle over the bandaged forehead, and blue crescents mottled the flesh below his eyes.

"About time. Aren't you going to invite me in for coffee? Or don't you have water yet? Better still—get cleaned up as best you can, and we'll drive out the highway to the diner. Come on. Cops always know the best places to have breakfast."

"Oh." Tully's face barely focused. "It's you." The effects of medication still showed in his sluggish expression, and his clothes looked like he'd been sleeping in them. "Sorry. I don't want to go out . . . now." His laugh sounded like he was choking on ice cubes. "Or ever. Please, go away."

"C'mon. We'll sit and talk, listen to each other make plans. Maybe you'll help me figure out what I'm going to do with the rest of my life. Maybe I'll help you." She grinned then, and it made her face feel strange. "C'mon. You can't just hide in there, you know."

He shrugged stiffly. "Why not?"

"Look. No, not at me, idiot. Look out there. The sun is shining. It's all over, and we're what's left. That's all. We survived. Right? So let's go. Time to move on. C'mon now." She tried to smile encouragingly. "Don't be afraid."

THE
PINES

Deep within the desolate Pine Barrens, a series of macabre murders draws ever nearer to an isolated farmhouse where a woman struggles to raise her disturbed son. The boy has a psychic connection to something in the dark forest, something unseen... and evil.

The old-timers in the region know the truth of the legendary creature that stalks these woods. And they know the savagery it's capable of.

ROBERT
DUNBAR

ISBN 13: 978-0-8439-6165-2

Five-Time Winner of the Bram Stoker Award

GARY A. BRAUNBECK

Hoopsticks will get you if you don't watch out!

More than three decades ago high-school senior Andy Leonard snapped. When he stopped shooting, thirty-two people were dead. But not little Geoff Conover. Andy spared Geoff for reasons no one ever knew. Now, all these years later, tragedy has struck again. Bruce Dyson too has gone on a murder spree, leaving nine dead in his wake. Even though they never met, there's only one person Dyson will speak to—Geoff Conover. And what he tells Geoff will shake him to his core. With one word, Dyson will reveal that he knows the dark truth behind the legendary bogeyman used to terrify local children for years, the deformed creature known as Hoopsticks…and the final, shocking secret of Cedar Hill, Ohio.

FAR DARK FIELDS

"Braunbeck's fiction stirs the mind as it chills the marrow."
—*Publishers Weekly*

ISBN 13: 978-0-8439-6190-4

Bram Stoker Award–Winning Author of *Castaways*

BRIAN KEENE

"One of horror's most impressive new literary talents."
—*Rue Morgue*

When their car broke down in a dangerous neighborhood of the inner city, Kerri and her friends thought they would find shelter in the old dark row house. They thought it was abandoned. They thought they would be safe there until morning. They were wrong on all counts. The residents of the row house live in the cellar and rarely come out in the light of day. They're far worse than anything on the streets outside. And they don't like intruders. Before the sun comes up, Kerri and her friends will fight for their very lives…though death is only part of their nightmare.

URBAN GOTHIC

ISBN 13: 978-0-8439-6090-7

NATE KENYON

**Finalist for the Bram Stoker Award
and author of *The Reach***

The biggest news in the small northern town of
Jackson was the reopening of the local hydropow-
er plant. Until the deaths. First a farmer was found
horribly mutilated in his field. Then a little girl disappeared from her home. Deep in the woods a
deputy came upon a chamber of horrors straight
from a nightmare. And through it all, one child is
haunted by visions of the mysterious "blue man,"
a madman who brings with him blood and pain
and terror, a terror spawned by forces no one can
understand.

THE BONE FACTORY

ISBN 13: 978-0-8439-6287-1

From author **David Robbins**
comes an explosive series of survival in a
postapocalyptic age.

The Time: 100 years after World War III

The Place: What used to be called America

The Family: The descendents of those few survivors
of the nuclear holocaust that annihilated most life on
earth, they struggle to rebuild a vanished civilization
within the walls of the compound known as the Home.

The Problem: People are not living as long as they
used to. Mutations are becoming more common. To
ensure their survival, there's only one thing the Family
can do: venture outside the compound wall for help...

ENDWORLD

DOOMSDAY—Now Available

#1: THE FOX RUN—Now Available

#2: THIEF RIVER FALLS RUN—Coming Soon

#3: TWIN CITIES RUN—Coming Soon

☐ **YES!**

Sign me up for the Leisure Horror Book Club and send my FREE BOOKS! If I choose to stay in the club, I will pay only $8.50* each month, a savings of $7.48!

NAME: _____

ADDRESS: _____

TELEPHONE: _____

EMAIL: _____

☐ I want to pay by credit card.

☐ VISA   ☐ MasterCard.   ☐ DISCOVER

ACCOUNT #: _____

EXPIRATION DATE: _____

SIGNATURE: _____

Mail this page along with $2.00 shipping and handling to:
Leisure Horror Book Club
PO Box 6640
Wayne, PA 19087
Or fax (must include credit card information) to:
610-995-9274
You can also sign up online at **www.dorchesterpub.com**.
*Plus $2.00 for shipping. Offer open to residents of the U.S. and Canada only.
Canadian residents please call 1-800-481-9191 for pricing information.
If under 18, a parent or guardian must sign. Terms, prices and conditions subject to
change. Subscription subject to acceptance. Dorchester Publishing reserves the right
to reject any order or cancel any subscription.

GET FREE BOOKS!

You can have the best fiction delivered to your door for less than what you'd pay in a bookstore or online. Sign up for one of our book clubs today, and we'll send you *FREE* BOOKS* just for trying it out... **with no obligation to buy, ever!**

As a member of the Leisure Horror Book Club, you'll receive books by authors such as **RICHARD LAYMON, JACK KETCHUM, JOHN SKIPP, BRIAN KEENE** and many more.

As a book club member you also receive the following special benefits:
- **30% off all orders!**
- **Exclusive access to special discounts!**
- **Convenient home delivery and 10 days to return any books you don't want to keep.**

Visit **www.dorchesterpub.com** or call **1-800-481-9191**

There is no minimum number of books to buy, and you may cancel membership at any time.
*Please include $2.00 for shipping and handling.